PERFORMANCE AND THE AFTERLIVES OF INJUSTICE

Performance and the Afterlives of Injustice

Catherine M. Cole

UNIVERSITY OF MICHIGAN PRESS

Ann Arbor

Published in the United States of America by the
University of Michigan Press
Manufactured in the United States of America
Printed on acid-free paper

A CIP catalog record for this book is available from the British Library.

Library of Congress Cataloging-in-Publication data has been applied for.

First published September 2020

ISBN: 978-0-472-07458-7 (Hardcover : alk paper)
ISBN: 978-0-472-05458-9 (Paper : alk paper)
ISBN: 978-0-472-12701-6 (ebook)

To Professor Sandra Richards, who helped me come to voice.
And to my son Aaron, who gives me hope.

Contents

Digital materials related to this title can be found on the Fulcrum platform via the following citable URL: https://doi.org/10.3998/mpub.9751634

Prologue: Returning to Remains

I dive in—water a bit too warm, lanes generously wide. Longer than most yet short by Olympic standards, this pool is graciously appointed.[1] Variegated gray marble tiles grace the deck. Plaster figurines of white women in diaphanous gowns and fat babies in repose line its perimeter. Underwater one finds an exquisite universe—brown marble streaked with gold, sunlight undulating and refracting through the water. I see but I don't hear in this place. It is elemental: constant motion abuts permanence, water against rock, light against darkness. And then there is me: a fragile human body floating free, a harried academic seeking refuge from a glut of emails, petitioning students, and bureaucratic meetings.

But swimming here is no longer the respite for me that it once was. Human remains under this pool have unsettled things.

At the center of this story are body parts—bodies that became objects, and humans who did not count as humans, who were not considered worthy of grief in life or death.[2] This story is about awareness and heedlessness, about a deeply repressed history, about my own university's unresolved connection to a genocide, about the perils of speech acts—including essays and plays—that attempt to address a long silence about long-denied atrocities. These are the afterlives of injustice.

What exactly counts as an "intervention" when profound injustices—such as genocide and slavery—have not been widely recognized? Acknowledgment is a complex performative act. Without acknowledgment, there can be no apology. Without apology, there can be no redress. Without any of the above, what can a piece of theater, performance, or art actually *do*? Without any of the above, what art can wield the toxic surfeit of this unfinished business without succumbing to its corrosiveness? As Toni Morrison asks, "How to enunciate race while depriving it of its lethal cling?"[3] Even when there has been a formal state acknowledgment, as happened when South Africa's Truth and Reconciliation Commission publicly recognized that apartheid perpetrated gross violations of human rights, legacies of injustice continue today, volatile and unpredictable in their impact, disrupting both life and art. Some experience the afterlives of injustice as social death. Others may careen from insight to sustained amnesia, being "woke" only momentarily, if at all, before customary obliviousness sets in.

Contradiction, says the narrator of Ralph Ellison's *Invisible Man*, "is how the world moves: not like an arrow, but a boomerang."[4] The boomerangs of history bear down with little warning. They crack across the head so fast. Some experience the blow as a sudden awakening. The pain may last, but too often the insights are fleeting. And there is an endless repetition of empire, an acting out of old dramas, over and over again, with nauseating predictability.

The gym in which I swim is a memorial to Phoebe Hearst. It was built on the University of California, Berkeley campus, in 1927 by her son, William Randolph Hearst, the newspaper tycoon. It was intended to provide a hospitable and welcoming space for women on a college campus that was otherwise a male bastion.[5] Phoebe was a remarkably progressive woman. She sponsored an architectural master plan for the campus, founded and funded the anthropology and archaeology departments, underwrote expeditions to collect art and artifacts throughout the world, and endowed scholarships for women long before most universities even admitted them.[6] And she created a museum. "This museum," I once told an audience sitting in its gallery, "the one we are sitting in today"—the Phoebe A. Hearst Museum of Anthropology.[7]

The Hearst family's fortune was first made from mining California gold, an industry that came as a boon to some and a catastrophe for others. In California, the word "genocide" was rarely spoken in relationship to our state's history. From 1845, just before the discovery of gold, to 1900, the native population had gone from seven hundred thousand to twenty thousand. Less than 3 percent survived. This decimation was deliberately perpetrated through a governor-endorsed war of extermination. As Alex Alvarez has argued, "The case of the Natives of California illustrates one of the clearest examples of genocide in North America."[8] Even though I had lived half my life in California, I could not recall people speaking about the state's genocide.

Likewise, in the nine years I worked at Berkeley, people did not speak about what, until recently, lay under Phoebe Hearst's pool. What neither I nor most people on campus did not know until 2012 was that to swim in Phoebe Hearst's spectacular marble-lined pool was to swim above ten thousand Native American human remains, for the Phoebe A. Hearst Museum of Anthropology had, at the time, more unrepatriated Native American human remains than any US institution besides the Smithsonian.[9] During the busy development of the state of California, many sites excavated for new roads or buildings would unearth bones, often the bones of Native Americans. The Hearst Museum became the place to send them. These accumulated bones were stacked in metal containers under the Hearst Pool. "There are rows and rows and rows and rows of bodies," a worker at the Hearst Museum told Tony Platt, author of *Grave Matters: Excavating California's Buried Past*. "It's hard for me to go there, but I have to do it when native groups want to see the remains of their people. It's very depressing."[10]

I dive in. Water a bit too warm, lanes generously wide. I try to imagine them: ten thousand is a lot of people. Arlington Cemetery has four hundred thousand graves that cover 624 acres. That's 641 bodies per acre. How much less than an acre is a swimming pool?

August 1911 was late in the genocide of California Native America, a genocide that began with the arrival of settlers and reached high pitch in the decades after California's discovery of gold in 1849. In August 1911, a Native American survivor was found hiding in a slaughterhouse in the northern Sierra country near Oroville, California. The man was thought to be the last surviving member of his tribe, the Yahi, the southernmost tribe of Yana Indians. Anthropologists and Indian Affairs officials had estimated many years earlier, in 1872, that there were then only a dozen surviving Yahi, so the emergence of this man in 1911 was an astonishing curiosity. No one knew his name, nor would he speak it, for Yahi custom prohibits speaking one's own name, and there was no one left alive who knew his. So he was called "Ishi," which meant simply "man." Ishi was brought to live and work at Berkeley's Phoebe A. Hearst Museum under the watchful examination and "care" of anthropologist Alfred Kroeber. Ishi became, much like South Africa's Sara Baartman when she was taken to Europe, a scientific and ethnological curiosity and exhibited specimen that was avidly studied and analyzed by experts. He was also paraded in public for popular amusement. Ultimately, when he died of tuberculosis in 1916, Ishi was dissected, as was Baartman.

A member of California's Yahi tribe, Ishi lived at the Phoebe A. Hearst Museum for a few years in the early twentieth century.[11] As a living person, he was put on display. He demonstrated skills—how to cut arrowheads, how to make a fire, how to hunt salmon. He died of tuberculosis within four years of leaving Lassen National Forest in northern California and coming to the densely populated settler town of San Francisco. Upon his death and against his wishes, Ishi's brain was removed and clandestinely sent off to the Smithsonian Institution, a fact that was denied for decades, until someone found a paper trail in Berkeley's Bancroft Library in the late 1990s. Then Ishi's brain was located and returned, repatriated finally to Native people who buried him respectfully. Some faculty in Berkeley's anthropology department apologized. Others objected to this apology, believing that the quest for knowledge gives license to possess others. Ten years later, Berkeley still dragged its feet about returning the many Native remains in its museum's holdings, despite federal law compelling their repatriation. A play about Ishi was mounted at Berkeley in 2012 by the theater department, where I worked at the time. Despite the producer's intentions to be on the "right" side of history, the play misfired colossally, as it unwittingly repeated many habits of empire: extracting a story to exploit an opportunity, failing to consult Native peoples, neglecting to make use of the great range of relevant expertise on the Berkeley campus, failing to imagine Native peoples in the audience, failing to even be aware of those unsettled thousands of bones that lay under Phoebe Hearst's pool just several hundred feet from the theater. When theater folk self-righteously assume they are "woke," they may, like a sleepwalker, not recognize their own somnolence.

Empire, argues South African historian Ciraj Rassool, is premised on extractive, hierarchical, and stratified relations of knowledge.[12] Empire is a story both of South Africa, the place where I have conducted research for the past twenty years, and California, the place where I lived and worked for half my life. While this book is about performance and the afterlives of injustice in Africa, I begin by acknowledging the land on which I live and its many unresolved histories that, unlike apartheid in South Africa, have only just begun to be acknowledged by the state of California and its settlers.[13]

In one of the few direct imprints that Ishi left in the historical record, he recorded on a wax cylinder some thoughts about the dead:

> To tell about the dead, the dead,
> They see, the dead,
> They see a little at a time,
> See in the west, keep going, the dead.
> Seeing, they see.
> They don't hear, the dead, the dead.
> So many dead,
> Dead people, rolled up,
> Their bodies rolled up, flexed, stiff and cold.[14]

Did the dead hear, I wonder, when Berkeley's chancellor refused in 2007 to meet with tribal elders, even though he himself claimed Native ancestry?[15]

Did the dead hear, I wonder, when in 2008 an associate vice chancellor for research explained to the *Los Angeles Times* Berkeley's decision to exclude Native Americans from the federally mandated deliberations that would compel repatriation of Berkeley's holdings of human remains to lineal descendants? He said: "We didn't go out and seek a Native American because what we were trying to study, Native American tribes would have had no knowledge or expertise to bring to the table." According to him, Native Americans "don't know how museums are organized or how our staff relates to each other or many of those questions."[16] Yet Berkeley has been granting doctoral degrees to Native Americans in the fields of anthropology and linguistics for decades.

The narrator of *Invisible Man* was right—contradiction *is* how the world moves. He also advises, "Beware of those who speak of the *spiral* of history; they are preparing a boomerang. Keep a steel helmet handy." [17] From Kroeber Hall and the Hearst Gym to Ishi Court in Dwinelle Hall, Ishi's story is as central to Berkeley's present as it is to its past. Likewise, the legacies of colonialism, empire, and apartheid are far too vast and enduring in contemporary South Africa to be seen in the rearview mirror. There is far too much unfinished business to view such histories in retrospect. The artists who tangle with such histories are wise to keep those steel helmets at the ready.

When I learned about the human remains under the pool where I loved to swim, I considered whether I should stop swimming there. Would such a boycott have any impact? Would such an act in any way disentangle me from the sordid institutional history of my employer? What was I exposing myself to by swimming regularly above these unsettled remains? And how did those ancestors below experience my blithe aquatic to and fro? I swam first in a state of settler oblivion and later wracked by settler angst. Of what consequence was either? In the end, I decided that as long as I worked at Berkeley, I was *in* this pool. And even now that I no longer work there, I am *still* in this pool. We all are.

I swim another lap
I flip and turn
I push off from the granite and paddle back to the other side

The living, the living
They see a little at a time
They don't hear, the living, the living.
So many living,
Living people, rolled up
Their minds rolled up, flexed, stiff and cold

How is it
That in a place of knowledge
So many prefer not to know?

In 2016, the Hearst Museum's holdings of ancestral Native remains, along with other precious possessions stored in the underbelly of Phoebe Hearst's pool, were moved, part of a renovation intended to consolidate the museum's holdings and place them in more suitable, climate controlled, and respectful locations. Objects collected (and looted) from throughout the world over decades went to a facility in the neighboring town of Richmond in a climate-controlled facility shared with Berkeley's Bancroft Library and the Berkeley Art Museum. However, the bones of Native ancestors were moved to a building right next to the Hearst Pool—to Kroeber Hall, home of the anthropology department. New storage facilities were created directly underneath the Hearst Museum. A separate entrance was created in a small corner, back by a parking lot with a lone redwood, a place for Native peoples to enter when they wished to visit their ancestors, a place to perform rituals of cleansing and to offer prayers of respect. But this renovation is not a story that the museum chooses to foreground. Many who enter Kroeber Hall and the Phoebe A. Hearst Museum today do not know what is under their feet. Visitors usually do not know that they walk over the unsettled dead.

In 2018, the museum hosted a reading of a play titled *Antíkoni* by Native American author and Berkeley professor Beth Piatote. An adaptation of the ancient play *Antigone* by Sophocles, *Antíkoni* casts Creon (here named "Kreon") as a Native American museum director who articulates an accommodationist position about anthropology museums' penchant for collecting and holding Native American remains and ceremonial objects. He argues that it is better to have a Native American than a settler directing such a museum and that, anyway, stories matter more than bones and objects:

I return to the departed their flesh, their humanity.
It is the story, not the body, that matters, that endures.[18]

Antigone, or Antíkoni, as she is called in this play, takes a more radical position, arguing that the ancestral remains should be rescued and repatriated by any means necessary, including outright theft, a crime in which she colludes.

On November 8, 2018, the day after the *Antíkoni* readings, a panel about the play was held that featured the playwright, the director, and two scholars, of which I was one. When I entered the Phoebe A. Hearst Museum in Kroeber Hall, where the panel was held that day, it was a warm and sunny afternoon, uncannily summerlike for November. While pleasant, this unseasonal weather was also disturbing, evidence to many people of climate change. The air was slightly acrid, with a hint of wood smoke that left grit in the mouth, a parched feeling on the skin. Hot air whipped my hair with occasional gusts. When I came out of the panel a few hours later, the air was choked with smoke, obscuring my view even of the neighboring Boalt Hall, home of the law school (named for a man responsible for fomenting anti-Chinese sentiment in California in the nineteenth century, a man who believed American white settlers had an "unconquerable repulsion" to Chinese immigrants).[19]

As the panelists and audience went to our respective meals and engagements that evening, groping our way through the haze and gray gloaming, we learned that the city of Paradise, some 172 miles northeast of Berkeley, had been incinerated that day. The Camp Fire: a tsunami of flame. At peak strength, this colossal blaze devoured an area the size of a football field each and every second. That's sixty football fields a minute—a ravenous inferno consuming everything in its path: cars, trees, pools, dogs, bikes, garbage trucks, signs, houses, air, and people. Lots of people. With few exits out of town, the roads became choked and impassable. Torched and stalled cars had to be removed by bulldozers to make way for the surge of vehicles behind them. The "vehicular equivalent of a stampede," the *New York Times* called it.[20] Some abandoned their cars and tried to walk or run to safety. There were few roads out of Paradise, each a corridor through hellfires raging on either side.

Ten days later, the number of people missing approached 1,300. A desperate search for human remains was carried out by otherworldly figures in white hazmat suits, bulging respirators affixed to their faces like industrial tusks. The workers poked and prodded the blasted, smoldering detritus—melted tires, collapsed roofs, toppled chimneys, twisted gutters, poisonous and billowing ash, and the skeletal remains of scorched and gutted cars. Over a thousand people were unaccounted for—evaporated, it seemed, without a trace. A chaplain in Chico commented that when you don't know what has happened to those who have disappeared, when there are no remains, grief is suspended: "It's like treading water and you can't get to one side of the pool or the other."[21] This powerful metaphor struck me—once again, in the pool, not swimming above unsettled remains, but rather treading water without them.

Paradise, California is in Ishi country, halfway between the Ishi Wilderness—where Ishi lived his life in the hills, until he was the sole remaining member of his entire family and tribe—and Oroville, where he was "discovered," alone, emaciated, and huddling in a slaughterhouse in 1911. Butte County sheriffs put Ishi in jail "for his own protection"—the same Butte County that was consumed by the massive 2018 Camp Fire, the largest and most destructive fire in California history.

A heavy cloud of acrid smoke descended on the Bay Area for over a week after the Camp Fire ignited. This tenacious conflagration defied containment for days. Air quality vacillated between "unhealthy" and "very unhealthy," climbing to "hazardous" in Sacramento and Chico. Over seventeen million people in the surrounding area were essentially put on house arrest, exhorted to remain indoors to avoid the unsafe air. A week after the fire began, the Berkeley campus was forced to close due to poor air quality. Even Saturday's big game with Stanford University was called off. A few forlorn students wandered Sproul Plaza wearing N-95 particulate respirator masks, items sure to be museum curios one day, or precious equipment in a future pandemic.

Paradise is gone. And now no one could breathe.

On Sunday, the campus announced it would remain closed through the following week, a partial week anyway due to the upcoming holiday. Rain was eagerly expected just before Thanksgiving, that strange settlers' holiday that supposedly commemorates when the Pilgrims and the Wampanoag Indians feasted together in 1621 in Plymouth, Massachusetts. The rains presented both relief—from smoke and the fire season—and anxiety that the charred human remains not yet found would simply condense, turn to soil, and wash away without a trace, leaving loved ones searching for them in a perpetual state of suspended grief, treading water. Unsettled remains disrupt the living, regardless of who they are.

At various public events like play readings and panels at the Phoebe A. Hearst Museum today, land acknowledgments are dutifully recited: "Let's begin by acknowledging that we gather today on the unceded lands of the Muwekma Ohlone People," a statement that really only conveys a recognition that the speaker and audience are on stolen land. But there is no acknowledgment of the ancestors under foot in the Phoebe A. Hearst

Museum. These ancestors, a village a third the size of Paradise before its decimation are not named. But there is no acknowledgment of them. No commemorative placard to indicate that unsettled ancestors lie below. No informed consent release that visitors can sign acknowledging that they know what is under them, that they occupy this space on their own recognizance. Without acknowledgment, there can be no apology. Without apology, there can be no redress.

With so much unfinished business, with such a toxic surfeit under foot, how do artists acknowledge and thoughtfully engage with the highly charged remains of the afterlives of injustice in our times? And why? Through what aesthetic strategies do they do so? These questions are at the center of this book. Artists, like the rest of us, are "in the pool"—in places like California, where I have lived half my life, or in South Africa, the place from which most of the artists featured in this book hail. Performance artists whose medium is the body, those who make performances about unresolved embodied histories in and through living bodies, may help us inhabit spaces shot through with the noxious remains of the afterlives of injustice. And they may lead us to do so with greater knowledge, insight, and care. They may help us see otherwise, even if a little at a time, and provide means for us to become a little less rolled up, flexed, stiff, and cold.

While this book begins in America, its central focus is South Africa. That said, its animating questions are equally resonant and relevant in both places. The United States shares with Canada, New Zealand, Australia, and South Africa deep-settler status—all are locations of white conquest wrought by violent white rule. Deep-settler states vary, each with its own distinctive historical trajectory and racialized practices of dispossession and dehumanization.[22] But they also share certain commonalities, as historian George M. Fredericksson demonstrated so persuasively in his landmark 1981 study *White Supremacy: A Comparative Study in American and South African History*:

> More than the other multi-racial societies resulting from the "expansion of Europe" that took place between the sixteenth century and the twentieth, South Africa and the United States (most obviously the southern United States during the era of slavery and segregation) have manifested over long periods of time a tendency to push the principle of differentiation by race to its logical outcome—a kind of *Herrenvolk* society in which people of color, however numerous or acculturated they may be, are treated as permanent aliens or outsiders.[23]

In California, white conquest was achieved through a state-endorsed war of extermination against Native Americans that was not formally acknowledged until 2019.[24] I began this book with a story about how I came to discover remains of genocide that were, quite literally, underneath me. Through this awakening to local afterlives of injustice, I came to see South Africa with new insight. Unresolved histories insert themselves in our times, yet their excess and surfeit often surpass both our comprehension and our ability to do something productive in the face of them, at least in a linear fashion. In such circumstances, the voices and visions of artists—such as those featured in this book—can help us see what otherwise evades perception. Their art also has the capacity to disorder the toxic real and wedge open spaces where necessary new fictions can take root, gestate, and become sentient, living, breathing realities in the now.

Introduction

> These questions, which have engaged so many, have troubled all of my work. How to be both free and situated; how to convert a racist house into a race-specific yet nonracist home. How to enunciate race while depriving it of its lethal cling?
>
> —Toni Morrison

Unresolved pasts tend to return. In the aftermath of gross state-perpetrated injustice, a facade of peace can suddenly give way. For instance, the semblance of peace created through South Africa's negotiated settlement in 1994 thinly veils the persistence of structural inequality and endemic violence even now, a quarter-century into a new democracy. Recent eruptions include the Marikana mining massacre and several waves of xenophobic violence and student protests on South African campuses against the iconic status of figures such as Cecil Rhodes and prohibitive student fees. As Achille Mbembe writes, the time of waiting is giving way to a time of doing—or perhaps more accurately, a time of undoing: "The winds blowing from our campuses can be felt afar, in a different idiom, in those territories of abandonment where the violence of poverty and demoralization having become the norm, many have nothing to lose and are now more than ever willing to risk a fight. They simply can no longer wait, having waited for too long now."[1] When heavily armed, militarized, private campus security forces are deployed to face down protesters and are prepared to shoot these students—even in the back, even as they flee—the word "transition" rings especially hollow.[2] There is nothing new about peaceful protesters being shot in the back. From the 1960 Sharpeville massacre to the 2012 Marikana mine massacre, such atrocities haunt as a disturbing and toxic repertoire. Some say South Africa is now dangling on the edge of a failed state.[3] Others say the postapartheid order is only now beginning.[4] Whether things are at an end or at a new beginning, the present is clearly a time of disruption. There is a core tension between movement and stasis in the country's current state of suspended revolution, and it is this core tension that commands my focus when considering bodies onstage, both those that move and those that do not, and the ways in which these bodies depict and enact change, transformation, stasis, and protracted intervals.

The edited collection *Remains of the Social: Desiring the Postapartheid* identifies the post-1994 era in South Africa as apartheid's wake.[5] Whether this wake is like the waves that a boat leaves behind as it cuts through the water or like a ritual that follows death, apartheid still affects the present. It lingers . . . persistent, pervasive, disruptive, and tenacious. As the editors of *Remains of the Social* state, one always feels the "visceral articulation of lived experience ordered by the undercurrents of apartheid," including its violent patterns of inclusion and exclusion.[6] Navigating apartheid's wake demands vigilance and wakefulness: one must cultivate an awareness of how profound wrongs have a potent afterlife. Wakefulness means not just being woke but actively engaging in what African American scholar Christina Sharpe calls "wake work," a "mode of inhabiting *and* rupturing [the] episteme [of slavery and its anti-blackness] with our own lived and un/imaginable lives."[7] The ultimate purpose of both vigilance and wake work is not to mourn, but rather, Sharpe urges, to "imagine otherwise from what we know *now* in the wake."[8] The epigraph from Toni Morrison frames the questions that have galvanized so many artists, including those featured in this book: "How to be both free and situated; how to convert a racist house into a race-specific yet nonracist home. How to enunciate race while depriving it of its lethal cling?"[9]

Performance and the Afterlives of Injustice brings the most social of art forms—live performance—together with questions about how societies change in the wake of state-perpetrated atrocities. Arguing that a performance-centered study is necessary in order to understand the inherent performativity of subjects, subjectivities, and social formations in post-conflict societies, this book places live performance at the center of cross-disciplinary conversations within theater, dance, performance studies, and cultural studies. How do unresolved racialized histories of state-perpetrated violence create particular conditions of possibility and impossibility for performance artists, choreographers, and theater makers? What aesthetic strategies do artists use to activate and shape live performance's unique corporeality and sociability as a medium, its distinctive capacities for expressing and representing volatile content? How, and how well, do various aesthetic strategies work? When and why do performances in such contexts misfire, or reach their limit?

This book considers key works by contemporary South African artists

Brett Bailey, Gregory Maqoma, Mamela Nyamza, Robyn Orlin, Jay Pather, and Sello Pesa, as well as choreographer Faustin Linyekula from the Democratic Republic of Congo. Even as I highlight performances from Africa's "now," this book begins in 1972 with Athol Fugard's play *Statements after an Arrest under the Immorality Act*, part of a trilogy known as the *Statement Plays*. I set my analysis of contemporary works against this historical backdrop both to illuminate the role that performance formerly played in South Africa's past and to reveal how the present arose from this past, how past and present bleed into each other, how the past returns, not always invited. If we are to understand the afterlives of injustice, we must first identify the life of injustices: to what are these contemporary artists responding? Fugard's play from the height of apartheid powerfully establishes the conditions of racialized subjectivity, both for white and black people.

Embodied performance in South Africa has particular potency because apartheid was so centrally focused on the body: classifying bodies into racial categories, legislating where certain bodies could move and which bathrooms and drinking fountains certain bodies could use, and determining how different bodies carried meaning. "Apartheid was not only a physical or spatial regime," Gavin Steingo reminds us, "but also an intervention at the level of the body and the sensorium."[10] Given the centrality of the body and the senses to the apparatus of apartheid, it is especially pertinent to examine the corporeal habitus of South Africa's current era.

In thinking about bodies both under apartheid and in its aftermath, I am inspired by the work of theorists Susan Leigh Foster and Alexander G. Weheliye. From Foster, I focus on the question of "corporeal epistemes," the ways choreography, kinesthesia, and empathy function to "construct corporeality in a given and historical cultural moment."[11] Corporeal epistemes participate in the production of knowledge and the structuring of power. They are specific to a place and time. What were the racialized corporeal epistemes of apartheid? How and how much have these changed in the postapartheid era? From Weheliye, I am prompted to focus on how enfleshment can point the way to freedom. For Weheliye, the concept of *habeas viscus* represents one "significant mechanism" for anticipating freedom, a state he contrasts with bare life and biopolitical discourse as theorized by Giorgio Agamben and Michel Foucault: "The conjoining of flesh and habeas corpus in the compound *habeas viscus* brings into view an articulated assemblage of the human (viscus/flesh) borne of political violence, while at the same time not losing sight of the different ways the law pugnaciously adjudicates who is deserving of personhood and who is not (habeas)."[12] Weheliye's approach highlights the potential of "minuscule movements, glimmers of hope, scraps of food, the interrupted dreams of freedom found in those spaces deemed devoid of full human life."[13] Hieroglyphics of the flesh are embedded in bone and synapses, held in repeated but often unexamined muscle memories, habituated through impulses and recurrent actions the purposes of which may have been lost in time. Artists who work with the body—choreographers, dancers, performance artists—are particularly attentive to the hieroglyphics of the flesh and often have a heightened capacity to notice and interpret what those hieroglyphics might be trying to tell us.

The majority of artists I analyze in this book are people of color. This is a necessary corrective to the still very white-dominated nature of South African performance scholarship. Some of the artists featured here are considered choreographers or makers of dance theater. Others might be labeled performance artists or creators of "live art." But many defy genre categorization, for they have exploded existing genre categories. The uncertainty about where to place performances by Sello Pesa or Robyn Orlin on festival programs is a sign that they have disrupted received aesthetic categories.

As they imagine new forms, these artists are helping audiences see the contemporary moment as it is: an important intervention in a country long predicated on denial. They are also helping conjure, anticipate, and dream a world that is otherwise. "Otherwise," as articulated by Ashon Crawley, is "a word that names plurality as its core operation."[14] Otherwise conveys that "It does not have to be this way. This can change. We can be something other than this."[15] Otherwise does not collapse into false utopias, rainbow chimeras, or coercive expectations of healing and cure. Working in the wake of apartheid, when all is still not well for South Africa's majority, these artists imagine an otherwise. They acknowledge both history and racism, but their performances are defined by neither of these.[16] While excavating apartheid's legacies, they do not rush to reconcile among factions that in South Africa have no previous history of conciliation, so how can they possibly "re"-concile?

Many contemporary South African performing artists could have been included in this book and are not, among them Nelisiwe Xaba, Athi-Patra Ruga, Steven Cohen, Boyzi Cekwana, Nhlanhla Mahlangu, Peter Van Heerden, Tossie van Tonder, and Dada Masilo, to name but a few. I privileged artists whose work spoke to me, whose performances resonated with this book's key theoretical questions and themes. I am also dependent on my own access to the artworks as live performances and through video documentation. Given my geographically remote location in Berkeley and Seattle, access to time and the opportunity to travel play a somewhat arbitrary and influential role in which works and artists got my attention.

The inclusion of Faustin Linyekula from the Democratic Republic of Congo testifies to transnational artistic relationships and the opening up of South Africa's borders after apartheid. Gregory Maqoma, the other key subject of my final chapter, has collaborated with Linyekula for several decades, something that would have been impossible under apartheid. *Beautiful Me*, Maqoma's signature work, lists Linyekula as a creative collaborator and co-choreographer. Maqoma's international collaborations are extensive; he works with artists from other parts of Africa and with those in and from other parts of the Global South. These transnational artistic connections are a decolonizing corrective to the afterlives of injustice that fundamentally isolated black South Africans from the rest of the continent and the world.

Why *Afterlives of Injustice*? In part, this title reflects my exhaustion with terms like postcolonial and postapartheid. The "post" is never accurate, as these regimes are not over. I object to the linear presumptions about time embedded in such words, as if there were progression from one state to another. Many of the artists I examine also express profound frustration with these ideas. South African choreographer Mamela Nyamza has said of her country's present that now is "too soon to say everything is fine; no we're not free yet."[17] As I sought a conceptual frame for this book that could hold the range of questions, themes, insights, and preoccupations that are central to the artists considered here, I was influenced by several scholars. First, I am indebted to African American scholar Saidiya V. Hartman for her phrase "afterlives of slavery."[18] Beginning with her book *Lose Your Mother*, a memoir about her diasporic travels to Ghana to trace slave routes and histories, Hartman illuminates how even though slavery has formally ended, its afterlives permeate America's present with disruptive, truncating, caustic, and distorting legacies. The afterlife of US slavery is evident today in "skewed life chances, limited access to health and education, premature death, incarceration, and impoverishment."[19] A related phrase, "afterlives of injustice," comes from Robert Meister's *After Evil: A Politics of Human Rights*, a formidable critique of global human rights projects and transitional justice endeavors. And of course, South Africa is a paradigmatic example of global transitional justice. Meister argues that instead of focusing on victims and seeing them as revolutionaries who are on a path toward social justice, more recent Human Rights Discourse[20] focuses on beneficiaries who do not wish to identify with past perpetrators:

> A beneficiary who bears witness to the innocence of past victims can thus conceive of himself as a would-have-been rescuer rather than a would-be perpetrator. The question for the human rights convert is always whether it is already too late to rescue or still too soon. By agonizing over questions of his own potential guilt as bystander, the witness to human suffering tries to save his soul without necessarily relinquishing his position of advantage.[21]

According to this argument, the contemporary Human Rights Discourse project includes an inherent attempt to deflect attention away from present demands for social justice by focusing instead on what *might have been* in the past. One also can read a presumed archetypal framing of both victim and perpetrator and an avoidance of examining the bystander's significant role in past conflict. Meister's argument is that Human Rights Discourse too often operates on an implicit presumption that the beneficiary of today *would have* sided with opposition to past atrocity instead of standing by passively as a complicit bystander and/or beneficiary. Within this structure, injustices of the present still go unattended.

Finally, Jennifer Wenzel's *Bulletproof: Afterlives of Anticolonial Prophecy in South Africa and Beyond* served as a pivotal and formative text for me. Wenzel argues that even failed decolonization movements in places like South Africa have productive afterlives: "If decolonization is a story of failure, for what contemporary or future projects might its continuing promise be mobilized?"[22] Wenzel helped me see that it is not just profound and unsettled injustices that live on in the present but also the vestiges of failed decolonial mobilizations. These too have afterlives that can be accessed and summoned in myriad ways today.

For the artists featured in this book, past injustices are multiple: slavery, of course, but also and more recently colonization and apartheid, both of which endure in neoliberal economies of extraction and exploitation in the contemporary so-called postcolonial world. None of these histories are over yet, but these artists presume it is not too late to imagine otherwise. Whether the afterlives of injustice are acknowledged or denied, whether they serve as a backdrop or a catalyst for dramatic action, the continued vitality of unresolved wrongs creates volatile, dynamic conditions. For artists working in such contexts, afterlives of injustice are forces with which to be reckoned.

PERFORMANCE CONTEXTS

Some readers will know my previous work as a scholar of theater. My shift to dance and movement-based performances with this book is a response to the artistic works I have found most galvanizing over the last ten years of attending performing arts events in South Africa, particularly during regular trips to the National Arts Festival in Grahamstown. Dance, dance theater, live art, and performance art have seemed to me especially resonant in and with the contemporary moment in South Africa, sometimes much more so than theater, which has had more of a need to replay revivals from the "struggle days," caught in a kind of nostalgic trap. Arguably the present moment has more shades of gray than can be accommodated by the moral certainties and presentational aesthetic styles so commonly seen in what is known as antiapartheid protest theater. Its signature mode of creation, the workshop method for collectively devising new works, and its broad aesthetics for storytelling, characterization, and acting styles remain well known and widely practiced. But the artists featured in this book are pursuing new modes of performance making. Their modalities are much more focused on the body, on kinesthetic memories, and on the upending of narrative and genre expectations and the refusal of audience appetites for coherence.

Dance, like theater, has a complex and often problematic inheritance from the apartheid era. A racially polarized and segregated form prior to 1994, concert dance privileged ballet and modern forms that were overwhelmingly associated with white culture, artists, and audiences. These genres were separate from the prolific range of dance forms that one might label traditional. Some of these "traditional" forms are associated with particular ethnic groups, such as *ngoma* among the Zulu, and Bharatanatyam among South Africa's Indian populations.[23] Novel cross-cultural forms developed in the crucible of apartheid, especially those such as gumboot dancing and *isicathamiya* forged in multicultural migrant hostels for mine workers (readers may have witnessed *isicathamiya* in the performances of the international touring group Ladysmith Black Mambazo). While much about dance under apartheid was racially segregated, in the 1970s there began to be small pockets of integrated dance that labeled itself contemporary (as opposed to modern). Dance scholar and journalist Adrienne Sichel notes that dancers, teachers, choreographers, and activists built artistic connections across racial divides, "often openly defying apartheid segregation laws and taking huge personal risks" to do so.[24] Key figures in this artistic integration were pioneers Sylvia Glasser and Alfred Hinkel, who trained many of the artists who went on to become celebrated choreographers of the postapartheid era, some of whom are featured in the present book. Yet under apartheid, dance did not enjoy the same international and global prominence as did plays like *Sizwe Banzi Is Dead,* which had high-profile tours in London and New York. Actors John Kani and Winston Ntshona won a Tony Award for their performances in that play, co-authored with Athol Fugard. Such protest theater played an important role in raising international awareness about apartheid and rallying activists to participate in the international boycott that was ultimately crucial to ending this regime. In contrast, South African dance did not reach global visibility under apartheid, and perhaps as a result, there was less of an impulse in the postapartheid era to revive struggle classics like *The Island, Woza Albert!* and *Asinamali*. Dance in the postapartheid years has rather been informed by an urgent sense that it needed to lean in to the new—to redefine itself, integrate, find new ways to disrupt inherited legacies, bring together disparate traditions, and share the stage across former divides.

This book aims to correct a racialized imbalance in scholarship on South African performance. A disproportionate amount of research has focused on white artists, despite the fact that South African contemporary artists of color have produced an abundance of dance, theater, live art, and performance works of tremendous complexity, sophistication, innovation, and insight in recent years. In addition, theater scholarship is segregated from dance scholarship, and these, in turn, are separate from research on performance art and live art. In this book, I quite deliberately bridge and intermix theater analysis with dance analysis and close readings of pieces labeled live art. I contend that moving among these forms is true to the South African current arts scene and to audience experiences of these works and to the artists' own working processes. But in the end, I privilege dance and dance theater.

Only a few book-length studies on contemporary South African dance exist, including: Sharon Friedman's edited volume *Post-Apartheid Dance* (2012), Adrienne Sichel's *Body Politics* (2018), and Ketu H. Katrak's *Jay Pather, Performance and Spatial Politics in South Africa* (2021).[25] South African performance art and live art have only recently begun getting scholarly attention. Jay Pather and Catherine Boule's edited collection *Acts of Transgression* (2018) is a welcome contribution.[26] Kim Gurney has published the only extant monograph on South African live arts, *The Art of Public Space* (2015).[27] In terms of theater scholarship, the last chapter of Loren Kruger's *The Drama of South Africa* (1999) covers the early years of the "interregnum," while Anton Krueger's *Experiments in Freedom* (2010) is entirely devoted to the postapartheid era.[28] Krueger focuses predominantly on white artists, though rather unselfconsciously so. Megan Lewis's *Performing Whitely in the Postcolony* (2016) is more deliberate about its white racial lens.[29] April Sizemore-Barber's *Prismatic Performances: Queer South Africa and the Fragmentation of the Rainbow Nation* (2020) provides a welcome and much-needed contribution by examining contemporary queer performances that have altered ideas of the normative.[30] *The Methuen Drama Guide to Contemporary South African Theatre* (2015), edited by Martin Middeke, Peter Paul Schnierer, and Greg Homann, offers a valuable overview of recent theater endeavors, though with necessarily abbreviated analysis, given the book's survey format.[31] More problematically, of the thirteen artists featured in individual chapters of the *Methuen Drama Guide*, only four are artists of color. Given that white people represent only approximately 8.4 percent of South Africa's population, the underrepresentation of scholarship on performance artists of color a quarter-century after the end of apartheid is especially notable and problematic. My book aims to address these lacunae.

In South Africa, especially in the dance world, there has been an avid debate in recent decades about what it means for disparate movement forms, traditions, and styles to share the same stage.[32] Many terms have been bandied about to represent postapartheid dance aesthetics that try to mediate cultural divisions: fusion, Afro-fusion, frisson, infusion, multiculturalism, syncretism, hybridity, cross-culturalism, interculturalism, melting pots, and cultural cocktails, to name but a few. Many have tried to facilitate a fusion of dance cultures but with unsatisfactory results, as choreographer Lliane Loots describes:

> We saw *Bharatha Natyam* dancers stand next to traditional *ngoma* dancers, and ballerinas in tutu and pointe shoe all moving to the sound of the same African drum beat. We sighed collectively as [we] saw how possible it was to all live side-by-side in rhythmic harmony. No one questioned the "side-by-side" and the fact that no real mixing and integration was taking place; the ballerina's tutu remained pink and the skins of the traditional *ngoma* dancer remained firmly cow-hide. This multiculturalism saw no mixing in its dance steps and styles, and we did not ask who owned this melting pot. Who *allowed* the *ngoma* dancer onto stage, and who asked the *Bharatha Natyam* dancers to join in? Multiculturalism, while a contested concept, for all its pretense at cultural tolerance, proved to be an economic and political power game where tradition and popu-

> lar performance forms were finally *allowed* to join the adults at the bottom of the dinner table. No one really stopped to question whose dinner party it was and, indeed, who owned the dinner table.[33]

As scholarship on interculturalism has long contended, such questions—which at their core are about ethics, economics, ownership, power, respect, and appropriation—inevitably arise amid attempts to mediate cultural differences that are thoroughly entangled with structural inequalities and unresolved histories of injustice.[34]

There is nothing terribly new or original about the idea of interculturalism in South Africa, a place where, for several centuries, a multitude of different cultures have collided, migrated, taken root, invaded, fled, resisted, and been transformed. "Black South Africans have practiced interculturalism from the onset of colonialism," says Jay Pather. "We had no choice."[35] But now that black South Africans *do* have a choice, what will they choose? While people often presume that mixing and integration among cultures formerly separated by apartheid is a positive aspiration, Pather approaches this view with skepticism:

> Is this infusion of cultures such a big deal anyway? I think the more we ask those questions honestly, the more we are going to be able to catapult ourselves into some kind of infusion. Because I think that's the big question: "Why is this important?" "Why should I know about your culture? I should tolerate you as a human being, [but] why do I need to know more about you?" And I think when one asks those questions, then one can figure out whether this whole experience is a worthwhile one. What are those moments all about?[36]

"Those moments" are the centerpiece of Pather's choreography: carefully crafted occasions of encounter with various "others" whom apartheid divided. By way of contrast, intercultural elements in Robyn Orlin's and Brett Bailey's work are more often collisions or competing realms or a composite of multiple others that can rapidly collapse from a spectrum of cultural affiliations and identities into a binary of black and white, especially when the work travels overseas.

Dance in South Africa has been perhaps uniquely positioned to explore new registers of interculturalism. Why? I posit four reasons: First, dance is generally liberated from the constraints of language, which otherwise present formidable communication challenges in a context like South Africa, with its eleven official languages. I may not understand a movement vocabulary from a different culture, but I can kinesthetically apprehend and respond to it. Second, bodies are dance's primary medium of expression, and South Africa has a heightened awareness of the potency of the body given the centrality of bodies to the very essence of apartheid. Third, kinesis is indeed, as Joseph Roach has argued, the new mimesis in the contemporary performance world globally. Roach argues that "as the arts proliferate within the mediated and multicultural languages of transnational space, expressive movement is becoming a lingua franca, the basis of a newly experienced affective cognition and corporeal empathy. Mimesis, rooted in drama, imitates action; kinesis embodies it."[37]

Finally, the inherited forms of dance in South Africa remained polarized and separated under apartheid; ballet and modern dance were affiliated with white identities and were largely segregated from a whole spectrum of dances associated with people of color. Even among people of color, these communities as well as their various dance forms were often isolated from one another. And then there was a whole slew of popular social dance forms that might be practiced by people of different races (but usually in isolation from one another), ranging from ballroom and *langarm* to gumboot and *pantsula*. Under apartheid, dance lacked the kind of prominent interracial collaborations and forums that we see in the history of South African theater. Beginning with the landmark dramatic works created by Athol Fugard, John Kani, and Winston Ntshona in the early 1970s, for example *Sizwe Banzi Is Dead*, South African theater spawned a whole range of workshopped, or devised, plays that were created in collaboration and across racial lines. After *Sizwe*, the interracial collaborative workshop method was also attached to a style of theater that was used to directly protest apartheid. The popularity of the workshop method eventually led to the founding of landmark interracial theater institutions such as the Market Theatre in Johannesburg and interracial companies such as the Junction Avenue Theatre Company.[38]

Yet the trajectory of dance was quite different. Except for a few specific instances of interracial collaboration, South African dance did not have a comprehensive platform that truly embraced interracial performances until the inception of the Dance Umbrella in Johannesburg in 1989. In the 1970s and 1980s, there were significant, innovative, daring interventions that crossed racial lines. For instance, Jazzart, the oldest contemporary dance company in Cape Town, founded in 1973, pioneered a number of truly groundbreaking racially integrated works in the 1980s, especially under the direction of Sue Parker. Particularly notable was a piece called *Abhamanyani*.[39] In Durban, the dances of Suria Govender and Irene Oakley as well as Jay Pather's *Duel in Black and White* worked in a similar vein. These were early interventions across racial lines. Yet it was the advent of Dance Umbrella that brought questions of interculturalism to the fore in the early postapartheid years, these questions energized by a sense that this interculturalism was not only new for the genre of dance but also timely in the history of South Africa. Dance's embrace of intercultural collaboration coincided with a national mandate for South Africa to become integrated, nonracial, culturally mixed, deliberately disrupting and dispensing with the boundaries and separations apartheid had imposed.

Robyn Orlin's 1999 *Daddy, I've seen this piece six times before and I still don't know why they're hurting each other*, a legendary postapartheid performance work, has endured in part because it posed with such acerbic wit questions about cultural ownership, empowerment, and appropriation that have remained paradigmatic and pivotal ever since South Africa's first elections in 1994. Reflecting on the extraordinary national and international success and endurance of *Daddy*, South African dance critic Adrienne Sichel identifies the show's relocation from Dance Umbrella to the Market Theatre in 2000 as evidence that South African dance at the turn of the century was "where SA theatre was in the 1980s."[40] In other words, dance had finally "caught up" with antiapartheid interracial protest theater.

While dance may once have lagged behind theater in terms of its cross-racial artistic collaboration, I would also contend that in the postapartheid years, dance has shot way ahead of theater in terms of bold inventions in form and content that speak directly to and with current times. Dance has generally resisted the vexing and tiresome tendency of postapartheid performance to mount nostalgic returns to the former antiapartheid theatrical triumphs, telling old struggle stories that are now eclipsed by an uncertain present.[41] Perhaps because theater reinvented itself formally under apartheid, it was less agile and responsive to the need to reinvent itself yet again once apartheid ended. However, dance, which remained a segregated and siloed practice under apartheid, with separate cultures doing their dances separately, has assumed wide-ranging license to reinvent itself.

In talking about the relation of dance and theater (and all the artists under consideration here work in crossover genres), one must also consider "physical theater," which arrived in South Africa through such pioneers as Jennie Reznek, a performer who trained with Jacques Lacoq and cofounded Magnet Theatre in Cape Town, and Gary Gordon at Rhodes University who, in 1993, founded the First Physical Theatre Company.[42] Physical theater in many ways bridged the worlds of theater and dance, which apartheid had kept apart. In their cross-pollination in the late 1980s and early 1990s, new styles enticed many formally trained dancers and choreographers to work in more conceptual ways. Many of the artists associated with this crossover between dance and theater are covered in this book: Gregory Vuyani Maqoma, Sello Pesa and his Ntsoana Contemporary Dance Theatre, Mamela Nyamza, Nelisiwe Xaba, and Jay Pather and his Siwela Sonke Dance Theatre, among others.[43]

Starting in the 1990s, there were many experiments in South African dance that brought previously segregated people together. As Gerard Samuel has written, "Blurring of differences of self and other was welcomed in the euphoria of the collapse of apartheid. White selves and Black others found one another in heady dance fusion experiments. But, 21 years later," Samuel argues, "this neutralizing can be equally obscure or nurture a false egalitarianism."[44] Samuel speaks to a growing wariness among politically engaged contemporary South African artists about collapsing into facile and highly problematic multiculturalism. Popularized South African slogans such as "ubuntu" (I am because you are), "simunye" (we are one), "rainbow nation," and "social cohesion" articulated desires for harmonious cultural integration.[45] State-endorsed projects of unity have met with growing suspicion and fatigue, especially as so little about the material conditions of black people's lives has changed. A long-standing muscle memory around separateness and separation is reinforced daily. While facile homogenizing slogans such as "simunye" attempt to mask these realities, at best such terms evoke a thin layer of "rainbowness" that is quickly exposed as an insubstantial chimera. South Africa's gaping inequalities and continued violence are far too extreme to say blithely, "We are all one."[46]

Dance scholar Sharon Friedman writes that "while the search for a 'South African' identity in the performing arts was and remains both a necessary and desirable aspect of social transformation in South Africa, there remains the danger that what is perceived as desirable and politically correct by both policy makers and funders . . . can lead to work that is made in a hodgepodge of styles."[47] The problem with the hodgepodge is not just the loss of cultural specificity and integrity, not just its homogenizing operations, but more troublingly its depoliticizing qualities as it attempts to erase a long history of racialized injustice before justice has been served. As choreographer Mamela Nyamza has said, "The laws have changed but the reality has not changed."[48] Gugu Hlongwane sees apartheid as "a stain that refuses to disappear."[49]

Theater—and theater scholarship—has followed a different track. Anton Krueger's *Experiments in Freedom* (2010), a key scholarly book that widely surveys postapartheid South African theater, focuses on the first ten years of democracy, 1994 to 2004. It takes up where Loren Kruger's monumental *The Drama of South Africa* (1999) left off (though her most recent book *A Century of South African Theatre* includes coverage up to 2018). Anton Krueger notes a sense of dis-ease that came with the "loss of clarity" at the end of apartheid. Aesthetics that were salient during the "struggle years"—such as political agitprop art and a focus on racial injustice—seem less relevant now. Krueger identifies what he sees as the paradox of South Africa's postapartheid freedom: artists must "learn to let go" of past artistic proclivities, repertories, aesthetics, and, most particularly, their commitment to "racialized categories" that were imposed and that structured all human relationships under apartheid.[50] He asserts that more recent plays are successful because they "let go"—that is, the authors do not "discover or fix identities" but rather show the failings of a too-rigid adherence to past identifications.[51] It is not identity differences that are the problem, according to this view, but rather the style, tone, and attitude with which they are articulated. Theatrical experiments in freedom, in Krueger's view, require artists to relinquish "faithful adherence" to specific identities.[52] In other words, one must let go of race, as a construct, as a rubric of analysis, and as a lived reality. Of course racism is lived oppression for some and lived privilege for others, so one's capacity to relinquish identity formations and the terms under which one might do so vary widely depending on key power differentials, ones that Krueger unfortunately does not turn his attention to.

Notably, Krueger's "letting go" approach has produced a book that focuses predominantly on white artists and gives only brief and cursory attention to playwrights of color such as Zakes Mda, Mpumelelo Paul Grootboom, and Ronnie Govender, all of whom are crammed into two chapters of the book's twenty-eight. Krueger ends chapter 24 by announcing the inadmissibility of race as a valid line of inquiry:

> Despite this very brief mention of writers divided according to racial categories, I must re-iterate that I have deliberately tried to avoid raising issues of racial identity since I feel that focusing on issues of race and trying to restore an essentialized racial identity are antithetical to the demands of democracy. It is astonishing that twenty years since the National Party raised the white flag and signaled the beginning of the end of apartheid, issues of race are still routinely debated and legislated.[53]

This quote models a predictable (usually white) liberal deflection that uses nonracial discourse to rationalize an attempt at race blindness while simultaneously refusing to acknowledge that racism—both interpersonal and structural—is still widely prevalent in South Africa today. As Melissa Steyn, who has written on postapartheid race identity, has argued of South Africa: "Nonracialism is . . . often recast in the mold of liberal color-blindness, with the consequence that middle class South Africans, both black and white, frequently express the belief that drawing attention to race as a societal issue is anachronistic and harmful. To name race is taken to be racist. The most frequent comment I receive when asked about my work is 'Aren't we beyond this?'"[54] Obsession with race was the fundamental evil of apartheid, so the argument goes, such that the best or more progressive or enlightened response today is to ignore race (which requires a refusal to acknowledge the intransigence of the continued manifestations of racism in the present). Yet if racism is still widely experienced by people of color (and race privilege, conversely, still widely enjoyed by white people), then surely race is a worthy subject of both art making and cultural analysis.[55] "Letting go" as a strategy for Krueger's book has reproduced the same old result: racial segregation and racialized disparity in how playwrights are covered—who gets airtime, focus, analysis, celebration, and discussion, and who does not. But there is one way in which the "new thing" of this race-blind approach does not take after the old: the new discourse attempts to remove explicit language about race altogether, the very language needed to name, identify, and describe such disparities.

Whereas Krueger asserts that "in order to be free, it may be necessary to abandon the pursuit of who we think we are," more recent discourse and happenings in South Africa have decisively and violently swung in the opposite direction. Theorist Achille Mbembe noted in 2015 that terms like "whiteness," "white power," "white supremacy," and "white monopoly capital" are "firmly back on the political and cultural agenda and to be white in South Africa now is to face a new-old kind of trial although with new judges—the so-called 'born-free.'"[56] Given the trajectory of so many African nations in the 1960s and 1970s as they transitioned from colonies into newly independent nations, it is no surprise that today, nearly twenty-five years into its new democracy, South Africa is experiencing profound disillusionment with the unfulfilled promises of Nelson Mandela's rainbow nation. Significant segments of the population experience the stark daily realities of unreliable delivery of water, electricity, and basic sanitation, and these segments are overwhelming people of color, as was true under apartheid. Lack of employment and escalating university fees are also flash points. Unequal and inadequate material realities have sparked massive protests in many sectors. Overall there is a growing rejection of the slow pace of transformation and the persistence of colonial and apartheid paradigms, profound socioeconomic inequalities, and pervasive violence. One sees today in the postapartheid era familiar scenes: street barricades, armored vehicles, rock throwing, and the burning of tires, all reminiscent of apartheid-era protests.[57] Universities are particularly volatile arenas; the #FeesMustFall and #RhodesMustFall movements are asserting urgent demands for everything from curricular reform and an increase in the number of faculty members of color to a reduction in student tuition, increased access for multiracial students, and the removal of offending statues and building names.[58] Confrontations between protesting students and law enforcement have led to the suspension of classes, violent encounters involving stun grenades and rubber bullets, and even the torching of libraries.[59] Clearly, the afterlives of apartheid's racialized practices are far from resolved. Instead of letting go, the disenfranchised may be more inclined to seize, take possession, and destroy.

The postapartheid decades have seen many cul-de-sacs and conflagrations and misfires as dramatists, choreographers, and performance artists have tried to devise new aesthetics that resonate with the country's complex cultural and political realities.[60] Some performances have been trapped: in nostalgia or in protest aesthetics that polarize in spectacular ways that no longer speak to the current moment, or in a reconciliation-induced conflict avoidance that tends to be singularly undramatic.[61] In addition, the enticements of the commercial marketplace often demand ossified images of black cultures for exploitation and profit.[62] Other South African artistic misfires have hinged on the propensity for heroic narratives and the ways these flatten, distort, and elide complexity.[63] Likewise, representations of violence can collapse into reinscriptions of violence, and cultural depictions meant to awaken historical sensibilities can erroneously promulgate amnesia.[64] These are the boomerangs that Ralph Ellison warned of.[65]

Of the present moment, Achille Mbembe has said that "a surplus of toxic energy has been aroused," evident in increased polarization and balkanization, as well as a resurgence of "deep-seated, repressed or denied racial anger."[66] The contemporary climate is a tinderbox, and some artists have chosen to light a fire under this tinder, sometimes using satire, parody, and even blasphemy as means of ignition. Most notorious in this regard was Brett Murray's painting *The Spear*, which depicted South African president (and president of the African National Congress [ANC]) Jacob Zuma posed as Lenin. Stylistically a cross between a Soviet propaganda poster and a Warhol-inspired action movie advertisement, the painting showed Zuma's body clothed and jauntily turned at an angle, poised for action, yet with his genitals exposed, flaccid and drooping between his legs. When it was exhibited at the Johannesburg Goodman Gallery in 2012, the painting was vandalized. It became the focus of intense debate and public marches, a target for protests, and the subject of a lawsuit. The ANC issued a press release expressing outrage at the painting, and the Goodman Gallery issued a statement saying that "it was never the Goodman Gallery nor Brett Murray's intention to hurt anyone or harm their dignity" and that "the gallery regrets the pain that the display of the painting has caused."[67] This controversy has been a defining one for contemporary arts in South Africa, as Shireen Hassim attests: "Art and politics met in a heightened clash that embodied all the tensions of a country moving imperfectly towards an imagined state of democracy."[68]

The conflagration surrounding *The Spear* followed a now-familiar repertoire that has been seen elsewhere in deep colonies such as America and Canada. One is reminded of controversies around Mike Daisey's 2011 play *The Agony and Ecstasy of Steve Jobs* or Robert Lepage's 2018 performance of the *Kantata* project, which was accused of appropriating Indigenous history, or the aborted Minneapolis Walker Art Center installation of Sam Durant's sculpture *Scaffold* (2017), which represented the 1862 mass execution of Dakota Native American men. The pattern is familiar: defenders of artistic license and the constitutional right to freedom of expression are pitted against defenders of the right to dignity, populist outrage seethes on all sides, press releases and counter press releases are issued, lawsuits are threatened and sometimes filed, emotional testimonies are aired about the intent of the artist or producer, these are countered with emotional expressions attesting to harm and negative impacts, agreements are made to withdraw or postpone or there are righteous refusals to do so, apologies or pseudoapologies are issued or refusals to apologize are defiantly proclaimed. Meanwhile, the whole tempest is fueled and amplified by a constant media storm that churns across internet clouds, picking up velocity with each tweet, blog post, article, and Facebook rant. The current cultural volatility in South Africa is especially extreme, for it is a place where, as one artist stated, "Everything is fucking political—puppies are political."[69] These challenges are among many that contemporary South African artists must face. In some ways, the stakes are highest for embodied performance because of its visceral immediacy. It calls a community forth, with live bodies, to meet face to face. It relies on freedom of expression, freedom of movement, and freedom of assembly both for performers and audience members.

LINES OF INQUIRY

This book is organized around several arguments and lines of inquiry. Following the provocative work of Jean Comaroff and John Comaroff on theorizing from the Global South, I approach the artists featured here as thinkers who are themselves theorizing in and through their performances while they are also located in and theorizing from the Global South.[70] First, I argue that embodied performing arts contribute importantly to postapartheid cultural studies by excavating submerged registers of understanding through the body. Second, I analyze how these performers disrupt linear framings of time as well as teleological assumptions about change, resolution, reconciliation, and cure. Third, I examine how these artists approach questions of interculturalism, what it means for one culture to encounter another given the complexities of difference in South Africa and its fraught histories of racialized separation, inequality, and violence. Finally, I argue that performance theory in general must grapple with the force fields surrounding the afterlives of injustice. If we are to consider how performance cultures flow into one another, permeate one another, confront one another, entangle, clash, and interweave with one another, then we need a method for understanding the politics of the permeation of past histories with present realities.

Corporeal Epistemes

Many scholars who have reflected on the predicaments of contemporary South African culture have focused on literature.[71] Much less scholarship has been devoted to theater and performance art, and astonishingly little has focused on South African dance. This book contributes to scholarship on South African culture in the wake of 1994 by focusing on the body and embodied artworks. Apartheid ruled its subjects in myriad ways, but it was within the regimes of the body that it most intimately invaded people's lives. Apartheid laws of separateness determined where certain bodies could work, where they could sleep and travel, where they could defecate and drink. Apartheid legislated whether and how certain bodies could or could not fraternize. In the bedroom, the boardroom, the theater, or the restaurant, and even in the court of law, segregation of bodies held sway. As dance critic Adrienne Sichel has written, "It is easy to forget that intrinsically apartheid policy and mind-sets politicized, even dehumanized, the human body. In essence the dancing, performing, body had the ability to humanize the 'other.' It offered the opportunity to see a fellow South African as a human being and not merely as a racially classified statistic shrouded in cultural stereotyping."[72] As scholars think through apartheid's remains while also desiring an otherwise postapartheid world, the body emerges as a primary site for incorporating and instantiating new paradigms and ways of being. Annemarie Lawless explores ideas of the social in South Africa that have congealed around calls for empathy among people whom apartheid had divided. She asks, "What is it for one thinking, feeling, breathing body to encounter another thinking, feeling, breathing body—not a subject-to-subject encounter, still less a human-to-human one, but rather a creaturely one, epidermis to epidermis?"[73] Of all the many mechanisms of apartheid—including substandard Bantu education, detentions, imprisonment, unwarranted searches, influx control, work permits, segregated housing, and pass laws—it was the prohibition against skin contact that went to the "very core of the heart of South African racism," Jeanne Colleran argues.[74]

If regulation of the body was central to apartheid's operations, what is the place of the body in a postapartheid world? Can embodied contact likewise be central to new senses of difference, desire, and wakefulness? At a visceral, kinesthetic level and in the presence of other bodies in space and time, might the body be central to new senses of difference, desire, and wakefulness in the South African present? Artistic expression of and through the body occupies an especially charged space in apartheid's wake. The South African performance works I examine excavate histories of violence with the body and within the body, for the corporeal serves as a container of memories, a forensic archive, and a potent site for reclamation. Through the performances considered here, we see striving bodies, struggling bodies, habituated bodies, bodies that move with entrenched muscle memories, and bodies discovering new ways of being, moving, encountering others, and letting go of things once tightly held. Bodies become primary sites for resisting old orders and disorders and for awakening new sensibilities, for activating and instantiating otherwise possibilities.

In addition to somatic and kinesthetic questions of being inside a body, there is the question of how bodies are seen. Sabine Sörgel's book *Contemporary African Dance Theatre* (2020) examines these questions in great detail.[75] Most critical for readers to understand, I think, are the complicated aesthetic conditions faced by black artists whose bodies onstage must automatically contend with a long history of objectification, of being seen as a racialized "other" rather than as a subject who offers others access through performances to their experiences, perspectives, and points of view. Some artists, such as Brett Bailey, have responded to this history by crafting works that directly confront the white gaze with the black gaze. Bailey's controversial work *Exhibit B* (2012), examined in chapter 3, references the history of Africans being put on display in human zoos. Bailey puts black performers in static exhibition vitrines with dramatically racialized tableaux. In their arresting stillness, performers make direct eye contact with each visitor who enters the exhibit, a flow that is stage managed so that spectators enter one at a time. The power of the gaze was really the center of this work, as visitors and critics often commented. Theater scholar Megan Lewis reported,

> To me, the power in this piece, given the history of the staging of human bodies across Europe and America, is that the live actors' bodies are given the power of the gaze. It is . . . that eye contact that absolutely blew me away. I found myself at different moments either trying to make eye contact or feeling so uncomfortable that I would look anywhere else and then realize I'm looking at objects when there's a live body here and now I have to make eye contact with the body. . . . That negotiation back and forth—what was most powerful was that they were set up as tableaux, as static images, and yet it's the body with the *eyes* who are returning the gaze.[76]

There was an uncontestable, riveting power in this returned gaze in performance, a staging element that was key to this white artist's entire *Exhibit* series. But the work of several of the artists of color in this book takes an entirely different tack in the face of the gaze. A recurrent motif across several performers places them center stage with their back to the audience, refusing the gaze. Gregory Maqoma's piece *Exit/Exist* (2013) and Mamela Nyamza's works *Hatched (2009)* and *Isingqala* (2011) all begin with long sequences in which the audience sees only the performer's back (figures 1 and 2). The performers deliberately withhold the audience's visual access to their faces. At the same time, this staging invites audiences to see from the artist's point of view. The stance is at once a refusal and an invitation.

This excavation of embodied knowledge in South African performance has significance beyond South Africa. Elizabeth S. Anker's pivotal work *Fictions of Dignity: Embodying Human Rights in World Literature* argues that a profound ambivalence toward embodiment is at the core of liberal human rights discourses and norms. She argues that although human rights were founded in the "dual fictions" of human dignity and bodily integrity, they produce a "highly truncated, decorporealized vision of the subject."[77] Yet

Fig. 1. Gregory Maqoma in *Exit/Exist,* 2013. (Photo by John Hogg.)

Fig. 2. Mamela Nyamza in *Hatched*, 2010. (Photo by John Hogg.)

Anker's objects of analysis are entirely literary (novels by Salman Rushdie, Nawal El Saadawi, J. M. Coetzee, and Arundhati Roy). The distance between the implications of Anker's theory and the sites of her application provoked me to think more deeply about how dance, physical theater, and live art as embodied art forms might be ideal sites for "tracking how aesthetic experience can map the unfolding of an embodied consciousness, in the process suspending ordinary thought and discourse to excavate submerged registers of understanding," the project that Anker proposes as paramount for a reimagining of predominantly liberal understandings of human rights.[78] Access to embodied consciousness and submerged unconsciousness is precisely what the performance works analyzed in this book do. I argue that embodied performances are uniquely capable of undoing apartheid's afterlives through kinesthetic means.

Refusing Closure, Disrupting Time

The artists under consideration here disrupt the assumptions of a desired destination embedded in the ubiquitous notions of transition and healing that have dominated the postapartheid era. Inaugurated by the now-paradigmatic transitional justice experience of the Truth and Reconciliation Commission (TRC), South Africa in the last quarter-century has focused on narratives that posit the nation as transitioning from one state (apartheid) to a new, liberated, nonracial democracy. Yet the destination is elusive. The country has clearly not yet reached this desired future state, which was once figured as Mandela's rainbow nation or Thabo Mbeki's African renaissance or the TRC's "road to reconciliation," which imagined a terminus where presumably all the races that apartheid divided would live in harmony. While the term "transition" may not be sufficiently capacious to describe the expanse of time since South Africa's first democratic election in 1994, a host of authors writing on contemporary South Africa underscore the overall sense of things having been stalled or suspended during this time; Adam Habib's *South Africa's Suspended Revolution* is perhaps the most obvious example. Writing in 2013, Habib talked about "the transition to date" with a clear sense that it was still ongoing.[79] He also said, "In many ways, South Africa has hardly moved since the end of Mbeki's presidential tenure, and the country is no closer to the prosperous cosmopolitan vision Mbeki projected in his speech to the constituent assembly in 1996."[80] Power has shifted subtly since the ANC's momentous Polokwane conference in 2007, the black middle class has been growing, and multiple new laws ensure employment equity and improved labor relations. But continued racialization of identities and growing socioeconomic inequality remain the defining characteristics of contemporary South Africa, according to Habib. Why? This question, in Habib's view, "is fundamental not only for scholars, but also for the architects of the transition."[81] While the artists I analyze do not attempt to answer this question, their artworks illuminate the experiential, embodied, and affective dimensions of a suspended revolution. What does stalled "progress" look and feel like? How is it kinesthetically experienced? What capacity for agency is possible, even during such a suspended state?

Transition is, by definition, a time in between. Robert Meister sees Human Rights Discourse, of which South Africa in the aftermath of apartheid has been the epicenter, as framing transition as a time between times—"when evil has ended but before justice has begun."[82] This understanding resonates also with the notion of interregnum, Antonio Gramsci's term, one often invoked in South Africa in the 1980s: "The crisis consists precisely in the fact that the old is dying and the new cannot be born: in this interregnum, morbid phenomena of the most varied kind come to pass."[83] Are the morbid symptoms of South Africa's interregnum of the 1980s different from the pathologies of the post-1994 "transition" and the ailments of the contemporary era, which some have called a time of "post-transition"? And if so, how? Perhaps the differences are matters of degree: morbidity versus chronic debility. Transitions are eventually meant to end, and likewise cure and healing imply that suffering will eventual resolve. In the mid-1990s, there seemed to be an assumption that a country could talk its way to psychic wellness or that the present-day legacies of apartheid are like festering wounds that simply need to be lanced and drained and then all would be well. While metaphors of healing and the supposed therapeutic effects of opening old wounds swirled around the TRC, this discourse inevitably excited expectations for a cure. As disability studies has shown, promises of miraculous cures usually both disappoint and coerce.[84] They also erroneously frame certain conditions as individual misfortunes rather than as a systemic societal failure to accommodate a greater range of human ways of being in the world. Likewise, the TRC individualized both the perpetrators and victims of apartheid, sidestepping the compelling question of the systemic nature of apartheid and the structural legacies it left behind.

Many monikers have been used for the years after 1994 in South Africa: postapartheid, post-antiapartheid, the transition, and post-transition among them. They all share an underlying sense of moving from here to there and temporal frames that separate "back then" from "now," along with hints of aspired futures, even if these are not yet realized. Postapartheid, post-antiapartheid, and transition (and TRC-fueled notions of healing) are all predicated on what Leon de Kock identifies as a teleological thrust, a linear thinking in which there is an ultimate object or aim. Yet de Kock argues that creative South African writers have consistently resisted any notion of a telos in the past three decades:

> Despite the efflorescence of postapartheid writing, its apparent release from the straitjacket of political themes, it is also true that much of the new writing consists of narratives and counter-narratives that set up a dialectic around the very notion of a fresh start. That is to say, the idea of a *transition* itself, in its denotation as a process or period of change from one state to another, a linear path that somehow yields the telos, or end point, of postapartheid . . . is questioned, problematized, cast in doubt or rendered ironic.[85]

The performing artists featured here both implicitly and explicitly convey that postapartheid framings of change have exceeded their limits. What is needed are new analytics with greater agility and a capacity to handle the elliptical returns of history, the resurfacings of atrocities thought to be passed, while also holding history's remains in dynamic tension with the promise of a future that is otherwise. As Elizabeth Maddock Dillon contends, "the signifying economy of the theater operates in two registers: one that is *ontic* (thingly, material, resolutely present) and one that is *mimetic* (referential, immaterial, gesturing toward a scene located elsewhere)."[86] So performers are not just articulating new analytics; they are doing them, they are performing them, they are putting them onstage before our eyes and making them so.

Intercultural Entanglements

Of the postapartheid years, choreographer and curator Jay Pather has said that "people are trying to decide: 'Are we going to come out of one Group Area and walk into another Group Area,' you know, one kind of tradition into another kind of tradition, or come to terms with fluidity and malleability."[87] Here Pather refers to apartheid's Group Areas Act, which segregated living areas based on race and ethnicity. Is it desirable for people who were formerly separated by apartheid to come together in the new South Africa? Can people connect across entrenched lines of separation and yet not step on one another's toes? And are we really sure that coming together is a good and desirable thing? The Truth and Reconciliation Commission touted that idea, but are rainbows really the future of freedom?

The politics of intercultural performance in a place like South Africa are precisely in the fact that colonialism is not yet "post."[88] Interweaving is a recent concept for thinking about intercultural performance globally, a theory that tries to make everything fit together, to be woven according to a pattern. I find theories about interweaving of performance cultures both useful and insufficient.[89] Interweaving strikes me as too mild, too neutral, too malleable, too flexible, and even flimsy. To analyze performances in places where there is a potent and toxic afterlife of injustice, we need analytic tools with more teeth and greater tensile strength. We need to extend our theories about the recursive nature of time in and through performance, to consider how caustic, inflammatory, churning remains of unresolved racialized pasts shape and even limit the potential of performance.

I see much more promise in the notion of entanglement. In a place like South Africa, entanglement captures the moral ambiguities, distortions, ironies, paradoxes, complexities, and repressions of the past and the kinks and frayed ends that remain today far better than current intercultural performance theories such as interweaving. In her book *Entanglement: Literary and Cultural Reflections on Post-Apartheid*, South African cultural studies scholar Sarah Nuttall writes,

> Entanglement is a condition of being twisted together or entwined, involved with; it speaks of an intimacy gained, even if it was resisted, or ignored or uninvited. Entanglement is a term which may gesture towards a relationship or set of social relationships that is complicated, ensnaring, in a tangle, but which also implies a human foldedness. It works with difference and sameness but also with their limits, their predicaments, their moments of complication.[90]

As Nuttall argues, apartheid was a regime of entanglement inasmuch as it relied on complicities, imbrications of people and things, interlocking modes of time, and pervasive and latent racial snarls. South Africa has not been a place where two forces—warp and weft—came together. It is not a place where a new fabric can be simply woven from the distorted fibers of yesterday's cloth. In the postapartheid rainbow dispensation there has been pressure to quickly unify as a new nation.[91] Yet, as Sharon Friedman has written, "The idea of 'simunye' is largely one that has been imposed to create the idea of unity. But we are not one, in fact we are one of the most heterogeneous societies in the world."[92]

Entanglement indicates connection among elements, people, and cultures without necessarily imposing the normative expectation that they *should* be interwoven. The question of agency is less fixed: there is no weaver because entanglements generally lack a coherent master plan or overall design. Tangles are produced by multiple forces, not all of them known. There are no "mistakes" with entanglement. Just tangles. The term also suggests a tension, a complication that was not predicted or expected. The term harbors at its core a dynamic agon that resonates with the fraught realities of the afterlives of injustice. Entanglement can be life threatening, as when an animal at sea dangerously becomes entangled in an abandoned net, yet entanglement can also be life giving, as in the human entanglements of love, family, and friendship that enfold us and lift us up.

Theorizing Afterlives of Injustice in and from the Global South

This book aims to discern theories that animate the contemporary African performances covered here, and to connect these with theories from elsewhere, particularly American-based black studies and Euro-American-based performance studies. I believe there is much to be gained by such cross-pollination. Saidiya V. Hartman's concept of the "afterlives of slavery" potentially has deep resonance in South Africa, a place with a long and complicated history of slavery and a long and complicated history of subsequent waves of state-perpetrated racialized violence. I want to open up a deeper consideration of the implications of Hartman's theorization of diasporic black experience. Christina Sharpe's notion of "wake work" is also relevant for South Africa, where black people constitute the majority and where the history of white supremacy has such uncanny links and resonances with that of the United States, as George Frederickson so persuasively demonstrated in *White Supremacy*.[93] Given the synergy between the histories of racialization in these two countries and their notable divergences, there is tremendous opportunity for greater connection between black performance theory, which has been a prolific and vibrant area of contemporary scholarship in the United States, and black performers in South Africa.[94] In her book *Illegible Will*, Hershini Bhana Young has done pioneering work in this regard, asking the important question "How well does black performance theory travel, given that there is no universal, transparent notion of the (black) body?"[95]

The anthology *Black Performance Theory*, edited by Thomas DeFrantz and Anita Gonzalez, explores how foundational assumptions may need to be revised when black people are centered.[96] Yet I share the question Mlondolozi B. Zondi raises about the role of Africa in that book: "What is elided or made possible by [an] invocation of Africa primarily as a site of folkloric tropes, aesthetic inspiration, and a *past* through which to trace elements of contemporary performance repertoires in the diaspora?"[97] The performance works of artists such as Mamela Nyamza, Gregory Maqoma, Jay Pather, and Sello Pesa place black artists in contemporary Africa as central and important interlocutors who are speaking of an Africa very much in the now rather than in some primordial folkloric past, even as the past remains a visible and palpable residue.

Just as US-based theater and performance studies tends to cast Africa as a place frozen in the past, as a source of inspiration rather than an active agent in the present, the field has also been impaired by linear framings of time. As is Rebecca Schneider in her book *Performing Remains*, I am interested in questioning our linear expectations of time.[98] I share Schneider's sense that we should perceive history not as linearity but rather as a constant resurfacing. Schneider asks, "What happens to linear history if nothing is ever fully completed or discretely begun?"[99] She focuses on people who intentionally and deliberately perform the remains of history through things like Civil War reenactment. Schneider intervenes in debates among performance studies scholars such as Philip Auslander, Peggy Phelan, and Diana Taylor about whether and how performance can be archived.[100] She argues that performance does not disappear but rather remains, especially through the "doing" of history as one sees in historical reenactments. My concern is with how unresolved histories exert their own performative force—that is, how unresolved histories do things, impact the now, insert forces and interruptions in our times in ways that we cannot always predict or control.

American-based theater and performance studies scholarship has often analyzed how performers affect—or intend to affect—a society or community. There has been much reflection on theater's utopian aspirations, what Dani Snyder-Young calls the "theater of good intentions," including work by Jill Dolan, James Thompson, and Laura Edmonson.[101] In addition, the work of Marvin Carlson on the haunted stage, Rebecca Schneider's work on performing remains, and Joseph R. Roach's scholarship on surrogation provide a rich array of theories for analyzing the relationship of past and present in performance and the ways in which theater participates in collective memory and the imagining of new futures.[102] But I believe we have underestimated the ways that the nonlinear nature of time, to use Schneider's concept, operates according to force fields that may be determined, perhaps even overdetermined, by the afterlives of injustice. The nonlinearity of time in *Performance and the Afterlives of Injustice* is about urgent political concerns and demands. A lack of restitution, acknowledgment, reparation, redress, and atonement in the wake of massive state-perpetrated atrocity produces a toxic surfeit that has a potent performative force. Our theories of performance must reckon with this excess.

Within theater and performance studies, we need to devise analytic tools that are strong enough to grapple with the cultural encounters that occur in the context of the afterlives of massive injustices such as apartheid, slavery, and genocide. These afterlives often inhabit what Sarah Nuttall would call the "underneath," a place out of public view in the hidden operations of a nation's cities, institutions, environments, and bureaucracies. Afterlives of injustice are also capable of suddenly erupting with remarkable velocity and force. A theoretical rubric that focuses on surface and depth is more revealing than time-based framings such as "post" and "beyond." The implied teleology in phrases such as "beyond postcolonialism" is misleading. Yes, one can point to certain historical moments when, say, mass atrocities were said to have ended: emancipation day in the United States on January 1, 1863, or the first democratic elections in South Africa, which signaled the end of apartheid, on April 26–29, 1994. But these gross injustices leave a legacy that is enduring. We do not get beyond the performing remains of unresolved histories of atrocity, certainly not without the deep work of excavation, atonement, redress, reparation, and repair. This work must be structural and material repair and symbolic and cultural reparation. Even then, it may be better to operate on the assumption that one does not get over such histories. The legacies of white supremacy in the United States and South Africa may be more realistically conceived of as enduring conditions. One can imagine otherwise possibilities while at the same time remaining clear eyed about the power of resurgent potentials, the tenacity of latent forces, and the enduring impact and presence of traumatic pasts—all of which require active care.

METHODOLOGY AND STRUCTURE

Performance and the Afterlives of Injustice is organized around close readings of pivotal contemporary performances. Readers familiar with my previous books may be expecting extensive interviews with artists, performers, producers, and communities, or in-depth archival evidence.[103] Neither are present in abundance here, as I have chosen instead to provide close readings of complex, richly suggestive performances, especially since several of these artists are so little known outside South Africa. I have had the privilege of witnessing in person nearly all of the works analyzed here, but I recognize that most readers will not have seen these performances and will typically not have access to videos, scripts, or other documentation. The majority of the featured performances are body based and ephemeral and have left limited traces in the archive. (I am especially grateful to the Ar(t) chive at the University of the Witwatersrand and Mime Centrum in Berlin for the video recordings they made available to me.) In the absence of widely available primary texts and documentation to which I can send the reader to consult and form their own opinions of these artworks, I have tried to provide rich, evocative, and illuminating descriptions, to conjure vivid moments from the performances, and to weave these closely with my critical analysis and arguments. I write about dance with acute sensitivity to the stakes of a body moving through space, the miracle of standing, and the inexorable forces of gravity. I abruptly experienced a heightened sense of body awareness twenty years ago when I was diagnosed with a tumor in my leg that ultimately led to an amputation. While I had not been a particularly kinesthetically astute person before that ordeal, my entire life after my diagnosis required that I train my body in ways that are similar to how a dancer trains: I had to cultivate balance, coordination, flexibility, and stamina. All of this has made me very aware of bodies and kinesthetics, giving me visceral appreciation of dance.

Many additional questions can and should be asked about the artists who are my focus—about their biographies, their histories, their aesthetics, their audiences, their collaborators, their producers, and their communities, especially considering the widely varied cultural, national, and international contexts in which many of their creative works have circulated. I hope this book will inspire other scholars to do research along these lines, which requires more time on the ground than I could afford over the last six years. As a non–South African, I am humbled by the challenge of writing about a culture not my own, knowing that there will be much that I will miss and not see and things that I will get wrong, despite my best efforts. Yet I also hope that my perspective as an outsider allows me to see some things that scholars and artists located in South Africa, who are fully immersed in the thick of a country so urgently and dynamically remaking itself, may not have the distance to perceive.

The book begins with Athol Fugard's play *Statements after an Arrest under the Immorality Act* and explores the relation of performance and the law in apartheid South Africa during the early 1970s—a time in between the nonviolent resistance of the 1950s and the escalation of open combat that characterized the wake of the 1976 Soweto uprising. In the 1970s, South African theater artists of all hues had to navigate a gauntlet of ever-escalating apartheid legislation, a cascade of laws that limited their capacity to assemble, to move through space, to fraternize across racial lines, and to express ideas. Chapter 1 illuminates how apartheid laws invaded the most intimate domains of the body, of love and sex, and of psyches and subjectivities. Just as the play's characters are literally and figuratively undone by an arrest, so too did apartheid's escalating laws disrupt, distort, and complicate theater artists' attempts to mount this play and, indeed, any live theater and performance during this era.

The next chapter considers several performance works created in the postapartheid years, including Jay Pather's *Body of Evidence*, Mamela Nyamza's *De-Apart-Hate*, and Sello Pesa's *Bag Beatings*. One sees in these performances paralysis and stasis. Yet one can also see emergent movements—sometimes inchoate, sometimes trapped in old paradigms and muscle memories, sometimes holding tight to ways of being that isolate and confine. Rediscovering the ordinary, as Njabulo S. Ndebele exhorted artists to do in the early years of South Africa's new democracy, sometimes requires one to set up seats on a sidewalk in a downtown intersection in Johannesburg, as Sello Pesa does, and then, through the disruptive potential of insurgent performances that masquerade as the everyday, to see what is hiding in plain sight but may have somehow eluded conscious observation.[104] The power of the performances studied here resides in the artists' capacity to trouble linear framings of time and to forge emergent aesthetics capable of wielding apartheid's toxic remains without succumbing to their corrosiveness.[105]

Chapter 3 interrogates notions of the intercultural, which is a charged and fraught topic in South Africa given the myriad cultures within its borders and the radioactive afterlife of apartheid's rule, which conquered by dividing races and ethnicities. Can the stage be shared? Can South Africa's many cultures and its legacies of racialized injustice be negotiated on contemporary stages—and if so, how? Can the breathtaking heterogeneity of South Africa's cultures—its rich inheritance of movement practices, aesthetics, languages, and people—occupy the same space, literally and metaphorically, in the contemporary political order? The chapter analyzes the disparate approaches that Robyn Orlin, Jay Pather, and Brett Bailey take to these questions.

The final chapter considers performances by Faustin Linyekula from the Democratic Republic of Congo and Gregory Maqoma from South Africa. These two artists met in Kenya in 1996, and their conversations over the years have led them to parallel artistic explorations and direct collaborations. In both countries, the afterlives of colonial injustice continue to exert a corrosive force in myriad ways today, but perhaps nowhere more ubiquitously and subtlety than in the realm of proper nouns. This chapter explores the performativity of names and the performativity of the proscenium stage. While both artists have often had to wrestle with the problematic labels "African dance" or "contemporary African dance," they are both more interested in locating their creative inquiries in the local and the individual rather than the continental. Names—whether one's own name, or the name of a city or country—are a way to investigate identity that is at once personal and part of a much larger network of relationships and histories. Is one Zairean or Congolese? It depends on when in history the question is asked: the country's name has changed several times. Likewise, much ink has been spilled on the idea of decolonization. But how does one actually accomplish decolonization? If the question of decolonization is about a reconsideration of what is in the center, Maqoma and Linyekula take up this question quite literally in the way that they use and occupy theatrical space. What is to be featured center stage?

The artists considered here eschew facile solutions and hasty moves toward closure and reconciliation. Their creative processes and expressions are often elliptical, approaching their topics associatively rather than directly. They sometimes refuse to say clearly what the work "means," but rather stage a process that invites audiences into a journey where we must engage with a willing sense not of "disbelief," as is so often referenced in the theater, but rather of tolerance for the unknown, the unfamiliar, the unconventional, and even the unnamed. My own writing style has mirrored their approach. I see my representations of dance through words not simply as thick description, but actually as its own kind of dance. Jay Pather theorizes that when one dance tradition or culture encounters another onstage, together they produce a third: the dance between dances. My text in this book is its own expression of a dance between dances, it is an expression of my mental, emotional, and kinesthetic response to encountering these provocative performance works. Hence I am not in a hurry to say what the works "mean," or to foreclose the possibility that readers may experience my representation of the dance through words and come to different conclusions than would I. In other words, the writing style may not be what is expected. Bear with me reader, for I am trying to give access to artists who are fully disrupting conventions and revising expectations.

The overarching questions for artists featured here are enormous. How does a decades-long official state policy of apartness premised on violently enforced white supremacy become something different—something democratic, inclusive, liberated, and not racist—in the new South Africa? What aesthetic strategies are contemporary African artists using to make performances that resonate deeply with the "now," with all of its paradoxes, ironies, and transitional ambivalences? How might live, embodied, visceral, kinesthetic performances in specific places and times navigate a fraught landscape of entanglements and help people cross over to a new place that is, if not "beyond" apartheid, then at least a place where fresh and liberating energies steadily flow? Performances, unlike novels, are time based and ephemeral. They are happenings with real people, real bodies, and assembled communities who share, for a finite duration, a common space. Sharing a common space has rarely been simple in South Africa, especially when those who have assembled come from disparate communities, races, and backgrounds. Things in contemporary South Africa and the Democratic Republic of Congo are entangled, and they are likely to remain morally ambiguous, distended, enfolded, and enmeshed for the foreseeable future. This situation does not necessarily imply a nihilistic position or even an Afro-pessimistic one.[106] The hope for a better future remains a vibrant expectation and a demand, certainly by the artists featured in this book. But theirs is a quest, a dedication to the ongoing necessary work of otherwise. It requires the ability to dwell in complexity, to endure a lack of resolution, to consider the heterogeneity of cultures without forcing a false oneness, and to inhabit a place where the afterlives of injustice are likely to endure.

The artists analyzed in this book negotiate these conditions by crafting performance works that often demand a *dwelling in* the palimpsest that constitutes the contradictions of the present, a resistance to impulses to simply *move on* from colonialism or apartheid. At the same time, they operate with an insistent and persistent expectation that things *should be otherwise* than what they are or have been.

ONE | Athol Fugard's Statements Before and After Arrests: Performing at the Edge of the Law in Apartheid South Africa

> It seems to me both poignant and striking how the effect of racialism on the subject has been avoided and unanalyzed. The scholarship that looks into the mind, the imagination, and the behavior of slaves is valuable; equally so is a serious intellectual examination of what racial ideology did and does to the mind, the imagination, and the behavior of the master.
>
> —Toni Morrison

I begin with analysis of a play by Athol Fugard, *Statements after an Arrest under the Immorality Act*, produced in the early 1970s, when apartheid had tightened its stranglehold, severely restricting freedoms of movement, assembly, and speech. The play stages an encounter between a white female librarian and a coloured male lover.[1] Partway through their tender assignation, the law intrudes: the police raid the scene, and the lovers are separated. This is what apartheid did: it separated people, in unequal ways, according to race. Through parallel monologues delivered after the arrest, Fugard dramatizes the disparate subjectivities that apartheid's white supremacy produced, both for the colonizer and for the colonized. How does this play reveal the effects of racialism on both black and white South African subjects? What access can this play provide to the interior, subjective experience of racialization specifically at the moment of arrest? I argue that Fugard's *Statements after an Arrest* illuminates with precision and nuance differential racial responses to interpellation in a racist state. We see how white and black characters react to an arrest in completely different—though racially structured—ways. The play's representation of racial differentiation at the moment when apartheid law intrudes on the most intimate sphere of human relationships provides an important window onto the racialized nature of subjectivity in a society dominated by white supremacy. This chapter also introduces theater produced at the edge of the law in apartheid South Africa, and the ways in which white theater artists and producers responded to the increasingly oppressive laws of apartheid in the 1970s.

I begin here in order to historically and theoretically situate the performance works covered later in this book. This apartheid-era play provides a strategic point of entry for it frames core issues that have remained salient in the quarter-century since the end of apartheid. South Africa is presently located in what Achille Mbembe describes a "historical interval," caught "between an intractable present and an irrecoverable past; between things that are no longer and things that are not yet."[2] The artists covered in subsequent chapters of this book are all working in that historical interval. To understand its dynamics and contours, we need to understand what came before, how apartheid law produced racialized subjectivities.

This chapter focuses on arrests during apartheid as a situation where the law hailed subjects by seizing and detaining them. Louis Althusser long ago showed us that subjects are "always already" interpellated by the law. The scene of the arrest or a hailing by a police officer make explicit the law's dependence on subjects to affirm its legitimacy. Arrests are highly performative: three-dimensional, durational, visceral, and kinetic. An arrest is a paradigmatic moment of interpellation as Althusser theorized it:

> I shall then suggest that ideology "acts" or "functions" in such a way that it "recruits" subjects among the individuals (it recruits them all), or "transforms" the individuals into subjects (it transforms them all) by that very precise operation which I have called interpellation or hailing, and which can be imagined along the lines of the most commonplace everyday police (or other) hailing: "Hey, you there!" [Note: Hailing as an everyday practice subject to a precise ritual takes a quite "special" form in the policeman's practice of "hailing" which concerns the hailing of "suspects."][3]

The minute that individual turns their body 180 degrees, they become a subject.

Sometimes an arrest is witnessed by third parties, other times only the officer(s) making the arrest and the accused see it. Today many arrests include witnesses who wield cell phone cameras, and these documents become additional witnesses with the capacity to circulate across space and time, providing the basis for other narratives and truth claims. They offer both a proliferation of perspectives and (potentially) a narrowing of the range of permissible lies. Yet arrests are rarely understood from a position that provides insight into the intersubjectivity of the arrest, the interiorized experience of an interpellation, *how* one becomes a very particular subject before the law, how it feels to be arrested. I am interested in the subjective experience of a *racialized* subject standing before the law. What is the psychic life of power, as theorized by Judith Butler, for those who are arrested or who are living with the perpetual threat of imminent arrest in a racist regime?[4] How is the psychic life of power constituted differently according to race within a racist regime? How should we think about the performativity of the apartheid-era legal prohibitions (nakedness on stage, mixed-race audiences without separate accommodations, etc.) that had to be defied in order for this play to be staged in Cape Town in 1972?

Mladen Dolar and Judith Butler took up the concept of interpellation after Althusser.[5] Dolar's critique of Althusser asks us to consider the role of subjectivity. He explores whether there is a "kernel of interiority" that is outside of subjection, an inner register of the subject that is beyond interpellation.[6] Dolar asks provocatively, "Could one say that love is what we find beyond interpellation?"[7] Judith Butler responds to this question by asserting that in fact, the scene of subjection involves a passionate attachment to the law, a "strange scene of love," as the subject comes to embrace the very conditions of subjection. She says, "That the subject turns round toward the law suggests that the subject lives in passionate expectation of the law. Such love is not beyond interpellation; rather it forms the passionate circle in which the subject becomes ensnared by its own state."[8] Mary Bunch's more recent intervention introduces the concept of "unbecoming"—not only to behave in ways that are, for instance, "unbecoming of a woman," but also to consider "unbecoming" as a space of resistance to the law because, as she argues, "one is also always already something other than the subject one is expected to be."[9] Bunch puts forth for queer theory the concept of an "unbecoming subject," one that inherently exposes subjectivity as a double performative—both law and the subject granting the other the conditions of its possibility and threatening the withdrawal of those conditions.[10]

I am interested in exploring the possibilities of an *unbecoming* subject, one who refuses subjection, particularly racialized subjection. Is it possible to refuse or disrupt the dual performativity of the subject and the law? In order to think through these questions about agency, we must consider how the law as a technology of race is performatively realized in scenes of subjection. Ancient Greek distinguishes the manner in which life is lived (*bios*) from the biological core of life (*zoē*). Philosopher Giorgio Agamben has taken up the latter, defined as "bare life," to explore "precisely this hidden point of intersection between the juridico-institutional and biopolitical models of power"—that is, how bare life constitutes a nucleus of sovereign power.[11] As Alexander G. Weheliye has argued, both Agamben's work on bare life and Michel Foucault's theories of biopolitics, despite their enormously important and field-transforming implications, are notably subdued on questions of race:

> Bare life and biopolitics discourse not only misconstrues how profoundly race and racism shape the modern idea of the human, it also overlooks or perfunctorily writes off theorizations of race, subjection, and humanity found in black and ethnic studies, allowing bare life and biopolitics to imagine an indivisible biological substance anterior to racialization. The idea of racializing assemblages, in contrast, construes race not as a biological and cultural classification but as a set of sociopolitical processes that discipline humanity into full humans, not quite humans, and non-humans.[12]

Weheliye echoes Judith Butler's meditations on the concept of bare life. Within general claims that bare life is the foundation of political arrangements in which we live, Butler argues, there is not yet clarity about how one becomes reduced to the condition of bare life or *how* certain lives are treated differentially on the basis of ethnicity and race.[13] In answer to these questions, the moment of arrest and its legal interpellations, its ontic reality and its mimetic representation in performance, can give us a privileged and provocative vantage point from which to consider arrests as "scenes of subjection," to use a phrase from Saidiya V. Hartman. If arrests are scenes of subjection, what do they stage? What can be learned from (re)staging them theatrically?[14] What happens to theatrical events that summon both artists and audiences to a scene that is illegal, where spectators themselves may be arrested?

"I FUCK, THEREFORE I AM"

The racialized legal habitus of the arrest has been brought spectacularly into public awareness in the United States through the "Hands Up, Don't Shoot" and #BlackLivesMatter campaigns in the wake of the fatalities at the hands of police during arrests in Ferguson, Missouri (Michael Brown); Staten Island, New York (Eric Garner); Oakland, California (Oscar Grant); and Summerville, South Carolina (Walter L. Scott), to name but a few in a long, disgraceful list. However, the arrest that commands my attention for this essay happened in South Africa under apartheid. This fictionalized arrest appears in Athol Fugard's 1972 play *Statements after an Arrest under the Immorality Act*. Fugard's inspiration for the play was an actual arrest the playwright recorded in his notebook in 1966:

> Immorality Act case at De Aar [a town in Northern Cape]. Coloured Anglican missionary and a forty-year-old white woman, a librarian. The police caught them in bed, pulled back the sheets and took photographs.
>
> Darkness. Suddenly a blinking flash of light like a photographer's flash; a split second later a woman screams. Then stage lights up to reveal an office desk, chair and—to one side—a filing cabinet. Standing at the desk, examining a police file, Sergeant. . . . He takes out a set of photographs—"They'll get four months' suspended."
>
> De Aar. Heat. Dust.
>
> "Three statements after an arrest under the Immorality Act"—Woman Man Sergeant.[15]

This shard of a dramatic idea from 1966 eventually became a one-act play that opened at the Space Theatre in Cape Town on March 27, 1972, starring Fugard himself as "Man," or "Errol," and Yvonne Bryceland as "Woman," or "Frieda."

Born in 1932 and the author of over thirty plays, Athol Fugard is one of South Africa's most prolific and internationally renowned playwrights and theater makers. Fugard was the son of an Afrikaner mother and English father, his lineage fusing the two major genealogies of white presence in South Africa, and he described himself as an Afrikaner writing in English. Since the 1950s, his plays, films, theater projects, and other writings have depicted the changing social and political landscape of his country, particularly the rise of apartheid and the many corruptions, distortions, and traumas it brought to human relationships. His gift as a writer is often said to come from the specificity and intimacy of his visions and the dimensionality of his characters. As Russell Vandenbroucke has written, "Fugard understands the characters and world of his plays as intimately as the drops of pond water he studies for hours with his daughter's microscope. His characters possess such concrete quirks, compulsions, and ways of expressing themselves that they persist in the imagination as tangible entities."[16] An outspoken voice of antiapartheid opposition, Fugard has seen his status as a writer shift in the years since 1994, in part because his own liberalism did not shift, but the times and circumstances did. As Jeanne Colleran argues, "Put bluntly: Fugard has never abandoned the liberal view, but the Left to which he formerly belonged has abandoned both liberalism and him."[17] While the post-1994 years have led to many in South Africa seeing Fugard and liberalism as outmoded, *Statements after an Arrest* spoke powerfully in and to its times in the 1970s. And what we do not see in this play are the depoliticizing moves of liberalism that become so prominent in Fugard's later plays: an assertion of human values that transcend political ideology, a reliance on altruism as an agent of social change, an emphasis on fairness and ethics as a corrective to political wrongs, or an advancement of a utopian fantasy of amicable race relations. Instead, *Statements after an Arrest* lays bare the way the law hails and forms subjects along racialized lines. The play's dissection and exposure of racialized subjectivities offers no attempt to suture things up, to produce a reassuring resolution.

Statements after an Arrest under the Immorality Act is one of Fugard's so-called Statement Plays, which were first performed in Cape Town in 1972 and then published together in 1974 as a trilogy. The other two, cowritten with John Kani and Winston Ntshona, were *Sizwe Banzi Is Dead* and *The Island*.[18] What ties the three plays together is the law, for it serves as the fulcrum of each drama. Passbooks—the identity card system so crucial to the apartheid legal apparatus—are at the center of *Sizwe Banzi Is Dead*; the ubiquitous incarceration of black individuals in such notorious prisons as Robben Island is the focus of *The Island*; and the Immorality Act, the apartheid law banning interracial sex, drives the action of *Statements after an Arrest under the Immorality Act*. *Sizwe Banzi Is Dead* and *The Island* are still widely performed in repertoire today; they are two of the most famous South African struggle plays. However, *Statements after an Arrest* is a relatively little-known play. It is seen as one of Fugard's "most ambitions and difficult works," Albert Wertheim says.[19] Highly stylized and experimental, the play when first presented in 1972 was an aberration in terms of Fugard's other dramatic works and in terms of the aesthetics of South African theater generally. Perhaps it was because of the play's radical formal experimentation that South African critics didn't know how to receive it in 1972.[20] When the show traveled abroad in 1974, London audiences may have had the context to understand and appreciate the play's fractured, Brechtian style, but they did not have an understanding of key context that was crucial to the play's action: specifically, the Immorality Act and the Group Areas Act. Success with this play eluded Fugard, and in frustration after the 1972 opening, he described the script in his journal as "at many levels, possibly unavoidably because of the circumstances, the most uncompleted, even careless, work I have yet done on a stage."[21] The multiple versions of the script in the Papers of Athol Fugard at Indiana University's Lilly Library reveal that the version of the play performed in Cape Town in 1972 was quite different from the one that was performed in London in 1974. I would have to agree with Fugard's self-reflection that the 1972 version consisted of notes for a play rather than a well-crafted script. However, by the time the show got through the rehearsal process in London two years later, the underlying structure of the piece had emerged with great clarity, as had the play's center of gravity and enunciation of theme. While *Statements after an Arrest* has been seen as a minor work in Fugard's oeuvre, I would argue that it is far more sophisticated dramaturgically and thematically than has been previously understood.

In addition, *Statements after an Arrest under the Immorality Act* provides a provocative vantage point from which to consider questions of subjectivity and the racialized psychic life of power. It is also an opportunity to reflect on the law's intrusion into intimate acts. The play depicts the clandestine relationship of an interracial couple in a small town in the Karoo in the Eastern Cape, a forty-two-year-old unmarried white librarian named Frieda Joubert and a thirty-six-year-old married, coloured (i.e., mixed-race) man, a school principal named Errol Philander. They have an affair that involves Errol sneaking into the all-white neighborhood under cover of darkness to make love to Frieda on the floor of the library where she works. The couple creates a temporary sanctuary, a cherished yet fragile oasis where love and affection across racial lines can flourish.

The play is divided into two parts, one before and one after an arrest, the halves radically divergent in style. The first part unfolds naturalistically, consistent with Fugard's other works: it features realistic, quotidian dialogue between lovers conducted in the intimacy of a domestic space. However, halfway through the play, the action is fractured in form at the moment when a policeman intrudes. Just before he enters, the lovers have impulsively come together in an embrace:

> [*Against this image of the two lovers, a plain-clothes policeman,* Detective Sergeant J. du Preez, *walks on. He carries a police dossier and notebook. His statement is dictated to the audience.*]
>
> POLICEMAN. Frieda Joubert. Ten, Conradie Street. European.
> Errol Philander. Bontrug Location. Coloured.
> Charge: Immorality Act.[22]

The first thing the sergeant does is hail the lovers by name, address, race, and their alleged crime. (And, of course, in apartheid South Africa, to hail by home address is to hail by race since the Group Areas Act prescribed where each race could live.) While the policeman seems to enter the same space and time that the lovers had occupied earlier in the play, he speaks from another time and place, narrating his experience in retrospect as he recites from his police report. He is the first character in the play to break the fourth wall, to directly address the audience, thereby interpellating spectators and implicitly suggesting their complicity with the action. Have they, like he, been lurking in the shadows, surveilling the lovers' clandestine relationship? Or perhaps the audience members, like Frieda's neighbor Mrs. Buys, have been spying on the couple, even summoning the police? Following the police raid of the "private" sanctuary created on the floor of the public library, the three characters—the sergeant, Errol, and Frieda—all provide statements. Each of these is stylistically distinct, providing a window into how the arrest performs authority and subjection in ways that expose the uneven racialization of the law.

In his notebooks, Fugard described *Statements after an Arrest* as fundamentally about the loneliness and isolation of the lovers—a lonely white librarian living in the arid Karoo and a downtrodden coloured teacher struggling to make ends meet and find human fulfillment in a world tightly circumscribed by poverty, lack of water, lack of books, and lack of respect. As Fugard saw it, the play stages an "encounter between two totally different worlds—both experienced as a 'loneliness'—and the slow, painful building of a 'no-mans' land where they are briefly together."[23] Errol and Frieda's illicit relationship is provoked by desperation about their respective lives. Fugard writes:

> Two people frightened of dying.
>
> One fate inside the room, another outside.
>
> The mistake of moving from being allies, to being lovers.
>
> What is the first incident or remark that provokes Philander to his final bitter sense of self? . . . What moved Philander from the center of his life—where he was living with a hollow sense of self—to its perimeter—because that is how, as a lover, he finally faces Frieda, his back turned on all he really is, and why it cannot work (the relationship), why it progresses into a self-destructive sterility.
>
> Frieda's sexual provocation (not by virtue of anything done deliberately, simply by being what she is) as the relationship devel-

> ops. The initial affirmation of "self" in an affair. Love = one of our useless defences against Death.
>
> Two things happen to Philander. He wakes up in the middle of his life, and he falls in love with Frieda.
>
> Frieda = charity, then excitement and admiration, then love.
>
> Fear?[24]

If what propels Frieda and Errol together is a desperate realization that their lives are running out, what drives them apart is the law that structures where each can live, where each can work, what access each has to resources, and whom each can sleep with. Their after-hours library no-man's-land, as Fugard calls it, is not actually a no-man's-land but rather one fully under apartheid sovereignty. But once the law formally intrudes, once the police burst in, their fragile, temporary sanctuary is utterly destroyed.

Frieda and Errol's affair violates South Africa's Immorality Act. This law—first created in 1927 and then amended in 1950, 1957, 1969, 1985, and 1988—prohibited "illicit carnal intercourse between Europeans and natives and other acts in relation thereto."[25] The act's amendment of 1950 clarified its terms: "'Illicit carnal intercourse' means carnal intercourse other than between husband and wife."[26] Section 20A of that amendment introduced the "men at a party" clause, thereby conflating in one law prohibitions on heterosexual interracial relations and homosexual sex regardless of race, which should lead us to reflect on the legacy of the apartheid state's regulation of both queer and hetero sexuality. The proliferation of amendments to the Immorality Act over many decades was symptomatic of the apartheid state's attempt to control one of the basic human acts: skin on skin, the connection of Self and Other. Jeanne Colleran asserts that of the many mechanisms of apartheid—including substandard Bantu "education, detentions, imprisonment, unwarranted searches, poverty, unemployment, housing and pass laws"—it was the prohibition against skin contact that went to the "very core of the heart of South African racism." She observes that the juridical obsession with interracial sex reflected "a fear of skin contact so immense that it became pathology."[27] While antiapartheid theater in the 1970s and 1980s bravely took on a whole range of apartheid's many pathologies and obsessions, Athol Fugard's *Statements after an Arrest under the Immorality Act* is unique in its bold focus on interracial sex. In Fugard's notebooks, he wrote, "Sex provide[s] the most primitive experience of 'self'—the double aspect/mystery of discovery and loss, both the self and 'the other.'"[28] In his rehearsal notes for the 1974 London production of this play, he wrote, "Sex is one of the most primitive acts of self-assertion of 'being' in relation to 'another.' 'I fuck, therefore I am.'"[29] So if one cannot fuck—and fuck the partner of one's own desire—does one cease to be? And if one ceases to be, is one still a subject?

STATEMENTS BEFORE AN ARREST

The play begins with two naked lovers in near-total darkness on a blanket on the floor in the stacks of a library. In a languid, tender scene of postcoital intimacy, the lovers converse. Soon the man will have to make a furtive, dangerous, and what he describes as "shameful" trek back home to the township where his family resides. The script's character list identifies the two by gender and race: "A Coloured Man" and "A White Woman." In parentheses each is given greater personalization with a name: Errol Philander and Frieda Joubert.[30] Yet in the script the dialogue lists them only as MAN and WOMAN, symbolic figures that some have read as alluding to a prelapsarian Adam and Eve.[31] The opening stage directions read: "A *man* and a *woman* on a blanket on the floor. Both of them are naked. He is caressing her. Dim light."[32]

The woman is the first to speak—a monologue about her hair drying in the sun, the way the texture of her hair changes as the water evaporates and the smell of shampoo intensifies. She describes a small breeze lifting a floating strand (the first clue about her racial identity). This monologue is a phenomenological narrative outside time, intensely sensual, spoken from a body in a space of safety and repose. And yet these individuals are two naked people of different races lying on a blanket in apartheid South Africa. There is nothing safe about that, even behind closed doors and certainly not on a theatrical stage. Given the extraordinary legal constraints on South African theater in the 1960s and 1970s, it is remarkable that the playwright imagined that the police and censors would allow two people of *any* race to be naked for the duration of this show, much less a mixed-race couple. The apartheid state's stranglehold on theater tightened significantly after 1965, when, as Martin Orkin writes, the Group Areas Act prohibited "racially mixed casts or audiences" from all public entertainments unless a permit was secured. Orkin has also written about how "theater practitioners were further inhibited by the rapid succession of wide-ranging laws intensifying the process of censorship in the country."[33] From 1974 to 1981, the censors considered 15,333 plays and declared 9,819 of them "undesirable."[34] Producers, playwrights, and actors, in addition to passing the censor, had to

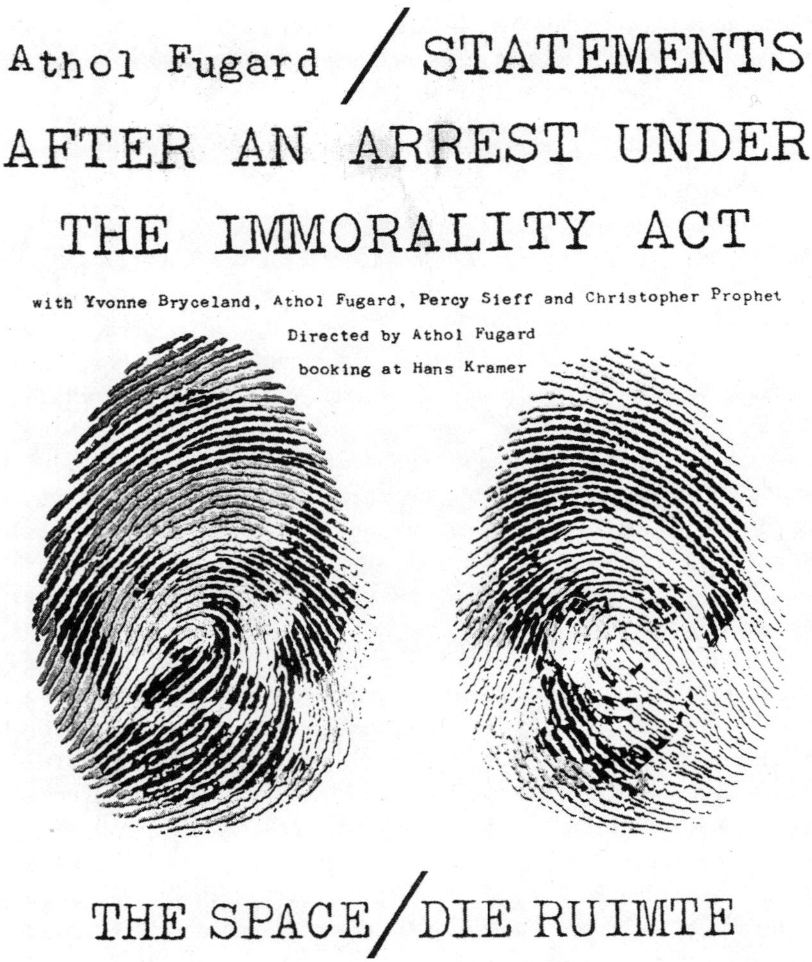

Fig. 3. Original poster for *Statements after an Arrest under the Immorality Act*, designed and screen printed by Margaret Hillhorst, 1972. The fingerprints are those of Athol Fugard and Yvonne Bryceland. (Image courtesy of Brian Astbury.)

contend with police harassment, surveillance, interruptions of performances, and demands that all theaters have separate accommodations for different races. The Space Theatre was run as a social club rather than as a theater in an attempt to skirt some of the racist regulations that limited theaters. In addition, artists were subject to harassment and personal intimidation that included house raids, arrests, and confiscation of personal identity documents. Fugard's *Notebooks, 1960–1977* provides evidence of recurrent police raids on his company's rehearsals and performances, multiple arrests and even imprisonment of actors, and intense censorship and withholding of permits. Notably, the two actors who performed the lovers in the original production were both white: Athol Fugard and Yvonne Bryceland (figure 3). There is no evidence that the police interfered with the first production of *Statements after an Arrest*, which had, as was typical, a six-week run.[35] Still, the performance broke the law because its audiences were interracial (but more on that later).

From the beginning of the play, the couple's conversation is intimate, familiar, and affectionate. She says "I love you" in the first few moments of the play. Their repartee moves easily between everyday details and larger philosophical questions as they talk expansively about the origins of the universe, books they've read, daily encounters on the street, reminiscences about the early days of their relationship, and playful imaginative digressions. Despite this calm and ease, recurring tensions thread through the dialogue. They are afraid of something, an unidentified "them" outside their oasis; they are afraid of being seen, of being exposed. There is a wedge in their relationship, of which his marriage and his family are only part. Neither feels fully understood:

> WOMAN: You don't understand.
> MAN: Understand what? There is seeing, and being seen. Which one are you frightened of? Me or you?
> WOMAN: It's not as simple as that!
> MAN: Yes, it is![36]

The first half of the play narrates scenes of world making: discussion of an imaginary house, an imaginary day of spending the money in one's pocket, and an expansive meditation on the creation of the world. But these idyllic moments are countered by disturbing stories of dismemberment, especially through animal motifs. She tells a story about two snakes that were caught in a neighbor's backyard while mating and were then killed. "Their . . . pieces kept moving . . . for a long time afterwards."[37] Errol remembers a story about his father bringing him a jackal's foot. "The animal had escaped that way . . . chewed off the foot caught in the trap. . . . I didn't know anything yet about being so frightened of something else, that you would do that to yourself. [*Pause*] That's what we're doing . . . chewing away, chewing away."[38] Disturbing images of dismemberment in the animal world are echoed by another disruption in the natural world: the town where they live is experiencing a drought that threatens both livestock and people, and water is being rationed. As Errol and Frieda discuss the water scarcity, the conflict between them, which had been, until then, subterranean and diffuse, finally ignites into a direct confrontation:

> MAN. The location dam is empty. Little mud left for the goats. They're going to start bringing in [*sic*] for us on Monday. Got to be ready with our buckets at twelve. Two for each house.
> WOMAN. Then why won't you let me send you some of mine? The borehole is still very strong. Please! It would be so easy.
> MAN. Thanks, but I'll go along with Bontrug.
> WOMAN. Don't thank me for something you won't take.
> MAN. For the thought, then.
> WOMAN. To hell with the thought! I'm not trying to be kind. It's only water, and you need it.
> MAN. We all do.
> WOMAN. Exactly! So your family must suffer because of your pride?
> MAN. [*Disbelief*]. Pride?
> WOMAN. It sounds like it.
> MAN: Pride doesn't use back doors!
> WOMAN: Sssh, please!
> MAN: Or wait until it's dark. You don't walk the way I do between the location and town with pride.[39]

Errol and Frieda are separated by differences in who does and does not have access to water or the right to enter front doors or which member of the couple must do the work of transgressing the treacherous territory of segregated living spaces between her address in a white neighborhood and his in the coloured township. Once the submerged conflict arising from their unequal subject positions under apartheid law finally erupts, Errol bursts into one of the longest speeches in the play, a torrent of words about pride and guilt, about shame and the difference between them, about solidarity with other people in the township who are suffering, who are so internally wrung out they are like "rags." Frieda finally confesses that she doesn't understand anything, and Errol retorts, "Then you can't. Don't even try."[40]

In the play's first half, dreams, reading, and learning emerge as an *oasis of possibility* for both characters. Errol recalls counseling a young boy playing in the sand to use his imagination to make a house, not by replicating the constraints of his own small township home but by being more expansive: "If you're going to dream, give yourself five rooms, man."[41] Errol narrates how (clandestine) access to the library and books has opened his world and placed him in a larger universe, despite the severe constraints of the coloured township where he lives. As he read at night in his home, the words on the page remade him as a subject:

> They weren't just words, it wasn't just that I understood that somebody had said . . . I'm expressing myself badly. It's hard to describe. It was almost like having a . . . No! . . . it was a "comprehension"—*ja*, of life and time . . . and there in the middle of it . . . at that precise moment . . . in Bontrug, was me. Being me, just being me there in that little room was . . . [*choosing his words carefully*] . . . the most exciting thing that had ever happened to me. I wanted that moment to last forever! It was so intense it almost hurt. I couldn't sit still.[42]

Even as spoken words elude Errol in his attempt to express his inner transformation, it is clear that the discovery of the library has given him access to otherwise possibilities, a change in subjectivity as radical as the impact of his budding love and relationship with Frieda. Through books, which she has shared with him (he is not part of the public given access to this "public" library), he gains a new sense of autonomy, personhood, and self-possession, a subjectivity full of excitement, a sense of optimistic possibility: "I read, therefore I am." He lives also for Frieda, for the world of love she has opened him to. But their relation is always fraught, undercut by her sense of entitlement to *her* water, her role as the one who initiates their sexual relationship, unlocks the door to *her* space. To access everything in this new world—the books and Frieda—he must turn his back on his own family and their life in the township.

Both Frieda and Errol profess love at different moments in the play. Clearly, for both of them the affair is a sanctuary from the deprivations of their respective environments, whether material, emotional, or intellectual. Yet even love cannot shield them from the social distortions of race. Overt acknowledgment of race happens only once in the first half of the play, just before the policeman bursts in and arrests them. Errol has just informed Frieda that he won't leave his wife, and she responds:

> WOMAN. Go home. Take your conscience and your guilt and go back to Bontrug and look after your family. I've also got problems. I can't add your adultery to them. If you haven't got the courage to say No . . . to anybody . . . to me or her . . . I'll do it for you. Go home.

> MAN [*viciously*]. It would be better if I waited until it's dark . . . remember! [*Pause*] My adultery? And yours? *Ja*. Yours! If that's true of me because of you and my wife, then just as much for you because of me and your white skin. Maybe you are married to that the way I am to Bontrug.[43]

He insists that their respective fidelities to race (his to the coloured township where the Group Areas Act prescribes that he live, hers to her white skin) are paramount over any fidelities based on choice or affection.[44]

Depending on how designers interpret the script's lighting directions, the stage may be lit so darkly in the first scene that the racial difference between the characters would be visually imperceptible to the audience for the first half of the play. Without a visual cue, the inequality in their social status emerges only gradually, elliptically through dialogue, or sonically through voice and accent. Race is not mentioned explicitly until well into the first scene. The play's bifurcated structure is also a sensorially divided one: the first half is about listening, the second half about seeing and being seen. The intrusion of the law brings exposure, light, and a sequence of six photographic images, suggesting evidence to be used later in court. These frozen stop-action, two-dimensional images contrast with the actors' continuous, embodied, three-dimensional live action before the audience.

AFTER THE ARREST

The police invasion incites a profound and thorough break in the play's style, character, tone, rhythm, and psychological representation. It is a violent disruption, although it is performed without violence. The sergeant speaks initially in truncated partial sentences that describe the individuals he's arresting: "Been living here for six years." "Born here." As the representative and face of the law, he also ventriloquizes other voices: he recites a statement given by a neighbor, Mrs. Buys, who had been suspicious about Errol's comings and goings at the back door of Frieda's library. He gives a cold and affectless speech that culminates in a description of the moment of the raid: "I saw Joubert and Philander lying side by side on a blanket on the floor. She was naked and he appeared to be wearing a vest. Sergeant Smitt started to take photographs."[45] What follows this statement is the first of six surrealistic sequences with flashing lights and the wielding of torches (flashlights). The blinding exposures, meant to evoke camera flashes, pin the accused couple against the wall, startle them in their nakedness as they scurry about for blankets and clothing items to shield their vulnerability. Fugard was inspired to write the play by newspaper stories about police raids on mixed-race couples' intimacy and the role of photography in those raids. In his notebooks he wrote, "The Immorality Act—at one level this country's one and unique contribution to the world of pornography. A guilt-ridden inversion of the celebration of the erect penis and moist vagina. . . . The camera flashes short-circuit the experience. . . . The point of view changes."[46] Fugard sees these staged photographic stills as

> the central image in their story—those six terrible photographs of Joubert and Philander scrambling around in the dark; twenty seconds of Hell which start with them together and end with them irrevocably apart; the twenty seconds that it takes to pass from an experience of life to an intimation of death. Those photographs were, and remain for me, the essence of the experience I wanted to explore. As I said repeatedly to Y. in Cape Town, and then again here [in London], the experience we ask an audience to share with us must be an exploration of the subtext to those photographs, and six scenes must in a sense be "Captions."[47]

Through the intrusion of the police and their flashes of light, Errol and Frieda are torn asunder; they become isolated individuals. The law becomes at times a voice, a light, a flash that intrudes on the subject and fixes both Frieda and Errol in preconceived assumptions, interpellations they must engage with, dispute, concede, or contest. But there is no place to hide. The self is thoroughly interpellated by a state that forbids their sexuality and intimacy across racial lines. The intrusion of the camera creates a cinematic and Brechtian element in this play, freezing the action and precipitating a different point of identification for the audience.

There is no place to hide. Errol and Frieda scramble around. The flashlights are "relentless, but we never see anything of the men behind them."[48] The stage directions report: "These 'flash-sequences' are nightmare excursions into the split second of exposure and must be approached as 'subtext' rather than 'reality.'"[49] At first the man tries to speak, but his words fracture with desperation:

> MAN [*terrified. Covering his genitals with his trousers he talks desperately to the torch shining on him.*] Look . . . look—before you make up your mind let me tell you something . . . I'm . . . I'm Principal . . . I . . . I won't do it again . . . I'm frightened. *Ja,* I'm frightened.[50]

He asserts the legitimacy of his job and social role (school principal), promises the officer he won't "do it" again (commit adultery across racial lines), and then simply confesses his present fright. As he continues to try to get his pants on without exposing himself, the whole operation becomes a "nightmare." The woman then comes forward, trying to shield the man with a blanket. The flashlights follow her as she speaks. Her response is rambling and almost incoherent, talking about biscuits and tea. Her speech is fractured but not panicked. She does not feel compelled to assert her credentials or promise not to "do it" again. Instead, her monologue becomes almost like a therapy session. She speaks of feeling unhappiness, of being hurt, of feeling "sorry" for him. This woman is an accused who doesn't feel the need to defend herself but rather wants to rationalize her behavior, to explain it. Her monologue soon begins to disclose far too much, becoming almost an erotic narrative: "We were whispering. Whispering makes you sweat. He loosened his tie and said . . ."[51] The stage directions say that "the man realizes that he must stop, and correct, this vein of intimate confession." The stakes of such admissions are entirely different for him as a coloured man; Frieda is clueless about that inequality. He tries to distract her from her overdisclosure by acting the role of the deferential black supplicant pleading with a white woman for water. His performance desperately escalates and intensifies, eventually becoming what the stage directions describe as "a grotesque parody of the servile, cringing 'Coloured,'" a bowing and scraping servitude haunted by minstrel "darkey" stereotypes.[52] His sentences become staccato fragments: "Dam's empty. Little mud left. For the goats." He calls her "Miss Frieda" and gradually degenerates into begging. However, Frieda is completely unable to recognize or acknowledge Errol's role-playing. She doesn't recognize *what* this performance is, much less *why* he is doing it. She rejects his shift in character and seems irritated by it. When he doesn't obey her order to stop, she becomes hysterical.

Here the play's action is once again interrupted by a camera flash sequence, an interlude that inaugurates yet another attempt to tell what happened, another iteration of "statements" after the arrest. This one is told contrapuntally, with the two lovers speaking, overlapping, conveying more about the intersubjective discoveries of their unfolding relationship, their shared excitement of books and learning, their companionship found through intellectual communion. They confess to a shared excitement about shared *learning* rather than shared sex. Their mutual confession pauses at one moment, abruptly, waiting for a response—from the sergeant? from the audience? The spectators are interpellated into the play as

Frieda and Errol seem to acknowledge the audience directly for the first time. There is an awkward pause. In this caesura, the playwright conveys that the intensity of the lovers' fear of their interrogators is equal, if not greater, to the intensity of their desire for each other. Implicitly the play performs a question: What is the audience's role in this scene? To witness? Spy? Conspire?

We next learn about the intimate moments when Frieda and Errol's sexual relationship first began—a relationship that she had to initiate, given the enormous stakes for Errol if he had read her amorous signals incorrectly. To her credit, Frieda is very clear about her role in initiating the love affair. Without this confession, Errol's fate at the hands of the law would surely have become much worse. The action is once again cut through with camera flashes, this time trapping the woman. She seems to be unaware of the flashlights, unashamed of her nakedness, and she rather launches into a private and self-absorbed reverie: "Ugly feet. The soles have got hard patches. My legs are bandy. Good calf muscles . . . probably got them riding to school on my bicycle up a very steep hill each day. Skin around my knees is just starting to get slack. I enjoy making the muscles in my thighs move. Hair is very mousy."[53] Like the opening monologue of the play about Frieda's drying hair in the sun, her speech conveys an embodied experience, intimately narrating what it means to be inside her body, a gendered body that is accustomed to being viewed. But her experience of surveillance is wholly unlike that of the coloured man. She is being appraised for beauty, not guilt, for conformity to an ideal, not a negative stereotype. She may be concerned about her hair or "ashamed" of her hands, and her skin may look "very old." But nevertheless, she says, "I think there is a whole lot of me in my hands somehow," a line that contrasts starkly with how Errol comes to perceive his own hands later in this scene.[54] Her internalization of the interpellative process is revealed in dialogue: she becomes both the interrogator asking questions and the one answering them. She asks herself about her own complicity, her guilt, and the possibility of coercion or shame. Her answers to her own questions are clipped, monosyllabic, until finally she begins to narrate the scene of seduction. For her, there is no fear in this statement of confession. She is a subject not in *subjection* but in *possession* of her body, her story, her self, and she is able to confess defiantly, even proudly: "So . . . so then . . . yes. . . . So then then we made love."[55]

Errol's trajectory through the fractured interpellative process of the arrest rides a course that is entirely different from Frieda's. Near the end of the play the policeman once again speaks, reciting a statement and showing "Exhibit A" and "Exhibit B," which are presumably the photographs that are being captured and staged before our eyes with all the camera flashes. He tells us that at the actual moment of arrest, Frieda spoke but a few choice words: "I am not ashamed of myself," which she said she would repeat to anyone. She then apologized to Philander. But "Philander said nothing."[56] She is defiant, in possession of herself, fully present in her body, even as she has internalized the questions of her interrogator.

Errol, however, becomes increasingly desperate. He first asserts his good character, then performs the role of the bowing and scraping subservient. He gets one brief period in the interrogation where he can speak about how much it meant for him to go the library "and use the encyclopedias, and read."[57] What is so remarkable about the final segment of Fugard's play is that Errol becomes a person before the law by becoming *not* a person at all. This drama is one of *unbecoming*. His dissolution throughout the scene is not even seen by his lover, so caught up is she in her own narcissistic reverie. Her final speech narrates what it means to lose him, how she must move autonomously now. "I must be my hands again, my eyes, my ears . . . all of me but now, without you. All of me that found you must now lose you."[58] The outcome of the arrest for her is that she must shed herself of him, wash his sweat from her body, his memory from her mind. In contrast, the outcome of the arrest for Errol is dismemberment, annihilation. Whereas the arrest prompts her to take possession of herself and rid herself of the Other, for him the arrest is a process of ridding himself of his very being:

> Now I must understand it.
> If they take away your eyes you can't see.
> If they take away your tongue you can't taste.
> If they take away your hands you can't feel.
> If they take away your nose you can't smell.
> If they take away your ears you can't hear.
> I can see.
> I can taste.
> I can feel.
> I can smell.
> I can hear.
> [*Pause.*]
> I can't love.[59]

This poetic sequence rehearses what it would mean if "they" take away your legs, arms, and head. He can still walk, work, and think, but he cannot love.[60] Next are the appetites: eating, drinking and sleeping. Stripped of these, what is he? Here he shifts from saying he *can't* love to asserting that he *won't* love:

> I will eat.
> I will drink.
> I will sleep.
> I won't love.[61]

The speech compresses, narrows, and condenses. Broken, wounded language conveys his undoing as he is reduced to bare life and even less than the bare life Agamben theorized: he becomes a subject without a body or a name:

> An arm without a hand.
> A leg without a foot.
> A head without a body.
> A man without name.[62]

Who is this force—this "they"—that takes limbs and body parts and locks a man away? The adversary is unnamed. Gradually this "they" becomes "God," a force of interpellation even greater than the law:

> So I tell God I don't smoke and I don't drink and I know the price of bread. But he says it makes no difference and that he wants back what is left. And then I start to give him the other parts. I give him my feet and my legs, I give him my head and body, I give him my arms, until at last there is nothing left, just my hands and they are empty. But he takes them back too. And then there is only the emptiness left. But he doesn't want that. Because it's me. It's all that is left of me. They arrest it all the same.[63]

Errol's statements after the arrest divest him of everything. The law makes him less than human, less than animal, less than a sentient being. Even after he is reduced to a dismembered, disembodied emptiness, he still does not possess his own "emptiness," for "they" arrest that too.[64]

Errol's monologue prefigures Judith Butler's speculations about the possibility of agency for the slave through desubjectivation. Butler concludes her meditation on interpellation in *The Psychic Life of Power* by saying,

> In a Nietzschean vein, such a slave morality may be predicated upon the sober calculation that it is better to "be" enslaved in such a way than not to "be" at all. But the terms that constrain the option to being versus no being "call for" another kind of response. Under what conditions does a law monopolize the terms of existence in so thorough a way? Or is this a theological fantasy of the law? Is there a possibility of being elsewhere or otherwise, without denying our complicity in the law that we oppose? Such possibility would require a different kind of turn, one that, enabled by the law, turns away from the law, resisting its lure of identity, an agency that outruns and counters the conditions of its emergence. Such a turn demands a willingness *not* to be—a critical desubjectivation—in order to expose the law as less powerful than it seems. What forms might linguistic survival take in this desubjectivized domain? How would one know one's existence?[65]

Errol's unbecoming performs the strategic calculation that it is better not to be at all than to be a coloured man arrested under the Immorality Act in apartheid South Africa.

UNSEEN AND UNBECOMING

Statements after an Arrest under the Immorality Act dramatizes the vastly different impact the law's racialized interpellation has on each character according to race. And yet it does not show us *how* that inequality is created, beyond the sergeant's initial hailing of each suspect by race at the very moment of the arrest. Just as we never see the men behind the cameras and flashlights, we never see law enforcement in this play actually arresting anyone or conducting an interrogation. We also do not see how apartheid's racialized law affects these two suspects, one white, the other coloured. The psychic life of power for the oppressor, the sergeant, also remains unseen. The playwright withholds this information. Why? The play raises the question of what is unseen. By withholding mimetic representation, it may provide its most potent representation of all.

In her book *New World Drama*, Elizabeth Maddock Dillon asserts that "the signifying economy of the theater operates in two registers: one that is *ontic* (thingly, material, resolutely present) and one that is *mimetic* (referential, immaterial, gesturing toward a scene located elsewhere)."[66] Here she is amplifying the pathbreaking work of theorist Bert O. States, who famously wrote, "There is a sense in which signs [in the theater] . . . achieve their vitality . . . not simply by signifying the world but by being of it."[67] The simultaneity of the mimetic and ontic is a defining quality of the theater, one that distinguishes it from, say, novels. Novels have received far greater attention in recent scholarship on questions of human rights and the law. I am thinking here in particular of the work of Joseph Slaughter and Elizabeth S. Anker, both of whom focus on human rights issues in relation to the novel.[68] How does the genre of theater compare with that of the novel in terms of its relationship to law and human rights? As a genre, theater (as opposed to "drama," meaning only the script) "has the body" (habeas corpus). What does this body do? What does it reveal? What does it withhold? How does it function in both ontic and mimetic ways simultaneously, and what are the consequences of the fundamental instability between these two dimensions? How and what do theater's ontic and mimetic dimensions perform?

The performance of Fugard's *Statements after an Arrest* in South Africa *defied* the law. Theater's potency during apartheid was equaled by its vulnerability. At the opening of *Statements after an Arrest*, the audience surely would have felt that vulnerability as much as the actors and producers did. The Space Theatre in Cape Town, where *Statements after an Arrest* premiered in 1972, was a new fringe theater that staged plays to mixed-race audiences in defiance of myriad prohibitions, pervasive censorship, and relentless police surveillance, raids, and harassment. In fact, *Statements after an Arrest* was the Space Theatre's first production. The Space can be seen as a "white" institution inasmuch as white liberals funded it and dominated its artistic leadership. However, the founders made a deliberate decision to admit all races, and in its assembly of persons normally segregated, its fostering of forbidden intimacies across color lines, it functioned as potent ontic instantiation of the transgressions mimetically represented by the characters Frieda and Errol in *Statements after an Arrest*. From its inception, the Space Theatre violated the law. According to the Separate Amenities Act of 1955 and Proclamation R26 of 1965, both racially mixed audiences and racially mixed casts were prohibited in public entertainments without a permit.[69] In the unlikely event that a permit for mixed-race audiences was issued, a theater had to have separate accommodations for each race: separate entrances, separate seats, and separate restrooms. In addition, apartheid law stipulated that event spaces that had been used by one race could not then be used by another. The first performance of *Statements after an Arrest* was entirely cast with white actors; Fugard played the role of the coloured man, Errol Philander. So on the casting front, the producers were legally in the clear. However, the audience was racially mixed, and that was a calculated gamble. As Brian Astbury, founder of the Space Theatre, recalls,

> Then during the run [of *Statements after an Arrest*] our final problem arose. Those that—in this country—shouldn't have been allowed entrance came to buy tickets. And we had, at the beginning, determined that if we were going to have to turn people away we were going to have to be forced to do so by the full and visible weight of the law. So from the start, everybody was allowed in. And we waited for the law to stop us.[70]

From its premiere, *Statements after an Arrest* raised the possibility that its title would become predictive—that the audience might end up arrested, giving statements for being in the theater that night. In the meantime, the theater waited for the law in the form of the police or Special Branch to show up, for arrests of actors and spectators. Theater was a space for doing what the law disallowed, not just for imagining such acts. Like the library after hours for Frieda and Errol, the Space Theatre was for many an oasis of possibility for imagining what the law disallowed, but the law could intrude and unmake things at any moment.

When policemen as characters burst into a dimly lit scene of love in *Statements after an Arrest,* wielding cameras and blinding flashlights, law enforcement announced itself mimetically as light, exposure, a blinding glare. The police completely disrupt the artificial no-man's-land that Errol and Frieda have created. The police expose this affair as being fully subject to apartheid law. This mimetic reality in the play was paralleled, even more potently, by the ontic reality of the Space Theatre itself. Just as Errol and Frieda were fully aware that their clandestine affair was never "outside" the law, South African theater audiences knew very well they risked arrest by attending this show, and that feeling may well have added drama and anxiety to the moment of the police raid in the script. Was this raid mimetic or ontic? There was likely to be confusion. Immorality *acted*: the live performance of the play *did something* with words, and bodies, and time, and space, and light and darkness.

From early in the play, Frieda and Errol are jumpy and anxious, despite their surface calm and equanimity. They are worried about exposure, about discovery, about who might be lighting a match that suddenly flares in the darkness. The two have created a bubble where a coloured man and a white woman can lie naked on a blanket in a tender embrace of love, but they know that this private space is a play world that can be destroyed in an instant. Yet still, Errol's affair is expansive. In Frieda, he has given himself the equivalent of the five-room house he had advised the child playing in the sand to build. Errol knows that fantasies and works of imagination are performative: they create *spaces of possibility*, experiences of how things could be otherwise.

South African minister of justice (1994–2004) Dullah Omar once described apartheid as a dual state whereby white people enjoyed parliamentary democracy and black people lived under dictatorship. International studies scholar Jens Meierhenrich has pursued this line of analysis at length. The country's "schizophrenic institutional structure," Meierhenrich writes, created conditions whereby contrasting legal norms for white and nonwhite people had to be repeatedly instantiated, enacted, made performatively manifest.[71] Especially in the wake of the 1960 Sharpeville massacre, the law became at once unstable and increasingly rigid, enforced in capricious ways through repeated declarations of states of emergency. Normal legal procedures were suspended through states of exception, the authorization of ever-escalating periods of detention without trial, the proliferation of bannings, and a host of other legal intrusions into daily life. The condition of the law in this period of apartheid South Africa was inherently unstable and dualistic, and that instability created the potential for performative moments of intervention and defiance.

The law as depicted in *Statements after an Arrest* appears to treat Errol and Frieda equally. Other than hailing them by their race, the arresting officer doesn't single out either Frieda or Errol or treat them in different ways—at least that we *see*. We don't see the actual arrest; it is only narrated. We don't see the actual interrogation, only snippets of it, particularly as Frieda internalizes the interrogator's voice. In early versions of the play—including the version performed in Cape Town in 1972—Fugard gave the police a far more prominent role. The early play had two policemen, both of whom were introduced from the very beginning of the play instead of entering halfway through. In the 1972 version of the play, the police were as central as Errol and Frieda became in the final version. What Fugard shows us in the revised script is how the two accused have internalized the stakes of this arrest in radically different ways. Clarity about this focus emerged during the London rehearsals in 1974, when actor Ben Kingsley played Errol, and Yvonne Bryceland, Fugard's longtime South African collaborator, played Frieda. Here Fugard discovered the play's final form. We see in the revisions a telescoping of focus so that Frieda and Errol's relationship, subjectivity, intersubjectivity, and thwarted love are clearly the center of the play.[72] Errol's narrative of his desubjectivization after his arrest becomes the play's true center of gravity. Fugard's choice to minimize representation of law enforcement implicitly intensified a questioning of the audience. Do the spectators become, in effect, aligned with the unseen wielders of the flashlights and cameras, the intruders on an act of intimacy, the interrogators, the judges to whom the two accused address their statements?

Fugard's notebooks reveal that he was most interested in the couple: their relationship, their interior lives, their loneliness, their impeded attempt to connect with an Other, and the way a racist set of laws shapes their individual characters and fractures their relationship. He dramatizes the police as an inciting incident, which is not to say that Fugard failed to grasp the perversion and gross immorality of the Immorality Act itself. If Fugard had been interested in focusing more on the police, *Statements after an Arrest* would most likely have been banned. As Martin Orkin reminds us, apartheid legislation forbade "any real discussion or representation of police and prison conditions in South Africa."[73]

Instead, Fugard casts a light on Frieda and Errol. What does this light reveal? We see that Frieda stands before the law as a full person. She is defiant, confessional, introspective, free to disclose. For Errol, the arrest instigates a rapid devolution into panic, stereotype, and disintegration of self that reduces him to bare life and even less—a subject with no body, no limbs, no soul, whose only possession is his own emptiness, and even that—that emptiness—can be incarcerated. Errol and Frieda begin the play with the appearance of Edenic purity and equality. Once they are caught in their act of love, there is a dual state of play. For her the way forward is that "all of me that found you must now lose you"; for him the way forward has nothing to do with dependence or confession or guilt or even shame. For him, there is no place from which to speak, no role to be in. His only possible strategy is a dissolution of his very being. He is reduced to pure will.

This conclusion is devastating in a play that begins with such tender intimacy, a love story that began with nakedness, honest intimacy in a darkened room, a tender embrace. The intrusion of the policeman, the policeman's dictation, and photographs, camera flashes, and flashlights wielded by unseen forces representing the law violently annihilates a precarious bond. In the dual state, fragile moments of tenderness and equanimity across racial lines could exist, but law's intrusion (magnified in the play's bifurcated structure and style) violently tears the two apart. Performatively, the law strips Frieda of entanglement with the racial Other. She becomes again a solo being. Performatively, the law strips Errol of his very being. In all of this, the audience is ambiguously cast as witness, spy, accomplice, interrogator, or potential fellow arrestees.

Two key ideas animated Fugard's revisions of this manuscript after the play opened in 1972. First, he said, "I want *their* [the couple's] story to contain the policeman's statement, rather than have the *policeman's* statement contain their story."[74] He also was exploring having the couple's fear and apology and explanation to the audience be "equal, if not greater, to their relationship to each other."[75] Fugard stages a reframing of the performative elements of interpellation during arrest. Instead of the law hailing the subjects, the subjects (Frieda and Errol) hail the law through the "statement" of the play itself. This inversion is a radical reframing in the context of apartheid South Africa, where the law so routinely, pervasively, and insidiously subjected people's lives to its force. Fugard also wanted the play to reframe the complicity and intersubjectivity of each lover's relationship with the other. In the course of the play, their intimacy and infidelity becomes echoed by a bond between them and the audience, a bond of intimacy, violation of the law, and legal vulnerability. For the audience, this vulnerability is more real than anything represented onstage. Audience members were hailed by the performance at the Space Theatre, and by attending, they broke the law.

Willfulness drove the theater artists who ran the Space Theatre on Long Street in Cape Town, the venue that staged as its first production *Statements after an Arrest under the Immorality Act* in March 1972. The theater's ontic reality provided a mimetic space not only to represent the world of apartheid South Africa otherwise but also to hail and interpellate its apartheid-era audience into an aspired nonracist future. The theater operated in defiance of apartheid laws about segregation and separate amenities. It danced around prohibitions about freedom of assembly across racial lines. It willfully asserted freedom of expression.

In a one-man show entitled *No Space on Long Street* that in 1997 retrospectively celebrated the twenty-fifth anniversary of the founding of the Space Theatre, actor, comedian, and Space founding veteran Pieter-Dirk Uys recalled the opening of the theater:

> The Space / Die Ruimte opened round the 27th march 1972 with a new play by Athol Fugard: *Statements after an arrest under the Immorality Act*.
>
> The Space's colours were nailed to the mast.
> The impossible was probable.
> It was the beginning of freedom of expression in the theatre. . . .
> The Space became the conscience of a generation.[76]

There was much about the Space that was improbable: its fiscal viability; its production timelines; its lack of technical support, stable staffing, finalized scripts, adequate electricity, proper plumbing, or a living wage for its artists. Disruptions by security police and the censors were so pervasive and capricious that the law almost became a kind of coproducing agent, inserting unpredictable provocations that the theater's producers and artists constantly improvised around. As Uys recalled in *No Space on Long Street*, "We did a season of my plays: *Selle Ou Storie*—they banned the script but you could see the play; *Karnaval*—they banned the play but you could read the script; and *God's Forgotten*[—]the play that should have been banned but wasn't. The pressures of three productions, no money, censorship and fear, exhaustion and the silly feeling of not being loved."[77]

Of course, the apartheid state had the capacity to shut down the theater entirely at any time. But the censors and Special Branch did not wish to make the Space Theatre into a political martyr. Their strategy seems to have been rather to tire the artists out, to undermine them with a kind of "slow censorship," a bureaucratic bloodletting as an endurance act. As one censor says in Uys's 1997 retrospective play, "We will just ban you for 'obscenity' and 'blasphemy' and bankrupt you! We know how to do our job."[78] Slow oppression undermined the theater through exhaustion rather than outright extermination. John Vorster, who was the actual South African prime minister, tells fictional Elsabe, a censor who routinely surveils the Space Theatre and is a key character in Uys's *No Space on Long Street*, "You see, Elsabe, we in power are also artists in what we do."[79]

Despite all that was improbable about the Space, the artists made theater and broke apartheid laws for ten years. The state, too, played its part—banning, raiding, spying, infiltrating, arresting, and undermining revenue streams. Raids were the most overt insertions of the law, and, just like the raid on Errol and Frieda in *Statements*, raids on the Space Theatre were usually prompted by a nosy neighbor. Speaking in Uys's play, Elsabe recalls,

> It was during the performance of Tennessee Williams's *Glass Menagerie*. One of my favourite plays. A wonderful production by Bill Tanner. I could've killed them! With Yvonne Bryceland at her most moving moment, suddenly like the Gestapo, these barbarians storm in. And why? Because some fool phoned them that there are blacks in the theatre and it is against the law! . . . The lights went on, and the magic was gone.[80]

Elsabe's own subject position was complicated: a "prominent member" of the censor board, she had the duty to attend the Space Theatre on a regular basis. But what the state may not have realized, she confesses, is that it had put a "chocoholic in charge of a chocolate factory."[81] She loved and supported much of what the Space was doing. Theater is a volatile, capricious, and unpredictable zone: in performing some roles we may unbecome them. In this case, the chief censor of the Space became one of its biggest fans. Her objection to the police interrupting the production of *Glass Menagerie* was at core a jurisdictional question—who has the authority to make such decisions, the police or the censors? Whose opinion about the tolerability or intolerability of infractions will prevail? The law has many agents with many different opinions.

The Space's willful defiance and improbable tenacity provided an incubation space for at least some people in South Africa to perform, enact, rehearse, and make belief through the make believe. Like Errol and Frieda, the artists at the Space Theatre created a temporary sanctuary, a cherished yet fragile oasis where love and affection across racial lines could flourish. Such a space, however vulnerable, was nevertheless potent. In this space, alternate realities came to appear not just *possible* but *probable*. As Uys recalls in *No Space on Long Street*,

> Twenty-five years ago. Before sanctions, before the Mandela t-shirts [*sic*], before it was fashionable and right to be anti-apartheid, there was a dream that came true. It was called The Space Theatre and it started its journey in a sprawling warehouse off Long Street, between Bloem and Buiten. It was the place where the alphabet of South African Theatre was reinvented. It was poor and yet gave great riches to the community. It was one of the beginnings of freedom of expression. It was the end of apartheid in the arts.[82]

Theater is a form that requires for its very existence freedom of assembly, freedom of expression, and the presence of the body. As such, theaters like the Space that pitch up at the edge of the law—that must defy the law in order to exist—have the capacity to incubate potential futures, contingent realities that not only make visible the law's reach, but rehearse and reveal the law's limits. Theater has the capacity to perform something else—something not yet seen, known, or understood.

CONCLUSION: LAWS OF PROBABILITY

While the three Statement Plays are not generally performed as a trilogy, their publication together in one book suggests a trilogy. These plays *are* statements—uttered performances at the edge of the law between the human and the inhumane, aesthetic representations of moments of legal interpellation that give insight into legal habitus, the interiority of the psychic life of power, and the capacity of dreams, relationships, and imagination to carve out finite worlds of respite where agency is envisioned and *rehearsed*. Given that all three scripts were composed and premiered in a climate of intense censorship that routinely subjected the theater to editorial interference, bannings, surveillance by spies, raids by the Special Branch, and arrests of playwrights and actors, the Statement Plays provide a provocative point of entry for thinking about how racialized individuals become—and *unbecome*—subjects before the law, and how the law and race were tightly imbricated in apartheid South Africa.

The most searing image of *Statements after an Arrest* is the final monologue by Errol. Through his extraordinary and poetically distilled language, we witness an implosion of self. He tells of the disintegration of his body, the loss of limbs, the erasure of his entire material realty, his corporeal being. Yet even as Errol describes the disintegration of his corporeal being, he asserts his will:

> Now I'm here.
> There is nothing here.
> They can't interfere with God any more.[83]

In these final moments after Errol's arrest, his speech echoes, unwittingly, ideas of theorists who have wrestled with the paradoxes of interpellation. Does the divine provide a space outside interpellation? Does love or desire offer a sanctuary beyond the reach of interpellation? In Errol's narrative we see several turns that hearken back to Althusser's interpellation scene of the policeman's hail: Errol turns away from Frieda, his lover, and we know that in turning *to* her previously, he had implicitly turned away from the rest of his life: his wife, his family, and his community in the coloured township. Caught between these worlds at the moment of his arrest, Errol turns yet again, this time away from Frieda, away from his family, and away from the law. His refuge is to become an *unbecoming* subject, a consciousness without flesh, a will without materiality. He says, "Now I'm here," and at the same time, "there is nothing here." Errol's self-negation dramatizes a subject refusing interpellation in a racist state, an unbecoming, an attempt to become not a subject at all.

Live performance is potent space in which the differential effects of racialism on subjects can be staged, framed, and seen. Fugard's *Statements after an arrest under the Immorality Act* represented the mind, the imagination, and the behavior of the racially colonized subject, Errol, while it also depicted what racial ideology does to the mind, the imagination, and the behavior of the master, here represented as Frieda. As a consequence of this arrest, Errol, as a black man, loses everything: his home, children, wife, dreams, job, masculinity, freedom, and body. Frieda, as a white woman, is entirely unconcerned by his loss and fate. She rather takes refuge in an inventory of her own position, gender, and body, and these remain intact. While the arrest may result in professional and social consequences for Frieda, she will be able to recover.

In *Willful Subjects*, Sara Ahmed argues that "to queer the will is to show how the will has already been given a queer potential. . . . Willfulness might be a conversion point: How a potential is converted into a threat."[84] She also posits that "perhaps self-certainty is not how the will becomes what is given to a subject, but how a subject can become itself: 'I have a will' understood not only as a sign of existence, 'I will *therefore* I am[,]' but as an impulse to existence: 'I will *then* I am.'"[85] Errol is a willful subject whose unbecoming performs "I am *not*—and yet still, *I will*." His disintegration can hardly be seen as liberation—it is a reduction of self, a distillation to a pure essence of will, devoid of body. However, we may read in his final monologue an insistence on another way of being, one that preserves something of the epiphanies he experienced through engaging in the affair, through reading books, through using his imagination, through creating a no-man's-land sanctuary in a darkened room on a library floor with a lover of his own choice, even if that choice destroys his life. Might Errol eventually, after the action of this play concludes, become something else altogether? He asserts, if not agency, then at least a willfulness, first through a becoming tied to sexuality, intimacy, and self-discovery, and then, when his becoming is arrested, literally stopped midstream by the invasion of apartheid law, his unbecoming contains the seeds of something else, something not yet seen, known, or understood, where "they" can no longer interfere. Errol's will at the end of *Statements after an Arrest* is all he has; it's all he is. Pushed, conscripted, reduced, annihilated, in a corner that is a space of nonbeing, his will lives on, makes a claim to agency beyond all sovereign forces. His will persists as a dematerialized essence that continues to exert a performative force after all else is gone. In the following chapters we will see how will as a dematerialized but performatively potent essence animates and propels many of the artists working to stage black subjects differently in the "new" South Africa.

TWO | Movement and Stasis in the Protracted Interval: Jay Pather, Mamela Nyamza, and Sello Pesa

> The old politics of waiting is therefore gradually replaced by a new politics of impatience and, if necessary, of disruption.
>
> —Achille Mbembe

> It was a lyric that dreamed, strove, and agitated to disorder the real and wedge open a space in the social where the necessary fictions of blackness and queerness could ascend to something that was and was not a fiction, but was, nonetheless, utterly heard.
>
> —José Esteban Muñoz

In 1994, South Africa's first democratic elections marked the formal end of apartheid, a change hastened by the adoption of a new constitution said to be one of the most progressive in the world. But even before 1994, South Africa had become a state in transition as it moved from authoritarian to democratic rule, from an epoch of intense internal armed conflict to a negotiated settlement brokered by the Convention for a Democratic South Africa.[1] The transition was further stage managed through the operations of South Africa's Truth and Reconciliation Commission, however unwieldy and unsatisfactory that "impossible machine," as Adam Sitze has called it, turned out to be.[2] Even in the early 1990s, ambivalence about the commission and about the many political compromises of South Africa's settlement was high. This ambivalence has only grown with time.

As with slavery and Jim Crow in the United States, apartheid in South Africa has a flourishing afterlife today, as is evident in the lack of a substantive redistribution of wealth and land, continued pervasive violence, and extreme material inequality.[3] Although the postapartheid era was founded on a desire for and commitment to nonracial emancipation, the cloth of the new South Africa has been woven with some of the fibers that once held apartheid's white supremacy tightly in place. Today, racism, inequality, physical violence, legacies of settler colonialism and dispossession, and continued structural "slow violence" are all still embedded in the warp and the weft of the country.[4] According to both the Gini index and the Palma ratio for 2017, two widely used global measures of inequality, South Africa is the most unequal country in the world.[5] As Thiven Reddy has forcefully argued, South Africa is essentially a former settler colony where the colonizing power is still present and powerful today.[6] South Africa also remains a violent place; an average of 50 murders and 142 sexual offences were committed every day in 2015–16, and one in four men admitted to having raped someone.[7] Crime statistics need to be viewed next to employment data. As Okwui Enwezor points out, these are two sides of one coin.[8] In 2017, the overall unemployment rate in South Africa was 27.7 percent. Among young people, the rate jumps is a staggering 60 percent.[9] These caustic realities are still deeply felt by many who remain disenfranchised, including the 53 percent of South Africans who today currently "fall under the widest definition of poverty."[10]

From these statistics, the aggregate patterns of apartheid's afterlives emerge. Richard Pithouse sees these in impulses to contain and control that together comprise a "unifying drive that links spatial segregation, brutal policing methods, anxieties about the free flow of information, and the increasing degree to which access to work and welfare is tied, for the most vulnerable people, to the performance of political obedience."[11] Historian Colin Bundy identifies the most toxic legacies of apartheid in the realm of culture, behavior, and experience: "Arguably the single most intractable, most toxic presence of the past is in how profoundly racialized South African society remains. The discriminatory divisions and hierarchies of apartheid into everyday experience and impacted on the psyche of all South Africans."[12] South Africa's transition promised change—that is, a shift from the "here" of apartheid to a "there," alternately imagined as someplace better—a place not racialized, a land of reconciliation, a nation with greater economic equality. But the postapartheid era delivered not revolution but "transformation"—a vague, nebulous, corporate concept that divested revolution of radicalism.[13] Colin Bundy offers a concise explanation for how this happened: "The negotiated settlement combined significant restructuring of the political sphere and broad continuity in the economic sphere."[14]

Many cultural critics, thinkers, artists, and writers have reflected on what Ashraf Jamal has called the "predicaments of culture" in contemporary South Africa. At their core, those predicaments center on the fact that the present era is after apartheid but is not yet "post."[15] A "suspended revolution" is how Adam Habib describes it, using this phrase as a title of his recent book.[16] "In many ways, South Africa has hardly moved since the end of Mbeki's presidential tenure," says Habib. "And the country is no closer to the prosperous cosmopolitan vision Mbeki projected in his speech to the constituent assembly in 1996."[17] There have been subtle shifts of power from the Polokwane conference; there has been a growing black middle class; multiple new laws ensure employment equity and improved labor relations, and so forth. But continued racialization of identities and growing socioeconomic inequality remain the defining characteristics of contemporary South Africa.

Another metaphor for South Africa's present is the "interval," as articulated by Achille Mbembe:

> One of the main tensions in South African politics and culture today is the realisation that there is something unresolved in the constitutional democratic settlement that suspended the "revolution" in 1994 but did not erase apartheid from the social, economic and mental landscape. This settlement led neither to final victory nor to crippling defeat for any of the protagonists in the historical drama. Rather, South Africa entered a historical interval. It is still caught in this interval, between an intractable present and an irrecoverable past; between things that are no longer and things that are not yet. This is the stalemate many would now like to end.[18]

What are the cultural and aesthetic implications of life in the protracted interval? What does it mean to live in a time that is not the aftermath of apartheid so much as its wake—a trailing path in which the vestiges of an authoritarian and racist former regime remain pervasive, churning, and alive today?[19] What aesthetics can insightfully express and effectively intervene in South Africa's suspended revolution, its interval, its experiential gulf between things that are no longer and things that are not yet?

As early as 1984, South African scholar Njabulo S. Ndebele said that artists facing the "immense challenging responsibility to create a new society" must shift from a single-minded focus on the representation of what he called the monstrous spectacle of apartheid and must instead "rediscover the ordinary," the ways that quotidian lives should be of political interest because "they constitute the *very content* of the struggle."[20] In the early 1990s, ANC leader Albie Sachs issued a provocative and controversial call along similar lines, saying that South Africans must prepare for freedom. He argued that an entrenched oppositional culture in which art itself was seen as a weapon would inhibit the imaginative capaciousness needed to make a new South Africa genuinely liberated.[21] The decades since these opening salvos in the debates about the "new" South Africa were fired have brought only less clarity.

What, to begin with, is this period called? Many reject the term "post-apartheid" when so much of the legacy of apartheid remains embedded in the foundations and structures of the country today. The partitions of space, neighborhoods, cities, and towns that were so fundamental to apartheid are not easily transformed, for instance. As geographer Edgar Pieterse wrote in 2009, "South African cities have remained profoundly divided, segregated and unequal despite sixteen years of concerted government efforts to extend development opportunities to the urban poor."[22] Apartheid's separations are literally written in stone, in concrete roads, street partitions, foundations, sidewalks (or lack of them), and highways, one of the reasons that racialized segregation is still a dominant feature of contemporary South Africa.[23] Loren Kruger argued in 2001 that the era after South Africa's first democratic elections should be called post-antiapartheid rather than post-apartheid because "the consequences of the enforced poverty and displacement of the majority are pressing, while the moral conviction and commitment of antiapartheid solidarity have waned, and in their place has come postcolonial uneven development, which has created a new black elite but not eased the lives of the black majority."[24] Nearly a decade later, in 2010, a special issue of *English Studies in Africa* asserted that South Africa had entered a "post-transitional" phase.[25] The volume's editors, Ronit Frenkel and Craig MacKenzie, contend that the hallmarks of protest-style writing of the apartheid era (such as literary realism, moral earnestness, and the dominance of race) have been "largely swept aside" by a new generation of writers.[26] In that same issue, Miki Flockeman argues that nevertheless, "restlessness, dissonance, and disjunction are frequently used to describe the experience of constitutional democracy as it co-exists with the emerging new apartheid of poverty."[27] In other words, "post-transition" by no means indicates that things are settled, resolved, or reconciled. Nor does being "post-anti" preclude the emergence of neoapartheid. Arguably, it is precisely the disbanding of overt liberationist opposition that may presage the arrival of the "neo."

The artists I analyze in this and subsequent chapters illuminate the experiential, embodied, and affective dimensions of living in a protracted interval. They help audiences understand what stalled "progress" looks and feels like, how it is kinesthetically experienced, how the body itself has capacity and agency, despite the lack of movement one experiences in a suspended state. I examine works spanning a decade: *Body of Evidence* (2009) by Jay Pather and Siwela Sonke Dance Theatre, *De-Apart-Hate* (2016) and several other works by Mamela Nyamza, and *Bag Beatings* (2018) by Sello Pesa and Ntsoana Contemporary Dance Theatre. All present visceral, potent, embodied works that attempt to intervene productively and provocatively in the protracted interval. They do so by excavating memories and epistemes embedded in habeas viscus, as theorized by Alexander G. Weheliye. That is, these are performances that illuminate "how race becomes pinioned to human physiology, exposing how the politicization of the biological always already represents a racializing assemblage."[28]

Of these artists, I ask: through what aesthetic strategies do their performances represent, interrogate, dramatize, undermine, and embody ideas about contemporary South Africa? How do these works depict the relationship between stasis and movement, between stagnation and transformation? I argue that these works begin to unravel an inherited corporeal habitus; to disorder perceptions of the "real" by breaking actions and inherited habits into component part. One of the techniques that each of these artists uses is something I call "delamination"—that is, a mode of deconstruction in which the material of the now, the substance of "ordinary" life that is otherwise taken as given, as being natural, normal and fused, fractures in performance into separate layers. Revealed in these works is that "normal" and the "real" fuse together disparate parts, some of which are toxic. Jay Pather's *Body of Evidence* looks at the way violence becomes part of one's body at a cellular level. Mamela Nyamza's *De-Apart-Hate* exposes the homophobia and racism embedded in practices of charismatic Christianity. Sello Pesa's *Bag Beatings* reveals an appetite for violence, and how this hunger can become unmoored from any particular purpose, goal, or political struggle. Through delamination of component parts that are otherwise sutured together in ordinary life, these artists open up otherwise possibilities. Their works suggest that the fused layers of contemporary South African life do not *have* to be stuck together. Delamination flakes, peels and pares away disparate layers, opening up the possibility of choice, the potential to separate valuable from toxic substances.

Embodied violence looms large in this chapter, a reflection of the ubiquity of violence in the spatial distributions and apparatuses of capture of both apartheid and contemporary life in South Africa. When violence converges with performance, the combination produces particular dynamics and problematics. Patrick Anderson and Jisha Menon have argued that "enactments of violence are both *spectacular* in their cultural impact and embodied in their transaction and effect."[29] When violence surrounds whole communities and engulfs individuals at the most intimate and psychic levels, when it is both exteriorized and interiorized, both visual spectacle and somatic experience, artists representing these conditions face a formidable challenge: to represent violence without contributing to its pervasiveness, ubiquity, and normalization. This is the formidable challenge artists Jay Pather, Mamela Nyamza, and Sello Pesa unflinchingly confront.

Histories of violence and racialized oppression are embedded in the ways certain bodies move—in the nuances of gait, in the authority or uncertainty with which certain bodies occupy space, in the habits of muscle memory, and, on a cellular level, in the tissues. The artists under consideration here help expose what lies within, unseen but deeply felt; what is held tightly in muscles even if toxic; what drives violence forward, what perpetuates it, including an investment in a context that one expects can neither be ultimately won nor lost. Corporeal epistemes are specific to time and space; they are fully imbricated in power and memory. Through the corporeal, these artists reveal a new ordinary by bringing nascent ideas and insights more clearly and overtly into the flesh. We see in their works embodied habitus of the old apartheid order shaking loose, unearthing certain freedoms that exist but are latent in the hieroglyphics of the flesh.[30]

JAY PATHER'S *BODY OF EVIDENCE*: FORENSIC REVELATIONS AND DREAMSCAPES

Since the 1980s, Jay Pather has been making dance, theater, and performance works of astonishing magnitude and range while also serving as the curator and producer for several vanguard festivals, such the Live Art Festival and the Infecting the City Festival, both of which occur in Cape Town. While the scope of his oeuvre and his own personal history will be covered in more detail in the next chapter, here I focus on just one of his works, arguably one of his most ambitious and complex performances. Created over a decade after the Truth and Reconciliation Commission commenced its transitional justice work in 1996, *Body of Evidence* (2008) by Jay Pather and his Siwela Sonke Dance Theatre is a conceptually challenging piece that interrogates the legacy of South Africa's negotiated settlement and the embodied, kinesthetic legacies of apartheid. Originally commissioned for the 2008 FNB Dance Umbrella in Johannesburg, the work subsequently appeared at the 2009 National Arts Festival in Grahamstown.

Like an ultrasonic rendering of what normally goes unseen, *Body of Evidence* is an invasive work. If South Africans are to "rediscover the ordinary," as Njabulo Ndebele has exhorted them to do, *Body of Evidence* suggests that this rediscovery should probe beneath the skin and on the other side of human consciousness. *Body of Evidence* is an intimate and jarring journey through the human body, probing both the physical body and its psychic dimensions. Unearthing memories embedded in bone, flesh, muscle memory, synapses, and scar tissue, the work also surfaces doubts about the country's transition, its "miraculous" utopian promises and hopes that truth telling could somehow heal the wounds of the past. *Body of Evidence* reveals the underneath of things, providing glimpses of how the past and its traumas remain embedded not only in scar tissue and bones but also in recurrent dreams, specters, apparitions, and tightly held muscle memories. These are the hieroglyphics of the flesh that Alexander Weheliye has theorized.[31]

Exposed in the cold harsh light, the scenography of *Body of Evidence* features video projections on the back wall and stage floor of images based on Henry Gray's ink drawings of brains, inner ears, muscles, ligaments, spines, vertebrae, pelvises, and feet bones in his classic 1918 work *Gray's Anatomy*. Gray's drawings are idealizations rather than faithful renderings of flesh and bone as they actually are. But the gulf between idealization and actualization is part of the point: the ideal is not real. Rights written into the constitution are not necessarily rights honored in daily life. South Africa's postapartheid multiracial dream has proven to be a mirage. While the medicalized frame of *Body of Evidence* suggests scientific positivism or forensic criminal inquiry, both of which presume that truth can be known, what actually appears on stage are visions and revelations that thwart and defy comprehension even as they present images of arresting strangeness that burrow deep into a spectator's psyche, seeding dreamscapes that remain vivid long after the show has ended.

With a cast of nine dancers, a string of loosely linked scenarios, cacophonous sounds, a succession of propulsive movement sequences, and a constant onslaught of images, *Body of Evidence* is a busy work. As one reviewer described, "We are bewitched by light and sound, learn about the origins of geraniums, enjoy rural masculinity boosted by feminine wiles, witness a traditional versus contemporary 'boxing' match, observe a moving scene where a body rises from the grave and relate to strong comments on the government's attention to suitable housing."[32] The anatomy projections on stage gradually move during the course of the show from head to foot, first isolating the top of the body then gradually moving to its base. Sometimes the images flash all at once, other times they are slowly revealed in a swipe from one side to another, as if generated in real time by radiographic imaging. The soundscape of *Body of Evidence* also invokes medical registers with assaultive clanking sounds like those produced by MRI machines. Composer James Webb's score uses recordings of visceral organs, surging fluids, pulsing heartbeats, and panicked breathing, interspersed with the sounds of call bells and the alarm that announces "code blue."

Body of Evidence begins with a fully clothed Mxolisi Nkomonde standing among other five other men, all of whom are in their underwear. Each is standing in a white baby bath that is filled with red clay and tabloid newspapers. Are they strangers? Brothers? Disassociated parts of Nkomonde himself? We do not know. The red clay that also covers their bodies symbolizes, as choreographer Pather explains, "a rite as well as a reinforcement of their death; their bodies as emptied out cavities that will soon be filled."[33] These figures are truly in the halfway of things—neither dead nor alive, neither clearly separate entities nor fragments of one self. They initially appear lifeless, inert, and frozen, while listing to one side. Soon the men begin devolving, melting like ice sculptures, toppling then collapsing downward, wilting. Abruptly, a zaftig woman played by Ntombi Gasa scurries onstage in red high heels, a mink coat, and, incongruously, a maid's outfit; flashlights dangle from her knees. She is a helpmate, a caretaker, or a stagehand, running among the frozen men trying futily to reverse the natural progression of their degradation. She adjusts, supports, props up, and tries to restore them. Nkomonde, stands as a puzzled witness among the other men.

Soon a didactic guide comes to mansplain it all: a white septuagenarian played by John Cartwright. He wears a dark suit, a red tie, a snappy hat, and sunglasses and is holding an armful of brilliant pink and red flowers in pots. The lights come up fully onstage and we see five men in tubs and Nkomonde more clearly. Nkomonde listens attentively to Cartwright's character as he directly addresses the audience: "Good evening. I would like to talk to you about geraniums." He hands some flowers to Gasa and she distributes them to the men in tubs. Cartwright holds forth in a pedantic way about the geographic origins and properties of geraniums: "They look so bright and cheery in hanging baskets and window boxes all over Europe in the summertime. But they are actually a South African flower, you know? Yep! They grow in the wild here. And they're really tough—hardy, the botanists call them." His speech is apropos of nothing, vaguely nativist, botanically deterministic, and certainly presumptuous—as though everyone should care about this topic when there is so much else to explained about what we are seeing on stage. Are the men in tubs supposed to be South African geraniums? If so, why are they wilting? Why are they not hardy?

Cartwright's character eventually fades, obscured and upstaged as the men in tubs come to life, move, step out of their tubs, and interact with each other. Over the course of the performance, they engage in a series of private encounters in duos and trios and in larger, more abstract ensemble movements. Some moments of *Body of Evidence* suggest scenes among characters—between a father and son or between a child and a mother or perhaps between brothers or between the living and the dead. Yet there is no dialogue or narrative to prove or disprove our interpretive speculations about who these people are or who they are to each other. Other moments are more abstract modern dance ensemble sequences anchored in shared ensemble movement patterns and repeated phrasings.

Cartwright, the white patriarch, returns periodically throughout the show, sometimes slowly processing upstage, other times cheerily singing ditties about cocaine. Later he is pushed onstage in a rolling desk chair suggesting a wheelchair and infirmity. Draped in white holiday lights, his feet resting in a white baby bath, he seems both lit up and infirm. Cartwright gradually undresses as he recites narratives about torture. He is delivering real first-person testimony from perpetrators' hearings at the Truth and Reconciliation Commission. We hear snippets about burning bodies, but his words are acoustically crowded out by other sounds. For Pather, the content of his confession is clearly not the point: it's merely a symbolic gesture of confession, a performance of sickness, a grab for center-stage focus, a white patriarch's implicit claim to his own victimhood. At the very end of *Body of Evidence,* Cartwright's character returns upstage and off center in an otherwise expansive operatic scene in which all the dancers move in flourishing, though often absurd and disconnected, ways. Cartwright slowly kneels by one of the performers, who is reclining on a beach chair, wearing long swimming flippers on his feet and sunglasses and blue ointment on his face. Cartwright washes this man's feet—or rather his swimming flippers.

This foot-washing gesture is a very specific and topical reference that would likely have been legible to all South Africans spectators in 2008. Unpacking this reference reveals a great deal about Pather's vision. Feet washing evokes the notorious apartheid police minister Adriaan Vlok, a man associated with a secret apartheid counterinsurgency unit called Vlakplass that was responsible for kidnapping, torturing, drugging, and murdering dozens of anti-apartheid fighters, sometimes burning victims on open flames as if at a brai (barbeque). Under Vlok, Vlakplass was responsible also for chemical warfare and assassinations, including the attempted murder of Rev. Frank Chikane by lacing his underpants with insecticide. In the postapartheid era, in the middle of South Africa's transition in 2006 (two years before *Body of Evidence* premiered and several years after the TRC had concluded its work), Adriaan Vlok approached Chikane, who was then chief of staff for President Thabo Mbeki. His sole purpose was to wash Chikane's feet, a gesture ostensibly inspired by Christian devotion and piety. Vlok arrived at the Pretoria Union Building with a Bible under his arm and a briefcase containing a rag and bowl. He slid to his knees, asking: "Frank, please, would you allow me to wash your feet?"[34] Was this a genuine act of repentance and contrition or mere posturing? Given the way the TRC individualized guilt and victimhood, and failed to address larger systems of oppression and inequality, does the question of Vlok's sincerity even matter? This performed act of atonement led him to be vilified as a traitor and ridiculed as a "quivering dog" in the Afrikaner press.[35] But Vlok, who lost his wife to suicide shortly after South Africa entered its new democratic dispensation, discovered a renewed faith in Christianity through his grief. After this episode with Chikane, Vlok made foot washing a regular practice: he washed the feet of mothers of activists that Vlakplaas had killed, of a group of black taxi drivers, of members of a black church, and even his own maid.[36] Vlok's habitual foot washing was provocative and controversial and many were suspicious of his motives, skeptical that these were acts of genuine contrition. In Pather's *Body of Evidence*, foot washing represents the afterlife of the TRC, the ghosts of its discourse of forgiveness and reconciliation, a remnant that was both symbolically potent and dramaturgically insignificant to the action.

The character of Vlok wafts through the performance and thus through the psyche of the show's protagonist, but he does little to fundamentally alter its recurrent conditions, which are jarring, confusing, and eclectic. On one hand, Cartwright's character is central: he opens the show, he is the only one to directly address the audience, and he holds forth as an expert. He often takes the focus when he is on stage, and he presumes that everyone will care about what he has to say. But on the other hand, in the overall staging of *Body of Evidence*, this character is relatively inconsequential and marginal. He is sonically upstaged, he is ineffectual, and he is impotent. The center of the action is the black performers, and specifically Mxolisi Nkomonde's character. Cartwright's character perpetuates whiteness and patriarchy as a persistent force. In the first half of the show, although he attempts to occupy center stage, he has limited impact on or relevance to the assemblage of others on stage, who go on about their movements and struggles and celebrations as they dance, fight with demons, drag themselves across the floor with miniature houses strapped to their backs (a likely reference to South Africa's perennial housing crisis), box with seen and unseen opponents, or holler from behind bamboo screens. By the end of the play, Cartwright has been sidelined and perhaps somehow personally transformed from oblivious, self-important expert to contrite supplicant and ostensible confessor. But he has not gone away.

At one point in the middle of the show two ethereal black spirit figures covered in white body paint emerge from within the projected image of a ribcage. One dancer carries an inverted white parasol (obviously ineffectual at sheltering from either rain or sun) and the other carries a glaring industrial work light (very practical and utilitarian). These characters are at once ethereal and earthy. They are from another world, another time. The woman is draped in a diaphanous gray gown whose length and structure evokes Marie Antoinette and her head is wrapped in a white turban that rises several feet in the air into a towering narrow conical shape, a plume of blond hair sprouting out the top. These two ghostly apparitions shuffle toward the audience slowly, expectantly. They seem to be in command of hidden powers or knowledge. They seem to be fascinated to watch the quintet of performers downstage as they go through various routines, such as a gumboot dance with buckets on their heads.[37] And yet these spirit figures are shaky and uncertain: they walk with a hesitant gait with quizzical expressions on their faces. We sense that something is coming into being with their tentative yet persistent emergence from the projected skeleton of a torso. They shuffle toward the audience downstage. They seem about to do something but we don't know what. It's not clear whether they will make any difference or have any impact on the events unfolding on the stage. But these intriguing apparitions in the process of arrival are quite beautiful.

Body of Evidence builds to a final crescendo as Mozart's *Requiem Mass in D Minor* blares and we see a busy flurry of disparate activity. The large black woman in whiteface makeup, the one with blond hair peeping out of her headdress who has paraded throughout the performance like a ghostly regal apparition, is hammering the stage floor, the young man is sunbathing on a beach chair as old white man Cartwright washes his feet, two dancers are running into each other repeatedly, and several others lie on the floor wearing enormous swimming flippers that quiver like fish out of water. All of this action does anything but cohere. Everything builds to a moment of crescendo and then suddenly there is silence and solitude. All but Mxolisi Nkomonde disappear from the stage.

Fig. 4. Siyanda Duma, Ntombi Gasa, and Neliswa Rushualang in a scene from Jay Pather's *Body of Evidence*, 2008. (Photo by Val Adamson, courtesy of Jay Pather.)

In contrast to the surfeit of visual and acoustic stimuli throughout the 90 minutes of this performance, its final moments stand in remarkable contrast: a single performer is left alone in stunned silence. Nkomonde seems surprised and disoriented to discover himself there. He climbs up from the floor and stands, peering in astonishment around him at the darkened, empty stage, his eyes straining as if he has just woken from a dream. A negative reverse image of Gray's drawing of a foot is projected on the screen behind him and on the floor below. We realize that the tempest of confounding and sometimes inscrutable images, scenarios that careen from the surreal to the banal, the ironic to the earnest, the absurd to the terrifying; the parade of characters familiar and strange; the bodies and spirits, the cries from muezzins amid snippets from Brenda Fassie's hit song "Weekend Special"; men boxing while dancing; dancers tap dancing in long swimming flippers; spirit-like figures engaged in elaborate though seemingly ineffectual ceremonies of healing; a father and son locked in an interminable Manichean battle; a goddess-like character dragging behind her a trail of bread loaves tied to her dress with ribbons; injured characters wearing bandages and hospital robes; and gumboot dancers in bras with buckets on their head—all of this has actually been a tour through one man's mind and body.

Body of Evidence is an anti-bildungsroman representing not a protagonist's gradual enlightenment but rather his ongoing fragmentation and bewilderment. Nkomonde's character finally emerges by the end of the show as an individuated person, although he is no more coherent than he was at the start. One senses acutely that this is not the end. What we have witnessed is a recurring cycle. The scenes, images, reenactments, old patterns paraded onstage throughout the performance are loops in his mind. These hauntings are puzzling, sometimes physically beautiful, often uncanny and abruptly mercurial in their shifting tone. Occasionally they are ominous or frightening, but for the most part they are not violent or deeply disturbing so much as puzzling and busy. The most violent moment happens when three men descend on a motorized small vehicle as they are trying to catch it and one of them smashes the car to smithereens with a hammer, an action so unexpected that the audience gasped the night I saw the show. But this one moment of actual violence seemed more a lashing out against an annoying insentient irritant than a premeditated act of destruction or rage.

What *Body of Evidence* reveals through its references to forensic autopsy and radiological diagnosis and its aesthetic of surveillance is that this person in the present is the sum of his past—a past that is very much alive in the here and now, asserting itself within and on the body, through psyche, dreams, and unconsciousness, erupting, disrupting, and thwarting any sense of calm or equanimity, although none of this may be apparent to the casual observer in daily life. The reality underneath the surface that is exposed through the forensic inquiry of *Body of Evidence* is not necessarily an alarming pathology, something to be "cured." Nor is this a body of evidence that seems focused on making a finding or proving anything or discovering who is to blame. This evidence is rather presented as a revelation, a cause for rumination. This body of evidence lacks interpretation or structuring narrative. To be sure, there are gestures toward confession, rituals of atonement, and attempted rapprochement between long-feuding duos. There are also otherworldly apparitions that seem to be attempting some kind of ritual of healing or cleansing. But these all seem largely ineffectual and irrelevant, more unresolved detritus, grist for the dream mill and memory machine of the unconscious.

Disillusion with the TRC and with the so-called postapartheid transition provoked Pather to create *Body of Evidence*. He saw the work as a way to shift temporal frames, to stop seeing the past as past.[38] The wounds and scars and traumas of the past live on in the bodies of now, in today's bodies, in their flesh and bone and skin and psyches. Pather says:

> The body remembers more than through the head. Nerve and vessel, artery and synapse all carry information from point to point suffusing muscle, bone and cell with a plethora of image and sound, a flicker of light, a scream or a touch. Sometimes we wish that a delete button might annihilate some of this information. But the body instead stores relentlessly, file upon file, bottomless cabinets of memory, individual and collective. What does the body do with this ebb and flow of knowledge?[39]

The afterlives of apartheid as portrayed in *Body of Evidence* are as cellular and enduring as they are overwhelming and loud—a cacophony and surfeit of confusing, inscrutable, dreamlike apparitions that resonate as deeply familiar but also defiantly strange. The characters onstage exist in the protracted interval: between a dream state and consciousness, between terror and hilarity, between paralysis and exuberant movement. In their multiplicity, the many dancers represent a fragmentation of the self that is indeed a kind of fallout from the past. When our protagonist arises in solitude at the show's end, his body appears very much intact and healthy, even virile. We are forced to reconcile his hale external visage with the sprawl of inscrutable, haunting phantasms that have populated the stage during the previous hour and twenty minutes. This confusion is what lies within him. Yet if this last image was our first impression of this man, who would suspect that such turbulence lies within?

When considered next to the other works analyzed in this chapter, Pather contributes a medicalizing gaze and pathological and forensic registers that ultimately foreground epistemological questions, signaling positivism and a moral and religious framing (through the reference to Vlok's foot washing and confession). At times, *Body of Evidence* invokes a postmortem. At one point we see a projection of a Nkomonde's face, his eyes closed as though he is lying on a table in a morgue. The performance also signals diagnostic tracking, as if there is an external agent trying to detect the patient's main complaint. Who is the doctor, the external inquisitor to whom this body of evidence is being presented? It may be us, the audience. But the performance disrupts the binary framing of subject and object by inserting moments, at least in the Grahamstown performance that I saw, when spectators had to leave their seats and race around the theater to follow the action. What *Body of Evidence* does not offer is any notion of cure. If it is pathology we are witnessing, this pathology is presented as a condition that *just is*.

Ideas of cure and metaphors about the need to "open the wounds" of apartheid in order for the country to heal were central to the discourses both in the operations of the TRC and in the public discourse that swirled around it. Cure is a contested concept in the field of disability studies, and while Pather's performance does not overtly connect to disability studies, I wish to make that link here, for I think it provides a valuable way of understanding the misalignment of the teleological thrust created by terms like "transition" and the lived and embodied experience of state and cultural transformation in the wake of an authoritarian regime.

Disability studies has long noted the pervasiveness and persistence of narratives of miracle cures—the belief, hope, and expectation that a particular impairment can be eliminated by some heroic new medical intervention that may reverse paralysis or make the blind able to see or the deaf able to hear. Narrative tropes about cure of disability are sometimes labeled as the medical model, a way of seeing disability that individualizes impairment and enforces on each person an expectation of compulsory "normality," an ablest ideal to which everyone should aspire. Disability studies has countered this medical model with what it calls the social model, which posits, as Tom Shakespeare summarizes, that "disability is about social barriers and social oppression, not impairment."[40] Instead of forcing individuals to conform to social norms, society should create barrier-free environments that are inclusive of the range of human ways of being and operating in the world. In this view, impairment is a difference, not a deficit. As many disability studies scholars have argued, broadly speaking, the medical model and social model overlap considerably and there is ambiguity and even potential complementarity between them. But what most agree on is the damage of the hyperbole and raised expectations that a rhetoric of miracle cure creates, such as the inflated expectations created by Christopher Reeve's campaign for medical interventions to cure paralysis or corrective childhood surgeries to lengthen limbs or the "cure" of Cochlear implants for hearing impairment. These practices mobilize assumptions that disability is a problem to be solved.[41] They presume that the individual must be "corrected" so that he or she will fit within a norm. This is a very different approach to making schools, curricula, buildings, roads, transportation, architecture, and art that is widely accessible, which is the underlying principle guiding universal design. What is most problematic about the medical discourse of cure is the heightened expectations that implicitly reject the condition of impairment. Disability studies rather posits disability as valuable, a quality that contributes to the richness of society and human experience. Embodiment comes in many forms and some aspects of human diversity not only cannot but should not be changed.

So how is this exploration of disability and cure relevant to South Africa and its political transition? As with temporal frames of before and after, as with the proliferation of "posts" in South Africa (post-apartheid, post-antiapartheid, post-transition), as with narratives about "truth, the road to reconciliation," there is an underlying utopian promise in the notion of cure that a condition can be permanently fixed and repaired. The ideology of cure has, as Rosemarie Garland-Thompson argues, "an aggressive intent to fix, regulate or eradicate" what is seen as deviant, a "pervasive will-to-normalize."[42] Just as the medical model promotes and sustains an essential separation between nondisabled and disabled, the discourse of transitional justice promotes and sustains a fundamental separation between an authoritarian past and a presumed liberated, democratic, and "healed" future state. The oft-touted "miracle" of South Africa's state transition created inflated expectations of a miracle cure for apartheid.[43] But both disability studies and Pather's *Body of Evidence* illuminate the fact that neither the medical model as symbolized by those drawings from *Gray's Anatomy* nor the moral model of dealing with the apartheid past as seen in the confessions of Cartwright's character are adequate. The afterlives of apartheid's injustice continue to fundamentally transform individuals, bodies, minds, and social formations and this will persist. To rediscover *this* ordinary is to experience the recursive and the nonlinear imbrication of past and present. Sometimes it appears that stasis is the same as stagnation, but *Body of Evidence* suggests that to stay in one place and to dig deeply—excavating the hidden, the unseen, and the misunderstood—can produce disruptive and unexpected journeys.

MAMELA NYAMZA: LEGIBLE WILL, UNBECOMING SUBJECT

I turn now to choreographer Mamela Nyamza, a prolific artist working on the edge between dance and theater, between performance and installation, between dance and undance, between adversarial confrontation and captivating self-discovery.[44] Born in 1976, the year of the Soweto uprisings, to a large family in the Gugulethu township of Cape Town, Nyamza began training in ballet as a young girl, when family members identified and encouraged her extraordinary gifts as a dancer. She trained at the Zama Dance School under the guidance of its principal, Arlene Westergaard.

Nyamza then went on to become the only black female ballet dancer at the Pretoria Dance Technicon. In 1998, she received a scholarship to attend the Alvin Ailey American Dance Center in New York City, which turned out to be utterly transformative and momentous. For the first time, Nyamza was able to study and train with black teachers, an experience of enormous significance in ballet, a dance form with strict expectations about body comportment, norms, and types—expectations that have not been particularly welcoming for black bodies and black ways of moving in South Africa or, indeed, anywhere.[45] While training with Ailey in New York, Nyamza also began to explore her sexuality and experienced a same-sex relationship for the first time. But living in New York was hard for Nyamza; it was a lonely place a long way from her home. She returned to South Africa a year later and soon thereafter traumatically lost her mother, who was brutally raped and murdered. In the wake of this tragedy, young relatives needed care, and Nyamza soon found herself locked into domestic duties.[46] This was compounded when she became unexpectedly pregnant by her old high school boyfriend. With the impending expectations of motherhood and mounting family obligations, Nyamza's career as a performer seemed to hang in the balance.

Out of this time of uncertainty, grief, loss, and what seemed to be a narrowing of possibilities, Nyamza's signature work *Hatched* was born. This autobiographical work expressed personal discoveries and transformations as Nyamza came out as a gay woman and a lesbian mother, divorced her husband, and proclaimed herself to be an independent performance artist—one with ballet training, yes, but one also set on imploding that training and making something altogether new with ballet's scattered remains. Mamela Nyamza came to prominence in 2008 at the Johannesburg Dance Umbrella with a piece initially called *Hatch*. A revised version of the work, retitled *Hatched*, opened at the National Arts Festival in Grahamstown two years later in 2010, a time when the hopes for South Africa's rainbow had faded and optimism about transition had worn thin. But in contrast to the country's growing sense of stagnation, *Hatched* depicts metamorphosis and positive self-actualization, portraying Nyamza "hatching" as a new mother who continues to perform, as a lesbian who has recently announced and embraced what is still in South Africa a nonconforming and often violently persecuted sexuality, and as a dancer who is deconstructing ballet's problematic embodied pedigree. In her intimate and kinesthetically potent works—*Hatched* and later *De-Apart-Hate*—Nyamza stages a subject becoming queer, a mother, an artist, a woman who is liberated from black female traditions of domestic labor and from ballet's kinesthetic colonization. They also stage a subject unbecoming: they upend decorum and inherited embodied values tightly held in muscle memory. As such, these works provide an important contrast and corrective to the loss of subjectivity evident in Errol Philander's experience in *Statements after an Arrest under the Immorality Act* of psychic dissolution and reduction to pure will, nothing else, when he was hailed and arrested by the apartheid state. While that play represented the psychic life of apartheid power for a person of color under arrest, Nyamza stages, many decades later, the psychic life of power for a black subject in the process of decolonization in apartheid's wake.

Hatched begins with Nyamza standing tall and erect, magisterially *en pointe* on her ballet shoes, her bare muscular back exposed to the audience as she balances a bucket on her head and edges gingerly on tiptoe along a laundry line, her long muslin skirt covered with wooden laundry pegs pinned up and down it like truncated feathers. This image "reads like a struggle between two antithetical yet recognizable worlds," says Alude Mahali, "that of the Westernized ballerina and the archetypal rural black African woman."[47] Nyamza's demeanor shifts with mercurial swiftness. Her mood and tone pivot many times with disarming directness: "She hungers; she accuses; she explains; she spites; she learns; she rejects; she *implores*," as one reviewer noted.[48] Nyamza performs *Hatched* with her son, Amkele Mandla. When the show premiered in 2010, he was a young child. He would quietly sit on the floor under a table, painting seascapes onstage. By the time of Nyamza's most recent iteration of *Hatched* at the 2018 National Arts Festival in Grahamstown, Mandla had become a strapping eighteen-year-old and his performance had evolved: he filled pages with charcoal drawings one reviewer found "sinister" while also rapping over background music.[49] *Hatched* is as much about personal transformation as it is about personal refusal—a refusal of domestic servitude; a refusal of expected gender roles and relationships; a refusal to show the audience her eyes, her face, and the most winning of smiles you have ever seen. Although the audience can see from her back that Nyamza's entire torso is bare, she withholds the exposure of her front from their gaze until well into the performance. Not only does *Hatched* signal Nyamza's conflicted relationship with ballet, it also depicts her emerging identity as a lesbian. Nyamza performs an emergent willful subject, as Sara Ahmed has theorized: "Perhaps self-certainty is not how the will becomes what is given to a subject, but how a subject can become itself: 'I have a will' understood not only as a sign of existence, 'I will *therefore* I am'[,]but as an impulse to existence: 'I will *then* I am."[50] In other words, will is something one asserts and claims, and through that, the subject becomes. Through the course of *Hatched*, Nyamza eventually dons and takes full possession of a brilliant red coat, a symbol of her newly blossoming identity, assertion of her will, and radiant transcendence.

While *Hatched* announced the arrival of Nyamza as a lesbian, a choreographer, and a performance artist, it also foreshadowed how she would explode genre expectations not only related to her ballet training but also to concert dance in general. Her mastery of technique was evident as she sustained her long legs *en pointe*, but she refused to give the audience any *grand jetés, Arabeques, attitude derrière*, or *grand pas de chats*. *Hatched* was the first of several works which Nyamza deconstructed ballet's physical vocabulary and grammar. Another performance along these lines was *The Last Attitude* (2015), a piece Nyamza created with Nelisiwe Xaba, who has performed internationally as a ballet-trained dancer in full command of technique.[51] Xaba is willfully in command of her license to unmake ballet and violate its elitist, racist, and gendered norms. *The Last Attitude* dismantles ballet with the aid of dismembered mannequins, as Nyamza and Xaba take possession of male dance moves, enacting a gradual demolition of ballet throughout what one reviewer called their "matador-like" characters.[52]

Okuya Phantsi Kwempula/The Meal (2015) continued Nyamza's dissection of ballet. This work autobiographically reflects on her introduction to ballet in childhood under the tutelage of Arlene Westergaard. The performance begins with Nyamza crouched on the floor of the theater entryway while writing on a long scroll over and over again: "I must not have a big bum," "I must not have a big bum." Once the performance formally begins in the theater, she kneels at the feet of actress Dinnah Eppel, here playing Nyamza's white teacher, who instructs and models precise ballet moves and comportment: chin up, shoulder down, back tall, bottom clenched, and hair twisted high into a bun. Later Eppel's presence gradually recedes as Nyamza's ascends: she becomes the senior teacher, instructing a younger black ballet dancer, Kirsty Ndawo. Nyamza imparts the same tutelage she has imbibed and internalized: chin up, shoulder down, back tall, bottom clenched, and hair twisted high into a bun. But gradually both dancers' bodies erupt, rebel, and give way to different kinds of comportment, musicality, movement, and athleticism. These alternate impulses well up, at first repressed but later exploding the bounds of ballet with Tswane dance rhythms. Eventually Nyamza and Ndawo arrive at a place of defiant mockery of ballet. As they passionately embrace, Ndawo jumps up on Nyamza's waist, forcefully wrapping her arms and legs around the elder dancer. Nyamza then removes the pins that bind Ndawao's hair. Later she burns *impepho*, an herb intended both for healing and summoning of the ancestors.

Okuya Phantsi Kwempulo/The Meal is about much more than ballet. It is about Nyamza's own body and her relationship to her first ballet teacher, and the parallels between this and South Africa's transformation from colonizing white power to a yet-to-be-fully-discovered liberated and decolonized dispensation. Ballet represents problematic inherited rules, constraints, judgements, muscle memories, and embodied patterns and the ways such traditions and habits are passed on from one generation to the next. Just as her white teacher schools Nyamza, Nyamza in turn schools black student Kristy Ndawo in the rigors of ballet comportment. But in Nyamza's transition from student to teacher, another force—an energy, an impulse—erupts, one that is both destructive and constructive, one that unmakes and remakes, even as it releases African movement patterns long held and suppressed.

As with *Hatched*, *The Meal* stages a metamorphosis, providing glimpses of Mamela Nyamza's ballet training while also staging her refusal. She thwarts the desire of her audiences, and these desires are impulsive, carnal, and often unexamined. Canadian reviewer Steven Weisz commented that the brief moments he saw of Nyamza's "beautiful lines and flowing movements" left what he calls "traditionalists" like himself "just wanting to see her dance."[53] But this desire to visually consume Nyamza's dancing body is precisely what *Okuya Phantsi Kwempulo/The Meal* declines to fulfill. While Weisz found parts of the performance satisfying, the whole did not cohere for him: "After an evening of dining on *The Meal*, I found the individual components to be full of flavor but somehow the ingredients just never combined to give me a fully composed dining experience, leaving me in the end still hungry."[54] What Weisz does not seem to contemplate is that this meal was never intended to satisfy him.

In much of Africa, meals may be prepared by one person and consumed by another. It is precisely this inequitable balance of exchange that Nyamza questions: "Before a meal can be eaten, preparation is necessary," says Nyamza in her artist's statement. "The most basic division is between the creator of the meal and those who are being served. This work examines the process in which the eater becomes one with the meal, though the process of reaching satisfaction can take many forms."[55] *Okuya Phantsi Kwempulo/The Meal* disrupts the usual relationship between the artist's generative labor of creation and the spectator's privilege of consumption. The work posits that those who laboriously prepare the "meal" of the dance should also be the ones to consume it. When performances like *The Meal* are staged for audiences who are overwhelmingly unlike the performers—in terms of race, class, nationality, etc.—there is a fundamental rift in the encounter. If art, like a meal, sustains, for whose benefit is the meal prepared and served?

Nyamza's subsequent performance works have moved in different directions. Instead of staging metamorphosis and self-actualization, these works foreground uncertainty, waiting, and stasis. She sometimes depicts worlds that do not change or that have changes one can barely perceive—changes we come to recognize only through endurance and careful and attentive observation. These works often demand a suspension of conventional expectations about development, genre, style, and structure and a refusal of the dance connoisseur's appetite for trained bodies moving in beautiful ways to music and rhythm with phrasings and partnering and prettiness. Nyamza's performances offer a patient excavation of time. With surgical precision, she sometimes introduces changes so slowly and subtlety that audiences may fail to perceive them. In describing these works in Nyamza's oeuvre, terms like "post-apartheid," "post-antiapartheid," "transition," and "post-transition" do not resonate. Instead, she leverages the power of undoing: deconstruction, decolonization, delamination, and defiance. Nyamza tangles with the afterlives of injustice by patiently lying in wait and then capturing, taming, and redirecting energies along provocative new trajectories. In *Phuma-Langa*, for instance, the Ndebele-inspired costumes worn by the dancers gradually, slowly, almost imperceptibly fall apart each time their names are mispronounced on soundtrack. In *Isingqala*, Nyamza performs a repeated cycle of grief many times, a frantic circling of the room, before the meaning of this repetition of this action reveals. In *De-Apart-Hate*, the performance begins with a long, seemingly unstructured worship segment that only through patient accretion of actions exposes itself as being an upending of Christianity's problematic embrace of anti-blackness and homophobia.

In addition to her sustained deconstruction of ballet and colonial performance aesthetics, Nyamza has also been preoccupied with gender violence and homophobia. Her work *Kutheni* (2009) is about homophobia in the townships and the double murder of two lesbians in Meadowlands. A year later she created *Shift* (2010), a performance about the murder of gender non-gender-conforming soccer player Eudy Simelane, who was stabbed twenty-seven times for acting like a man.[56] *Shift* strikes an unexpected tone at its opening. Nyamza first appears with only her bare feet exposed. They poke out from beneath an obscuring scrim, lofted in the air, not quite touching the floor, with canvas sneakers tied at the ankles and dangling below.

Her feet initially are inert, as though we are seeing a body that has been hung. But soon these feet spring to life, running, slightly raised up in the air, and gradually they kick off the tennis shoes. Nyamza reaches down and puts on five-inch high, open-toed sling back silver pumps, her muscular calves glistening with oil. Right from the start, this performance shifts several times—from a possible death scene to a recreational jog to a flirtatious expression of female sensuality through footwear while also exhibiting formidable muscle and strength. Eventually Nyamza's whole body is revealed and the audience sees she's wearing a simple tennis-like costume, a short white shift and swim goggles. She snaps bubblegum while cheerily, impishly smiling and waving at the audience whom she begins to address directly. She coaches and persuades them to throw twenty-seven ping-pong balls at her. But only in their mass propulsion at the appointed moment does the murderous symbolism of these balls become clear. As she is hit, Nyamza spastically contorts and ultimately collapses. She disintegrates before our eyes, finally climbing into a small refrigerator. The door closes and the performance ends, leaving audience members aghast at the work's abrupt shifts in tone and their own role in its conclusion. *Shift* features a character who transitions, who changes during the course of the show, but this is an experience of dehumanizing annihilation, not self-actualization. We are seeing another iteration of Errol Philander's devolution from *Statements After an Arrest*. The remains of apartheid's afterlives rear up and perform to a conclusion that is perhaps even more devastating than Errol's: not even *will* remains at the end of *Shift*.

Nyamza's next work, *Isingqala* (2011), was an intimate and inwardly-focused performance that debuted at the National Arts Festival in July 2011.[57] *Isingqala,* which is an isiXhosa word meaning sorrow, begins in darkness, forcing the audience to grope their way to metal bleachers in dim light. As a person with a mobility impairment, my entry to this *Isingqala* performance was particularly challenging and disorienting in the darkness. But gradually I located an empty seat and shimmied to an upper riser. As my eyes adjusted, I noticed that the person sitting next to me had just one arm, and only when I saw his face in profile did I realize I was sitting next to legendary anti-apartheid activist and Constitutional Court justice Albie Sachs, someone I had interviewed for my previous book. As my eyes adjusted to the theater's shadowy nocturne, Nyamza gradually became visible standing center stage, her back to the audience, wearing a shimmering silver male leisure suit. Her opening anticipates the opening moments of Gregory Maqoma's *Exit/Exist,* in which he also begins in a luminous silver suit, his back to the audience (see Fig. 1).

The show commences with a primal screech. "With the scream the choreographer sets the scene for the *isingqala*, the frenetic heaving of the chest and shoulders after heavy sobbing," one reviewer described. "The heaving turns into a chilling waving of her arms as if a bird is setting flight, as a form of absolution from a painful experience."[58] Nyamza breaks into a jog as she runs laps around the stage. *Isingqala* is visually and sonically spare. Its only light comes from flashlights and its only set piece is a box the size of a coffin that hangs from the ceiling, suspended at approximately the height of a table. Its soundtrack consists of screams and occasional wailing, the sound of jingling coins in Nyamza's pocket, and the clacking of her feet shod in male dress shoes as she jogs around the perimeter of the stage. Occasionally we hear something like the sound of a coin dropping followed by the whirring sound of a child's top that Nyamza drops on the floor periodically and lets spin as we collectively watch its trajectory of chance.

Nothing about *Isingqala* is easy. In an interview with the festival newspaper, Nyamza said she was "not on stage to entertain," adding that audiences might find "me self-indulgent, so be it. . . . I'm working from the inside out."[59] *Isingqala* is about what happens when private crying and grief become public. The work can also be read autobiographically in relation to Nyamza's grief in the face of the gendered violence that so tragically ended her own mother's life, although one has to access that story outside the theater, as she provides no such anchoring details in the show or its program. Nyamza is living her life and her career in the wake of a violent, traumatic loss—a direct, profound, and personal injustice. *Isingqala* vividly and achingly portrays the profound grief that is its afterlife.

Outside the theater after the show, I greeted Justice Sachs. He shook his head, expressing perplexity and exasperation with what we had just seen. He declared that he did not understand the point of Nyamza's "undance." In his 1991 essay "Preparing Ourselves for Freedom," Sachs had famously opined that South African artists needed to prepare themselves for freedom by allowing for greater ambiguity and complexity in art, by jettisoning the straitjacket of political correctness and the limits of overt protest art that demanded clear, unambiguous meanings and objectives. However, it seems that the ambiguity and complexity of *Isingqala* was not what he had had in mind.[60]

In 2012, a year after *Isingqala*, Nyamza made another work about gender violence, a show called *I Stand Corrected*, created in collaboration with London-based artist Mojisola Adebayo.[61] The play begins with a lesbian fiancé, Charlie, who has been stood up at the altar. We eventually learn that her lover has been "correctively" raped and murdered in a homophobic hate crime. *I Stand Corrected* is the most theatrical of Nyamza's works—it has characters, dialogue, story, and plot development. This is perhaps due to Nyamza's collaboration with writer Mojisola Adebayo, who plays the role of the lesbian lover, the surviving fiancé, who speaks throughout the work in long soliloquys. Adebayo also imaginatively reenacts scenes with other characters, such as encounters Charlie has with a homophobic police officer who refuses to file a missing-persons report because he won't countenance a lesbian identity as valid. He derogatorily ridicules the "unnaturalness" of Charlie's same-sex relationship, which she refutes by discussing how "unnatural" it is for humans to fly in airplanes.

While *I Stand Corrected* is marketed more as theater than as dance, the work certainly features moving bodies prominently, particularly Nyamza's. She plays the role of Zodwa, a woman who is first discovered onstage head down in a trash bin. We watch as she comes to life, animated, confused, and inquisitive. We eventually realize she is the spirit of Zodwa, who has been raped and murdered. *I Stand Corrected* stages her afterlife of injustice as she literally rises after death, seemingly somehow "corrected" by the trauma and sexual violence she has endured so that she now imbibes without hesitation female gender norms promulgated in the women's fashion magazines she finds in a rubbish pile. Zodwa awkwardly strikes poses mimicking the magazine models and she crudely, awkwardly puts on lipstick. The show eventually stages an encounter between the living abandoned bride Charlie and the spirit of her deceased partner Zodwa as they recall with nostalgia their budding romance and courtship.

Zodwa and Charlie occupy two separate but parallel universes. *I Stand Corrected* thwarts audience appetites for closure: this is a queer wedding that wasn't; this is a play about a ritual that has been abruptly and violently interrupted, an attempted gay marriage that turned out to be a most unhappy and infelicitous performative. The ideal of the new South Africa—which has a constitution that progressively inscribes the right of lesbians and gays to live freely and safely as full-fledged citizens, to take up with and marry sexual partners of their own choosing—cannot be realized within the reality of pervasive homophobia. As Richard Pithouse states, gay rights in South Africa are "only protected on paper" and, as with so many aspects of the constitution's thwarted promise, "winning rights in principle is a different thing from realizing them in practice."[62] By staging unhappy performatives, *I Stand Corrected* stands apart from the ringing declarations of South Africa's constitution. Thwarted promise through murder is quite literally a "morbid symptom," one that arises in a time that can no longer be called the "interregnum," to reference Gramsci, though still is fraught with pathologies.[63]

I see two major trajectories in Mamela Nyamza's creative oeuvre. On one hand, she has produced works like *Hatched, The Last Attitude,* and *Okuya Phantsi Kwempulo/The Meal* that represent self-actualization, self-realization, and positive personal transformations and discoveries while at the same time deconstructing what is inherited. These works depict liberation through the divestment or deconstruction of colonizing practices such as the white supremacy embedded in ballet's policing of "big bums" and imposition of tight hair buns or the rigid domestic expectations of compulsorily heterosexual African motherhood. We see a personal transformation on stage from one state to another along a trajectory of progress. On the other hand, a second major theme goes in another direction, depicting changes that are destructive or annihilating or situations of stagnation that freeze individuals in terminal states of grief, isolation, or separation. Performances like *Shift, Isingqala,* and *I Stand Corrected* are about *unbecoming* subjects, even when the new South Africa has promised something that is so radically at odds with what Nyamza has experienced.

As gender-based violence became a more dominant and prevalent theme in Nyamza's oeuvre, it upstaged the emergent sensibility of metamorphosis that she so effervescently portrayed in her earlier works. Over the course of ten years of her career, utopian promise, emergent hope, and the prospect of positive transition seemed to become ever more remote. However, these two trajectories—metamorphosis and nihilistic paralysis—converged most dynamically in her 2017 performance *De-Apart-Hate,* first performed at the Johannesburg Dance Umbrella. Both celebratory and defiant, confrontational and seductively enticing, *De-Apart-Hate* deconstructs the apartheid past by delaminating or ungluing its component parts: "apartheid" becomes "apart-hate," a hyphenated phrase preceded by the prefix "de-," which marks a further undoing. "Apart" and "hate" still stand but they are also breaking apart and in that delamination of component parts, something new emerges that is both blasphemous and libidinous.

We begin in "church"—the small Wits University Amphitheatre transformed into a house of charismatic worship.[64] As audience members enter the theater, an audio recording of choral worship, "Indumiso 84," from a small Presbyterian church somewhere in South Africa, blares over the sound system, rocking the house. The room pulsates with an underlying rhythm that is marked out on hand bells and a low bass thumping that we eventually learn (when one performer planted in the audience contributes live accompaniment) comes from the slapping of a leather pillow. ONE-

TWO- and then an unstressed third beat. ONE-TWO (three). ONE-TWO (three)—a racing and rollicking asymmetrical three-part heartbeat. Individual voices in the chorus soar above others at various moments, creating a musical texture of loose-knit synchronicity that fully inhabits the off-beat, punctuated by occasional shouts of "hallelujah" and a few harmonic progressions and rhythmic shifts. Otherwise this opening soundtrack is a continuous, mesmerizing loop—a groove, a vamp of incantation without transitions.[65]

Audience members looking for empty seats step around and past a woman dancing in the main aisle: Mamela Nyamza dressed formally in a black sleeveless sheath that wraps like a tight leather book cover around her slender, athletic body. Her toned hourglass torso undulates to the music while her elbows jut out rhythmically while wrists remain firmly held at her hips. The beat seems to well up from within her: ONE-TWO (three). Nyamza's head is shaven, save for a tightly cropped patch on top. Her loosely held arms, bare and muscular, swing in time to the music, elbows fluttering out from a swaying torso. The confining tightness of the black dress gives way just below her knees to a flair of white tulle that flares outward from the knees like a mermaid's tail. At one point, Nyamza's knees, tightly bound together by the dress, bend in time to the music almost as if she is stooping to kneel. At the same time, her torso rhythmically drops forward along a horizontal plane. Legs and torso form interlocking but contrasting undulations, moving both horizontally and laterally. Nyamza seems to be singing along to the music, her face concentrated and radiant with an expression of intense ecstasy and joy. Sometimes she extends a single arm upward and outward in forceful punctuation of an emotional musical crescendo. A slight shift in the tempo of the music or a slight modulation in the melody prompts Nyamza to lift her right arm above her head and bring it downward at the elbow, as if pulling on a rope. The congregation, which is what the audience has become, is submerged in a sea of sound without any clear destination or shore.

Nyamza then leans over the thrust stage and begins banging on it like a drum: ONE-TWO (three). ONE-TWO (three). ONE-TWO (three), amplifying the beat held steady by the clanging bells and thumping leather pillows. Spectators still streaming into the theater walk past Nyamza, sometimes swaying to the music, sometimes looking at their cell phones or furtively trying to find an empty seat, alarmed that the performance seems to have already begun. At one performance, the celebrated South African choreographer Robyn Orlin entered the theater as a spectator and Nyamza rose for a quick embrace and air kiss, signaling that the boundaries between performer and audience are porous at this event, which is more like church than theater. Nyamza decisively shakes hands with a few spectators in the front row. Some patrons look positively stricken by the unexpected congregation in which they find themselves. Others join in with the spirit of the scene—swaying, singing, exclaiming, ululating, and clapping. For some, this opening scene taps deeply held somatic memories, accessing well-inhabited practices of worship in black churches. For others, this ritual is out of place and out of context at a Johannesburg dance festival.

For Mamela Nyamza, this scene evokes a weekly ritual from her childhood. As dance critic Adrienne Sichel writes: "Historically this context and setting has huge resonance for a Gugulethu dancer who as a little girl had her first classical ballet and contemporary training with Zama Dance's the late Arlene Westergaard and the late CAPAB Ballet star John Simons in a Moravian church in her neighbourhood. The pews were pushed aside for the classes."[66] But for Nyamza, church was more than a site for makeshift dance classes. As she narrates in an autobiographical video documentary, recollections of her childhood are filled with memories of attending church weekly with her grandmother. The charismatic singing, ecstatic worship, mesmerizing dancing, and continuous praise she summons at the start of *De-Apart-Hate* emulate how she spent Sundays during her childhood and, indeed, much of her adulthood.[67] But for those who know Mamela Nyamza, the turn to Christian ritual is not without ambivalence. Coming out as a queer woman, divorcing her husband, and claiming a new life as a performance artist do not find ready convergence with conservative church values. Nyamza has cast off so many of the constraints of her previous life that a scene of Christian worship is not an obvious beginning for her new performance work.

A second performer enters, Aphiwe Livi, dressed formally in a black suit and white shirt unbuttoned at the neck. Like Nyamza, he sways and undulates, seemingly possessed by the beat. He follows and surrenders to the rhythm as his arms loosely flow at his sides. He hinges at the waist and slightly crouches over, his knees bending momentarily. Livi then changes direction, rises up, straightens his body as his chest opens upward and outward, a single arm jutting up in the air. ONE-TWO (three). ONE-TWO (three). Eventually these two dancers converge downstage center, gracefully sliding past each other, possessed by the groove in simultaneity. A few audience members clap along as we hear bells ringing and leather pillows thumping. The music flows in cascading paroxysms, a seamless river of movement and song with occasional crescendos and punctuating gestures: a raised arm, a pointed index finger, worship without end.

Eventually Nyamza and Livi join arms and step together onto the stage.

They continue to move to the music while progressing upstage, their backs to the audience, working side by side in tight synchronicity. They move from left to right, right to left—his steps deftly placed in his shiny patent leather shoes, her steps gingerly touching the floor with her elegant five-inch silver pumps. The dancers' elbows pump in and out, wrists close at their sides. A deeper grind in the rhythm pulls them left, left, left, left, left, left—a step at a time, until they circle fully around. Inching in a semicircle, their right sides become exposed to the audience. While staying in place, they slowly crouch downward and then rise back up, their arms bent at the elbows with their forearms straight up in the air, like sprinters. Their arms keep pumping slowly up and down as their bodies gradually descend and ascend, as if they are moving into and out of a starting block in slow motion. Then they begin moving forward again, each holding a right arm out high in the air, swaying their hands as though showering blessings on a crowd. Each places a right hand on their right ear and twists sideways, obliquely opening their torsos toward the audience then quickly pulling downward and away.

The dancers' movements seem trance-like, internally motivated; their eyes are often closed, faces beaming and focused. Some movements draw the performers inward as the body coils in on itself, as if in prayer. Other times their bodies extend upward and outward as they exuberantly lift their arms, their joyful faces radiant with ecstasy. Even though they are moving in tight synchronization, Nyamza and Livi are not dancing *together*, per se. The music loops and loops. Fourteen minutes into this hour-long performance, the show is far more groove than action. Slow escalation of tension is Nyamza's métier. She is entirely comfortable with making audiences uncomfortable.

Finally, something changes. Nyamza moves upstage to the only piece of furniture on the stage: a wooden bench painted in bright rainbow colors. Instead of having the normal four legs, it is poised on a triangular base. Nyamza is the first to sit on this bench, carefully placing herself at the center while continuing to thump out the praise music rhythm, her hands slapping the seat. The bench sways and shakes; it's clearly not stable. The man gradually backs upstage, bent over in a worshipful undulation until he finally sits next to Nyamza, causing her to shift slightly to the right. Even as they continue to sing and sway while seated, they situate themselves carefully on the bench, attempting to reach equilibrium. The recording fades out. For a brief time, the two performers and some audience members continue to hum and clap until the sound fades to silence. This is the performance's first major transition.

Mamela Nyamza's performances often feature a few well-chosen quotidian objects, such as the trash can that appears in the opening scene of *I Stand Corrected*; the clothespins, clothesline, and washbasin she used in *Hatched*; and the ping-pong balls and refrigerator that feature in *Shift*. In *De-Apart-Hate*, the focal object is a bench, which for South Africans conjures histories of separate amenities for different races under apartheid: one bench for blacks and another for whites. But the single bench in *De-Apart-Hate* is decidedly postapartheid, painted with a flourish of cheery rainbow colors that evoke both gay pride and Mandela's "rainbow nation" of utopian interracial harmony. So what is this bench? Whether it signifies the "old" apartheid South Africa or the new inclusive South Africa, one thing is clear: as a bench, it does not work. It is precarious and unstable, constantly threatening to topple over, pivoting on a central balance point that causes it to teeter from side to side like a seesaw or to rock from front to back like a boat without a centerboard. In the course of the show, this bench transforms into a pew, a cage, a coffin, a blockade, and a burden. Its cheery colors suggest optimism, but functionally it seems poised to disappoint and possibly to cause harm. Its precarity causes discomfort, and that discomfort and the effort that must be exerted to stay on the bench consumes the next twenty-three minutes of this show, during which Nyamza and Livi wait and wait and wait, always in silence and sometimes in stillness, sometimes making small adjustments in posture and position, with the bench sometimes tipping one way, then the other, sometimes crowding one person and elevating another. She clasps her hands, he winces and screws his face up to the side. They both look forward and out, her eyes cast downward while he looks at a distant horizon. Their stillness is almost unbearable, but it is never dull. Focused and working in tight, coordinated precision, theirs is not a wait of ease or relaxation or lethargy, but rather one of active readiness, its exertions evident in the sweat streaming down their faces and dampening their clothing.

While much of this section, which I will call "phase two" of the performance, is defined by stasis, the scene is also abruptly transformed on occasion with explosions of activity. Prompted by a cue that is decisive for the two of them but undetectable to the audience, Nyamza and Livi periodically explode into a flurry of action with flawless synchronicity. Abruptly, Nyamza whirls around to the left while Livi spins past and over her to the right. This repeats over and over again, as though they are in some kind of amped-up version of musical chairs. Eventually their movements become fatigued and lethargic. This continuous reshuffle takes so much energy that eventually they are practically crawling over each other in exhaustion.

Fig. 5. Mamela Nyamza and Aphiwe Livi in *De-Apart-Hate*, performed at JOMBA! Contemporary Dance Experience, 2017. (Photo by Val Adamson.)

Once again the piece reaches stasis as the performers carefully resituate on the bench, adjusting their clothing, inching into an equilibrium far too active to be called stagnation. They are waiting. Nothing happens. The wait seems fatiguing, even exasperating, but no one is about to fall asleep. Gradually Nyamza and Livi focus directly ahead and they begin panning the room, watching. Are they watching the audience? No, it seems more like they are watching imaginary people who are walking and moving, enjoying mobility in a world where these two must wait in stillness. Do they look with envy? Resentment? Hostility? Rage? Their faces are inscrutable but their intensity is unmistakable. Then suddenly, as abruptly as before, they both pop up and down, their arms pumping furiously at their sides. Livi becomes exhausted before Nyamza does and flops down on the bench in repose. Meanwhile she keeps bouncing up and down, causing the whole bench to rock like a teeter-totter. She lands on the bench and Liv's end of the bench pops up, and when she bounces off, Livi and his end of the bench sink to the floor. The bench creaks. The audience laughs, the humor of this sound breaking an unbearable tension that has been building throughout, the tension of *De-Apart-Hate*'s fastidious contrast between unproductive stillness and futile exertion.

In an unexpected gesture, Livi takes out a handkerchief from his coat and offers it to Nyamza. She delicately dabs the sweat from her face, then hands him back the handkerchief as they both smile. So they like each other. Even if we don't know yet what their relationship is, they are cordial, respectful, helpful with each other. After a time of waiting, they each again begin to stand up, whirl in place and then sit down, again and again. So much effort, so little traction. Then they slide off the bench, turn around, go on their knees, and bow their heads on the bench, as if in prayer at a pew. While their heads are down, the bench continues to bob and wiggle like a dinghy in turbulent water. Then the two rise and sit side by side, hands clasped reverently in their laps. Their arms cross at the elbows in a pose of defiance. At one moment they each mark the sign of the cross from head to heart, right shoulder to left shoulder. Church and Christianity are never far from the scene. But one does feel a mounting subterranean rage.

This is challenging work to endure. As reviewer Sarah Roberson writes, "Nyamza's work isn't ever easy to watch. It's never easy to understand. She makes us uncomfortable, she draws out stillness and silence to an unbearable point, her provocative imagery oozes through the space and leaves us bare."[68] Robyn Sassen concurs: "It's a piece about imprisonment and boldness, rules and taboos that will insinuate itself in your thinking with a deliberately gradual flow of energies. It becomes difficult to watch because of the stasis presented, giving an ear to Dance Umbrella critics who reflect on some Dance Umbrella pieces as being conceptually and actually stripped of all movement."[69] Sassen underscores the genre-defying nature of Nyamza's choreography. This accomplished professional dancer has performed internationally and yet after returning to South Africa, she has consistently thwarted expectations of dance, often creating works that she calls "un-dance." Nyamza demands that her audiences sit with precarity and stasis or with change that is so slow it is nearly imperceptible. In her piece *Phuma-Langa* (2017), for instance, dancers are clad in Ndebele-inspired costumes that gradually break down and malfunction every time there is a mispronunciation of their names over the soundtrack. But this deconstruction happens so slowly that, as reviewer Masego Panyane comments, "If you are not careful you'll miss" it. Yet the subtle crafting of dissolution, in aggregate, ultimately creates what Panyane calls this dance's "silent scream."[70]

As the performers in *De-Apart-Hate* sit and squirm on their unstable seat, the audience grows restless. The patience of Nyamza's dramaturgy gradually forces the audience into a deeper stillness beyond fidgeting anxiety. And it is in this stillness of the work, its refusal to cater to expectation, that the full impact of its metaphor becomes clear. As the audience and the performers wait in tense expectation, *De-Apart-Hate* condenses and crystallizes South Africa's suspended revolution not as an idea but as an experience. The hope of transition was change—that one would move from here to there, from the bad days of apartheid to a new promised land. The experience of suspended revolution, however, is time-based, requiring endurance, with no felt expectation that the tension will resolve. Collapse is both a constant threat and a seemingly likely outcome. Tedium is the daily reality. As critic Nicola van Straten notes: "While we wait, I realize the potency of this image and metaphor that Nyamza has created, all the more potent in the midst of the current political climate and social context in South Africa. I envision throughout the country, South Africans sitting on something that could collapse at any moment—and waiting."[71] Perhaps the most enduring impact of the work—through its painstaking contrasts of precarity and equilibrium, movement and stasis—is a heightened and acute perception of the potential for immanent ruination embedded in the tedium of stagnation.

Humor alleviates the scene's mounting tension. While Livi is seated on one side of the bench, his weight bringing his end to the floor, Nyamza tries to climb up on the high end. When she arrives up top, she modestly juts her feet off, "ladylike," to the side. The audience laughs. The tension is also somewhat alleviated by our growing curiosity about the relationship between these two. Are they husband and wife? Brother and sister? Lovers? Do they support each other? Are they in competition? While they constantly work to achieve equilibrium, is this also equality? Equity? But the building tension takes a different turn when a gendered disequilibrium between them finally comes to the fore. At one point, they end up both crowded on one end of the bench, struggling to share the limited space, trying to get their feet up off the floor. Maybe they are hoping to go to sleep? The space for both of them has suddenly become far too confined. Their contest becomes more slapstick and the audience starts chuckling. And then abruptly, Livi throws Nyamza off the bench and onto the floor. Someone in the audience exclaimed: "Woah!"

We now enter phase three: Mamela Nyamza is off the bench, on the floor on her hands and knees, a position of obeisance, vulnerability, and sexual subservience. Livi carefully and precisely removes each of his patent leather shoes and each of Nyamza's high, silver pumps, placing all four shoes precisely on the floor upstage. And then, after brushing off his pants and his bare feet, he steps onto her back, balancing there in a position of triumph. Both begin speaking contrapuntally: "Ephesians 6, Verse 5!"

"Ephesians 6, Verse 5!" "Hallelujah!" "Amen!" The rolling incantation between them accelerates and becomes more and more ecstatic and fervent. "Deuteronomy 32, verse 8!" "Leviticus 18, verse 22!" Their recitation becomes ever more passionate and frenzied, even enraged, with the amens and hallelujahs cascading in quick succession. Livi stands and then kneels on Nyamza's back for three full, excruciating minutes. Finally, she collapses, recoiling into child's pose on the ground while he pushes down on her back, as if doing cardiopulmonary resuscitation as they both intone: "John 8, verse 7." Her "Amens!" morph into a kind of delaminated version of that word—"A. Men." "A. Men." "A. Men."—while Livi recites repeatedly, "Oh my god, oh my god." They face off. She helps him put his shoes back on and then her own. They now enter the fourth and final phase of the performance.

After kneeling on the floor with Livi on her back, Nyamza stands and resumes singing a capella the praise song from the start of the show, swirling her torso as before, as a recording of a few women's voices plays on overhead speakers. The rhythm beaten on the leather pillow resumes insistently: ONE-TWO (three). ONE-TWO (three). Livi brings Mamela a white neck ruff and cap reminiscent of a Rembrandt-era Dutch painting, costume accessories that are at once austere and luxurious, chic and evocative of Afrikaner heritage in the Netherlands. Livi and Nyamza scoot the bench downstage, then turn it in several revolutions while their shoes stomp out and amplify the hymn. They stand behind the bench, which now becomes a pew. We are once again in church. Nyamza and Livi resume their dancing, gyrating in synchronicity side by side. The harmonies and rhythms propelling them become more complex, escalating, and syncopated. Shouts come from the audience: "Holy Fire! Holy Fire! *Hallelujah*!" Their dancing transforms into a kind of shaking and then dynamically recoils into restrained, quiet foot tapping with humming. Nyamza exits the stage for the first time and Livi remains, humming and tapping, his knees wobbling as he shakes a Bible in the air. He tries to stand on the bench and center it, but the bench wildly tips right and then left underneath him. Holding his arms to the side for balance, Livi begins preaching in isiXhosa and English, shaking his Bible at the "congregation." He shouts about the spirit of the Almighty God, which provokes responses of "hallelujah" from the audience. Livi becomes so seized by the spirit that he lies down on the floor, all the while continuing to preach. Nyamza returns to the stage and methodically, deliberately, lifts the bench off its pivot base, stands it on its end, and drags it across the stage while pounding out that incessant beat—ONE-TWO (three). For a time, the bench functions as a kind of barricade between her and Livi. Then she slowly lowers the bench over him, forming both a cage and a coffin. The music subsides as the coffin descends and a few audience members clap, perhaps thrilled that she has seemingly vanquished him.

Nyamza then turns to the audience, inches her snug skirt up around her thighs, crouches down on the edge of the overturned bench, reaches up by her crotch and pulls on a dangling pink ribbon. Is this a tampon string? No. It is the page marker of a book—the Bible, it turns out. The pink edges of the Bible's page trim also peek out, suggesting, in this context, labia. Nyamza quickly, deftly spreads the Bible open across her crotch while simultaneously spreading her legs wide in a *grand plie*, her silver fishnet–encased thighs leading to pointed outstretched feet shod in high silver pumps, her feet decisively turned out in ballet's second position. Nyamza stares at the audience fiercely, intensely, her nostrils flaring. She licks her finger with libidinous pleasure and begins thumbing through the Bible's pages, citing over and over again "Leviticus 18:22"—the anti-homosexuality verse: "Do not have sexual relations with a man as one does with a woman; that is detestable." There are murmurs and outraged exclamations and laughter from the audience at this most audacious and provocative juxtaposition of Bible, crotch, and homophobia. Nyamza continues to lick her finger with her pink tongue and flip through the Bible's pages while staring down the audience, declaiming: "Leviticus 18 verse 22." She mouths the words silently, incessantly licking her finger and stroking the pages with masturbatory relish. Audience titters and giggles well up. She flips and flips the pages, ruefully looking at us, her face and arms glowing with sweat. "Doesn't end, eh?" she asks, and the audience bursts into laughter. Is she talking about the Bible? Homosexual hatred? Masturbation? This performance? Or South Africa's unresolved political state? Nyamza finally pages through to the end of the book and closes it, along with her legs. She shoves the book again between her tightly held thighs while lowering her dress. One is reminded of Achille Mbembe's characterization of the tumult of recent times: "Brashness, disruption and a new *anti-decorum* ethos are meant to bring down the pretence of normality and the logics of normalization in this most 'abnormal' society."[72] Nyamza's mash-up of Christian worship and public masturbation, her placement of the Bible at her crotch, her thumbing through the holy scriptures while reciting repeatedly a particular problematic passage all perform an anti-decorum that fully disrupts the logics of normalization. Her will and defiance are fully legible. She is not going along with the flow of the hypnotic rhythms of worship, with decorum and expectation imposed on women. She is literally fucking the

Fig. 6. Mamela Nyamza in *De-Apart-Hate,* 2016. (Photo by John Hogg.)

Bible. Willfulness here is a conversion point. Or, as Sara Ahmed describes it, "how a potential is converted into a threat."[73] What is her performed, embodied willfulness doing?

De-Apart-Hate physically and symbolically poses many questions: What things do we hold most closely, in our most intimate regions? What do we use the strength of our most powerful muscles to grip? Looking defiantly at her audience, Nyamza launches into a contemporary song, "*Asiphelelanga,*" the lyrics of which say: "We are not complete, no no we are not complete, no no we are not complete, no no we are not complete."[74] The lyrics ostensibly lament the loss of so many musical luminaries who have passed away: Hugh Masekela, Lucky Dube, Queen Brenda Fassie, Mother [Miriam] Makeba. "*Asiphelelanga,*" which has a three-part rhythm not dissimilar to the Christian hymn that started the show, became politically contentious in the waning days of Jacob Zuma's presidency, a time concurrent with the premiere of *De-Apart-Hate*. At an event near the time of *De-Apart-Hate* performances, protesters disrupted what was supposed to be a tribute to Zuma by singings alternate versions of this song, with lyrics expressing impatience with the unfinished state of things. The crowd sang: "*Asiphelelanga. Kushoda umnotho, awukho la. Hayi hayi asiphelelanga* [We are not complete, we still need the economy, it's not here. No. No. We are not complete]."[75] An alternate translation is, "We aren't satisfied, we need economic liberation."[76] Within the context of *De-Apart-Hate*, it is the repetition of incompleteness that is most salient, as Nyamza sits near that upturned rainbow bench—at once a symbol of racial segregation under apartheid and the rainbow of change promised by Mandela's dispensation. The "church" *De-Apart-Hate* has summoned suddenly becomes a political gathering or a sports rally with Nyamza as our agent provocateur in chief. As she had with the Christian hymn, she grinds her body but with a new relish as the Bible pokes out between her legs, creating a long phallic indentation in the front of her dress. She thrusts her arms out, slowly bending, sitting, and inching her way along the upturned bench—Livi's "coffin"—as she gets on all fours and undulates, then lies on her back, wiggling with her legs as they cross over each other, all the while mouthing the song's words and doing sexualized contortions that eventually reveal peek-a-boo glimpses of the pink trim of that Bible, still held tightly between her thighs. "We are not complete." Has there been a transformation? Has she thrown off the patriarchy? Has she climaxed or reached sexual liberation? Has she vanquished her oppressor?

The Bible drops on the floor and Nyamza picks it up, lifts the cage/coffin off Livi, and they both stand as the football anthem blares. She hunkers down behind the bench, which is still off its precarious base, upturned and resting on the floor like a broken piece of furniture left over from a raucous party. Nyamza lifts her right leg high in the air and bends her knee out, raising her shin and knee like a dog at a hydrant while still holding the Bible to her opened crotch. She climbs up over the back of the bench, coming toward the audience, then crouches down in front of it, doing splits, her crotch grinding on top of the Bible as she collapses forward into the floor. A deflated Livi sits behind her, in retreat, reading his Bible, thoroughly upstaged.

Critic Robyn Sassen began her review of *De-Apart-Hate* by saying, "Seldom do you find yourself turning to the Bible in an attempt to access what you have just seen in a dance festival context."[77] The Bible verses themselves are hardly spoken in the performance, so it is up to spectators to either summon their own knowledge of these cited verses or to read about them on pieces of paper that Nyamza plastered on the walls of the theater.[78] When one connects the Bible passages to the stage action, the potency of Nyamza's vision emerges. The verses read: "Slaves, obey your earthly masters with respect and fear, and with sincerity of heart, just as you would obey Christ." The Bible endorses slavery. "When the Most High gave the nations their inheritance, when he divided all mankind, he set up boundaries for the peoples according to the number of the sons of Israel." The Bible endorses segregation, aka. apartness, aka. apartheid. "Do not have sexual relations with a man as one does with a woman; that is detestable." The Bible endorses homophobia. The one cited Bible verse that strikes a more conciliatory tone is John chapter 8, verse 7: "When they kept on questioning him, he straightened up and said to them, 'Let any one of you who is without sin be the first to throw a stone at her.'" In a show that begins by throwing its audience in the deep end of ecstatic Christian worship, religion appears as something that is imbibed and tightly, joyously held in long-entrenched repertoires of the body. The show is not anti-Christian or necessarily about religion or even necessarily about race. *De-Apart-Hate* is about what is held tightly, ideologies that are imbibed, ingested, and internalized but that may have quite poisonous elements mixed with what is pleasurable, laudable, holy, or sublime. The show is about balance, precarity, and equilibrium, about what fails to hold up, what inevitably holds and pushes down.

The work delaminates the now, separating component parts from each other, exposing the unbearable and intolerable circumstances that are borne with enthusiastic amens. "Apartheid" deconstructs into separate syllables: *De-Apart-Hate*. "De" is to undo. "Apart" is distanced from the word "hate," a delamination of "apartheid." The word "amen" likewise breaks apart: "A. Men." The performance enacts an unraveling, an undoing, a process of delamination that exposes composite elements. Apartheid was falsely represented by the former government as "good neighborliness." Here, in Nyamza's work, she reveals it to be the fusion of apart + hate.

De-Apart-Hate is not postapartheid art or post-anti-apartheid art. This performance symbolically intervenes in South Africa's protracted interval, its exhausting stasis and intensely non-productive movements. Yet Nyamza's aim is closer to decolonization, the undoing of the power structures that have created a whole range of oppressions and hatreds, including racism, sexism, and homophobia.[79] But even decolonization is not sufficient for Nyamza. On the entry about *De-Apart-Hate* on her website, Nyamza says, "We need a discourse that goes beyond 'decolonization,' a discourse that moves towards humanity, *ubuntu*, without being blinded by race and class, a discourse that I call a DE-APARTHEID PROCESS."[80] She continues, "The DE-APART-HATE process is a discourse that starts with the struggles of South Africa as a nation without dwelling on narrow particularities of race and ideology." The performance represents, instantiates, and promulgates a *process,* one that delaminates component parts of a word (from "apartheid" to "Apart-Hate") and mobilizes the power of the prefix "de"—meaning "down," "away," "removal," or "reversal." "De-apart-hate" as a process comes to fruition in the final segment of this performance, in the unexpected appearance of the pink edge painting on the pages and marking ribbon of a Bible in the most unlikely of places.

If we think back to Errol Philander in chapter 1 and the process of his unbecoming as a racialized subject arrested for engaging in an act of interracial "immorality," recall the centrality of will to his last moments:

> I will eat.
> I will drink.
> I will sleep.
> I won't love.[81]

We see in Nyamza's *De-Apart-Hate* a reverse transformation. In the aftermath of apartheid, in its turbulent wake, Nyamza articulates and performs on stage the potential and potency of the will. She chooses to interrupt habitual motions, her grinding possession in worshipful dance without end, in order to seize hold of that useless rainbow bench, to turn it over, to transform it into a cage to contain what oppresses her, and to change it yet again as platform and climbing structure on which to enact her defiant, libidinous self-discovery. She does this with such ferocity and intensity that the world around her is disrupted and transformed, even it if is not entirely deconstructed and disposed. Nyamza defiantly and literally fucks a Bible, yet she still goes on to sing worshipful Christian praises by the performance's end. The old is transformed but not gone: the bench, Bible, and Livi are still there. But the bench has been overturned and displaced, the symbolic rainbow has been dismantled from its unstable base and brought down low like a piece of architectural detritus, and Livi's prominence has been thoroughly upstaged by Nyamza's lusty explorations. She seizes her will and desire, and wields these powerful forces to overturn her world. Things long held close (a Bible) now produce, at least for Nyamza, different kinds of pleasures and different kinds of revelations. While Hershini Bhana Young has written poignantly about the illegibility of black women's will in the archives of southern Africa—in the records documenting Sara Baartman or the eighteenth-century slave Tryntjie of Madagascar—Mamela Nyamza's will is clearly and vividly legible by the end of this performance.[82] Nyamza wields the toxic remains of colonialism and apartheid but does not succumb to their corrosiveness. Her will has utterly changed everything. The past remains present, but clearly nothing remains what it once had been.

SELLO PESA: STRUGGLE WITHOUT END

Sello Pesa has been at the forefront of pushing the bounds of site-specific and site-responsive performances and installation works that happen in nontraditional venues. These strategies often making his performances more accessible to a greater range of audiences. Although Pesa initially trained as dancer, over time he has cultivated a distinctive style and approach to performance, often pushing at the boundaries of the genre of concert dance to take performance into unexpected places. Early in his career he was a member of the Soweto Dance Theatre, where he began teaching in 1997. He finally started doing his own choreography in 1999. In 2006 he founded the Ntsoana Contemporary Dance Theatre, a collective that often performs in unusual spaces, such as the decommissioned Johannesburg Stock Exchange, the Hector Peterson Museum, the streets of downtown Johannesburg in the gentrifying neighborhoods of Maboneng and Newtown, in people's homes, or in a narrow trading passage in Alexandra township where you can buy "everything from chicken to fruit to cellphone airtime."[83] Thematically, Ntsoana's preoccupations have included death as a big business that preys on the poor in South Africa (*Lime Light on Rites* 2010), the forces of gentrification (*Inhabitant* 2011), the fallacies of "discovery" in colonial scenarios (*Naka tša go rwešwa* 2010), and the dynamics that drive xenophobia (*AfriKa* 2015). In this chapter I want to focus on the piece *Bag Beatings*, which holds within its frame an implosion of the contradictory forces of concatenating movement and stasis while also bringing into focus impulsive, habituated reflexes, struggles that have become unmoored from a sense of larger purpose and objective. *Bag Beatings* depicts violence as the show's core action and sole subject. This is violence as pure physical act, unmoored from cause, motivation, explanation, or apparent underlying social structure; violence without a sentient victim; violence as a perpetrator's act of athleticism, endurance, and strength; spectacular violence as an active choice that depends on the willingness of spectators to wait and watch.

Premiering in 2017 during the first season of William Kentridge's new venue, the Centre for the Less Good Idea, *Bag Beatings* was subsequently performed at the 2018 Johannesburg Dance Umbrella in a much extended and transformed version that will be my focus here.[84] Performed in the Wits Downstairs Theatre at the University of Witwatersrand, the show arranged this intimate black box theater by positioning the bulk of the audience on risers on one side of the flat staging area. A second section of seating consisted of chairs placed directly opposite the risers with their backs along the theater's back wall. This created a kind of tennis-style theater with the two banks of spectators able to see each other, as they would in a boxing ring.

Bag Beatings disrupts and violates boundaries at every turn. Through watching the tenacious beating, kicking, burning, tasing, and whipping of a boxing bag, we get up close and personal with the extreme physical exertion, strength, and endurance required to thrash a sack that approximates the size and density of a human being in its mass and weight. Most alarming is the way the performance casts its audience as potential victims: shrapnel that broke off from a whip when cracked on the floor lands on a spectator at one point, boiling water splashes within inches of others, and the swinging mass of a boxing bag being steadily beaten moves locations throughout the show, unsettling spatial dynamics and sometimes forcing audience members to leap out of their seats and flee to the side of the stage. The seats closest to the playing area were not for the faint of heart.

The tone of the piece swings as wildly as does that bag. Sello Pesa, Humphrey Maleka, and Brian Mtembu's violent evisceration of a boxing glove with the help of outsized tools provokes laughter at the start of the show, as does our growing sense that the performers' extreme efforts seem rather futile and at times even comically ineffectual. A refreshment station on the side of the playing area laden with bread and tea suggests a certain banal quality to the beatings we are witnessing, conveying implicitly that this happens all the time. South Africa is, after all, a country where apartheid-era state torturers notoriously held a barbecue at a site where the dead body of one of their victims was being incinerated.[85] This is a country that has one of the world's highest rates of murder and rape.[86] This is a country known for atrocities such as "corrective rape" of lesbians and xenophobic vigilante murders of immigrants from elsewhere in Africa.[87]

Bag Beatings highlights violence as a routine, commercialized transaction. The show begins with Sello Pesa approaching audience members while silently holding a rack of T-shirts for sale, like a streetside hawker at a traffic intersection or a merchandise vendor at a sporting event. When the seemingly all-male black cast begins beating the bag in earnest, a woman in the audience shrieks with derisive laughter. Eventually she comes into the performance space, wanders over to the amenity table, and pours herself

Fig. 7. Choreographer Sello Pesa tests movement and noise on the boxing bag with dancers and collaborators Humphrey Maleka and Brian Mtembu in *Bag Beatings*, 2016. (Photo by Stella Olivier, courtesy of the Centre for the Less Good Idea.)

some tea. Later the woman (performer Hlengiwe Lushaba Madlala) pours boiling water on the boxing bag and melts it with a hot steam iron. Objects of ordinary domesticity—a kettle, an iron, a belt—become instruments that threaten to both destroy the bag and harm the audience. The performance conveys these actions as quotidian events. We do not know why the performers are beating the bag, but we do know that they do so fiercely and intensely. Through sweat, kinesthetic energy, full-on blows, and the threat of a swinging bag that is tased with a taser, melted by an iron, and flayed by belts, whips, baseball bats, and fists, the performers' fierce commitment to destruction of the bag is ferocious.

This performance represents bag beatings as an extreme embodied experience for the perpetrator. By not featuring a sentient victim, *Bag Beatings* contrasts with a host of theatrical representations of violence that have been seen on South African stages in the several decades since the arrival of democracy; Mpumelo Paul Grootboom's plays are perhaps the most extreme examples.[88] Unlike Grootboom's plays such as *Cards* (2001) and *Relativity: Township Stories* (2005), Pesa's *Bag Beatings* stages violence without a link to a crime or personal violation, for it does not show or refer to the stuff of Grootboom's plays: rapes, serial killers, police brutality, dead bodies, or predators sniffing the panties of a dead woman's corpse.[89] In *Bag Beatings,* the "victim" is literally a thing: a bag. And not just any bag, but one specifically designed to be hit: a boxing bag.

Instead of performing violence as raw carnality and risking a capitulation to colonial fantasies of black lawlessness, *Bag Beatings* disrupts the colonial gaze by removing any sentient victim from the scenario and by staging violence as a protracted spectacle that a mixed-race audience witnesses in a state of passive waiting that is itself a choice. One can choose to leave the spectacle at any time, and some did leave the performance I attended. At one point about fifty minutes into the show, ushers entered the house and told the audience that they should go, that the show was over. Yet the performers continued to beat, whip, kick, punch, and burn that bag. It seemed that their opponent had not yet been vanquished. Did the ushers' announcement truly signal the end of the show or was this a plant by the show's creators, a fake ending that threw an even brighter spotlight on our own appetites, proclivities, agency and—dare one say—responsibility? Violence here becomes a ritual with a perverse structure that forces the audience to confront a most uncomfortable question: what are we waiting for? For the death of the bag? For the violence to spill across the boundaries of the stage and into our laps? No onlooker, bystander, spectator, or witness is free from the implications of the fact that witnessing and waiting for an end are choices, crucial aspects of violence as spectacle.

Group dynamics gradually emerge among the performers who are conjoined in a communal commitment to delivering this beating. Their camaraderie becomes evident as one of them holds the bag while another punches it, in their wordless coordination and pacing, and in the unnerving laughter and cackles of Hlengiwe Madlala, who is often sporting sunglasses, as if the violent scene before us is sport, joke, and source of sadistic pleasure. The performers' camaraderie is matched by group dynamics among spectators who are witnesses. Some left the theater within ten minutes, others had walked out by twenty minutes, and several others had to repeatedly leave their chairs and flee to the side of the stage, out of harm's way. Those of us who were still present at the end of the performance were united in a decision to stay, even as it became clear that we could not take refuge in anonymity behind the theater's fourth wall. *Bag Beatings* foregrounds time by refusing to end. The gamelike atmosphere of a boxing ring enlists and puts a spotlight on the audience's investment in their desire for an endgame. The show's structure, if we can call it that, offers no clear developmental arc or certainty of a terminus or point of closure. The work challenges the passivity of spectators and illuminates our complicity. Does the beating continue *because* we are staying? From start to finish, we cannot be confident in our safety or in our innocence.

The audience is repeatedly reminded that violence is only an arm's length away, sometimes even closer than that. Toying with audience uncertainty about the real and the staged around questions of violence is hardly new in South Africa. In 2007, Afrikaner performance artist Peter Van Heerden began his Dance Umbrella performance of *6 Minutes* by disrupting the preshow hubbub in the lobby with what was eventually discovered to be a staged attempted sexual assault of a white woman by a bearded white man. The rape scene in the lobby was followed by Van Heerden's performance in the theater, which dramatized even more graphic images of brutality: raping a plastic infant doll, chopping raw meat, and a kind of ritualistic hanging and beating of Van Heerden himself. Whereas Van Heerden seems to relish the taboo and explicit renderings of people and objects in an abject state, Pesa takes a different path in *Bag Beatings* by refusing any explicit representation of human violence against another living being—whether human, animal, or even plant. The result is a laser focus on violence as physical exertion and as a communal endeavor predicated on agreements that sustain it. The power of Pesa's approach is that he reveals the power of violence as both a lure and a threat. This is a very different "rediscovery of the ordinary" than what Njabulo Ndebele had in mind.[90] Instead of staging a monstrous spectacle (the stuff of anti-apartheid theater), Pesa stages an insidious, menacing spectacle that is at once highly unnerving and entirely banal.

Critic Robyn Sassen asks of *Bag Beatings*: "Is the work cathartic? In a sense, but with the house lights glaringly on, you in the audience feel completely exposed. There's water and electricity on stage and it feels like you are at the scene of the crime."[91] Pesa does not provide revelation of character or motive or explanation or words. He does not insert in the performance anything directly linked to contemporary or historical South African realities other than the ubiquity of violence and the pervasiveness of the constant threat of violence. Boxing has a particular historical resonance in South Africa: Nelson Mandela was a boxer as a young man, an experience that provided a literalized and contained notion of "struggle" and sportsmanship that ghosted the many other political battles he fought throughout his life.[92] But *Bag Beatings* feels like it is far away from South Africa's past political heroics. Through its refusals, its simplicity, and the way it toys with time as something the audience *gives*, *Bag Beatings* deftly makes manifest dynamics that are ubiquitous in contemporary South Africa yet are still somehow not fully seen—its realities of "corrective" rape, attacks on migrants, and all-too-frequent murders.[93]

Unlike some of Pesa's other works such as *No Man's Land* (2015), *Inhabitant* (2011), and *In House Project* (2010), *Bag Beatings* happens in a conventional performance venue, it sells tickets and distributes programs, and it has an agreed-upon starting time (although the end of the was not entirely clear). Several of his other works have been staged in outdoor venues—such as the streets of downtown Johannesburg, where the performers blend in with "normal" people going about their everyday lives: pedestrians holding umbrellas or young men pushing shopping carts filled with plastic for recycling. In Pesa's work *Inhabitant,* the performers pass as ordinary commuters, vendors, and pedestrians for the whole first part of the work. But eventually the performers rupture normal as they roll their bodies through busy street traffic. They did this first in Maboneng, a rapidly gentrifying arts district in Johannesburg, and later in a performance on the streets of Newtown, the historic heart of the city and the arts district where the Market Theatre is located.[94] Performers Sello Pesa and Vaughn Sadie took on an unnerving level of risk as they rolled, their bodies horizontal, across Main Reef Road in Johannesburg during rush hour. As unusual as it is to see a person tumble his body across a busy street, what was also notable to pedestrians and passing drivers was the rather strange, out-of-place installation of spectators sitting on the sidewalk in plastic chairs. *Inhabitant* inserted an audience among the to and fro of daily street traffic in Johannesburg's urban center. They were as notable a disruption of "normal" as a person rolling like a tumbleweed through an intersection was. Pesa and Sadie do not interact with these seated spectators; they work to blend in with the street scene among the regular inhabitants of this urban environment. Fiona Siegenthaler argues that *Inhabitant* "oscillated between the common and the unusual, movement and stagnation, disintegration and aggression, protection and risk."[95] While Pesa and Sadie pass for ordinary pedestrians at first, gradually they crack open the ordinary by doing exceptional things. These ruptures demarcate the zone of "performance" as being both the out-of-place spectators sitting on white plastic chairs by the roadside and the actors hurling their bodies across the street. Here performance is not a framed, separate staged event but rather something that little by little wells up through the ordinary, blurring boundaries, disordering the real, and forcing a new perception of that real.

Pesa's aesthetic contrasts starkly with the message-driven didacticism of earlier anti-apartheid theater. *Inhabitant* only gradually reveals itself to be a performance at all and it doesn't announce its meaning. Pesa *shows* rather than tells. As Kim Gurney notes, his work requires participants to "connect the dots."[96] His work promotes neither a specific politics nor a message; instead, it incites a heightened perception of the ordinary by revealing everyday dynamics that are pervasive yet somehow too ubiquitous and habitual to have otherwise drawn focus. Sello Pesa's approach can be thought of as a kind of delamination of the real: performances peel apart component parts that had been previously fused together in way that appeared "real." We might think that hard wood floor is solid, that it's one thing, but when saturated with water, the fused layers beging to peel away from each other. What formerly appeared solid is exposed as a composite of multiple elements, some of which are toxic. This operation disrupts and disorders perceptions of the ordinary—whether it's the ordinary of an urban street scene or the ordinary of a bounded event at the country's premier dance festival that gradually loses coherence, refuses narrative progression, and thwarts the audience's demand for an accessible meaning and a clear ending. The iconic phrase *a luta continua* a rallying cry of the anti-apartheid struggle, takes on a whole new meaning with an interminable bag beatings. For Pesa, performance is not a "weapon in the struggle," but rather a carefully calibrated instrument of revelation and deconstruction, one that exposes the deeper, enduring dynamics of *struggle* itself—regardless of whatever any particular struggle's objective, purpose, or name might be. Struggle continues (*a luta continua*) long after we remember what the struggle was about. Struggle is muscle memory. Struggle as agon. Struggle as habitual violence. Struggle as a perplexing and pointless commitment to destroying a hulking bag.

When I left the Wits Downstairs Theatre venue after *Bag Beatings*, it was late, close to 10 p.m., as I recall. The lobby was empty; only a few theater patrons remained with the refreshment stand workers who were closing up shop for the night. I tried to summon a car via Uber but my phone was nearly dead and strangely, no cars seemed to be available to pick me up at the Braamfontein venue in central Johannesburg. Such problems with Uber had also occurred when I was at the Dance Factory in nearby Newtown. That night after the performance at the Dance Factory, neither I nor any of my fellow patrons leaving the theater could seem to secure Uber drivers. Rumor had it that taxi wars between the metered taxis and Uber were the cause. Uber drivers were reluctant to cross certain street boundaries downtown and risk the ire and potential violence of their metered taxi colleagues. There had been recent attacks and some Uber cars had been set alight. I could have summoned a metered taxi and waited for it on the empty sidewalk outside the Wits Theatre. I am a single woman conspicuous not only for my whiteness but also for my disability: I am a leg amputee who often walks with crutches. My own precarity leaving the theater and my uncertainty about my path of travel home seemed to be a continuation of *Bag Beatings*. What this moment of my real life shared with the previous hour of theatrical life was this unnerving combination of the completely ordinary—trying to get home—and an acute sense of precarity, vulnerability, and apprehension about violence. Something so simple as a commute can be anything but simple. As I scanned the uninhabited sidewalk outside the theater, I felt I was a proxy—like a spectator waiting for that bag to abruptly swing my way. I also felt like a proxy for those spectators on plastic white chairs in Sello Pesa's *Inhabitant* who had pitched up, uncharacteristic and out of place, on a sidewalk in an ordinary urban scene, waiting to see a performance, their very strangeness and non-ordinariness broadcasting that they were *not* inhabitants of that place. They did not belong and neither did I. And yet, there I was, waiting for my own transition from "here" to "there" while the means of my locomotion remained elusive.[97]

CONCLUSION

Apartheid's remains are neither dormant nor inert; they are active elements of contemporary life that insert what is unresolved into the present with insistent disruptions, temporal drags, and pathological recurrences. In apartheid's wake, time is out of joint. The performance works by Jay Pather, Mamela Nyamza, and Sello Pesa analyzed in this chapter manipulate time by stretching, looping, isolating, bifurcating, and accelerating it in extraordinarily interesting ways. Scenarios of conflict endlessly repeat—until they finally give way. These performances create a fastidious contrast between unproductive stillness and futile exertion. Resisting narrative closure or a utopian notion of arrival, or false hopes of a "cure" for apartheid's remaining ailments in the present day, these artists dig down into the present, exposing the repressed, isolating the pervasively normalized, disidentifying with cultural elements that paradoxically and problematically may be both beloved and disempowering. They excavate through a kind of forensic autopsy on the psychic and physical afterlives of injustice embedded in the habits of today.

Caught in the interminable interval, stuck between an intractable present and an irrecoverable past, between "things that are no longer and things that are not yet,"[98] Pather, Nyamza, and Pesa deploy strategies that begin to suggest a way forward without simplistically claiming any singular way. Pather upends a discourse of scientific positivism and forensic criminal inquiry, and instead presents to his audience visions that defy comprehension but offer arresting strangeness. These images burrow deep into the psyche and seed for us alternative dreamscapes. Nyamza tangles with the afterlives of injustice by patiently lying in wait and then capturing, taming, and redirecting energies along provocative trajectories. She exposes what is held tightly, ideologies that are imbibed, ingested, and internalized that may have poisonous elements mixed in with what is pleasurable, laudable, holy, and sublime. Pesa stages the spectacle of violence as a habit, a game, an irresitable encounter that we instinctively watch. But Pesa as well as Nyamza delaminate the component parts of the ordinary—revealing, in Nyamza's case, the homophobia and racism embedded in Christian practices; or in Pesa's *Inhabitatnt* how racialized exclusions are shot through the substructure of a busy downtown intersection and the city's aspirations for urban renewal. These performances open up spaces where something new might emerge: perhaps something at once blasphemous and libidinous, or something that interrupts our instinctive commitment to playing out old scenarios to their end, even if no end exists.

The power of these performances resides in the artists' capacity to forge new, emergent aesthetics capable of wielding apartheid's toxic remains without succumbing to their corrosiveness. They take up the challenges articulated so effectively by African American writer Toni Morrison: "How to be both free and situated; how to convert a racist house into a race-specific yet non racist home? How to enunciate race while depriving it of its lethal cling?"[99] As with the U.S. queer performers of color José Esteban Muñoz analyzed in his influential work *Disidentifications*, the contemporary South African performing artists of color analyzed here are dreaming, striving, and agitating for disorders of the real. They are wedging open spaces in the country's stalled and even false transition. In these spaces, they project new and necessary visions that are simultaneously fictional and not; embodied expressions that can be utterly seen and kinesthetically felt, even if not always understood.[100]

In her book *Performing Remains*, Rebecca Schneider theorizes about the cross-temporal slippages of performance—the ways time (re)turns, repeats, recurs, and becomes tangled in and through performance.[101] The South African artists featured in this chapter also question and disrupt linear time. If, as Rosemarie K. Banks claims, "What has happened in a place is always happening," then what has happened in South Africa's apartheid past is still happening today.[102] These conditions demand that contemporary artists possess in their work a fierceness not unlike that wielded by artists under apartheid, who understood art as a weapon in the struggle against apartheid. Yet contemporary artists differ from their anti-apartheid predecessors by generally eschewing past techniques and aesthetics such as Manichean oppositions or an overt protest ethos based in certainty, moral earnestness, the dominance of race as a theme, the ossification of complex social problems into symbols, and a clear call to a particular political action. The contemporary performance works analyzed here can be characterized rather by the artists' restless tenacity and ability to open vistas of captivity and vistas of non-captivity.[103] They rediscover the ordinary as being itself a kind of spectacle, one that is no longer monstrous but continues today as a perverse and warped quotidian reality that has become so naturalized that people's aptitude for doing things differently has yet to be perceived, much less attempted.

THREE | Sharing the Stage, Breaking the Theater: Robyn Orlin, Jay Pather, and Brett Bailey

(*To technicians*) Cut! (*To performers*) We are the ambassadors for our country! We have got to show we can work together, right? We are from the *rainbow nation*! Alright? We are trying to work on the African Renaissance here! (*Shouting to technical crew*] Stand by for group dancing!

—Robyn Orlin, *Daddy, I've seen this piece six times before and I still don't know why they're hurting each other*

The sons of the nation were now in charge, after all. How completely the new thing took after the old.

—Ayi Kwei Armah

Standing on a raised platform, a white woman wearing a wig and a proper A-line dress speaks rhapsodically to the audience. She hyperventilates with excitement as she brags about her windup ducks, which are, for her, a precious troupe of highly trained performers. She removes them one by one from her handbag, places each on the floor, and calls them affectionately by name. Nearby, a black woman bends over, methodically placing red plastic plates in neat rows. As the ducks and plates jostle for space center stage, the white woman announces with self-congratulation that she's learned how to *negotiate* in the new South Africa. She then hisses with imperious irritation: So can they *please* just share the stage? This scene from Robyn Orlin's 1999 *Daddy, I've seen this piece six times before and I still don't know why they're hurting each other* is paradigmatic of the postapartheid era. It frames what have turned out to be critical questions: Can the stage be shared? Can South Africa's many cultures and its legacies of racialized injustice be "negotiated" on contemporary stages—and if so, how? Can the breathtaking heterogeneity of South Africa's cultures—its rich inheritance of movement practices, aesthetics, languages, and people—occupy the same space, literally and metaphorically, in the postapartheid political order? When the stage is occupied by those whom apartheid had previously divided, how do artists manage issues of respect, cultural appropriation, and unequal power relationships?

In addressing these questions, this chapter takes a comparative look at three pathbreaking South African performance artists who have very similar performance aesthetics: Robyn Orlin, Jay Pather, and Brett Bailey. Ever since the first democratic elections in 1994, these artists have been pushing boundaries, violating norms, and disrupting audience expectations while also inventing and defining new territories of postapartheid performance. Their works are notable for a profusion of images, abrupt shifts in tone, an aesthetic of excess, a collision of highbrow and lowbrow, arresting images of beauty cut through with irony, the handcrafted contrasted with the commercial, organic matter juxtaposed with the mass produced. All consistently refuse coherence and linearity. The formal experiments of Orlin, Pather, and Bailey have been matched by their bold engagement with topical South African content, specifically questions about the potential and perils of bringing together disparate cultures in South Africa's new dispensation. Since the early 1990s, Orlin, Pather, and Baily have regularly created intercultural performances, sometimes quite controversially. They have each also used self-reflexive techniques to simultaneously acknowledge potential criticisms around questions of cultural ownership and appropriation and redirect such questions through aesthetic layers dense enough to hold ambiguity. Their innovations have sometimes been so bold, so unexpected, that some spectators have stormed out of the theater while other spectators have scratched their heads in befuddlement. Bailey has provoked the most intense reactions, especially in Europe; teeming crowds of protesters in Berlin in 2012, in London in 2014, and in Paris in 2016, along with twenty-three thousand online petitioners, called for the closure of the European showings of his *Exhibit B*, a live art installation piece about the history of human zoos.[1]

Orlin, Pather, and Bailey share an aesthetic of hypertheatricality, which Keith Bain identifies as being "more theatrical than theatrical." In other words, hypertheatricality is a type of performance "that surpasses the framework of any theatrical forebear."[2] Manic collisions, unexpected venues, acts of breaking the fourth wall, insertion of metacommentary, and juxtaposition of incongruent elements are just some of the expressions of their hypertheatricality. Critic Matthew Krouse writes of Robyn Orlin that "her work satirizes the collision of worlds, as though Hannah Montana has finally met Hannah Arendt on the internet for a hot date at a lesbian sex club."[3] For Jay Pather, intercultural collisions are occasions for nuanced inquiry rather than satire. His multisited work *CityScapes*, which he has performed in public spaces throughout Durban and Johannesburg, brought widely disparate spheres and otherwise segregated populations into dynamic encounter. Critic Adrienne Sichel said of the 2003 Johannesburg version of *CityScapes*, "Whether at the Oriental Plaza on a bustling Saturday morning, the Carlton Centre escalators that afternoon, a Sandton piazza, or a steamy hotel room in Braamfontein the following day, people of all ages have been stopped in their tracks . . . by encounters of the conceptual kind."[4] Of Brett Bailey's early work *Ipi Zombi?* (1998), which is based on an actual incident where boys were killed in a rural bus accident and local women were accused of killing them through witchcraft, Daniel Larlham says that the play's "ritual elements and showbiz razzmatazz leap out in striking juxtaposition: a divination rite precedes a lip-synch version of Doris Day's 'Shaking the Blues Away,' complete with zombie back-up dancers, leaving the spectator jolted by the aesthetic and atmospheric switch."[5]

Because racialized legacies of apartheid's injustices remain very much alive, sharing the stage in contemporary South Africa is fraught with entanglements. While the revolution in South Africa was thwarted by a negotiated settlement in the early 1990s, the disingenuous way that some—such as the white woman in Orlin's *Daddy*—have "learned to negotiate" in the new South Africa provokes nagging questions. Is the current stage being shared? Will it be shared? Can or should it be shared? Perhaps the stage should rather be repossessed, decommissioned, destroyed, torn up, or broken to pieces. It certainly needs to be decolonized, but no one seems to know quite what that means.[6] The works of Orlin, Pather, and Bailey examined here broke open the performing arts in South Africa in pivotal ways after the end of apartheid. Their performances have exposed the knotty entanglements underneath things and revealed cultural fibers irrevocably bent and kinked from all that has happened in the past and all that remains to be addressed.

This chapter begins with a comparative analysis of all three artists, illuminating their aesthetics and establishing their respective artistic trajectories. I then discuss each artist separately, asking: what aesthetic strategies does each use to engage the afterlives of injustice, for what reasons, and to what ends?

MIXING GENRES, BREAKING FORM: INTRODUCING ORLIN, PATHER, AND BAILEY

The performances of Robyn Orlin, Jay Pather, and Brett Bailey are located at the confluence of multiple genres—dance, live art, installation, dance theater, performance art, and theater. They cannot be contained in any one of these categories. Indeed, their uncategorizable nature is evidence of the ways these artists have broken open performance, broadly conceived. These works explode as many aesthetic conventions as they deploy. All three artists share a penchant for vivid stage pictures; stylistic collage; nonlinear structure; the use of media, popular culture, and kitsch; politicized representations of race and cultural difference; and liberal doses of satire, camp, and irony. They all work in highly visual and body-centered ways; they subordinate the spoken word to the prominence of bodies, movement, and images. These artists consistently treat inherited traditions of Western theater and dance and their related pedigrees of training with iconoclastic irreverence. Ballet has been the focus of Orlin's fierce theatrical deconstructions and skewerings, especially the hegemonic and white supremacist legacies of ballet as practiced in South Africa. Pather and Bailey have often rejected conventional performance venues, preferring to mount works in spaces such as the Cape Town City Hall or in decommissioned power stations, stock exchanges, medical schools, or quarries, or in South Africa's present-day Constitutional Court, which itself is a repurposed apartheid-era prison, and in more quotidian sites such as railway stations, oceanside promenades, and the country's ubiquitous shopping malls. So sharing the stage, in the context of Pather's and Bailey's work, has sometimes meant expanding what we consider the stage to be.

Brett Bailey and Robyn Orlin are white and born of privilege; Jay Pather is Indian and comes from a family of modest means. Brett Bailey was born in 1967 in a white suburb of Cape Town, the third generation of an English family in South Africa. He attended an elite all-boys secondary school and attained a bachelor's degree in drama at the University of Cape Town in 1991.[7] Robyn Orlin, who was born in Johannesburg in 1955, is the descendent of Jewish refugees who came to South Africa fleeing Nazism, as is true for so many South African Jews. Her family lived in a genteel white suburb and ran a famous textile shop in Johannesburg known as Kays and Swanks. Orlin's mother taught dance classes in a large room attached to their family house, and when Orlin had the opportunity to study at the London School of Contemporary Dance at the age of twenty.[8] So she grew up very much immersed in the classical dance establishment of Johannesburg, a world Jewish girls participated in by hiding their cultural difference. As Matthew Krouse says, their Jewishness "hid behind straightened hair, dyed blonde, and they would sometimes even use Christian-sounding *noms de plume* and had to keep their weight to a minimum in order to effectively 'perform European.'"[9]

Pather was born in 1959 to a working-class Indian Hindu family in the city of Durban in KwaZulu-Natal. Like Orlin, he was socialized to conform to white supremacist expectations. As an undergraduate student at the Indian-only University of Durban-Westville in the late 1970s and early 1980s, Pather had to undergo instruction, as was expected of all students of color in the field of drama, to remove "deviant accents" from his speech, including erasing all traces of his South Asian speech and his South African speech patterns so that his diction would conform to an elite Anglophone ideal. While Pather loved dance, apartheid treated ballet as a white-only endeavor, so that particular pathway to dance training was technically closed to him, save for sporadic instruction from a few white teachers who would have him. It was not until he had a chance to go to New York in the 1980s that Pather came to fully understand, appreciate, and take possession of the artistic métier that would be his calling. Pather's multiple exposures—to the internationalism, cosmopolitanism, and artistic avant-garde of New York, to postmodern performance theory at New York University, and to the open and thriving gay culture of Greenwich Village—opened up for him an expansive world far beyond the repressions and censorship of apartheid.

While each of these artists experienced apartheid's racial divisions differently, all three came of age and came to voice as artists during the turbulent years of the 1980s, a time when the apartheid state declared numerous states of emergency, a time when performance makers who went to rehearsals and performances that crossed racial lines often did so at great personal risk. Orlin, Pather, and Bailey also received formative postgraduate education outside South Africa: Orlin attended the Art Institute of Chicago on a Fulbright Scholarship in the 1990s; Pather attained a master's degree in performance studies at New York University in 1984, also on a Fulbright Scholarship; and Brett Bailey earned his postgraduate degrees in performance studies in 2004 at Amsterdam's DAS Theatre, Academy of Theatre and Dance. This exposure to advanced education abroad certainly informed their subsequent artistic trajectories.

Bailey and Orlin are both controversial and polarizing figures, but Pather is not. The *New York Times* notes Orlin's "long history of annoying people," and South Africa's *Mail & Guardian* describes Orlin as both "adored and reviled."[10] The UK *Guardian* says that "Robyn Orlin was a thorn in the side of South Africa's apartheid rulers. The new government isn't too keen on her either."[11] Bailey is similarly referred to as the "bad boy" of contemporary South African theater, a whiz kid, an "edgy" director who engages in "representational recklessness and appropriation."[12] Pather is quite different from the other two in this regard: audiences are more often perplexed than offended by his performances. A reviewer at the Grahamstown Festival described Pather's *Body of Evidence* (2009) as a "weird, Peter Greenaway-meets-Derek Jarman exploration" that was compelling more for its opulent theatricality and excess than for its meaning. "So what's it all about?" the reviewer asked. "Good question."[13]

Each artist has devised a distinctive approach to the South African intercultural entanglements that compose his or her artistic palette. Performances by Orlin, Pather, and Bailey consistently invoke a palpable South African "real," even if these allusions are sometimes tongue firmly in cheek, even if this locational specificity can be drained away when shows tour abroad like a color photograph that is bleached of its vivid hues through exposure to ultraviolet rays. Orlin, Pather, and Bailey all draw on South Africa's prolific array of cultures, including multicultural dance forms, songs, and rituals. Orlin and Bailey have at times worked with iconic stories from southern African history (the Xhosa cattle killing of 1856–57; Chief Gcaleka's ill-fated quest to Scotland in 1996 to recover King Hintsa's skull, which British troops pillaged in 1835; Xhosa warrior Makana's attack on Grahamstown in the nineteenth century). Both Pather and Bailey invoke rituals that often have deep local roots, whether they are Zulu, Xhosa, Hindu, or Muslim. Bailey is the most extreme in his dallying with ritual elements, often blurring the line between representation and performativity to the extent that a chicken was once ceremonially slaughtered onstage by a *sangoma* priest during the Baxter Theatre's production of his *iMumbo Jumbo* (1997), much to the dismay and alarm of many theater patrons and the management, which had not been informed.[14]

Disrupting conventions and pushing boundaries, Orlin, Pather, and Bailey often muddle distinctions between audience and performers, between "pre-show" and actual performance, or between representation and the real. They all also create works that cross racial lines, although each does so differently. Orlin's performers often play themselves, inasmuch as the characters have the same names as the performers. Her casts mix black and white performers, and Orlin draws our attention to their racial identities, although she may give little sense of other aspects of identity such as ethnicity, sexuality, or class. Yet even with Orlin's interracial stagings, such as *Daddy*, one notes that it is the white characters who do a great deal of the talking. Pather's shows are often multiracial, and he regularly stages intercultural encounters as the centerpiece of his performances. He focuses on the exact moment when one culture bumps into another. Pather's company, Siwela Sonke Dance Theatre, began as a mixed-race company but over time became all black.[15] Brett Bailey tends to work with all-black casts, although there are occasional cameos by white actors, such as the "blond-haired boys of settler descent" who showed up in his *Ipi Zombi?*[16] The body-centric ways of all three artists innately foreground issues of race and difference. In both the "old" and the "new" South Africa, specific bodies render specific meanings, and Orlin, Pather, and Bailey rarely expect audiences to be blind to those specificities.

While Orlin, Pather, and Bailey share aesthetic similarities, their work diverges in terms of the artists' motivations, methodologies, aesthetic strategies, and critical reception. When Orlin and Bailey move their performances to the Global North, they are able to do so because they have designed their works with that relocation in mind. In contrast, Pather's performances are designed to resonate in South Africa, to disrupt long-standing habits, to tap into the subconscious elements that are part of the intercultural entanglements of South Africa. As a result, Bailey and Orlin are well known internationally, Pather much less so. Bailey and Orlin have both enjoyed careers abroad with steady touring engagements in Europe; in fact, their performances are now more widely seen outside of South Africa than within it.[17] When the European touring circuit picks up performance works from South Africa, what types of performances does it choose? How does Europe's appetite for black otherness and its general ignorance of the vast socioeconomic disparities in South Africa affect these geographically transplanted artistic works? Both Bailey and Orlin often make work with an eye toward Europe, especially in the later parts of their respective careers. They design their performances in a sort of multichannel way so they are capable of resonating differently in various geographic locations. One might receive the work in a kind of stereo complexity when it is presented in South Africa—at least in terms of reading specific South African cultural references—yet that signal may collapse into a mono channel in Europe, losing much of its richness and depth. The danger is that in geographic translation, the work can slip into flattened, stereotypical expectations that are overdetermined by European biases about Africa and South Africa. Specific South African cultural references may become illegible to foreign audiences for whom an array of unfamiliar signs may collapse into preconceived notions of otherness, exoticism, and a racialized difference that is simply black and white.

Pather's works are generally resistant to global circulation. He has sometimes presented his work internationally—in New York, Copenhagen, and India—but he has not entered the elite, first world festival circuit to the degree that Orlin and Baily have.[18] Pather has preferred to do most of his work in South Africa, prioritizing local audience development and creating theater literacies, which explains in part his preference for productions in public spaces.[19] While Pather values his international engagements as a way to challenge himself by swimming in a larger pond, ultimately his political commitment is to his home country. As Brenda Dixon Gottschild has argued, choosing to locate one's primary artistic activity in Africa is a path of "most resistance" because of the relative paucity of economic resources for artists there compared to those in Europe.[20] But Pather's commitment is to place, to belonging, to the making of an artistic future in South Africa and for South Africans. Pather's nuanced depiction of the complexity of intercultural encounters in his country makes his work resistant to facile consumption by outside audiences. His performances cannot be easily evacuated of their cultural specificities without depleting the work of its core substance.

The racialized nature of the circulations of global performance capital are well known.[21] However, it is not race alone that has produced such disparate professional trajectories for these three artists.

ROBYN ORLIN'S NEGOTIATIONS

While waiting for their director to arrive, six performers fight. It is five minutes before show time, and the director has still not shown up. The troupe frantically rehearses what South African choreographer Robyn Orlin calls the "collage of dances" that constitute her legendary work *Daddy, I've seen this piece six times before and I still don't know why they're hurting each other*.[22] This signature piece, which premiered at the Dance Umbrella in Johannesburg in 1999, has toured widely throughout Europe for many years since, garnering Orlin the prestigious Laurence Olivier Award for Outstanding Achievement in Dance in 2003, among other awards.[23] As with all Orlin pieces, the title is long and digressive, and its meaning is unclear (at least to those who have not yet seen the show) while also being evocatively playful. Orlin sees such titles as a kind of program note, providing clues that reveal themselves once a spectator has experienced the work.[24] As with many of Orlin's shows, the characters in *Daddy* share names with the real-life performers, and the boundaries between audience and playing area are thoroughly blurred. It's not even clear when the performance actually begins. Audiences might think they are waiting for the show to start and yet gradually realize that it already has. Waiting is part of the action. Matthew Krouse says of Orlin, "This act of waiting is the main ingredient of the diet she feeds her audience—waiting for 'them' to arrive. Waiting for 'them' to depart. Waiting for the actors to dress and undress, to take up their props and use them like children playing tirelessly, but with boredom, with the same toys they've played with for years, over and over."[25]

With a nod from Orlin to Pirandello's iconic play *Six Characters in Search of an Author*, the six characters in *Daddy* seem to be in search of a way to share a very small space. *Daddy*'s main playing area is a small raised platform like a boxing ring without ropes. The stage, which is bordered with white trim, also resembles an oversized ping-pong table. One thing is clear about this stage: it is too small. An energetic group of black and white performers (Gerard Bester, Thulani Zwane, Toni Morkel, Pule Molebatsi, Nelisiwe Xaba,[26] and Dudu Yende) rush about in a hectic frenzy.[27] Several television monitors are placed at the corners of the stage, suggesting a sports bar. They display closed-circuit images of the performance area shot from above. The audience, which is arrayed on all four sides, is encouraged to view the multiple television monitors, an indication of the need to witness whatever happens from multiple angles. In some venues where this piece was staged, the audience had no seats, so spectators were given agency to pick where they went and what they focused on throughout the show.

Daddy commences with Gerard Bester—who plays a combination of harried stage manager, officious master of ceremonies, anxious mother, earnest pedagogue, expert sports commentator, and bossy circus wrangler—exclaiming, "Let's keep the show going! I want lots of energy! I don't want any sulking!" Nelisiwe Xaba, a lithe young black dancer, enters carrying a bucket on her head, sliding her feet with both grace and a hint of truculence, creating an iconic visual image of black female servitude and looking precisely like someone who has good reason to sulk. Bester, Xaba, and other performers ascend the raised square stage, and Xaba begins placing red plastic plates on the floor in neat rows, helped by other black performers as African pop music blares. In the 1999 Johannesburg production, dancer Sello Pesa was a member of *Daddy*'s ensemble, and he commandeered a space upstage right, where he danced in free-flowing improvisation. Meanwhile, Bester narrates for the audience how this piece has toured internationally. Preposterously, he claims that the plates Xaba is dropping somehow represent the violent streets of Johannesburg, the sound of them dropping evoking gunfire.

The stage action is interrupted by Toni Morkel, a white woman dressed in a gray wig, modest dress, and ridiculous gag glasses with fake eyes, who bursts onto the stage shouting, "Sorry, sorry, sorry, can you please just stop this crap? This isn't *dance*! This is just rubbish! I mean, I've spent *years* studying at Sadler's Wells, I've studied *dance*! I've studied Cecchetti . . . RAD [Royal Academy of Dance] . . . classical ballet. Do you know how this is breaking my heart?!!" With imperious disregard for the performers onstage and a presumed conspiratorial collusion with the audience, she intrudes on the playing area, inserting herself center stage, kicking Xaba's careful arrangement of red plates out of the way with utter disregard while rambling on, talking to the audience about her suffering, her endurance of performances that are not *dance*, asserting herself as one of the few who has *real training*, and introducing us to creatures that represent what genuine dance actually is: her windup ducks.

Out of the ample handbag she clutches beneath her arm, Morkel removes several small yellow automaton ducks and unleashes them to spin and wobble center stage. She treats these identical, trite, mechanical objects as living wonders of extraordinary accomplishment. In the 1999 performance of *Daddy* at the Dance Factory in Johannesburg, Morkel introduced the ducks one at time—"Aurora . . . Odette . . . Odile"—the names of characters in the ballet *Swan Lake*. She shrilly exclaims their respective dance fortés and brags that the troupe has just flown in from Madagascar.[28] These are *cosmopolitan* globe-traveling ducks, it seems, even if their circuit is localized in southern Africa. In the Montpellier performance of *Daddy* in 2000, Morkel tells the audience that the ducks have just flown in from South Africa. Thus, their circuit had extended impressively in the intervening year—which is actually true, as *Daddy* immediately gained remarkable traction on the European touring circuit, particularly in France.[29] As Morkel blathers, shrieks, and crows about her ducks, she continues to kick Xaba's red plates out of the way. Xaba, folded over at the waist like a woman toiling in the fields, continues her methodical, deliberate, orderly arrangement, unthwarted by Morkel's heedlessness. But when Morkel steps on a plate and her heel suddenly slides out in front of her as though she has stepped on a banana peel, their peaceful coexistence ends (figure 8). The physical aggression onstage escalates, and Morkel pushes Xaba, shouting, "Excuse me! Sorry! Do you think we could just perhaps share the stage? Look, I have learnt *to negotiate* in the new South Africa. So just BLOODY

Fig. 8. Toni Morkel slipping on red plates in Robyn Orlin's *Daddy, I've seen this piece six times before and I still don't know why they're hurting each other*, 1999. (Photo by John Hogg.)

share the stage with me—*now*!" In an attempt to situate this squabble in larger, national, and optimistic terms, Bester confides to the audience, "It's very, very difficult in South Africa . . . *very* difficult history. But we are working towards it—ALL the time!"

South Africa won its transition from apartheid to democracy through negotiation. The country's relatively peaceful regime change was socially engineered over conference tables rather than won on the battlefield. Transition produced no clear winners or losers. No political party was evicted from the land; no leaders of the apartheid state were thrown in jail or executed. While desires for retribution and revolution were high in the waning days of apartheid, the negotiated settlement and its invented instrument of peaceful state transition, the Truth and Reconciliation Commission, redirected these impulses into more palatable pursuits. The commission's idea of "restorative justice" was to "restore" the humanity of both victim and perpetrator instead of capitulating to retributive justice and vengeance. Yet negotiation had its asymmetries and obfuscations, which *Daddy* satirizes brilliantly. Negotiation here means that a presumptuous, entitled, white cultural snob hijacks center stage and shoves a black woman out of the way while commanding her to "share." The new thing clearly resembles the old, as Ayi Kwei Armah (in this chapter's epigraph) predicted it would. Orlin's "new thing" overtly, self-consciously makes this racialized truth about the asymmetries of negotiation into something that the audience cannot fail to perceive, even as they are enticed to laugh.

With irony and self-mockery, *Daddy* constantly reminds the audience that the entire performance is a metaphor for the new nation. In this newfangled country, which was just five years old when *Daddy* premiered, things are not going as planned: it is not clear who is in charge, the whole world is watching, the stakes are high, and the show is not yet ready. Nevertheless, everyone is trying *really hard*. "Desperate to get their show on," the cast members flail around, wrote the London's *Guardian* reviewer, "putting together bits and pieces of material, rummaging through their available turns, exhorting each other to do better, and trying to explain themselves to the audience."[30] *Daddy*'s crowded group of anxious characters, bereft of their leader, furtively mount an array of scenes. They include a synchronous Busby Berkeley–like dance number called the "protea dance" that we can see from above on the overhead TV screens. Xaba has several solos, one as a prima donna elevated on a very high stool. At various moments, the whole ensemble breaks into kitschy synchronous numbers accompanied by saccharine songs like Karl Denver's sentimental version of "Mexicali Rose" or Bobby Vinton's sappy recording of "Roses Are

Red (My Love)." At one point, a troupe of unknown performers unexpectedly arrives doing a "tribal" dance, which prompts Bester to make a frantic cell phone call to the missing director Orlin: "Robyn if you get this message, there is a huge crises here. . . . There seems to be a bit of a scheduling problem. It's been a very bad day. First we didn't get the World Cup, and now this is happening to us!" In the many venues where *Daddy* has toured, the intrusion of unexpected dancers is sometimes locally sourced: perhaps a troupe of local sword dancers or British Morris dancers or dusky ladies in black skirts doing Zulu *indlamu* stamping. The whole performance ends with the troupe doing a spirited *cumbia* line dance to the accompaniment of the Latin American number "Soledad" by Combo Los Galleros.

Daddy's chaotic and overweening presentation is, on one level, a hilarious send-up of the emerging nation. The stage of the new South Africa is crowded with performers vying for the spotlight in a disorganized show. *Daddy*'s performers try desperately, despite all odds, to get their act together and mount a woefully under-rehearsed play for a gaping international audience that has great expectations of "miracles."[31] They hiss and shout at each other in furtive eruptions of exasperation and pique, and conflicts sometimes flare across racial lines. There are also other debates about color—literally about color gels on the lights. Yet Bester—as the nervous master of ceremonies who wears ridiculous leopard-print underwear, his bare, spindly white legs nervously twitching as he prances about—reassures the audience that color is no longer relevant in South Africa: "Anyway, we are all colorblind in South Africa now. So, it's after 1994. It's a huge relief for all of us. Um . . . we've really *dealt* with black and white issues," he says as he flicks his hands out to his side, as if flinging off dirty dishwater: "All *gone*. We're now the rainbow nation. It's a huge relief for all of us."

That gesture—that flick of the fingers, the dismissal of race as if it were a nagging irritant easily brushed off—is emblematic of a persistent and pernicious postcolonial tick. This gesture is habituated in deep-settler colonies where the afterlives of injustice continue to thrive. We see it in Anton Krueger's theory of the need to "let go" of identity and race, discussed in my introduction. We see it in the contemporary discussions of race in South Africa, as analyzed by Melissa Steyn, that commonly provoked the response, "Aren't we *beyond* this?"[32] The penchant to arrive prematurely at a "beyond" in the wake of profound injustice is by no means limited to South Africa. We see it internationally in, for instance, subtitles like *Beyond Postcolonialism* in a book that is supposed to be about the politics of intercultural performance.[33] Authors published within this very edited volume expressed their discomfort with the "beyond postcolonialism" framing. As Rustom Bharucha argues, new paradigms cannot ever fully eliminate old ones.[34] Likewise Margaret Werry asserts that no terminology is potent enough to "magic away the inequities that attend performance encounters across geopolitical difference."[35] In an American context, Brandi Wilkins Catanese identifies attempts to erase race as "the problem of the colorblind;" that is, "the unruly chin hair on the face of an otherwise unblemished America," something that one doesn't bring up in polite society."[36] Robyn Orlin puts onstage both white self-aggrandizement masquerading as nonracialism and the attempt to magic away those vexing, bedeviling "black and white" issues with gestures of dismissal that we can see are completely impotent; racial issues are anything but "all gone."

Ostensibly the performers in *Daddy* have been abandoned by the famous, cutting-edge white South African choreographer Robyn Orlin, whose name and reputation are satirically, self-reflexively invoked throughout *Daddy*. Bester dishes out equal doses of breathless sycophancy and snarky irritation about his missing auteur. When Nelisiwe Xaba comes onstage in ballet pointe shoes and tutu, Bester speaks sotto voce to the audience, like a sportscaster preparing us to watch a star turn by an Olympic gymnast: "Just to say, this next dance piece is very, very famous. This really is one of Robyn Orlin's most renowned pieces." Bester also snarls insults about Orlin in a steady stream of asides. In the video made of the premiere production in Johannesburg in 1999, the camera takes us backstage in the dressing-room area before the show as Gerard Bester searches frantically up and down the hallway, asking with neurotic panic whether anyone has seen Robyn, while he also exhorts the cast to hurry up and get ready for the performance, muttering: "Please just get ready, all right? I know it's difficult without Robin. But let's just pull it together. Okay, we know it's difficult. She's a fucking prima donna!" The larger-than-life internationally celebrated white artist is nowhere to be seen in *Daddy*. Yet even in her absence, she upstages everything. The "new" South Africa resembles the old inasmuch as white people are still the center of attention, even when they don't show up, and the white people who do show up do most of the talking. They are still the ones with the microphones.

But embedded in *Daddy*, nested like Russian dolls, are alternate scenes and vignettes that begin to suggest what a centering of black performers and artists might achieve. Here I think of Achille Mbembe's admonition that decolonizing is "not about closing the door to European or other traditions. It is about defining clearly *what the centre is*."[37] *Daddy* is a work about competing centers. The most arresting performance (one that produced an abiding and iconic image, figure 9) is by dancer Nelisiwe Xaba,[38] who wears a white tutu as she carefully, methodically dusts her feet, one at a time, while stepping forward, gently shaking a sieve filled with flour over each foot. Cascading on her black skin, the powder lands like snow as she moves deliberately, purposefully forward, one foot at a time, leaving behind a trail of reverse footprints. The silhouettes of her feet are exposed on the black vinyl floor, framed in white powder like so many snow angels. Through the overhead cameras and television monitors, one sees from above the striking abstract pattern Xaba produces as she moves in an ever-shrinking spiral on the stage, her body bent at the waist, white tutu flaring up in back, her left arm folded behind, the back of her hand patiently pressing against the small of her back. Nelisiwe Xaba is an accomplished dancer who trained in the mid-1990s at Rambert School of Ballet and Contemporary Dance in London, though in *Daddy* only the turnout of her feet reveals her command of ballet technique. This refusal to demonstrate command of dance technique and virtuosity is a signature feature of Orlin's performances, for she feels that dance technique leads to perfection and narcissism.[39]

At the climax of this white powder sequence, Xaba becomes an altogether different dancer. When she reaches center stage, Xaba shakes the powder over her knees and thighs, then blankets her arms and shoulders, as if dusting sugar on a bakery confection. She tosses the sieve offstage, reaches down to the ground, and spins in a circle to scrape up a large swath of flour in two fistfuls. She rises and shakes the powder in the air through her clenched fists while also shaking her tutu, now saturated with flour such that an ethereal white plume rises up in a diaphanous cloud that encircles her. Whether this action is a celebration, a ritual, or an exorcism we do not know, but her comportment throughout is focused, unwavering, and confident. In the final moments of this sequence, two chiffon Shangaan cloths are tossed to Xaba, and she dons them as sashes while shaking her hips continuously. As critic Adrienne Sichel wrote, Xaba then "surrenders her pelvis to the African dynamics," moving her tutu to the characteristic quick shakes and undulations of a Shangaan social dance known as *xibelani*, which is also performed with a tutu-like skirt.[40] From within that plume of whiteness encasing Xaba, emanating from her shaking hips and spreading outward from her raised, shaking hands, Xaba transforms the clinging, suffocating, pervasive, insidious whiteness and its historical repression of black hips, its coercion of black dancers to conform to Western vertical aspirations, into something she completely owns and commands.[41] As Brenda Dixon Gottschild argues, "The traditional and classical Europeanist aesthetic perspective for the dancing body is dominated and ruled by the erect

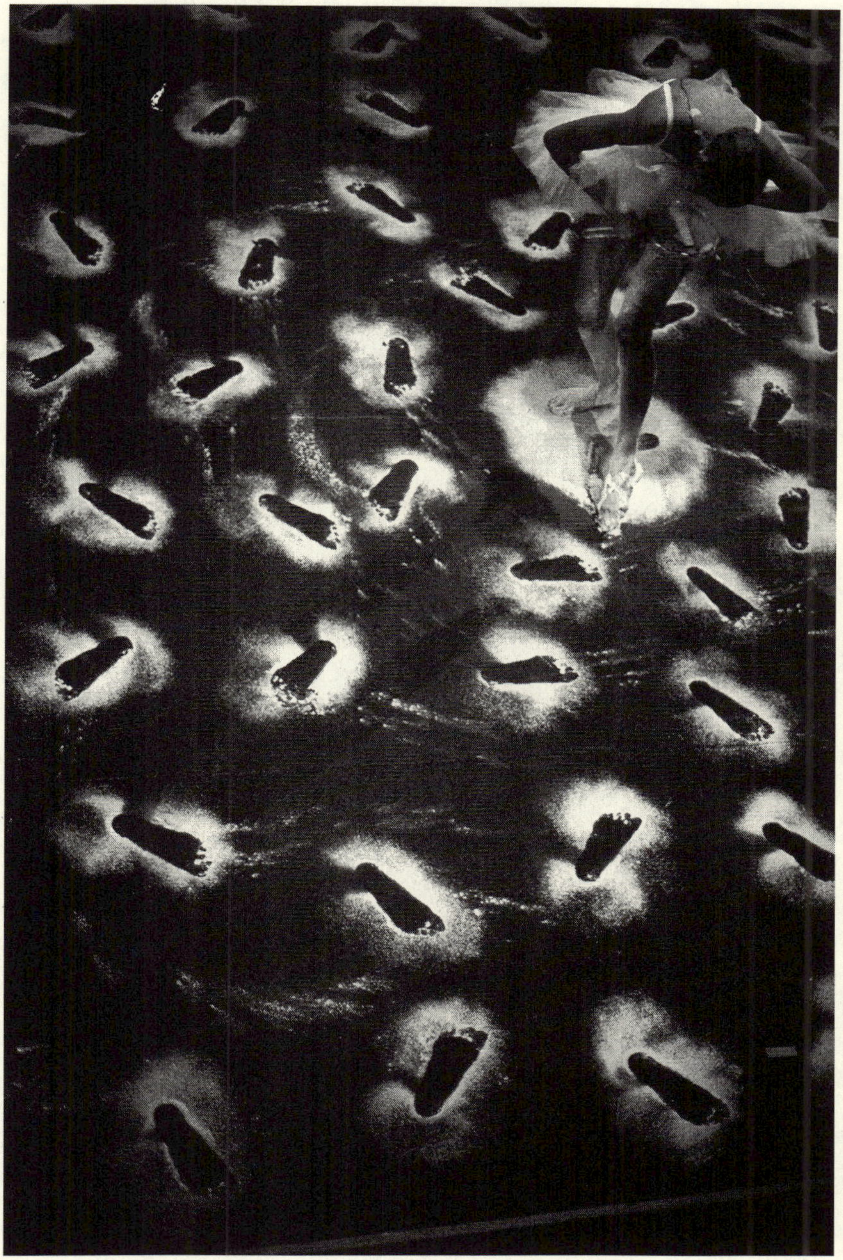

Fig. 9. Nelisiwe Xaba in Robyn Orlin's *Daddy, I've seen this piece six times before and I still don't know why they're hurting each other*, 1999. (Photo by John Hogg.)

spine. Verticality is a prime value, with the torso held erect, knees straight, body in vertical alignment."[42] Xaba's performance in *Daddy* subverts ballet's directionality. Her tutu jutting horizontally outward expresses ballet's paradoxical propensity to demand that dancers tuck their buttocks in and yet also emphasize their posterior with stiff white tulle. In Xaba's performance, this ballet paradox becomes a Shangaan dance in which she accentuates her hips, celebrating a round posterior with ecstatic motion that literally changes the air. As ballet becomes *xibelani* in the final moments of Xaba's solo, a black male dancer joins Xaba onstage, and they begin joyfully to bump their hips together. Xaba's flour dance in *Daddy* creates an arresting and iconic image. Even if most European audiences had no idea about the specific Shangaan traditions of *xibelani* alluded to by Xaba's movements and final costume, her liberating transformation was nevertheless unmistakable. The reviewer for the London *Guardian* saw this moment as a parable of "begetting new dance forms from the ashes of white ballet and traditional black dance."[43]

But Orlin's larger aesthetic and method in *Daddy* don't allow the audience to slip into contemplative ruminations on beautiful transformations. Instead, Xaba's solo is constantly reframed in ways that draw attention to the politics of touring, presentation, appropriation, and claims to originality and authorship. Through sideshows, commentary by Bester and Morkel, and other distractions during Xaba's solo, the spectators are forced to constantly recalibrate focus, as if they are watching the action through a zoom lens and the cinematographer has gone rogue on amphetamines. No performer is ever allowed an undistracted solo turn in *Daddy*. Gerard Bester, standing on the floor below the raised platform where Xaba's solo takes place, provides constant commentary about the importance of Orlin, making claims about her originality. At the top of this segment, when Xaba is introduced through a dramatic enlarged silhouette that is projected on a large translucent paper, Bester tells the audience: "Robin here working with shadows, again, this evening . . . [she] invented shadow work in South Africa eight years ago and then brought it to Europe," where, he says, many other choreographers copied it—a preposterous claim in all regards. Bester prattles that black and white issues are all gone in South Africa, so spectators should not invest too much meaning in Xaba's black-and-white color palette. Bester dedicates this dance to a "famous French artist, Jean-Luc Godard," saying that Godard and Robyn are "great friends" and have been for many, many years, and noting that they've shared a lot of ideas. "Unfortunately, Robyn does tend to steal quite a lot of ideas. And she comes to Europe and steals ideas here and brings them back to South Africa and pretends they are original. And then she wins prizes." Meanwhile, as Bester is disclosing Orlin's propensity for cultural appropriation, Morkel is doing laps around the raised platform on which Xaba performs, chattering on as she tries to capitalize on Xaba's talent and appropriate this performance for her own purposes: "Neli, this is the most *classical* thing that I have seen onstage all evening!" Morkel, the aging ballet diva, then tries to recruit Xaba to her dance company: "Please, reconsider joining the ducks. Me, you and the ducks can make a fantastic piece. . . . We can make a lot of money . . . with steps and style!" The emotional leitmotif of *Swan Lake* begins to swell, and Morkel warbles along while capering lightly around the edges of the playing area, waving a large piece of cloth like a victory flag, upstaging and distracting. Bester admonishes her: "This is Nelisiwe's solo, not yours!" Meanwhile, he is handing various performers in the ensemble rose-patterned slips, urging quick costume changes for the next number. He rushes the conclusion of Nelisiwe's solo, ushering her offstage without a bow. The solo ends hastily, unceremoniously, with a pressure to *move on*.

Orlin's nesting of images, her layering of performance spheres, and her refusal to let spectators ever *land* seems calibrated to keep the audience off balance. While viewers might wish to focus solely on Xaba's solo—for nothing quite like it had ever happened on dance stages under apartheid, and the image created was arrestingly beautiful—Orlin's staging does not allow Xaba to have her moment. Rather, Xaba is actively undermined by the white characters, even by Orlin herself, who does the most upstaging even though she is not physically present. The white characters appropriate, claim, aggrandize, manipulate, and make specious claims of all sorts. Active manipulation of perspective and interruptions provide opportunities for humor and satire and, one could argue, the Brechtian estrangement (Verfremdungseffekt) that is so crucial to political theater. Yet somehow, even with this openness, something essential of the old order stays firmly in place.

What are the limits of Orlin's satire? When does the incessant send-up of white appropriation and self-aggrandizement tiresomely and predictably replicate white power and privilege? When Hannah Montana hooks up with Hannah Arendt for a hot date at the lesbian bar, who is the top? And is their assignation more than a one-night stand? John Matshikiza critiqued Orlin's *Life after the credits roll: A piece for five performers in the spirit of Makana* (1999) for appropriating the black historical figure Makana for the purposes of white amusement, for providing little insight beyond stereotypes, and for failing to show "respect for the deeper meaning these images might have for the black community."[44] Matthew Krouse defends Orlin against her critics, contending that irony is sufficient deflection. According to this view, an embedded satirical comment in the performance about artists "who use political correctness to curry favour with officials who hold the funding purse-strings" functions as a kind of hall pass. In other words, this comment licenses Orlin to compress the Makana story to forty-five minutes in a production based on very thin research because the political correctness of the topic and the little time she has to create are, in fact, the conditions that the lack of artistic funding in South Africa has necessitated.[45] There is truth in this view. South African arts funding is horribly inadequate. Yet there is also a sleight of hand. Ironic scare quotes seem a flimsy cover for work that uses black bodies but gives them very little voice and makes a self-conscious joke out of the performance's shortcomings in this regard. One can understand Matshikiza's 2007 assessment of the paradox of South Africa's contemporary arts scene: "Everything has changed, and yet everything remains the same."[46] Apartheid does seem to be the stain that refuses to disappear, as Gugu Hlongwane has asserted.[47]

In the 1980s, through her pioneering explosion of the previous rigidities of dance in South Africa, Robyn Orlin forged connections between white-dominated modern dance and a range of black cultural groups, including the Soweto Dance Theatre. She established the multiracial City Theatre and Dance Group, giving practical and artistic development to young dancers, including facilitating ongoing workshops to develop and enhance their performance skills and providing them with new opportunities to market their work. Orlin has inspired other artists to work across multiple cultural forms and styles. Her performance works in the 1990s disrupted and further exploded genres and categories, to the degree that members of the dance community often stormed out of her performances because they were not sufficiently "dance." She was central to introducing performance art and live art in South Africa, new genres that liberated many artists to find fresh forms that were capable of expressing radically new content, or at least content that had not been previously given a platform. Furthermore, Orlin courageously trod on volatile and controversial subjects and did so with a great deal of wit and humor. With an oeuvre that has been abundant, sophisticated, and enormously successful, Orlin helped launch the careers of other performers, many of them black. Several have gone on to have remarkable independent careers, Nelisiwe Xaba chief among them.[48] Xaba's subsequent works have included *Plasticization* (2005), *They Look at Me and That's All They Think* (2006), *Sakhozi Says "NON" to the Venus* (2009), *Uncles & Angels* (2012), and *The Last Attitude* (2015), a collaborative

Fig. 10. Nelisiwe Xaba's *Uncles & Angels*, 2012. (Photo supplied by Goodman Gallery.)

work with Mamela Nyamza that was a deconstruction of the legacy of ballet. Many of Xaba's critically and internationally acclaimed self-generated performances are about voyeurism, the exotic, and exoticism; she has continued to explore themes and preoccupations she began to address during her time with Orlin (figure 10).

So it could be said that by "sharing the stage" with Xaba during the early phase of her career, Orlin provided professional and creative opportunities that Xaba then leveraged to launch her own independent path as a choreographer. An artistic tutelage model is certainly fraught with paternalistic power dynamics and inequalities of patronage, especially in a racialized context like South Africa. And where does this method ultimately lead? Orlin continues to mount shows that propel emerging black performers to new visibility. A recent case in point is the one-person show *and so you see . . . our honourable blue sky and ever enduring sun . . . can only be consumed slice by slice. . .*, starring Albert Silindokuhle Ibokwe Khoza, which premiered at the Montpellier Danse Festival in 2016 and had its South African debut at the Johannesburg Dance Umbrella in 2018.[49] In this stunning solo performance and meditation on the seven deadly sins, Khoza's ingenuity, charisma, personality, and extraordinary command of the stage are evident at every turn. *And so you see* is an initiation, a drag show, a healing ceremony, a frenzy of grunts, laughter, and animal sounds. It is an homage to Billie Holiday, Nina Simone, and Miriam Makeba, accompanied by music from Mozart and jazz singer Nono Nkoane. It is clear that the show would not have existed without Khoza, so central is his own larger-than-life personality, talent, movement, extraordinary body, voice, and sense of humor. It is less clear that Orlin should command sole authorial credit. Yet the program billing reads "a project by Robyn Orlin with Albert Silindokuhle Ibokwe Khoza."[50] The words *by* and *with* are doing significant work. There is a vast inequality between them: *by* is the lead, *with* is the backup singer. Is this framing an accurate depiction of the relative contributions of these two artists? Is this collaboration "sharing the stage"? And what might be the limits of such sharing? Regarding a different Orlin project, *Dressed to Kill/Killed to Dress*, Matthew Krouse poses the hypothetical question of whether it is Orlin's job to "parade African men in Europe." Krouse answers: "One thing is definite though, by relinquishing what she has worked for, Orlin would not necessarily be empowering a new force" (this achievement "she has worked for" being, presumably, her power and capacity to take South African artists with her on tour).[51] But would sharing—as in sharing authorial credit where such credit is due—necessarily mean relinquishing what Orlin has worked for? If that is true, what then is it that she has worked for?

Relinquishing solo authorship is something that theater artists began doing in South Africa back in the early 1970s, when white playwright Athol Fugard and black actors John Kani and Winston Ntshona began devising theater work together with the Serpent Players through what became known as the workshop method. While their billing as coauthors of *Sizwe Banzi Is Dead* has not been without its own frictions and inequalities over the years, this shared authorial credit was a true reflection of the creative workshop process.[52] And shared billing ultimately proved empowering to all three of them. Orlin's performances are also collaboratively created with her performers in a process that sounds very much like South African theater's workshop method. Longtime Orlin collaborator Gerard Bester describes their creative process: Orlin "asks the actors to bring their own material on certain themes."[53] Dudu Yende concurs: "You have to be creative. She gives you space to improvise. . . . Because of it, I now feel in a position to create my own work." Nicodemus Moremi also adds that Orlin "gives you a platform to be yourself, and a lot depends on what you, as an actor, offer." When asked in 2000 what about *Daddy* was "peculiarly" South African, Orlin answered:

> Everything about it is peculiarly South African. . . . It's quite difficult to really talk about this and I don't want to get too intellectual about it. One of my thrusts for the last few years since I've been working back here [in South Africa] has been how to empower the artist and so the way I work is that my performers take compete control and responsibility for everything that happens on stage. That's from the lights to the sound to [mess-ups] to whatever happens, they have to take complete control of it. There's a point at which I have to put myself outside.[54]

Orlin's stated desire is to empower her actors by giving them autonomy and agency to contribute to the generation of new creative works. According to her, they have "complete control and responsibility for everything that happens on stage." The unique and idiosyncratic contributions of the performers make Orlin's shows somehow distinctively South African, which is especially necessary since for so many years Orlin has lived in Europe. So it is the performers who possess the granular, daily, year-round immersion in present-day South African culture and realities, elements that are so crucial to making Orlin's work "authentically" South African. Her performers are not the windup automatons that Toni Morkel's character carries around in her handbag in *Daddy*. Her performers work very closely with their own identities and personalities, creating self-generated movement sequences and performance segments. So why not credit collectively authored works as being coauthored?

Orlin has learned to negotiate in the new South Africa, and the result is that she retains top billing. As much as her artistic sensibility of hypertheatricality may surpass the framework of her artistic forebears,[55] Orlin retains key frameworks from the past, most notably the centrality of the white auteur director/author even when the artistic work is generated collaboratively and across racial lines. Parodies within her performances about Orlin as a "genius" and frank onstage disclosures about her reputation for stealing other people's ideas and crediting them as her own—or references to how her international perambulations between Europe and South Africa increase her cultural capital in both places—only go so far. One can view these gestures as a type of performing "whitely," to use a concept from Megan Lewis: these performances do indeed allow audiences "to better see the construction of whiteness."[56] But this exposure does not necessarily progress to dismantling white supremacy. Orlin shares the stage with many others—black, queer, dancer, actor, *inyanga* (traditional healer). But it is *her* stage on which they perform, and they are *her* performers, even if they are a motley crew of diverse dancers and actors who often move and speak in ways that Orlin has not prescribed.

We can see that a "new" cloth of cultural production and artistic output in South Africa is being constructed using fibers from the old cloth. We can also see that whiteness clings to all that it touches, like the insidious and invasive powder that envelopes Nelisiwe Xaba in *Daddy*. Whiteness marks and possesses as its own even what does not belong to it. Yet whiteness, too, can be transformed, just as white ballet became black *xibelani* in Nelisiwe Xaba's memorable solo from *Daddy*, and just as Xaba's appearances in Orlin's performances became, in time, a launchpad for her own autonomous performance career. What is also clear is that those black and white issues that *Daddy*'s master of ceremonies Gerard Bester tried to flick off with his fingers are anything but "all gone."

JAY PATHER: CROSSING OVER BUT NOT BEYOND

"Crossing over to a new place altogether" is the isiZulu translation of Siwela Sonke Dance Theatre, the company Jay Pather directs.[57] Pather's choreographies "cross over" inasmuch as they interrogate layers of cultural coexistence, unravel specific performance genealogies, excavate the afterlives of injustice, and access the audience's latent dreams. But Pather refuses to fabricate a facile commonness. His work is not about getting "beyond" South Africa's many entanglements but rather about exposing them, unraveling them, and sometimes entangling them anew. He creates space where new forms and styles of dance may emerge from South Africa's fractured psyches. His work is about the need to find a way to live with those fractures, neither denying them nor allowing them to determine the future.

Pather's distinctive embodied creative aesthetics include his staging of what he calls the "dance between dances"—specific moments when one culture encounters another, occasions when one movement style bumps into another, or a near-miss when there is abundant opportunity for connection but it doesn't happen. What kind of dance wells up between disparate, previously isolated, and segregated dances? Pather's aesthetic practices include unraveling, palimpsestic layering, and questioning access to meaning, spaces, and audiences. Finally, Pather's creations offer poetic visions of transition and emergence.[58] Instead of focusing on what Pather's dance theater performances may mean, I wish to analyze *how* they mean—how certain techniques, recurrent images, movement genealogies, spatial dynamics, and tropes work to unravel the legacies of apartheid histories in the context of an entangled present. Without prescribing what a new dispensation should be, Pather's Siwela Sonke Dance Theatre creates occasions where something new *may* emerge. Even if that "new" turns out to be the same old fibers in a different tangle, Pather's choreography is animated by a drive to expose toxic histories and provide a space where a liberated dispensation is imaginable. These are dances of otherwise possibilities. In all of this, the body is central: the body as medium and message, the body as archive and repository, the body as the epicenter where notions of "ordinary" and "normal" are both inscribed against one's will and willfully revised to align with new dispensations and aspirations.[59]

Let us begin with an image, a situation, a scene without words, a surreal embodied apparition that might be a dream—not because the image is aspirational but rather because it taps a nerve, puts into tangible and material form deeply felt impulses that are otherwise inchoate and abstract. In Pather's 2005 site-specific performance *The Beautiful Ones Must Be Born*, a black male performer in a pinstripe suit walks on a treadmill in a courtyard where, decades before, antiapartheid political prisoners had been allowed to exercise during their incarceration. Pather's site-specific work was staged at South Africa's Constitutional Court in Johannesburg, which was formerly apartheid's notorious Old Fort prison. The man is flanked by two white ballet dancers in tutus who wield garden forks and poke at tufts of artificial green grass, a feeble attempt to groom a false lawn that itself is a feeble attempt to cover the courtyard's cracked floor.[60] The "new" has not yet taken root—because it can't. Projections on a screen above and behind the man show images of urban squalor in informal settlements, the shanty towns that still populate so much of postapartheid South Africa. Another performer, dressed in Indian clothing and nonchalantly sipping a Diet Coke, pushes buttons on the treadmill, accelerating the suited man's pace. As the runner's pace quickens independent of his will or agency, the tempo of the video above him slows down, isolating specific details of poverty and neglect. The man "runs at maximum speed on the spot, fleeing a horizon in sight," says choreographer Pather.[61] This work pivots on a paradox: frantic motion in stagnation.

This scene, called "Motion Sickness," typifies Pather's penchant for evocative imagery and unexpected juxtapositions. His performances often string together several scenes, tableaux vivants of the unconscious, uncanny living pictures without words that encapsulate the ironies of the present while also disrupting and unleashing their power. "Motion Sickness" both reflects and foretells. The location evokes a rich history: the heroism of antiapartheid political prisoners and South Africa's "miraculous" transition. This former prison once held defiant activists Mandela and Gandhi, and today it has been reclaimed and repurposed as South Africa's Constitutional Court. The renovated prison and adjacent new structures were designed to create "an iconic building, celebrated for its daring, its combination of dignity and accessibility, its warmth and light, and its embodiment of the hopes of a young country."[62] But the contemporary scene Pather stages on this site is not one of hope. One black man races in place while sharing the stage with various atomized others who enjoy a leisure that this man does not have. He is the quintessence of a man striving for upward social mobility: he wears a pinstripe suit and uses a treadmill to stay in shape, for his life, unlike that of so many black men in South Africa, does not demand manual labor. Yet he seems desperate. He is all sweat and exertion, but he doesn't get anywhere, especially in terms of addressing the poverty that hovers over him, haunting and pursuing him. Pather's choreographed meditation offers an image of Sisyphean exertion without progress. This man doesn't move forward, and the faster he races, the more the poverty above him comes into concentrated, sharp focus.

This evocative scene was one among six staged in *The Beautiful Ones Must Be Born*. As often happens with Pather's works, the performance required spectators to move locations as they tracked the evolving scenes mounted throughout the site—from the Great African Steps and Mandela Courtyard to the Constitutional Square and the Tower. Audiences witnessed multiple tableaux, each an amalgamation of dance, video art, movement, music, and spoken text. Each was created by Pather's company Siwela Sonke Dance Theatre in collaboration with Kathak Kendra from KwaZulu-Natal, Moving into Dance Mophatong from Johannesburg, and graduates of the South African Ballet Theatre. Intertexts for the work were multiple and wide ranging, exemplifying intercultural diplomacy and an interweaving of South Africa's many cultures: Zulu praise poetry and the story of Shaka Zulu, India's *Mahabharata*, and the Greek tragedy *Oresteia*. Movement vocabularies included Shembe dance, ballet, Indian Bharatanatyam, and San and Khoisan dance.[63]

The work's title references the Ghanaian novel by Ayi Kwei Armah, *The Beautyful Ones Are Not Yet Born*, a now paradigmatic novel of postcolonial disillusionment written in 1968. Armah's story transpires on the eve of Ghana's first coup and depicts a world of intransigent poverty and corruption in which there is little reason to expect genuine change with the overthrow of Ghana's first president, Kwame Nkrumah. Armah's novel is darkly pessimistic but has a cautious hint of optimism. The novel's title comes from its final scene, in which the narrator describes a slogan he sees on the back of an overloaded lorry going about its usual business in the fragile days after the coup: "the beautyful ones are not yet born."[64] In his allusion to Armah's novel, Pather asserts a new imperative: the beautiful ones *must* be born. This dynamic between a disappointing present (the beautiful is not now) and a desired future (a beautiful that must be) animates Pather's creative expressions.

Born in Durban in 1957, Pather is a choreographer, dancer, director, curator, performer, scholar, and writer. As a South African of Indian (Tamil) background, Pather self-identities as "Indian in heritage and black in ideology."[65] His understanding of blackness is very much informed by Steve Biko's Black Consciousness movement of the 1970s.[66] Pather is best known for his work as artistic director (1996–2016) and as executive artistic director (2016–present) of Siwela Sonke Dance Theatre. From its inception, Siwela Sonke has been dedicated to training black dancers who have no other access to formal training opportunities. In addition to producing dozens of original choreographic works from the 1980s through the present day—including highlights such as *The Beautiful Ones Must Be Born* (2005), *Body of Evidence* (2008), and *Qaphela Caesar* (2010)—Pather is also a prolific and internationally respected curator who serves as the current director of the Institute for Creative Arts (formerly the Gordon Institute for the Performing Arts) at the University of Cape Town, where he is also a professor. From 2008 to 2016, Pather curated the annual Infecting the City festival in Cape Town, and in 2012 he began curating Cape Town's biennial Live Art Festival.

Pather has been steadily making performances since the 1980s. Situating his work historically is crucial to unpacking it. The 1980s were a turbulent time characterized by multiple states of emergency, violent resistance at all borders, rural uprisings, urban demonstrations, and pervasive police raids. Yet by the end of that decade, a new vision had appeared: Mandela was freed from prison, and a path to some kind of negotiated settlement and transition to democracy was beginning to surface that eventually led to South Africa's first democratic elections in 1994. In the early 1990s, in the eye of the storm of this political transition, Pather wrote an essay entitled "Dance in Search of Commonality." It speaks eloquently of the traumas of this era and the euphoria about a postapartheid nation then in the making. He was incredulous about the freshly minted term "new South Africa," which he considered to be crafted in a "fit of desperate optimism."[67] Perversely, newspapers at the time were even publishing reports with phrases like "in the days of the struggle," as though the struggle was already in the past. Yet in the early 1990s more people died from political violence than in the previous four decades. What vexed Pather and galvanized his artistic explorations was his acute awareness of the pervasive violence of South African society, a seemingly endemic pathology for which he knew there would be no easy cure. Pather said:

> Fundamentally . . . we are a violent society. This is the essence of what we face. Mostly this is a bewildering time and there is very real confusion; people being burnt, whole families rendered extinct, the soaring crime rate, a creeping disregard for life, an almost unstoppable momentum of violence. The fabric of South African society is a disturbed one. To stay with and acknowledge the legacy of a violent and divided society is not merely to take the stance of the sulking school boy when we are being lauded with such "gifts" as Japan's lifting of trade sanctions or a visit by Miss World. These are instantaneous solutions, quick fixes that cover up long term and severe damage that has been wrought on collective and individual psyches concerned with the spine of things, the centre. There is a whirlwind of desperate euphoria but at the centre of that whirlwind, I see disease.[68]

The things Pather named in the South Africa of 1991—the whirlwind of desperate euphoria, the diseased spine of things, the country's scarred collective psyche—have remained his abiding preoccupations.

So how does Pather see South Africa today? A contemporary bookend to Pather's 1991 essay is one published in 2017, "Negotiating the Postcolonial Black Body as a Site of Paradox."[69] In this piece, Pather focuses on blackness in a transnational frame; race and blackness emerge more forcefully and explicitly than in his previous writings. He references the #FeesMustFall student uprisings in South Africa in which students across the country have protested the privatization of education, their diminishing access to higher education because of escalating fees, and the long-neglected project of decolonizing the university's curriculum and physical structures. Pather also engages the #BlackLivesMatter movement in the United States, which has protested the disproportionately high rates of African American deaths at the hands of police and the mass incarceration of black people that represents, as Michelle Alexander has argued, America's "new Jim Crow."[70] Just as the dreams of a post–civil rights United States have been intolerably deferred, the postapartheid rainbow nation dream in South Africa has evaporated in the unrelenting drought of continued inequality, segregation, and violence. In such a context, the idea of "postracial" discourse appears as an abomination. While in 1991, Pather was exploring the idea of commonalities in dance, in 2017, he demands that postracialism and the commonality it tries to normatively coerce be abandoned. He speaks about the entrenched paradoxes of the black body and writes with a more forcefully articulated black consciousness and a vivid African diaspora consciousness.

Pather states that South Africa is "trapped in the colonial paradigm."[71] He offers a range of stories about interventions and controversies in South Africa and asserts that these stories must be viewed in a larger context that includes the massacre of protesting mineworkers in Marikana in 2012 and profound inequality and pervasive poverty on a national scale: "The holders of South Africa's wealth and land remain largely unchanged since apartheid. There is an alarming disparity between the wealthiest and the poorest sectors of the population, and the number of people living on the poverty line has barely changed since apartheid."[72] In short, apartheid is not over. It has formally ended, yes. South Africa has a remarkably progressive and enlightened constitution, the press is relatively free, most people enjoy the freedom to assemble, black people have rights today that they did not have under apartheid, and the government's demographics appear far more diverse today than thirty years ago, certainly. But the pervasive structural violence that created and sustains racialized inequality is holding firm in the "new" South Africa that is not so "new" anymore. Maybe it never was really new anyway.

Pather is also interested in how the past, present, and future are thoroughly enmeshed and imbricated. His work is preoccupied with memory only inasmuch as the past in embedded in today's bodies: "Sometimes we wish that a delete button might annihilate some of this information," says Pather in his introductory note to his performance *Body of Evidence*. "But the body instead stores relentlessly, file upon file, bottomless cabinets of memory, individual and collective."[73] Because violence remains intimately woven into the social fabric at every level, no desirable future can be envisioned or fabricated without unraveling its toxic legacy. Some of the fibers may be hopelessly corrupted and thus dispensed with or, at the very least, quarantined. Others may be reclaimed, but the reclamation process may require acts of remediation, cleansing, and repair. In Pather's view,

> While memory and a traumatic past bleed inevitably into the present—a present that reenacts the deprivations of the past and allows memory visceral, graphic reimagining—a grip on the future is much

> more tenuous. South Africans live in a slippery state of postponed gratification by the real fruits of democracy so hard won. The future resembles a suspended malaise of broken political promises and a rapidly waning patience with national projects of social cohesion. The good life that government repeatedly urges its citizens to look toward renders present-day reality a kind of unreality—a distension, a floating above the ground. The constant rupturing of the narrative of material progress and development, articulated at the onset of our democracy in 1994, reinforces a state of stasis, impotence and inertia. The profound economic asymmetries that persist in South Africa, characterize our lived reality with a kind of schizophrenia, where the overwhelming presence of despair and the very human need to cling to hope gnaw away at each other.[74]

In thinking about the conditions of possibility for making art in contemporary South Africa, Pather invokes the metaphor of rape. A rape victim flees their attacker and may even fight back and then seek justice and recovery. The victim may eventually reclaim independence, recover a violated self. This process may happen in part through recourse to the legal system—through arrests, charges, trials, damages, or financial recompense—or through something like truth and reconciliation hearings that facilitate a reckoning through restorative justice. But as Pather says, "Even after all of this, in the most optimistic scenario of reconstruction and recovery, no one can deny that that person's life is forever changed."[75] If South Africa after apartheid is likewise forever changed—if the trauma of many centuries of conquest, colonialization, and apartheid have become embedded as cellular reality—then one must abandon teleological models of "beyond" and "post" and healing metaphors that deceive with a coercive demand for cure when cure is not always possible or even desirable. Even with recovery, there is a foreverness about certain histories that demands our recognition and acknowledgment. Disability studies has shown us that the reflexive reach for cure is often a depoliticizing gesture and a normative erasure of enduring conditions. Apartheid's afterlives remain, and all attempts to magic them away with rainbows and "oneness" are coercive denials of the enduring afterlives of injustice.[76]

Some have said that despite the Truth and Reconciliation Commission's many disappointments and failures, it succeeded in narrowing the range of permissible lies.[77] We might think of Pather's dance theater as a kind of analogous performative: these dances expand the range of accessible dreams. Not all of them are pleasing. In Pather's dance theater pieces, there may be characters with whom to identify or a story to be followed—kind of. He provides the audience with a few narrative lifelines, or what he calls "little islands" that one "can hang onto if one needs to."[78] But neither narrative nor character is Pather's main objective. Instead, he wishes to access the realm of dreams. Journalist Peter Machen once said in an interview with Pather, "Your work is usually accessible but seldom easy to interpret." Pather admits that this opacity is a source of anxiety for him. He says that when his family comes to see his dances, "they are trying so hard to be polite":

> They go, "Yeah, I really *liked* it! It was about *that*, and it was about *this*." And there is immediately a need to say *what it was*. What *is* the story. Well, I prefer to think of my dances as accessing your dreams. . . . If you think about the dream that you had last night, . . . I'm sure if you are trying to explain that to someone, the logic will defy them. In fact, you might reveal much more than you wish to reveal.[79]

Dreams haunt us. They resonate in our waking hours, reflecting both our subconscious processing of memories and our aspirations and fantasies. Surfacing memories from the day that has just ended and scenes and locations from long ago, dreams are embedded in the past, both distant and immediate. At the same time, dreams are enmeshed in the future, saturated with desire. Our dreams belong to us, but given our general lack of control over them, we might say rather that we belong to our dreams. Our instinctual sense of the authenticity or veracity of a dream, its connection to something that is "true," may often surpass our conscious ability to understand what the dream may actually be about. Sometimes we can lose our capacity to dream, perhaps through anxiety, shallow sleep, apnea, constant interruptions, or quite simply lack of sleep because one is working too hard, doing too many jobs in order to make ends meet.

Pather's performance works are, at their core, dreamscapes. As such, their impact accretes gradually over time: one has to immerse oneself in and marinate in the work in order to start to recognize the salient patterns.[80] Resolute meanings and neat conclusions are beside the point. As Pather says: "The flux, the suspended meanings, the non-sequiturs of an imposed system of classification, of traveling iconographies and the reach toward coherence is what the work foregrounds. The point then is not to obfuscate and gloss over the distension but to re-enact the submerged discourse that is present in a particular space, however rarified."[81] Meaning, in Pather's view, is "something that the body processes over time, and if making art is about accessing a subconscious field, meaning may not be immediate but it might occur later, perhaps in one's dreams."[82] So there is a circularity here: the choreography arises from the subconscious while also penetrating it, embedding itself in a subterranean field that will be carried into the future through the archive of the spectator's mind. Pather's objective is to "make contact with a subconscious depth and to give expression to that depth."[83] For instance, he has described his piece *Shifting Spaces Tilting Time* (1997) as a "fantasy world revealing a new South African subconscious."[84] This subconscious realm is both private and public; its visions express both the individual and the collective.

Pather's refusal of coherence is matched by his resistance to conventional venues. His oeuvre does include some concert dances, where one pays for a ticket, sits down in an assigned seat, and stays put in a darkened theater for an hour or two to watch a performance with carefully crafted entrances, exits, turns, leaps, positions, transitions, and lighting cues. However, much more of Pather's work in the last two decades has been site-specific—or, as he prefers to call it, "site responsive."[85] His performances may pop up outside a shopping mall or insinuate themselves in a town square or fully occupy a former prison or a stock exchange. Some Pather shows require one to sequentially sit down, walk, and stand, as spectators must relocate multiple times throughout the performance. The Igbo of Nigeria say, "You do not stand in one place to watch a masquerade."[86] The same is true of watching a Pather performance: even if your feet don't move, your consciousness will. His works are not for the lazy. When you see a performance by Pather, you may be sitting in a cafe or standing in a small hotel room with nine other spectators or racing through the poorly lit corridors of Cape Town City Hall at night. Or you may be in the great Transnet Hall at the Grahamstown National Arts Festival, sitting as comfortably as one can on those unforgiving cold metal bleachers in the middle of winter with no heat, when suddenly the center of the stage action radically changes and you must give up your seat and move to another part of the hall entirely, not quite sure whether or how you will be accommodated when you get there. As one reviewer of *Body of Evidence* wrote, "Pather moves his audience around the Great Hall not less than three times, from the bleachers to the performance floor to the area behind the screen, facing backwards toward the half-obscured bleachers."[87] Over the last two decades, Pather has become increasingly impatient with audience passivity and the class exclusivity of traditional concert dance genres. Pather says:

> Contemporary dance still has the stigma of an elitist art form that requires particular decoding available to a privileged few in order for the form to be enjoyed. There is clear evidence of this in the demographic representation of audiences at these events. Given the drastic lack of access to the arts during apartheid, the shifts in the postcolony are slow to augment these absences with clear strategies for developing audience literacy and access.[88]

His passion for site-specific choreography crystalized in 2002 with the multisited production of *CityScapes,* which transpired in host venues all around Durban.[89] His simultaneous disruption of the locations of performance and commitment to the specificity of place is another key to understanding Pather's work.

In rejecting the postelection euphoria of multiculturalism, interculturalism, and dance "fusion," Pather has positioned his work as being a staging of the dance between dances rather than a melding of forms. He has said, "The value in a multi-layered dance work with a variety of cultural influences has become more than just offering another point of view. I have found that in my work with Siwela Sonke Dance Theatre that this process is vital in developing a large enough palette to contain a vastly complex, multi- (dance) lingual culture, the dance *between* dances."[90] Sometimes how this works in practice is that Pather places two codified dance forms adjacent to one another, and what Pather frames is the space between them. This is a space in which to ask: Is there a connection? Can there be a connection? What does Pather's new form take? What is lost? What is gained? Perhaps the dance between dances is no dance at all. The outcome, for Pather, is not predetermined.

When you see a dance theater piece by Pather, you may see a white female ballet dancer en pointe, wearing a tutu sewn out of the new South African flag. She dances a pas de deux with a black man clad in an *amabheshu,* a ceremonial Zulu waist apron that is customarily made from goat- or cattle skin, but in Pather's 1997 dance *Shifting Spaces Tilting Time* it's made of hot pink fur. In this piece, Pather further queered traditional costumes through his unexpected twists on conventional dance styles. The woman performed ballet, its own kind of European "ethnic dance," as Joann Kealinohomoku has argued.[91] When ballet was adopted in apartheid South Africa, the genre was tightly fused with ideologies of white supremacy. "The apartheid government used ballet in much the same way that Nazi Germany did," Pather contends. "They took these really athletic forms; they made it the hallmark of rectitude: the ideal body," which in South Africa was, of course, white.[92] But when Pather brings ballet into his choreography, he focuses our eyes to perceive what was previously denied while also in plain sight. In *Shifting Spaces Tilting Time,* he partnered the ballerina with an *isicathamiya* dancer, not a male ballet dancer. A South African all-male choral and dance form that originated in the late nineteenth and early twentieth centuries, *isicathamiya* is intimately associated with fraternal support networks among black male migrant laborers. The form is thought to be a combination of traditional Zulu male group dancing and American minstrel dances, both of which are done in a line formation.[93] (Blackface minstrels from the United States and Britain sailed around the tip of Africa in the nineteenth century, leaving complex performance genealogies in their wake.) In *isicathamiya,* dancers walk softly, almost on tiptoe—a stylistic adaptation of older Zulu dance forms with loud foot stomping. When migrant workers from the KwaZulu-Natal region were forced to live in cramped conditions in hostels away from the open fields of their rural homes, they had to be quiet when dancing.[94] *Isicathamiya* is thus already a hybrid, synthetic, and transcultural form, one that is distinctively South African not only because of its roots in Zulu traditional dance, but also because of apartheid's distortions.

In *Shifting Spaces Tilting Time,* Pather used costume shifts and unexpected juxtapositions of movement styles to transform these two dance genres—ballet and *isicathamiya*—in ways that made each strange, that pulled the "fiber" out of its previous context but retained the shape and contours of its former knot. Whereas the ballerina teetered en pointe precariously and ungracefully, the *isicathamiya* dancer was outside of his normal context because he appeared without a larger group of male performers. The Zulu verb *cathama,* at the core of the word *isicathamiya,* means "to crawl like a cat."[95] In this pas de deux, the male dancer crawled like a cat and walked softly on tiptoe as he partnered with a woman who was also on tiptoe, but of a very different kind. In the course of the performance, her tutu was torn and her pointe shoes became bloody.[96] Ultimately the woman lost her pointe shoes.

We may ask: what is the point? As with so many potent images conjured in Pather's dance theater, the meaning of this scenario was ambiguous and layered. Clare Craighead found that this scene spoke "on many levels about the form (ballet) that was historically (and racially) privileged in a violent system (apartheid) that for so long governed South Africa."[97] Pather says that many spectators have interpreted the woman as "the last colonial outpost, or a white woman who has to throw away her shoes and become part of the new South Africa."[98] Yet he was not trying to promote a facile coexistence of disparate cultural dance styles or to suggest a pas de deux of European and African traditions in the new South Africa. As he explains,

> The ballerina in a tutu of the new South African flag is less a representative of white South Africa and more a symbol of the new South Africa, on pointe, teetering, fragile, a fairy tale democracy. So when she loses her pointe shoes at the end, this is less about the demise of European culture in Africa as it is representative of a post modern democracy struggling to deal with the realities beyond hyperbole and election promises.[99]

Especially in 1997, when *Shifting Spaces Tilting Time* premiered, South Africa was still a new country, a mere three years into the life of its new constitution. Already the nation was wobbling with the dawning recognition of the magnitude of unmet frustrations, the precarity of dreams deferred.

Throughout Pather's choreographic oeuvre, which has been largely created in the postapartheid era, he has distinguished himself by carefully crafting such moments of intercultural encounter. His aesthetic strategy is not so much one of intercultural interweaving as it is a thoughtful, nuanced, and methodical experiment with different substances. What are their distinctive properties? What level of charge can they carry? What repels? What attracts? What can hold water? What sinks? What happens if we connect this style and that one, link this form with that one, or perform this dance style but modify some crucial element? New insights about old forms combine with tentative moments of connection across difference. These moments appear alongside near misses of unrealized opportunities: people from different cultures—or even different realms of sentience and spirit—may occupy the same stage but coexist without mutual recognition or even awareness in disconnected parallel worlds.

Siwela Sonke Dance Theatre is based in Durban, where Pather was born and raised. While Pather has since relocated to Cape Town to assume a professorship and a distinguished leadership position at the University of Cape Town, Durban remains his artistic home, a signature for him as an artist and for his company: "Siwela Sonke has always been about bringing together the rich tradition of KwaZulu-Natal and merging this with contemporary dance," says Pather. "This is not artificial; it is who we are—a combination of our heritages and our global present."[100] Pather describes the spirit of eThekwini (the larger Durban metropolitan area) as "a very strong, intoxicating intense thing. You grow up with it, imbibe it, and it never leaves you, ever," he says. "It definitely pervades my work wherever I go."[101] With its arcades and an active pedestrian scene where many cultures collide in public, Durban is a city of street life. This observation is less true of other South African cities such as Cape Town, which was (and in many ways remains) a model apartheid city of racial separateness. Whereas Pather calls Cape Town "too beautiful and sometimes bland," he sees Durban as more prone to on-the-street intercultural and interracial encounters.[102] Durban is distinctive not just for its large population of people of Indian descent and its strong Zulu presence; it is also a city where urban and rural residents, lawyers and *sangomas* often share the same sidewalk. During the course of an interview with Pather, Peter Machen talked about these distinctive features of Durban and the way in which they inform Pather's work:

> This is one of the most wonderful things about Durban for me: seeing *sangomas* and *inyangas* in their traditional dress walking down the same streets as snappily dressed lawyers, Indian and African Moslems wearing kurtas and burkas, Zionists, Shembes and, of course, young people wearing South Africa's own sharply flamboyant interpretations of Western fashion. All of this comes through in your work. And while for you and I it represents our reality, for many South Africans who live in more compartmentalised realities, it is a foreign world.[103]

As an artist who has consistently presented visions that break through the socially engineered compartments of apartheid, Pather is energized by the way bodies in public space hold the potential for collisions and connection: a white urban skateboarder may collide with a black rural woman carrying a stack of kindling on her head. This very scene, which Pather staged in a part of *CityScapes* on a Durban beach, arose from an actual encounter.

The potential for such connections—across lines of race, class, ethnicity, gender, and urban versus rural cultures—is both highly possible in the new South Africa and seemingly impossible, or at least rarely realized beyond the briefest of encounters. "All the ingredients are there, you know," says Pather. "It's 'all dressed up and nowhere to go,' because the only way to go is into each other—and I don't think we are ready for that; or somehow we're not going into each other."[104] In his dance theater works, Pather may be interweaving cultures, revealing their entanglement, or exposing the lack of connection among people who pass each other every day. For instance, in *Body of Evidence,* an older white man wearing a suit and clutching a bouquet of flowers opens the show with an arcane speech about the botanical lineage of geraniums. He is surrounded by half a dozen black dancers, but he seems not to see or acknowledge them, with the exception of a black woman dressed as a maid. As she scurries around delivering props and tidying things up, the older white man distractedly hands her things to take care of. Later in *Body of Evidence,* a spirit figure clad in white coexists with a "living" sentient character. They dance a pas de deux seemingly without mutual awareness, bumping into each other, rolling over each other, encountering the obstacles each other presents but without actually *seeing,* recognizing, or acknowledging the other. Such scenes express the strange heedlessness that is its own dance between dances of South Africa's contemporary moment—a kind of dance of refusal.

Pather's performances feature a surfeit of uncanny and perplexing images: otherworldly and familiar, accessible yet opaque, disturbing while strangely comforting; dark, haunting, and arresting but also showing flashes of hilarity and lightness. Pather creates potent scenarios that speak of the instabilities and ironies of contemporary South African life. In *Qaphela Caesar,* a group of black men in formal suits who represent the new South African government blow up and deflate white balloons while their unzipped pants flop around their ankles, entangling their movements, undermining their dignity. They are the image of pretension and empty political bloviating (figure 11). In *CityScapes,* a large black woman with shopping bags and a hoopskirt (performer Hlengiwe Lushaba Madlala) rappelled down the exterior of the Musgrave shopping center in Durban. With ropes attached to her back, the dancer literally walked down the side of this building facing downward. ("She was very brave!" recalled Pather.)[105] An *isicathamiya* chorus on the pavement below sang praises: a South African version of Andrew Lloyd Webber's "Don't Cry for Me Argentina" from *Evita.* The Zulu lyrics praised eThekwini (the municipality), Calvin Klein, and Armani.[106] The image of this woman was "at once powerful and vulnerable," says Pather. "It was about the taking over of this white middle-class space by the black middle class."[107] Once the woman reached the ground, she and the singers interacted marginally, "making space for each other, negotiating survival in a middle class consumer paradise," as Pather said.[108] But then the woman and the singers rushed off in a battered, rusty Toyota Corolla. Gaffer tape secured a broken passenger door, and plastic sheeting covered a broken back window.[109] While this black woman may be the new middle class, a shopper from another dimension who enters confidently, unconventionally, and with great courage into

Fig. 11. *Qaphela Caesar* by Jay Pather and Siwela Sonke Dance Theatre, 2012. (Photo by Val Adamson, courtesy of Jay Pather.)

a space that historically would have excluded her, her daring entrance was followed by a prosaic, hasty departure that revealed the underlying precarity of the fledgling black middle class she represents.

One segment of *Body of Evidence* features a line of five black men wearing tight beige Lycra shorts, rubber boots on their feet, bras around their torsos, and plastic buckets on their heads (figure 12). They dance in a distinctive style known as gumboot, or *isicathulo*, which means "shoe." The men stamp, clap, and slap the sides of their knee-high Wellingtons as they kick their legs in the air in tight synchronicity. Some people say gumboot dance developed on the docklands of Durban. Others trace its source to South Africa's gold mines.[110] Still others believe it may have started among the night soil (human waste) collectors in Witwatersrand.[111] Whatever its actual derivation, gumboot dance can trace its roots to the extreme hardship and duress of black male migrant laborers before, during, and after the end of apartheid. Jane Osborne contends that the "all-black, all-male, white-controlled compound milieu provided a uniquely South African environment" in which the gumboot dance form arose.[112] The many cultural tributaries flowing into gumboot dance include Bhaca traditional

Fig. 12. *Body of Evidence* by Jay Pather and Siwela Sonke Dance Theatre, 2008. (Photo by Val Adamson, courtesy of Jay Pather.)

dances such as *ngoma*, social dance such as the jitterbug that came to South Africa with jazz music, regimented movements from the military, and tap dancing appropriated from Fred Astaire and Gene Kelly movies.[113]

While gumboot dance is clearly a highly syncretic form with many performance genealogies, it is not typically danced by men wearing tight Lycra shorts. Gumboot dancers typically wear the standard uniform of those who work in the mines: matching overalls and hard hats. Likewise, one never sees gumboot danced by men wearing bras or buckets on their heads. But in *Body of Evidence*, Pather turns gumboot dance inside out and upside down. Gumboot has long been appropriated by white mine owners keen to show "happy darkies" on the mines, and more recently the form has been exploited for tourist shows in the new South Africa for audiences who wish to experience South Africa's dynamic rainbow euphoria without having to endure the storms and tempests of racialized violence and inequality that are the basis of its climate. In *Body of Evidence*, the dancers are overtly dehumanized because their faces are covered with buckets—which we might read as oblique reference to the buckets of excrement lugged by Witwatersrand night soil collectors. The performers' bras subvert (or at least complicate) the intense masculinity of the traditional gumboot form. In a country that today has one of the highest rates of violence against women in the world, masculinities deserve to be questioned. But Pather poses questions that he does not resolve as the dance unravels its performative inheritance.

Pather's dance theater plumbs the violent histories, private traumas, public humiliations, and continued felt realities of apartheid. At the same time, his creations are full of unexpected moments of irony and levity that are often achieved through abrupt pivots in mood. In *Body of Evidence*, a dancer disappears behind a screen in a scene that is evocative of the ubiquity of state torture under apartheid. The dancer cries out. His screams escalate, becoming sharper, louder, and more desperate as the other dancers and we—the audience—look on. Suddenly a swimming flipper is tossed in the air, flopping on the floor with a definitive splat. A state of terror abruptly becomes a state of play, even frivolity. The man's screams cross over to peals of laughter. Such sudden pivots of mood are possible only because of Pather's assured navigation of a murky terrain, the acuity and precision with which he queries, tests, manipulates, excavates, and pushes on the submerged forces for which we have yet to find words.

What does it take to make art that tangles with the afterlives of injustice? Pather's creative method tenaciously pulls at various threads in the tangled mess that is the postapartheid state. Sometimes the line snaps, and we tumble into a new reality; at other times the thread unravels, revealing something else underneath. Not infrequently an even larger tangled mess is created. At other times, the line abruptly ends, unmoored yet kinked, knotted, and permanently snarled. And sometimes the line stays taut, an unbearable tension of dynamism and stasis. Pather's approach patiently dwells in a lack of coherence, finds revelation in unexpected juxtapositions, and gently pulls at the disorder of things. Yet he is also mindful of what is fragile, gentle with that which is wounded, and patient with what is emerging. This fragmentary aesthetic does not arise from postmodernism, nihilism, narcissism, or a deliberate formal experimentation per se. Pather argues that in much of African performance work, an aesthetic of alienation is not "born of privilege, but comes from poverty and a legacy of violence."[114] Pather's approach is embedded in the political context of South Africa's lack of resolution, its potent and continued revival of the afterlives of injustice. This approach, and his respect for the movement genealogies from which he draws, and his trenchant exploration of space, time, memory, and the archival repository of the body itself form the foundation of his unique artistic sensibility.

Pather's choreography has at times drawn on a prolific range of South African dance styles: *pantsula, isicathamiya,* ballet, Kathak, Celtic dance, *indlamu,* hip-hop, *kwasa kwasa,* gumboot, *namastap* from Namibia, Shembe from a Zulu Africanist sect of Christianity, *ngoma,* contemporary modern dance, and physical theater. However as often as Pather invokes any particular style, he also unravels it. Discrete cultural forms are not so much interwoven as undone, with single elements isolated and transformed: a ballet dancer loses her pointe shoes; a gumboot dancer appears on crutches; an Indian Kathak dancer is forced to perform with her hands bound.[115] Pather's approach demands, in his words, an "interrogation of the various ethnic dances from *isicathamiya* to ballet before they are juxtaposed."[116] While Pather's work may summon disparate cultural strands onto the same stage, he does not try to create a coherent whole. In the earlier days of South Africa's new democracy, there was a time when Pather had fantasized that South Africa could provide the world with the "ultimate in democratic choreography." In other words, he hoped "cultures in juxtaposition, complementing each other, sometimes in conflict, crashing with each other would produce a *frisson* that could in turn provide the passionate spark, something missing from contemporary Western nihilistic art."[117] But the reality of life in contemporary South Africa demands something different. Legacies of separateness, violence, and cultural denigration complicate any attempt to bring cultures together. Even invoking Indigenous traditional forms onstage has to be done with great care because, as Pather says, these forms:

> have been so disrespected in the past that they cannot just be played around with. One has to be quite careful how they are represented. The experience can be powerful and uplifting but, if not done with care, it can also be alienating and superficial. It is one of my missions to represent this rich diversity, some kind of truth. And truth in a matrix of such diversity is hard work.[118]

The "hard work" of this choreography is found in specific decisions about when and how various cultural strands come together and when and how specific elements are unraveled, or even bound and confined. In all of this, Pather avoids the coercive demand for a normative well-fabricated intercultural cloth. But at the same time, he doesn't fetishize a hopelessly entangled snarl. He engages in patient work that prioritizes dignity and respect and asks hard questions without a demand for immediate answers.[119]

In staging what he calls the dances between the dances, Pather speaks about respect as key to his method for choreographing encounters between cultural forms or even invoking them independently on stage. Precision and care are guiding imperatives. He says,

> It's about finding the exact fit. Finding its exact formation; really, really trying very hard—and very often it is about paying respect to that particular thing in a very fundamental way, and I very often have to really dig deep to the level of respect that I have for it. For instance, in *Shifting Spaces* . . . the original *Shifting Spaces*, Pravika did an entire piece with her hands bandaged . . . and I mean, how can an Indian dancer bandage her hands? . . . I do a lot of soul searching. . . . I have to be very, very clear.[120]

Respect seems to be key to any analysis of the integrity of intercultural creative work in a South African context, but respect can be hard to codify or distill into a methodology. How do we define respect? Who decides what is to be respected? How is respect expressed? What practices help foster respect in the creative process or in the audience's reception of the finished work? I will return to these questions later, when I examine the work of Brett Bailey.

The "crossing over" of Siwela Sonke Dance Theatre's work can be thought of in several different ways. First, it is the dance between the dances of South Africa's disparate cultures. Second, its dances cross over between past, present, and future. Temporalities themselves are entangled. What has happened in the past is not in the past: it is embedded in the muscle and bone of now, the synapses and arteries of the living. For Pather, the body is a living repository, a somatic archive. Third, Pather's performances often breach the separation of performance and audience in conventional Western theater, demanding that the audience itself do several literal "crossings" to experience the work. And finally, Pather crosses over from consciousness to the unconscious world of dream life. His choreographic works are ultimately dreamscapes for a sleep-deprived nation.

A character in a Milan Kundera novel said, "The struggle of man against power is the struggle of memory against forgetting."[121] In Pather's performances, recollections and subconscious memories are unearthed as apparitions. These visions intervene in the Manichaean battle between memory and forgetting, between hope and despair, while also staging an encounter between dreams and wakeful consciousness. Without invoking utopian expectations of "post" and "beyond" or a cure, these performances stage an unraveling. Pather's performances surface in the present continuous—the present moment's lack of clarity and resolution, its reflex actions and thwarted attempts, its ruptures and lack of coherence. Memory and the future overlap, things remain slippery and tenuous, but the flux suggests potential for change. In a world of paralyzed stasis, performing bodies that move stand out.

Pather's choreography patiently dwells in an inherent lack of resolution that may frustrate or confuse some but at the same time may help audiences dwell with new insight in the contemporary uncertainties of a South Africa that itself remains in flux. Pather does not force a narrative or resolution. There are no prefabricated visions of wholeness to be found here. One may cross over to a new place through the portal of these performances, but we don't get beyond South Africa's past. Pather's performances are as potent for their ability to build awareness of spectators' desire for coherence as they are at undermining this habitual expectation. This simultaneous invocation and refusal of coherence seems to me to be the point of Pather's dance theater: The whole does *not* cohere. The story does *not* add up. The promises of a liberated, nonracial postapartheid order have *not* yet been fulfilled. And yet, Pather's work asserts, they *must* be.

BRETT BAILEY: AESTHETIC BOOMERANGS

Among contemporary South African artists, Brett Bailey enjoys an extensive scholarly bibliography of research on his work.[122] While he is visionary, prolific, and innovative, I would argue that Bailey is no more distinguished and important than many of the other artists covered here. The disproportionate scholarly coverage of Bailey, who is the only contemporary white male artist featured in this book, is symptomatic of what I see as the need to decolonize South African theater and performance studies. The scholarly literature has developed unevenly, with notable neglect of significant contemporary artists of color. Nevertheless, there is value in considering Bailey's work comparatively, next to and as part of a cohort of artists working in a similar vein. Drawing on the rich literature about Bailey's performances, I offer here a compressed analysis, focusing in particular on the relationship of his performance works to those of Robyn Orlin and Jay Pather, with emphasis on questions of sharing the stage, cultural appropriation, and "breaking" the theater.

Brett Bailey rose to prominence in the late 1990s with a trilogy of extraordinary works based on South African current and historical events. Collectively called the *Plays of Miracle and Wonder* (a nod to the lyric "these are the days of miracle and wonder" from Paul Simon's legendary Afropop album *Graceland*), these performances unleashed Bailey's experimental aesthetic to great critical acclaim and critical dismay. His work traffics in the sensational, the irreverent, the holy, the anthropological, the commercial, the mass produced, and the supernatural. His is a theater of excess that creates visually striking, affectively potent concatenations of the unexpected. Bailey has a remarkable capacity to design arresting stage pictures, and his formidable design talent won him the gold medal for design at the prestigious Prague Quadrennial in 2007—a first, I believe, for any South African designer. His insatiable curiosity, his appetite for cultural syncretism, and his seeming lack of reflection about his own subject position have also sometimes gotten him into a great deal of hot water.

When Bailey first started making performance works, before he was lured by the enticements of international touring, his stated motivation was to have his performances be accessible to people across the social spectrum in South Africa, "from the highbrows who pay R50 for a ticket to those who scurry to their shacks to find 50c."[123] He also wanted to stimulate interest in the country's vast heritage of cultural forms and to develop the talent of young performers.[124] The *Plays of Miracle and Wonder* launched Bailey's company Third World Bunfight. The company's inaugural trilogy included *iMumbo Jumbo* (1997), about the 1996 pilgrimage of Chief Nicholas Gcaleka to the United Kingdom to try to reclaim and repatriate the skull of King Hintsa, which had been pillaged by the British in 1836 after they killed him. The next play, *Ipi Zombi?* (1998), was loosely based on a perplexing contemporary tragedy when fifteen boys died in a bus accident in Kokstad and the community broke out in a series of witch hunts, with mobs descending on and killing two women accused of supernatural intervention in the boys' deaths. Finally, *The Prophet* (1999) theatricalized an iconic story from the nineteenth century about the teenage prophetess Nongqawuse, who predicted the defeat of the British and the mobilization of ancestral powers if the Xhosa killed their own cattle. The *Plays of Miracle and Wonder* were arguably the first time a white playwright had so forthrightly and with such experimental daring tackled distinctive Xhosa stories. Bailey considers himself to be working in the spirit of French practitioner Antonin Artaud and his Theatre of Cruelty. Considering the colonial critiques that have been leveled against Artaud and his Orientalist adventures in Bali, it is no surprise that Bailey has had difficulties with accusations of intercultural appropriation.[125]

After this trilogy, Bailey began working with a more global palette. *Big Dada* (2001) featured Kenya's Idi Amin as a showman; *Macbeth: The Opera*

(2002) set Verdi's *Macbeth* in Africa; *Voudou Nation* (2004) was about Haiti; and *House of the Holy Afro* (2004) was a mash-up of Xhosa gospel, cabaret, drag show, Afropop, and house music that Anton Krueger described as "joyously frivolous."[126] Another reviewer described this late-night show, which began at eleven o'clock, as something that "sends up and celebrates universal stereotypes and archetypes of 'Africanness' with a manically mischievous glint in its eye."[127] It's hard to reconcile "joyfully frivolous" with stereotypes of blackness, but it is precisely the gulf between the two that is Bailey's métier.

Over time, Bailey began deliberately designing his shows to reach an international touring market, a shift that proved enormously successful. His later works toured Vienna, Brussels, Berlin, Amsterdam, Bern, Melbourne, Edinburgh, Umea, Zurich, Perth, Adelaide, and London, among many other cities. The seductions of the global touring circuit introduced new motivations that became paramount. As Kellen Hoxworth argues, citing interviews with Bailey, "Baily demonstrates both a profound desire to 'sell [his] work' and his 'ass' to (inter)national agents of World Bank Drama."[128] The lure and prestige of international touring proved so seductive that Bailey's productions are today rarely seen in South Africa. He is no longer reaching South Africans who "scurry to their shacks" to find a few pennies, people he once said were his core constituency. Bailey's work is not even that accessible to culturally elite circles of South Africans unless they are traveling in Europe.[129]

A transitional period in Bailey's oeuvre, the period when he was moving from Xhosa-specific stories to European canonical and global arenas, coincided with his time as a resident artist at the Stellenbosch Spier Estate (a notable South African winery) and with his budding relationships with the touring agent UK Arts International. As Hoxworth has argued, Bailey's dramaturgy at this point "began to shift from intracultural dialectics among various South African constituent groups towards a pronounced (inter)cultural theatrical framework spanning multiple continents and focused on production in international theatre festivals."[130] It was at this time that when he pivoted from framings of the intercultural in South Africa to concoctions of a global intercultural designed for a global market.

In 2009 Bailey began making a series of installation performances about the history of European human zoos called the *Exhibit Series*. The first iteration was called *Blood Diamonds: Terminal* and staged at the National Arts Festival in Grahamstown. This installation was followed by other installments: *Exhibit A: Deutsch-Südwestafrika*, which opened at the Vienna Festival and Festival Theaterformen in 2010, and *Exhibit B: Paradis perdu*, which premiered at the Kunstenfestivaldesarts 2012. Each installment presented tableaux vivants of black performers in still scenarios that evoked specific incidents of colonial atrocity. The underlying images and stories were adapted to the specific European nations where Bailey's performance was installed—the Dutch slave trade, the German extermination of the Herero in German South West Africa, the Belgian and French incursions in the Congo. In Vienna, for instance, they featured the story of Angelo Soliman, a black Austrian resident of notable accomplishment in the eighteenth century who was skinned, stuffed, and displayed as a specimen in an imperial curiosity cabinet when he died. The *Exhibit Series* required audiences to enter the performance venue one at a time as they processed to each installed tableau in which a single black performer in elaborate costume and a thoroughly designed scene posed mutely, but made unrelenting eye contact with each and every spectator. There was supposed to be an *Exhibit C* that addressed British colonization, but instead Bailey created an amalgam of scenes that toured under the now truncated title *Exhibit B* (figure 13).[131] Bailey intermixed the historical scenes with tableaux vivants representing contemporary African refugees in Europe, thereby conflating historical relations between Europe and Africa with contemporary ones.

Despite the shift in Bailey's work over time, his creations have consistently trafficked in the intercultural and forged various kinds of syncretism. He describes his creative method as follows: "Take township traditions and styles, throw them in the blender with rural performance and ceremony, black evangelism, a handful of Western avant-garde and a dash of showbiz, and flick the switch."[132] Bailey's irreverent approach to throwing together a potent intercultural African concoction has found avid consumers in international touring circuits. They have welcomed Bailey's site-specific creations, ritualistic invocations, stylization, irony, and prolific use of pigments and body paints on black performers.

Bailey's work, like Pather's, may quickly pivot in mood from the sacred to camp humor. As Daniel Larlham describes, "Tongue-in-cheek musical numbers can erupt unexpectedly out of moments of ritual intensity; heightened characterizations oscillate between playful caricature and the grotesque, and restrained performances of great simplicity and spiritual depth; an often dreamlike stage reality emerges."[133] Scholar Jennifer Wenzel has written insightfully about Bailey's *The Prophet*:

> The pantheon of benevolent gods called the "Juju," inspired by West African masquerades, is the tip of *The Prophet*'s syncretic iceberg. The Juju perform what Bailey calls "mudras," hand gestures of

Fig. 13. Brett Bailey's *Exhibit B*, 2016. (Photo by Cristos Sarris for Onassis Stegi.)

> Indian dance tradition. Their incantation borrows from Chinua Achebe's *Things Fall Apart* and *The Wizard of Oz*'s "Somewhere over the Rainbow." Characters sing in isiXhosa, Shona (from Zimbabwe), and buNyoro (from Uganda). Rejecting the "passive solitary watching" of contemporary theatre in the European tradition, Bailey seeks the atmosphere of a Hindu or Zen temple or a voodoo ceremony. This borrowed, New Agey spiritualism is awkward in its treatment of old fashioned anticolonial millennialism; Bailey sketches utopian impulses in MGM Technicolor imagery.[134]

The result, Wenzel describes, is "less rainbow nation than chaos nation."[135]

Anton Krueger asserts, quite validly, that Brett Bailey has blazed an aesthetic path that departs from the moralizations that were so overtly and heavily overworked in the tradition of antiapartheid protest that dominated South African theater in the 1970s and 1980s (and even in the 1990s and 2000s with so many nostalgic revivals).[136] While Bailey has certainly forged new paths in South African performance aesthetics, he has not been a lone trailblazer. Robyn Orlin and Jay Pather have long been bushwhacking this wild terrain, and they also eschew simplistic didacticism, causal narrative, and stylistic coherence. All three refuse consolidation, exoneration, and reprieve, and they traffic in potent images and tableaux vivants that draw eclectically from disparate sources, both sacred and profane. Orlin, Pather, and Bailey stage clashes of heterogeneities and irreconcilable differences that arise from South Africa's particular historical circumstances without trying to resolve difference into a coherent, reconciled unity. In some ways, Bailey's aesthetic approach is most closely aligned with Pather's. They both use multiple African languages onstage that are not necessarily translated into English, they both regularly breach the traditional European separation of audience and performers, and they both often force spectators into active physical movement. Both artists often stage their works in nontheatrical outdoor venues with complex histories. Both invoke elements of spiritualism, ritual, and animism onstage. Other similarities include the use of canonical postcolonial texts from West Africa (*Things Fall Apart* and *The Beautyful Ones Are Not Yet Born*), and reference to Broadway and Hollywood motifs ("Somewhere over the Rainbow" and "Don't Cry for Me Argentina").

And yet there is a crucial difference between Bailey and Pather, a fork in the road that leads to very different outcomes. While Pather's works never overtly moralize, they remain anchored by social consciousness and a commitment to imagining otherwise possibilities in South Africa's afterlives of injustice, specifically for people of color. Pather's performances are not about inciting white guilt or provoking white epiphanies. Although these things may happen in performance, they are not the point. Pather's commitment to the Black Consciousness movement serves as a touchstone, compass, and guide. He approaches with overt care cultures in South Africa that have been historically disrespected. His performance works may be infused with irreverence, but they are anchored in a commitment to the hard work of respect. That approach stands in stark contrast to Bailey's intercultural blender. It is Bailey's "potent dash of showbiz" and his cavalier flicking of the power switch that he can access as a privileged white South African man that has recently backfired on him in quite spectacular ways with *Exhibit B*.

In the view of South African critic John Matshikiza, too often respect has been lacking in the intercultural performances white South African performance artists such as Robyn Orlin and Brett Bailey have created. To him, Orlin's and Bailey's experimentation with African ritual and African historical figures such as Makana and King Hintsa have too easily appropriated black material "for white amusement, without any respect for the deeper meaning these images might have for the black community."[137] Matshikiza has said of Brett Bailey's *iMumbo Jumbo* that "most white audiences were stunned by the spectacle, a bold mix of *sangoma* ritual, stylized movement, and cartoon storytelling. Most black people I spoke to disapproved of exactly those combinations. The bottom line was the perceived lack of respect for black history and culture."[138] In contrast, Pather brings together disparate cultural elements with a more subtle hand. He is attentive to cultural nuance and is keen to present this material with precision and care while also plumbing the subconscious world of postapartheid dreamscapes, all of which makes his work resistant to consumption in the elite First World festival circuit, more apt to mystify than to polarize his audiences.

While Pather works to find the right fit for every gesture, movement, vocabulary, tradition, and ritual element he puts on his stage, he is not especially vexed by questions of ownership and cultural appropriation. Pather feels entitled to draw on a wide cultural palette without necessarily seeking permission. When "so-called cultural forms are appropriated, decontextualized and used as symbols within a theatrical context," says Pather, "I remain unprecious about their origin and sanctity."[139] For him the primary negotiation is with his dancers, who are generally people he has worked with for many years, in some cases over two decades. The longevity of those relationships lays a foundation for candor and honesty in the collaborative encounter that is simply not possible when dancers are brought in for one project. As Pather says, "There is an understanding around what kind of latitude they have for objecting to something."[140] Pather believes "strongly in the individual as a member of a nation. I cannot seek the approval of an entire group of people who I might assume as custodians of a traditional or classical form. I do however, negotiate directly with a dancer on the floor not as a representative but as an individual sufficiently aware of the discourse and issues involved."[141] While he is not particularly concerned about questions of cultural ownership, Pather feels an intense obligation to the performers; he describes their creative process as a "soul searching." For him, the integrity of each dance element must be explored with a great deal of specificity in order to discover the "exact fit" between elements.

And here we return to that key word: respect. To this word we must attach another key concept: intention. While scholars have long ago dispensed with the "intentional fallacy"—that is, reading creative works according to what an artist intended—I would argue that in the context of performances enacted in places that have potent afterlives of injustice, the impact of an artistic work must consider the creator's intent, especially when that creator is representing cultures that have experienced great harm. Even if an artist's intention in making art has little bearing on audience reception, intention invariably shapes decisions in the creative process, especially in a fraught cultural context where the afterlives of injustice are so pervasive and enduring.

Cultural critic Briahna Joy Gray proposes that instead of focusing on the concept of cultural appropriation, we should focus on the two separate issues of cultural exploitation and cultural disrespect.[142] Gray suggests four key questions that can help artists and critics think through questions of cultural exchange and injustice:

> 1) Is there a historic record of exploitation between the appropriator and the originating group? 2) Is the originating group and its culture being celebrated, appreciated, and respected, or are they being degraded, mocked and accessorized? . . . 3) Is the appropriator actually *claiming* to be the owner or innovator, or allowing the media to create a false origin narrative? . . . 4) Is differential economic enrichment occurring? Is the cultural product more valuable in the hands of the appropriator, and does that have wider financial or political consequences for certain groups?[143]

To these questions, we may add two more in the context of South African intercultural performance: How deep is an artist/creator's investment in forging decolonized forms when their work is about South African cultures that historically have been divided? And is knowing about each other's cultures really the primary step in decolonization? Pather has asked: "Why should I know about your culture? I should tolerate as you as a human being, [but] why do I need to know more about you?"[144] Recent work on friendship in South Africa has posed similar questions about the validity and possibility of ties that bind and whether such ties as friendship can be forged across violent histories. Jon Soske and Shannon Walsh conclude that "Thinking [about] white supremacy and anti-blackness requires that we confront a relationality that exceeds the language of relation: the constitutive violence of settler civil society works to render full, ethical reciprocity between white and black—that is, friendship in the classic, Aristotelian sense—impossible *in advance*."[145] If relational reciprocity is ipso facto impossible in South Africa, what are the implications for aesthetic relationality across cultures in artistic practice?

Pather's approach to art making—his irreverence, abrupt pivots of tone, combinations of radically disparate cultural motifs—diverges from that of both Orlin and Bailey around this question of respect. He excavates particular traditions of movement and brings them onstage with an awareness of and appreciation for elements that have historically been disrespected. He is very careful about toying with forms that under apartheid were demonized or commercially appropriated and distorted. And he is acutely aware of how quickly intercultural concoctions can become toxic.

Bailey's expressed motivations for making theatrical works in the early years of his career included creating works that are accessible to all South Africans and bringing spirit and spiritualism into the lives of all South Africans.[146] He has long taken umbrage at what he calls "political correctness," although sometimes the rejection of his work has come most viscerally from the underprivileged communities he claims to champion. His tone can be flippantly contemptuous of his critics, even if the negative responses come from Xhosa audiences who live in a world of profound material insecurity that they see as deeply imbricated with the spiritual insecurity his performances depict. When *Ipi Zombi?* was about to be performed in Bhongweni, a place near where the bus accident that was the source for the play occurred, this prospect was intolerable "for forty-seven women still on the hit-list, and their terrified relatives," according to Helen Bradford.[147] A play about a witch hunt is not likely to be helpful to those who are literally being hunted and killed as suspected witches. The mimetic and ontic realms of theater are occasionally entirely incompatible, even toxic, especially in the hands of a privileged white male auteur who is insulated by his economic privilege and whiteness. As Jennifer Wenzel has said, Bailey's "irreverence towards the politics of residual privilege and suffering" sometimes "borders on dilettantish callousness."[148]

The paradoxes of Bailey and his performances are striking and volatile. He has courageously (and/or foolhardily) plumbed the depths of the afterlives of injustice, not just in South Africa but also globally with his *Exhibit Series* about the ghastly history of the European human zoo. Some of his works have suggested the promise and potential of mobilizing the afterlives of previously aborted decolonial movements, such as the Xhosa cattle killing. As Wenzel contends, Bailey's *The Prophet* was actually *about* the problem of afterlives—that is, the living effects of violent histories of the Eastern Cape that are neither over nor resolved. But in her view, the play offered

> little sense of the specific ways in which contemporary South Africa ails from the sickness the play aims to heal. Instead the play's interest is in the restless past—its menacing presence in the form of the Dead, as well as the desire to undo error and defeat. The play's ceremony reverses the logic of cattle-killing prophecies; the Dead can

> save the living only by going away. *The Prophet* performs a strange kind of ghostdancing, inviting a haunting in order to posit a future perfect of a healed nation in which the past will have been laid to rest. The future's past, in this sense, will be a dead past.[149]

Bradford is less charitable in her assessment of Bailey's collected *Plays of Miracle and Wonder*:

> This is groundbreaking drama in a democratic South Africa? Smash-and-grab raids on audiences and actors, on history, religion, health and art, are the best that is on offer? Assuredly, affirm critics, dazzled by Africanization of a western genre. Others have seen crime. One does not have to be a rural pensioner, grimly advancing on Bailey and his guys, to sense the violence of male gangsterism lurking just beneath the surface of this glitzy book.[150]

While some people in rural areas where Bailey has conducted his "ethnographic research" have indeed physically attacked him and his company, Bailey has nevertheless continued to experience widespread international success, touring the world with his iconoclastic productions of "bewitching visions and primal high-jinx," to reference the subtitle of his own anthology of plays.[151]

While Brett Bailey has long been known as the bad boy of the South African theater scene, it was not until he created the incendiary *Exhibit Series*, which provoked protests and demands for its closure in France and England and other European venues, that he became notoriously controversial internationally (figure 14). *Exhibit A*, first staged in 2010 in Vienna in an abandoned wing of the Ethnographic Museum, focused on the history of German South West Africa (present-day Namibia), including the decapitation of Herero men. *Exhibit B* expanded to include Belgian and French colonial incursions in Africa. *Exhibit C* was intended to foreground the British and Portuguese colonial past.[152]

Scholars Chokri Ben Chikha and Karel Arnaut distill the various installations in Bailey's *Exhibit Series* into five types of characters:

> 1) a half-naked "Saartjie Baartman"–type of figure rotating on a plateau. The other types are: 2) a "Samira Adamu" (Brussels) or "Aamir Ageeb" (Berlin) figure of an illegal immigrant who died on a forced return flight home, strapped to an aircraft seat and gagged with white packing tape; 3) scenes referring to events in the Belgian or

Fig. 14. South African playwright and installation artist Brett Bailey (*right*), working with an actor during a rehearsal of *Exhibit B* at the Musée Sainte-Croix in Poitiers, France, 2014. (Photo by Marlene Awaad/*New York Times*/ Redux.)

> German colonial history which involve (sexual) violence; 4) figures in contemporary clothes who are identified as refugees or undocumented migrants, and staged as arrestees (sporting enlarged mug shots and record cards); and 5) a display comprising four singers whose bodies are encased and whose "heads" produce polyphonic songs that provide eerie background music for the entire installation.[153]

Bailey's *Exhibit Series* invariably collapses wide-ranging references, positing white Europe as a uniform totality that is contrasted with a flattened, totalized Africa. Black people are depicted as mute and without agency, on the receiving end of unrelenting violence and dehumanization. We do not see evidence of their resistance other than the performers' penetrating stare directed at those who gaze on them. The entire exhibit trafficked in a stark binary of black and white that allowed little room for spectators who come from a range of backgrounds to place themselves with nuance, specificity, and complexity into the situation. Some critics, such as Yvette Gresle, contend that neither Bailey nor his presenters took black audiences into account.[154] Bailey sees otherwise: "I do not portray the world in the binaries of black and white, wrong and right, good and evil. I am an artist who works with colours and shades."[155] It was a surprise to Bailey that the most vocal and activist protesters of *Exhibit B* were people of color.[156] He was further baffled about why so many of his critics were on the political left: "I thought it would provoke the right wing," he said. "I had no idea it would provoke the left wing."[157]

In artistic tumults such as this one, it can be valuable to disentangle intent from impact. What did Bailey intend to accomplish? He spoke at length about his motivations in a public statement published in the *Guardian*: "It has not been my intention to alienate people with this work. To challenge perceptions and histories, yes. Explicitly to offend, no. But I work in difficult and contested territory that is fraught with deep pain, anger and hatred. There are no clear paths through this territory, and it is littered with landmines."[158] If Bailey's statements about his intent in making *Exhibit B* are to be believed, then the distance between his intent and impact is one of the most notable performative misfires in recent theatrical history.[159] Protests, petitions, and sometimes-violent confrontations around this show in Berlin, London, and France mobilized many people of color, for whom the images Bailey summoned were intolerable, as were the underlying labor conditions for the black performers. While Bailey contests such accusations and takes exception to anyone who judges *Exhibit B* without seeing it, he nevertheless acknowledges that the impact of the performance was not what he had intended. And he regrets that. He wrote in a Facebook posting:

> I regret that EXHIBIT B has polarized people.
> I regret that a multidimensional performance piece, which has meaning in the intimate dynamic interaction between performers and spectators, has been judged on the basis of 2 dimensional photographs.
> I acknowledge that seeing a photograph of a shackled black woman and reading that it is the work of a white South African man can cause deep offence. I wish that photographs of EXHIBIT B had not been published, and that the only access that people had to the work is through the living, vibrating, profound experience of recognizing the equality and humanity in us all, and the horrors of systems that continue to stifle this.[160]

The explosive reception of the *Exhibit Series* could have been predicted, it seems to me, especially by an artist who has provoked firestorms of controversy throughout his entire career. Scholars Ben Chikha and Arnaut anticipated this controversy in their 2013 article about *Exhibit B*, well before the public firestorm about the work reached its climactic pitch the following year. They see *Exhibit B* as problematic for several reasons. First, different "types" on display "have the potential for eliciting different viewer positions. However, this is thwarted because the images end up being construed as a binary grid that is racial in nature."[161] Bailey's on-site adaptations did not incorporate local categories for debating and understanding alterity—whether among ex-colonial subjects, migrants, or members of ethnic groups. A range of culturally particular understandings of identity and race in various European contexts became subordinated to the performance's stark binary of black and white, Africa and Europe. Second, by putting black artists who represent human zoos on display before overwhelmingly white bourgeois European audiences, Bailey's representation too easily collapsed into a re-presentation of the very human zoos he intended to critique.

There seems to be no question that Bailey's arrow, which he designed to strike at the heart of European racism, became instead one of the historical boomerangs that Ralph Ellison predicted, striking the artist himself decisively across the head.[162] Peter Crawley, writing about *Exhibit B*'s production at the Galway International Arts Festival, commented: "It's surprising, given Bailey's determination to implicate the audience in his display of power and exploitation, that he has not fully considered his own place within it."[163] Bailey, the auteur director, professed that "*Exhibit B* is about the dynamics of people with power framing other people in a particular way so they can exploit them, take their territory and take profit from them." Crawley's response was that this statement seemed to be "a point on which both Bailey's admirers and his disapprovers finally agree."

CONCLUSION

When cultures that are saturated with the afterlives of injustice come together onstage, through what methods and terms can they engage with one another? Negotiation may be a hopelessly compromised concept since it so often leaves racialized power differentials, especially from white supremacy, firmly in place. If cross-racial friendship is not possible in

South Africa today, as Soske and Walsh contend, what are the implications for cross-racial artistic collaboration?[164] As I have argued, interweaving as a theoretical idea for how disparate cultures might come together in performance seems too invested in normative notions of reconciliation, in the act of bringing disparate strands together into something neat and tidy. What may be needed is rather a pulling apart—the undoing of white supremacy, the unmasking of how racialized power inequalities corrupt relationships, the exposure of recurrent inequities in collaboration, and a revelation of the subjective dreamscapes such conditions produce.

Orlin, Pather, and Bailey have addressed questions of sharing the stage in contemporary South Africa in quite different ways. Orlin has drawn attention to the persistence of white supremacy by framing black performances with white commentary. But in the end, she has held tightly to her place at the center, and as Achille Mbembe has argued, decolonization is fundamentally a question about (re)defining the center. Bailey has summoned cultural references in a busy chaotic jumble that sometimes stays all on the surface, at other times plumbs inchoate, potent depths. His method is irreverent and imprecise: "Take township traditions and styles, throw them in the blender with rural performance and ceremony, black evangelism, a handful of Western avant-garde and a dash of showbiz, and flick the switch."[165] He restaged historical human zoos with what he thought was a critical difference: the direct visual engagement between a lone performer and a lone spectator. But that eye contact was not enough for some audience members to undo the colonializing and racist legacies he was invoking. Pather's method for navigating these tricky issues is to discover the dances between the dances: what happens when one culture encounters, abuts, collides with, fuses with, or even destroys another? What guides his experimentation is a commitment to the subterranean depths of subjectivity, the body as an archive of the past traumas of apartheid, and performers as vessels of otherwise possibilities. He is also guided by questions of respect. But the line between respect and mockery isn't always clear. For instance, how do gumboot dancers and mine workers who practice this dance form feel about Pather's gender-bending send-up of gumboot in *Body of Evidence*? Briahna Joy Gray's reframing of the cultural appropriation question from a rights-based discourse of ownership to an examination of cultural exploitation and cultural disrespect is helpful, but it is not a panacea. It is not something that resolves these very tricky issues.

Works by Robyn Orlin, Jay Pather, and Brett Bailey reveal the complexity of "sharing" the stage in a new South Africa, the challenges of interculturalism in a radically heterogeneous place, especially one potently saturated with the afterlives of injustice. Their artistic careers also illuminate the enticements, seductions, and distortions created by the global marketplace of intercultural performance touring. Without a doubt, the works of Orlin, Pather, and Bailey are fresh, original, visually arresting, pathbreaking, and genre busting. Nevertheless, one can discern resonance with the epigraph from novelist Ayi Kwei Armah that opens this chapter: "How completely the new thing took after the old."[166]

When one considers the many collisions and abrupt pivots that Orlin, Pather, and Bailey unleash in their performances, one can almost hear Gerard Bester, the frantic master of ceremonies in Orlin's iconic work *Daddy, I've seen this piece six times before and I still don't know why they're hurting each other*, anxiously admonishing: "Don't break the theater!" But perhaps the theater needs to be broken or is already broken. This very brokenness may create necessary conditions for new dispensations and new ways of sharing on South African stages. Orlin, Pather, and Bailey share irreverence for received conventions, and a penchant for bold and disruptive interventions not just in content but in form. While they have not broken the theater, they have broken open the postapartheid performance world with inventions, disruptions, and new aesthetics that have pushed boundaries. They took performances to shopping malls where performers repelled off the side of buildings and onto hillsides where audiences sat on hay bales. They refused to fetishize technique and the mastery of artistic craft. They drew on South Africa's tremendous range of cultures, races, and identities, and they put a great tangle of references onstage with a high degree of tolerance for incoherence. Even when some experiments have misfired or mystified, or have led to impacts that radically diverged from the artist's stated intentions, they have wedged open a space for the potential that some new things may not take after the old.

FOUR | Of Names and Frames: Faustin Linyekula and Gregory Maqoma

> When you are serious about names, you cannot collapse into yourself.
> —Faustin Linyekula

> I could never pronounce my own name: Gregory.
> —Gregory Maqoma

> Why not use the fantastic energy of guitars and voices not to sustain dreams as thin as the cheap paper handkerchiefs sold in the streets of Kinshasa, but on the contrary to speak of the difficulties, dead ends, mistakes and the poor legacy of our fathers?
> —Faustin Linyekula

Jean Comaroff and John L. Comaroff's book *Theory from the South* provocatively asks whether in the present moment the Global South "affords privileged insight into the workings of the world at large."[1] They invite readers to theorize from the Global South, to work against the ubiquitous centrality of Europe in academic knowledge production, the tendency to perpetually see the North as epicenter of intellectual agendas, the wellspring of valued lines of inquiry. But what does it mean to actually theorize *from* the South? And what does it look like when artists are the ones doing the theorizing? The latter is not a question the Comaroffs ask, but it is one that I think we should ask. I contend that many of the artists covered in this book are theorizing in and from the Global South, in and through their art making and creative processes. This book is an attempt to distill theories embedded in the art making of the artists located in and working from the Global South, and to amplify these ideas, helping make them more widely accessible and known.

Colonization creates irreparable ruptures when invading forces denigrate existing cultural forms through regimes of violence and dispossession. Navigating colonialism's wake is fraught, the route unclear. In theorizing about aesthetics and creativity that must grapple with the afterlives of colonial injustice, both Faustin Linyekula and Gregory Maqoma gravitate toward concepts from Nigerian Nobel laureate writer Wole Soyinka. He has said:

> Once you have a break, a real rupture, whether it's a physical one or a mental one—because you can have a rupture when an invading force, a concrete force, persuades you, or persuades your leaders that what they had before was not valid—so you go through a period when either willingly or by force, you accept that there is a totally new matrix of conceptualization of creativity, of education, and consequently of reproducing your own existence. So you can't accept it as a rupture. On the other hand, and . . . and some artists are doing this—they try to reconstruct the past in its anterior form. That is a very painful process because cultures evolve. . . . I'm afraid it's a problem that has to be approached from many forms. I will never suggest one approach is superior to the other. I will like to judge what results from the approach as being valid, maybe, for that particular artist, or for that particular time. The important thing is always to remember that the past is not dead.[2]

Like Soyinka, Maqoma and Linyekula approach the problem of colonial legacies through multiple forms. They are searching to discover new matrices of conceptualizing creativity while at the same time selectively taking up "anterior" forms, those that predate colonization, but without romanticized assumptions that the past is inherently superior or fully recoverable.[3] One cannot, as Soyinka says, "reconstruct the past in its anterior form." Cultures evolve.

This chapter focuses on the theorizations and creative innovations embedded in the work of choreographers Faustin Linyekula Ngoy from the Democratic Republic of Congo (DRC) and Gregory Vuyani Maqoma from South Africa. These two performers have collaborated together intensively for over two decades. Each explores the afterlives of injustice through the performativity of names, especially as deployed, declaimed, and artistically deconstructed and remembered in performance. They focus on names and physical staging as charged nodal points, threads in a large, messy tangle that, if pulled insistently enough, can cause the tenacious knots of the afterlives of injustice to give way. Both artists approach names as verbs—a doing, a process, a performative action, and a springboard to artistic creativity. These can be personal names, names of cities or countries, or names of artistic genres—like, for instance, "contemporary African dance." They focus on the etymologies and genealogies of names, how names both carry history and remake history. Maqoma and Linyekula focus on how names sit in the mouth and sometimes demand our tongues to wrap around unfamiliar sounds. Names are at once intensely private (what could be more personal?) and highly public, for they serve as a key nodal point in a complex web of connections and relationships, the link between self and other. Names proclaim a unique identity for each individual while simultaneously connecting that individual to family and nation. Thus, as much as this chapter is about these two choreographers and their names, it is also about their relationship with each other, as well as with fellow artists, and their larger collectives and networks beyond the self. As Linyekula says, "When you are serious about names, you cannot collapse into yourself."[4]

Performance space is also a core preoccupation of both artists, especially the legacies and ideologies embedded in physical staging conventions. For instance, a proscenium staging that separates performer from audience is a European tradition. Circular formations are often seen as more communal and more "authentically" African. Like names, prosceniums and circles are frames that shape perception. Maqoma's and Linyekula's artistic works implicitly and explicitly question the ideologies that saturate theatrical staging, especially the proscenium stage as a spatial apparatus inherited from Western theater. The proscenium is generally a foreign import in much of Africa, with a performance genealogy that is thoroughly entangled in colonial histories.[5] Yet proscenium staging has been fully adopted throughout the continent, especially for concert dances and scripted dramas. Just as Ngũgĩ wa Thiong'o has argued that African writers must question the "fatalistic logic" by which authors adopted European languages in the early days of independence, Faustin Linyekula likewise argues that contemporary African artists should deeply interrogate the use of proscenium staging for African performances.[6] What ideologies are embedded in the proscenium? Linyekula sees the proscenium as a "clear extension of Europe—a colonial stage," one that ultimately defines everything from the perspective of an ideal spectator's eye, historically the king's.[7] When one puts African traditional dances, which often are organized with circle formations, on a proscenium stage without taking into account the question of "whose point of view you are constructing them from," says Linyekula, "then something's wrong from the onset."[8] But neither does Linyekula advocate an uncritical nativist reclamation of the circle, as though simply shifting from a proscenium to a circle would perform decolonization. He rather advocates that one should interrogate staging conventions and make deliberate choices. Linyekula says Congolese typically make circles when they dance. Circles, or cyphers, are likewise common in hip-hop dance. But in working with various dancers, Linyekula refuses to allow them to form a circle. His rationale is that circles create and express community, "but that is not the world we live in"—meaning especially the world of the DRC, his home country. The DRC's histories of wars, violence, exploitation, capitalist economies of extraction, and waves of related social traumas have profoundly strained communal ties. "The circle is broken," says Linyekula, "and if we want to make the circle again, we must take responsibility"—meaning the community must take responsibility for re-creating the ties that bind.[9]

In this chapter, I start by telling how these two artists met and began making performances together. I then focus on a dance theater piece Linyekula created in 2009 called *more more more . . . future*, which toured in Europe and the United States.[10] I also analyze a piece by Maqoma called *Beautiful Me*, a one-person show first commissioned by the FNB Dance Umbrella in Johannesburg, South Africa, where it premiered in March 2007. *Beautiful Me* toured internationally, debuting in the United States in 2009.[11] As much as the show is autobiographical, it is also a dialogic work, created collaboratively through a series of conversations, both verbal and embodied, with multiple choreographers, including Linyekula, Vincent Mantsoe of South Africa, and the London-based choreographer Akram Khan, who is of South Asian descent. *Beautiful Me* is very much a work in dialogue with other artists working in, from, or in relation to the Global South.

The genres, styles, movement vocabularies, and forms created by Linyekula and Maqoma disrupt existing, familiar categories. Is their work dance? Dance theater? African dance? Contemporary African dance? Performance art? The desire to place their work—to name its format—and the artists' disruption of these inherited categories creates dynamic tension. Why name or classify the work at all, one may ask? Because names matter, as Linyekula and Maqoma express so vividly. As problematic as names can be, we need them, we depend on them, they set expectations, and these tendencies cannot be avoided. At a conference on African and Afro-Caribbean theater at the University of California, Berkeley, in 2008, many of the African performing artists in attendance "declared that they wanted to be known simply as artists and not as Africans or black artists," as Frank B. Wilderson III recalls.[12] While scholars may debate the theoretical assumptions behind such claims, one must also acknowledge, as Wilderson does, that there can be "something in the force of the artists' cry just to be artists that resonate[s] with the force that first turned subjects into cargo."[13] What is at stake performatively and politically in the naming process and in its staging?

PAN-AFRICAN ENCOUNTERS: LINYEKULA AND MAQOMA

War, violence, and the closure of universities in Zaire (as the DRC was formerly known) led Faustin Linyekula to leave his home country and go into exile in 1993. He fled to East Africa, to Kenya, where he cofounded with Opiyo Okach and Afrah Tenambergen (from Germany/Ethiopia) Kenya's first contemporary dance company, La Compagnie Gàara. The group garnered a prize at Angola's International Dance Festival in 1998, putting Linyekula on the map for international presenters. He went to stay in Europe for a time, but he decided to return to his home country in 2001, by which time it had been renamed the Democratic Republic of Congo.

Gregory Maqoma happened to be on tour in Kenya in 1996 with South African choreographer Vincent Mantsoe and the Johannesburg-based company Moving into Dance Mophatong when he met Linyekula for the first time. The chemistry between them was visceral and electric, and they soon decided to collaborate artistically. As Maqoma recalls,

> We knew right away that we wanted to do something together. That was *Tales off the Mud Wall*, created in Vienna in 2000. Meeting Faustin Linyekula left a mark on me, touched me profoundly. I started to question the state of mind of an artist, a human being living in Africa with all of these atrocities. It has become a part of the weight that I carry. Yet there was extreme tension between the two of us because we also come from very different contexts, very different realities. I consider his realities to be unbearable, impossible for any human being to take on. But my realities were still bearable. Even though I experienced the apartheid era, I come from a fairly sheltered background. I always lived with my family, and I never had to go into exile. So I became very involved in this relationship. He had things that I had missed, and I wanted to be able to grasp them. It was very important for me to stay in contact, even after he returned to the Congo, to follow from afar his new life in that country.[14]

Maqoma and Linyekula got the opportunity to collaborate in 2000 when the Wiener Tanzwochen Festival in Vienna, Austria, accepted their proposal for a work called *Tales off the Mud Wall*. But the process of mounting the work was not smooth. Maqoma recalls that the Vienna organizers questioned their artistic choices and "bombarded us with press cuttings on wars and AIDS in Africa. It was very clear they wanted us to indulge in their formula and to feed their hunger."[15] However, Maqoma and Linyekula "chose to override" the producers' stereotypical projections and go against expectations.[16] Rather than focus on overtly African themes, or indeed on any geographically specific content, they went in a formalist direction by contrasting stillness and motion. "Faustin preferred not to move as a way of commenting through the work," says Maqoma. "So he decided to create this sense of a statue that carries a light on his back, a neon light."[17] Staying in one position without moving produced a tremendous tension; the effort required to perform such stasis became evident in the sweat pouring from Linyekula's brow. Maqoma went in a different direction: "I preferred . . . moving as a way of commenting." He was in constant motion. Each performer responded to the imposition of African stereotypes differently, but what they shared was a focus on "silence, tolerance, and honesty."[18] *Tales off the Mud Wall* refused to directly engage the themes and topics projected onto these two African artists. They refused both the perennial negative African stereotypes (about suffering, AIDS, genocide, war, poverty, and famine) and their Janus-face opposite (romanticized notions of Africa as exotic, colorful, primitive, and authentic, in touch with "real" identity and culture).[19]

Vienna audiences, which were overwhelmingly white, had to engage directly with Maqoma and Linyekula as two people, two bodies onstage. The artists decided to conclude this performance by going to the front of the stage and shining a light on the audience for a few minutes. Their desire was to disrupt the imposed otherness of the "African" identity that had been saddled on them by their Viennese producers. The result was unexpected: the audience stood and would not leave, caught in paroxysms of clapping and crying. The show could not come to an end, much to the surprise and consternation of the artists. Maqoma recalls,

> As the drama was unfolding in front of us, I stood there thinking: "Is Africa in so much pain? Why can't we see beyond what CNN reports?" I started crying because we had simply failed to change perceptions. People see what they want to see and they hear what they want to hear. I felt compromised. . . . The audience failed to see beyond what they knew of the African continent.[20]

This inaugural collaboration in a European city that labeled both Linyekula and Maqoma as African foundered because the audience could not see beyond that label. Names, it turns out, are more tenacious frames than prosceniums.

In dance works each choreographer created independently in subsequent years, motifs about names recur, as does the use of deliberate address to the audience, the breaking of the fourth wall, and attention drawn to the proscenium. I see these moments as, in essence, revised reperformances of that defining encounter in Vienna in 2000 at the edge of the proscenium stage. Partway through his solo work *Beautiful Me,* Gregory Maqoma says, "My name is Gregory Vuyani Maqoma. I have plenty of exotic stories to tell, so which one would you like to hear tonight? Which one? Which one? Which one? Come on. Come on. Come on, Mobutu, which one? I am an African dancer, I sell exotic stories to survive."[21] Faustin Linyekula makes a similar statement in his one-person show *Le Cargo* (2011), which also toured widely in the United States and Europe: "I am an African dancer! I have exotic stories to sell! Which one do you want to hear today?"[22] Yet outside of the performance venue where such lines are spoken, Linyekula completely rejects the label "African dancer." At a conference on contemporary African dance held in Durban in 2004, Linyekula lamented, "Every time there is a dance gathering somewhere, we discuss Africa. But really I don't care about Africa. As far as my dancing is concerned—when I'm creating—I care about myself. . . . I don't care about Africa because Africa—at least my portion of Africa—the one that I experience in my flesh, doesn't care about me."[23] "Africa" is a large, impersonal construct, shot through with stereotypes and preconceptions, defined and overdetermined by Western projections. This notion of Africa doesn't care about an individual like Linyekula because it is wrapped up in overdetermined ideas. Rather than discussing Africa, Linyekula wants to discuss something far more specific: names. For him, the excavation of the histories and meanings of names yields far more insights than a discussion of Africa, and this observation is equally true whether he is performing in his Studios Kabako in Kisangani in the DRC or in concert houses in Paris or New York. His approach is to name names, to illuminate their instability, to reveal their widely divergent claims. There is a patience and precision in this work, a demand that we, the audience, sit with names as utterances both simple and profound. He is interested in his own personal name, the name of his town and country, the name of his fathers and family members. The etymology of names, and the power invested in those who are able to name and rename. Names as a primary, founding act of colonization, and names as a primary, founding act of agency and individuation.

As with his patient excavation of names, Linyekula likewise demands that we sit with the enforced separation that the proscenium creates. Linyekula says,

> My blood is really blazing as if in flames, and my history is in ruins. What does it mean to create under such circumstances? What does it mean to come forward and say: my name is this and that—when just a few years back I was told that my name was not really [that] and overnight it changed? I don't know if I'm talking about dance here. I don't know if this is contemporary African dance or art—but whatever I do today, for me, it is simply trying to stay alive. Trying to look up, stand in front and say: "Hey, I'm still here—I haven't given up resisting." Maybe that's why the Western proscenium stage suits me because with that setting, I'm allowed to just stand, come forward and say: "Hello, here I am. Do you see me? And if I say my name is this, do you hear that?" And that applies whether I'm here in Europe and maybe more when I'm in Kinshasa.[24]

In coming to the edge of the stage and facing his audience, Linyekula is saying, "'Hello. I'm here.' And actually, you know what, I'm just as European as you are. I studied Latin for six years in high school with Reverend Father Lommel, who came to Congo in 1955 and stayed there until 2004. . . . I speak French, for god's sake, it's my first language."[25] Language, like a proscenium, or like a thrust or arena stage, is a way of shaping one's worldview. The reality, Linyekula asserts, is that he and Europe are entangled, yet only one party in this relationship readily acknowledges their mutual imbrication. He is asserting, "I'm just as European; but if you don't acknowledge it—too bad for you. How can we deal with this? Whether you like it or not, we are stuck together. We are stuck together."[26] He is simply stating a fact.

Names likewise galvanize Maqoma. In the middle of his one-person dance theater piece *Beautiful Me*, Maqoma leaps repeatedly into the air, almost as if he were jumping to dunk a basketball into a hoop, while striking to the left and right with his arms, as if swatting away, using the downward motion of his elbows to bring him back to the floor. He declaims, bestowing on himself not his own name but that of his long-term collaborator, "I am Faustin Linyekula Ngoy, I come from the Democratic Republic of Congo, the former Zaire, the former Free State of the Congo, the former Léopoldville, the former private property of Leopold the 2nd, King of Belgium: YES!" At that resounding affirmation—"YES!"—Maqoma lands with a thud.[27]

After an extended silence during which he crouches in a position of readiness and peers at the audience, Maqoma then vaults into the air again, landing in a way that punctuates his speech: "I am Gregory Vuyani

Maqoma, I come from the Republic of South Africa, the former Union of South Africa: YES!"

These contradictory enunciations—of individual names and of the ever-shifting names of two particular African countries—expose the unstable ground on which Faustin Linyekula and Gregory Maqoma stand. In their home countries of the DRC and South Africa, the afterlives of colonial injustice continue to exert a corrosive force in myriad ways, but perhaps nowhere more ubiquitously and subtlety than in the realm of proper nouns. Like land located in what seismologists call liquefaction zones, a name can quickly give way, losing its apparent solidity and becoming anything but terra firma, especially during periods of political transition and regime change in the postcolony. At such moments, names liquefy: the former private property of Leopold II of Belgium (from the mid-nineteenth century) becomes Léopoldville (1881) becomes the Free State of the Congo (1885) becomes Zaire (1971) becomes the Democratic Republic of Congo (1997), which is not to be confused with the neighboring Republic of Congo. Instability of names fundamentally erodes both the perceptions and conditions of identity, belonging, rights, citizenship, and kinship; it erodes their reality as well. "I name" is one of the commonest types of explicit performatives, according to speech act theorist J. L. Austin.[28] It is also one of the most foundational. Without a name, how can one get a birth certificate, a passport, or, under apartheid, a passbook—the so-called book of life or "dompas" that documented and controlled where black people could live, work, and travel? Without a name, to whom or what does one belong? Without a stable name, who are you?

The international careers of both Linyekula and Maqoma have been so successful that they could, if they so chose, locate their work primarily in Europe, where the funding models would be far more favorable than what they face at home. South African choreographers Robyn Orlin and Vincent Mantsoe, who have also attained international prominence, chose to make Europe a creative base.[29] Linyekula and Maqoma, however, have chosen to remain centered in the Global South, in their respective home countries. As Brenda Dixon Gottschild says of Linyekula, "He could have set up shop in some European locale—maybe Paris or London—and become the next new thing on the exotic-erotic block. Instead, Linyekula chose the path of most resistance and returned to work in his homeland."[30] Both Maqoma and Linyekula feel that their stories and distinctive visions as artists are based in Africa, and their primary political commitments are there as well. African artists, as with artists anywhere, should be at liberty to choose whichever part of the world proves most conducive to doing their creative work.

But the choice to be primarily located in the Global South represents a very particular commitment: it is a refusal of enticing opportunities to work in places with far more financial resources, and a choice to practice work in a way that is at once in, from, and *for* the Global South.

FAUSTIN LINYEKULA: BETWEEN A LULLABY AND A SCREAM

Born in Ubundu near Kisangani in the former Zaire in 1974, Faustin Linyekula comes from the farthest navigable point inland in the northeastern part of the Democratic Republic of Congo, a place made famous both by Joseph Conrad's 1899 *Heart of Darkness* (Kisangani is near Stanley Falls) and by V. S. Naipaul's 1979 *A Bend in the River*.[31] Linyekula is a prolific artist who works at the crossroads of cultures and forms. In addition to *more more more. . . future* (2009), major works by Linyekula and his Studios Kabako include *Spectacularly Empty II* (2003), about "'Life and a half' or 'half-life,' life and death within a single day";[32] *The Dialogue Series: i. Franco* (2006), a work focused on Linyekula's childhood hero, the legendary Congolese rhumba musician Franco, aka François Luambo Luanzo Makiadi; *Pour en finir avec Bérénice* (2010), a theatrical argument with Jean Racine's 1670 neoclassical tragedy *Bérénice; Le Cargo* (2011), Linyekula's first solo work, a meditation on the village of Oblio, where he spent part of his childhood and where his first memories of dance were sonic because he was forbidden to see the dances; *La creation du monde 1923–2012* (2012), a piece that Linyekula calls a "ballet of shame," created in conversation with a trilogy of 1920s "negro-Cubist ballets" by Swiss choreographer Blaise Cendrars and librettist Jean Börlin;[33] and *In Search of Dinozord / Sur les traces de Dinozord* (2012), which is in part a requiem about a "last tribe" of Congolese artists (including Linyekula's friend Kabako, who died of the plague, and other artists forced by politics to flee into exile, as was Linyekula himself in the period 1993 to 2001). The score of this last work includes Mozart's *Requiem*, organ music by Arvo Pärt, and "Voodoo Chile" by Jimi Hendrix.[34] Dinozord is also the name of one of Linyekula's dancers; it means "the last of my kind."[35]

Linyekula works with an aesthetic of survival, creating assemblages of elements at hand from what he calls the "ruins" around him. Driven by an urgent and pragmatic will to persist, Linyekula's performances fiercely seize on the possibility of dreams, hope, and visions of a future from within a place, a situation, a city, a country so devastated by destruction that, in Linyekula's view, "the only way of being subversive is to be positive."[36] He says: "The most important thing is not the aesthetic object. Art is not important. The most important thing is to believe in something in a context where it is impossible to believe in anything. The work is thus an act of faith."[37] The struggle at the core of the work is not over ownership of aesthetic sources or questions of cultural appropriation or anxieties about cultural authenticity. The battle is rather to *believe*. Linyekula mobilizes any and all useful sources in that urgent quest for not just *a* future, or *the* future but rather *more more more* future, without even waiting to insert commas in between each "more."

Throughout Linyekula's oeuvre, names have been both a preoccupation and a central component of his theorization. In several different writings, lectures, and performances, Linyekula has described the names attached to him and his land of birth over time. His focus in his performance work is on how names serve as an archive of relationships and networks. Names, he argues, are resources to combat and demystify the intense isolation of the individual in a situation such as his in the DRC. In his essay "Corks and Memories," Linyekula recalls "lines from a conversation with my fathers" from 1974, "just a minute after I was born":

> My fathers: Here is a name for you, here's your home.
>
> I (repeating after my fathers): My name is Linyekula, son of Mobutu, with pride I embrace thy glory, oh Zaire, immortal Land of my Ancestors.
>
> Thus I was born in a land called Zaire, the most caring hand I could ever find under the sunlight. I grew up believing in this, until . . .[38]

That "until" came three years later. Everything changed on a single day:

> I was born in a country called Zaire. On 16th May 1997, I was still a Zairean. On the 17th of May, 1997, I woke up to be told I was Congolese. That my name was Faustin. My name is everything that makes me. Under Mobutu Sese Seko, it was illegal to have a name that was not Zairean. Whoever had a foreign name was kicked out. Whoever wore a tie was put in jail.[39]

When Mobutu took over the country in 1965, he introduced the "postnom," the after name, which was intended to reject colonial heritage and embrace "authenticity."[40] Linyekula was an acceptable name, but Faustin—like Jean, Paul, or Marie—was not. When Mobutu was deposed in 1997, people were once again free to take names that had previously been forbidden. So Linyekula's family added to his name the ancestral name Faustin. His father's twin brother had been baptized Faustin by a Belgian priest many decades before. The Belgians had been in the Congo for over 130 years, long enough, in Linyekula's view, for a name like Faustin to attain its own claim to authenticity. Faustin Linyekula's birth country is now called the Democratic Republic of Congo, but in interviews and performative lectures he is quick to point out that there are two lies in the name of his country: one is "Democratic," and the other is "Republic."[41]

For Linyekula, names are unhappy performatives, infelicitous declarations that are too often unable to lay claim to what they proclaim, too unstable to serve as a foundation one can depend on. Yet names are at the same time too foundational to disregard. He approaches names as though on an archeological dig, bringing to the surface long-buried fragments, pieces of evidence that testify to prior worlds. He acknowledges that names are generative, a way to access one's own history and to connect with other people. In saying, "I like to talk about my dance as an attempt to remember my name," Linyekula is embracing names as sites of inquiry, artistic and otherwise: "When you are serious about names, you cannot collapse into yourself. It opens up a web of relationships to place, to history, to people. And negotiating that over and over, trying to understand the intricacies of those relationships becomes a project in itself, a lifelong project, an artistic project. My dance is a way of negotiating relationships. My dance is an attempt to discover another archive."[42] Names serve as networks of relationships, as archives of a history denied, as springboards to creativity through dance. They can change with time, with regime change, with the license of performance, where one can adopt the name of another. Sometimes the web of relationships embedded in names leads to kinship ties, and at other times Linyekula's tracing of names leads to disparate geographies of belonging, revelations about how laws and norms changed over time (especially in conversation with artists from elsewhere in Africa who share experiences of colonial occupation, even if the colonizers came from different countries and even if the label "African" is one that Linyekula eschews most of all).

To grasp the radical heterogeneity and genre-defying nature of Linyekula's work, let us consider *more more more . . . future* (2009), which Stacy Hardy calls a "rogue arsenal of displacements and delirious incantations."[43] Linyekula himself vacillates in describing the work, saying that it's "a fashion show and yet it is not," or that "it's a choreographic piece and yet, it is not. It's a concert and yet is not. It's somewhere between a scream and a lullaby."[44] The work includes spoken, sung, and projected English translations of French poetry by writer Antoine Vumilia Muhindo, who was a political prisoner at the time the show was created. His performed words are growled, shouted, spoken, screamed, chanted, whispered, and intoned in a deep-throated low bass voice. Other key elements include a sound track of distinctive Congolese dance music of infectious upbeat rhythms known as *ndombolo*, which Linyekula calls the "bastard daughter of rumba, traditional rhythms, church fanfares and Sex Machine funk,"[45] and performances by a trio of masterful musicians, including virtuoso guitarist Flamme Kapaya from Kinshasa and Paris, who is reputed to be one of the best guitar soloists of his generation. (Linyekula says that in the DRC "between 1997 and 2007, at least every year, you heard Flamme's guitar in a hit song that made the entire country dance."[46]) The sonic landscape of *more more more . . . future*, which changes in tone and style with surprising alacrity, is propelled by a pulsing score that Kapaya composed. It erects a kind of sonic wall as drums, electric guitar, and bass reach cataclysmic acoustic levels. This soundscape gradually settles into what one reviewer called "a single, heavy metal repeated lower chord that turns into an aggressive assault bordering on punk rock."[47] Equally memorable are moments of quiet delicacy, enchanting passages of unamplified a cappella singing, single fragments of melodic lines sometimes sung by one person and at other times sung by the entire ensemble of seven dancers, singers, and musicians. Mellifluous and gentle with luscious and seductive harmonies, these moments are surprising ruptures in a world otherwise dominated by assault and rage or nightlife glamour.

If *more more more . . . future* were a conventional piece of contemporary dance, this paragraph is where I would begin to describe the work's movement vocabulary and grammar. But given Linyekula's refusals of genre expectations, let me begin with his statement that it is a "fashion show and yet it is not." What can be said of its costumes? The three principal dancers wear fantastic chrysalis-like skins created by Parisian and Malian designer Xuly Bët—rotund costumes fabricated from a woven plastic material that is usually used for inexpensive luggage made in China. The effect is at once extravagant and frugal. Two of the dancers' costumes are red and gray plaid, and the third dancer's costume has a pattern that suggests multicolored currency bills plastered on top of one another like papier-mâché. Linyekula commissioned designer Bët to create a shell for dancing bodies, and the result was, in Stacy Hardy's words, "not clothes but literally skins, prosthetic forms, organic folds and metallic sheaths that transform the extended bodies."[48] Ariel Osterweiss describes these costumes as "bulbous layers of colorful reflective material (think Michelin Man meets crinkly

Fig. 15. Pappy Ebotani (*left*) with Faustin Linyekula in *more more more . . . future*, 2011. (Photo by John Hogg.)

detritus turned hip-hop sheen amidst grotesque, botanical blooms)" (figure 15).[49] When the three dancers shed their plastic shells early in the performance, their bodies emerge unadorned, their chests bare, Lycra tights their only clothing. The rippling musculature of each dancer's torso emerges and moves in mercurial, undulating, supple, and subtlety articulated ways. The nuance of the dancers' exposed, slender and muscular forms contrasts markedly with their previous cartoonish, rotund spinning and bouncing forms, when encased in their bulbous, Ubu-like skins. Something that was formerly hidden is being revealed. Something formerly dormant is coming to life. That "something" is both vulnerable and strong.

Linyekula says that *more more more . . . future* is a musical concert—and yet not. Most notable is the work's abrasive punk-like aesthetic, which is both acoustic and kinesthetic. We see catapulting, raging bodies that climb on top of and crash into one another with astonishing recklessness. At one

Fig. 16. Pepé Malumba Musema, aka Le Coq (*left*), and Patient Muftala Useni, aka Pasnas, in Faustin Linyekula's *more more more . . . future*, 2011. (Photo by John Hogg.)

moment Linyekula leaps onto the shoulders of the guitarist Kapaya, moving around his neck and head as if the musician were a jungle gym. All the while, Flamme Kapaya keeps playing his double-necked guitar, calmly and expertly, as though physical assaults like this were a routine experience for him. Grounded in a heavy metal, head-banging mix, *more more more . . . future* is dominated, at the same time, by another theme: that of bling and ostentatious strutting, with flashy and glittery jackets evoking the vibrant Kinshasa nightlife scene, a world full of posturing. The irrepressible, gleeful, even frantic aspirations of *ndombolo* that are paraded each night in Kinshasa's clubs are a stark contrast with the threadbare infrastructure so starkly exposed in the daytime hours.

Ndombolo is a musical form that is a subset of *soukous*, which translates as "shaking," a movement seen at multiple moments throughout the show. Two singers downstage left near a microphone, Pasnas and Le Coq, both clad in snappy, slick suits represent the club scene (figure 16). They are smooth, confident, elegant representations of what Linyekula calls the "masters" of Kinshasa's nightlife, those who enter the scene and then "disappear to come back again, singing their own praises, power, beautiful women and expensive stuff, designer cloth and luxury cars . . . a fantasy life, directly drawn from TV soap operas and American R&B videos."[50] Yet while *ndombolo* is upbeat and aspirational, it is also a flimsy artifice that masks profound depths of denial. Linyekula says that "this music is so so important for us": "It is part of the daily life and experience of being in the Congo, really. It's got incredible energy, but it's there actually to help us forget about our problems—so it's art as some kind of escape from reality. I started just questioning myself differently—like, 'No, I can't just play ndombolo, I have to investigate further what it means to us.'"[51] The result of Linyekula's investigation is *more more more . . . future*, a show that exposes how *ndombolo* exists only in the present tense—a *now* of consumption and pleasure seeking that attempts to keep the dark realities of the daytime and the bleak prospects for the Congo's future in abeyance. Club goers stay up all night, seeking joy and pleasure, behaving "as if everything was granted in a country where everything is to be built again each morning."[52] Linyekula wanted to see whether he could capture *ndombolo*'s irrepressible energies and then redirect them in a more meaningful direction. He asked, "Why not use the fantastic energy of guitars and voices not to sustain dreams as thin as the cheap paper handkerchiefs sold in the streets of Kinshasa, but on the contrary to speak of the difficulties, dead ends, mistakes and the poor legacy of our fathers?"[53]

More more more . . . future offers no solutions or roadmaps to a brighter future. But it does bring the ostentation and glitter of *ndombolo* out of a realm of denial and into conversation with a more sobering discourse, particularly through the poems by Antoine Vumilia Muhindo that serve as the work's libretto. Commissioned by Linyekula expressly for this show, Muhindo's French-language poems speak about "kicking the anthill," a provocation that risks self-sabotage.[54] Lines like "sowing discord in the middle of the festival" announce a decidedly killjoy spirit, but at the same time there is promise of catharsis ("we are going to do some ranting").[55] The speaker even declares, like a stage manager, that the music must be cut:

> Ndombolo, coupé-décalé, rumba, zoblazo—
> All are fine, but not at the expense of memory.
> So turn off the sound![56]

In other words, music cannot be celebrated at the expense of memory. The lyrics exhort listeners to awaken, to get woke, to see:

> Look, our ship is sinking
> Meanwhile eyes closed, we're still dancing the cha-cha-cha and the
> rumba of independence
> On the tiny raft of our cosmetic democracies.[57]

The solution?

> Just open your eyes and see
> How far we've gone now
> Just open your eyes and see
> How deep we've fallen down
> Just open your eyes
> And say yes to the future.[58]

The songs of *more more more . . . future* exhort audiences to leverage the power of *ndombolo* to do something more than seek escape from the Congo's harsh realities: to face the music, to see, to open one's eyes, to say yes to the future because that future is a legal *right*. "You have a right to future."[59] A right, that is, not just to *a* future or *the* future, but *to future*, as if it were a verb. After the hot nights in Kinshasa's lawless zone, day will come, the lyrics say. In fact, the day:

> Is already starting
> To wrest from us the cover of misery,
> Because tomorrow you do not know![60]

This right is an unknown, unstoppable, inevitable happening.

More more more . . . future also attempts to capture the anger and disillusionment encapsulated in British punk of the 1970s and 1980s. The punks rejected futurity: "no future" was their mantra.[61] Although Linyekula identifies with punk's rage and hardened aesthetic, he does not embrace its nihilism. "In a place of no hope," says Linyekula, "belief in a future is an act of resistance, because it's impossible for us to send to hell a future that we never had."[62] The show uses the gravity of heavy metal's anger and the determined upbeat rhythms of *ndombolo* to do something that neither of these forms otherwise accomplishes: to assert faith that one should demand a brighter future and to seize hold of this faith with fierce tenacity.

To this dense acoustic layering the show adds one more element. On top of the punk/heavy metal ethos and *ndombolo* is a crucial third layer: moments of surprising quiet and solitude, recurring passages of exquisite delicacy, unadorned and unplugged. The human voice emerges, sometimes rising up from a sea of sound or inserting itself lightly in the few moments of quiet interlude between screams. The voice in these moments is unamplified, accompanied only by single guitar notes, simple melodic riffs, or harmonic chord progressions, over which one hears occasional chirps, tweets, and whistles, like the sounds of birds or insects in a forest. This layer is the lullaby Linyekula promised—a grace note, a caesura in a sea of screams. One might also hear hand claps and the sounds of feet sliding, kicking, and tapping on the floor. The modulation between the three levels of punk, *ndombolo,* and unamplified human-produced sounds represents the experiential journey of *more more more . . . future*. The work is an acoustic and cultural palimpsest with dense layers of performance cultures that surface sometimes overtly and immediately, other times more gradually, seemingly having always been present but, until now, submerged, repressed, upstaged. Layers of despair and rage are tempered by lightness and joy. Layers of fragile, fleeting, and intimate human connection and companionship are lodged in unexpected gaps of an otherwise aggressive, loud, ostentatious, competitive, greedy, and violent world.

And what can we say of the show's movement style? How is this a "choreographic piece and yet, it is not"? I have struggled to find appropriate words to describe its choreography. For a time, I thought this struggle was my own failure as a scholar relatively new to the field of dance. But highly experienced dance scholars also find it difficult to describe Linyekula's choreographic style. Brenda Dixon Gottschild, one of the foremost scholars of black dance, notes that Linyekula "doesn't fit the box." In broad terms, how do we even consider his work? "Choreography? Improvisation? Theater? Performance Art? Installation? Dance? Hmmm . . ."[63] His works often have characters, set pieces, props, narrative, spoken text, and big thematic ideas, yet his performances are most often marketed and reviewed as dance when he tours internationally. Gottschild notes that "the prevailing non-African dance referents in his presentations are more European and expressionist (German, French) in nature than American minimalist. His somatically sophisticated movement style (that freely uses contact improvisation, an American invention) is driven by ideas and philosophical concepts."[64] Dance reviewers of *more more more . . . future* describe the movement in broad, nonspecific terms: "The three men skitter and slink, sometimes sliding through elegant, indeterminate gestures and phrases, sometimes trying out hip-hop power moves, sometimes undulating their bodies with frank eroticism," said the dance critic in the *New York Times*.[65] *Culturebot* critic Andy Horwitz noted that the dancers "start with simple, smallish moves but gradually expand out into sinuous, athletic and aggressive movement patterns. They seem to be blending little bits of 'traditional' dance with popular dance and contemporary movement, embodying the tension between worlds that is The Congo."[66] There are many elements in Linyekula's work that might be labeled "traditional" Congolese dance, but he will never label them that way. "If I go through my pile of ruins to build my temporary shelter," Linyekula says, "there are moments when I find tools that can be viewed as 'traditional African dance' or rituals. But I really don't ask myself the question whether it's traditional or not. That's what I need at that particular moment and I use it."[67] Dance critics trying to represent the choreography of *more more more . . . future* resort, like the poet Muhindo, to metaphor. Horwitz described the performers in the show: "They look like they are dancing at the apocalypse, summoning up the spirits of the End Times and struggling against forces much stronger than them and beyond their control."[68]

But perhaps even more central than words, music, and dance to the core theories embedded in Linyekula's performance is how the performers occupy the theatrical space. Linyekula creates a dynamic tension between the proscenium and the circle. Linyekula has long ruminated in his writings and lectures on the ideologies of physical staging. In two performative lecture demonstrations (one at the Walker Art Center in Minnesota in October 2011 and the other, a lecture titled "Knowing Dance More," as part of the Re-PLACE-ing Philadelphia Project in October 2015), Linyekula talks about the dynamics and meaning of the circle and the proscenium.[69] In both, he speaks about how, in much of African performance, circles are associated with storytelling, ritual, community assemblies, and impromptu dances. Circles represent connectedness; everyone in the circle has agency to participate, and everyone can be seen. But for Linyekula, the circle as a symbol of community has been broken, certainly in the DRC.

Linyekula begins his Philadelphia talk by telling how war sent him into exile. He left the Congo and went first to Kenya and then to Europe. What was surprising to him was that while he was in Europe, he spent all his time avoiding the proscenium in his creative work, since it represented colonization, but when he returned to the DRC eight years later, the proscenium became a place of safety, structure, and refuge for him. While he recognizes that the circle is the most common format for Congolese performance, he questions this formation, especially in light of the country's recent violent history. "We count our deaths in millions," says Linyekula. "How can we talk of a circle when we are killing one another?"[70] In his view, the circle connecting people has been broken. Back home in the Congo, the proscenium he had once vilified became rather a necessary form of shelter: "It's a frame, and the world is always shifting under my feet. I don't know which kind of space to occupy. I don't know which kind of form to make that art."[71] At the Walker Art Center in Minneapolis, his lecture demonstration was held in an open space, a lobby that became a kind of informal arena theater with audience members on all sides. As he spoke, Linyekula gradually made his way to a freight elevator, the doors of which had been fixed open. From within that stationary elevator, Linyekula spoke, claiming this space as his refuge, an unexpected "found" temporary proscenium. Linyekula himself uses words like refuge, shelter, and safety to describe his rediscovery or reappraisal of the value of the proscenium. He explained that when he returned to the DRC from exile, the proscenium became an anchoring structure in the otherwise formless situation where all structures and infrastructures had been broken or thoroughly compromised. The rending of the social fabric through violence is the most destructive of all. If the DRC counts its deaths in millions, then the social circle has been broken. It can only be restored if everyone takes responsibility for reforming the circle. Until then, the proscenium is an activist platform from which Linyekula can challenge those around him, to ask: "What do I do to make others around me to see that the circle is broken? And to motivate them to play a part?"—that is, to actively work to repair a social fabric that has been shredded into so many pieces that the original is no longer recognizable.[72]

More more more . . . future stages Linyekula's theory of theatrical space and its underlying meaning. Its choreography deliberately contrasts presentational moments downstage—moments that directly address the audience—with private, intimate moments upstage, occasions that offer the audience a fleeting glimpse of an unbroken circle where a community comes together in harmony. Intimacy and acoustic singing contrast markedly with the presentational-style of the punk, assaultive heavy metal, and infectiously hyperactive *ndombolo* downstage. Linyekula essentially creates a physical score in which different types of performers move and occupy the space in contrasting ways, just as various sonic layers coexist without being reconciled. And in a world where the afterlives of injustice haunt, disrupt, and distort the present, his refusal of reconciliation and rejection of stylistic coherence speaks to a persistence of rupture while expressing Linyekula's *refusal to refuse* a future he never had.

More more more . . . future is typically staged in proscenium theaters that clearly separate the audience and the performers. The musicians are placed center stage left, and the singers are placed downstage right near a microphone. All the musicians and singers face straight ahead toward the audience for most of the show as they switch between the fast rhythms and quick melodic guitar licks of *ndombolo* and the assaultive dissonance of punk. The dancers move laterally from side to side across the stage. Linyekula is the first dancer we see, illuminated in dappled light that suggests a moonlit forest. His calves, glowing with focused side light, are prominent as he carefully inches into the performance space wearing his Michelin Man suit. Linyekula stays upstage behind the musicians, moving slowly from left to right, like a giant caterpillar. His movements are temperate and tranquil, yet there is an impulse driving him to move. Two more dancers enter, undulating in their bulbous costumes, also in horizontal patterns from stage left to stage right. Gradually, in response to the music, they all begin to bounce and shake, bopping up and down. Eventually, one at a time, the dancers work their way downstage, where each sheds his costume, sometimes after collapsing on the floor with a sudden thud. Unlike the musicians, the dancers do not seem to acknowledge or perform for the audience. They perform for themselves. They are absorbed in their own world. As they vibrate, shake, tremble, and gyrate in response to the music, the dancers seem to be aware of each other, and they even interact once they have shed their plastic skins. At one point all three of them form a single inverted being—a piled-up assemblage with six arms and six legs, all on the floor, moving slowly and with great effort and internal struggle, reaching, pushing, shuffling, as if in a rugby scrum.[73]

About halfway through the show, when the music is reaching a raucous and dissonant crescendo, the dancers migrate far upstage right. They are mostly hidden from the audience's view behind the drum set. Despite this visual obstruction, we can nevertheless *see* that they are singing. We cannot hear them, for they are sonically upstaged by the musicians' acoustic wall of punk, heavy metal, and screaming. However, it is clear that they are making music in a different register, tone, and style altogether. They are clapping in slow motion, stomping methodically with their feet as they move in an intimate rotating circle. It is as if the three of them are in a Pentecostal church service in prayer, speaking in tongues.

Meanwhile, to the accompaniment of raging guitars, the two nightclub singers downstage shout and growl lyrics from Muhindo's poem "Like the Prophets":

We deserve more than the fleeting shadows of false promises
We deserve more than headlines and media compassion
More than the bogus happiness that dulls our minds
More than aid, we deserve justice
More than money, we deserve dignity
Rather than a glorious past, let us have a future.[74]

This insistent demand for justice comes in the form of imperatives. The song closes by saying "you have the right to future." At this cue, the musicians gradually leave their stations and make their way upstage to join the dancers behind the drum set. As each musician drops out of the raucous acoustic score, we begin to hear the dancers' delicate a cappella singing. There is a slow revelation of a scene that is intimate and coordinated, social and yet also intensely private. The performers seem to have forgotten about the audience. Linyekula says: "We've built in such a moment where we go back to ourselves. We close the circle. The audience might feel excluded, but we need to reassess where we are before we continue. It's negotiating a relationship amongst ourselves, because we need to move as a group. Maybe that's another statement about the future, because you cannot do it alone. We cannot do it alone."[75] This segment happens right in the middle of *more more more . . . future*, sandwiched on either side by segments that are loud and enacted by atomized individuals rather than a coherent ensemble, and delivered in a theatrical presentational style directly to the audience. This moment is an island, a vision of another world, another way of being together. This moment is for the performers, not the audience. The show has shifted from an assault to a circle that is not broken. The dancers form a cypher, a circle in which individual dancers, one at a time, come to the center to express their idiosyncratic style and signature moves. The other performers clap and sing, supporting and responding to the ingenuity of their dancing peer. The circle may have been forgotten, or repressed, or torn up, or submerged, but it still exists. For a brief moment, the audience becomes a remote witness looking at a horizon barely seen and heard. Whether this moment is future, present, or past, we do not know. But the moment is not for us, the audiences abroad where the show toured. And in this refusal to cater to us, to cater to the viewing desires of the audience on the other side of the proscenium, Linyekula frustrated some spectators. *Los Angeles Times* critic Laura Bleiburg complained that the "momentum sputtered three-fourths of the way through, when the entire cast gathered in an upstage circle of call and response."[76] I would argue that the performers' momentum in no way flagged at this moment, but rather the audience's access to it did.

The final moments of *more more more . . . future* shift the relationship between the audience and the performance yet again. All the performers come downstage toward the audience and then turn their backs abruptly. They sit down. It seems we are all the audience now. Upstage, projected on a screen like a family slide show or an outdoor cinema, clouds slowly migrate across a blue sky. Gradually photos of various leaders from the DRC's past emerge amid the clouds. This montage is a visual invocation of political personages so well known to the performers and the people of the DRC that no one needs to name names. The screen displays a sequence of outsized faces that implicitly proclaim their power: Mobutu Sese Seko, former military dictator and president of Zaire; King Leopold II of Belgium, the founder and brutal despot of the Congo Free State; Patrice Lumumba, hero of Congolese independence and first prime minister of the independent Republic of Congo who was assassinated by foreign forces; and President Laurent-Désiré Kabila, who overthrew Mobutu but was himself assassinated by his bodyguards. They appear in sequence, as specters, conjured but not named.

Then images of the performers are projected. The past becomes the present, and this present becomes the performers. As Adrian Kear has written of this moment, "These are the members of *this* company, present here and now, co-appearing as both audience and performers in a seemingly 'democratic' space of futurity. This space opens up as precisely something to be constructed through the political labour of re-imagining their own trajectory, fashioning the opportunity to navigate a route through the memory and patrimony of 'the dark alleys of history.'"[77] Through those dark alleys, through the screams, through the lullabies, through the careening shifts in tone from punk to *ndombolo* to acoustic song, at the very edge where stage meets audience, the future is envisioned by gazing on a past. The people of the present sit on the edge—of the stage, of time, of the unknown. "For already the day is breaking / To strip us of our hidden misery," says the poet Muhindo, "Because nobody knows about tomorrow!"[78] The shift that Linyekula enacts in the final moments of *more more more . . . future* literally stages a transformation: the performers, who have been the objects of the audience's gaze, become subjects who gaze at the leaders of the past, many of whom have led their country astray. This reversal of the gaze spotlights what Linyekula calls "the poor legacy of our fathers."[79] The performers then become both subjects and objects, seeing themselves cast into a future that is only here and now being imagined as they are poised on the threshold that separates the stage and the audience.

GREGORY MAQOMA'S *BEAUTIFUL ME*

Linyekula has argued that when you really explore names, you cannot collapse into yourself, that names are archives that lead to vast networks of relations. One of the members of Linyekula's networks is South African choreographer Gregory Maqoma. For Maqoma, as for Linyekula, names and frames anchor their artistic inquiry. Maqoma's one-person show *Beautiful Me* uses all four corners of the stage to interrogate names, histories, the dynamics of theatrical space, and the way Maqoma is constituted through innumerable others (figure 17). At its core, *Beautiful Me* is a dialogic piece in which fellow choreographers, writers, world leaders, Nobel laureates, pop stars, Maqoma's father, and we the audience all participate in becoming Maqoma's "me."[80]

Early in *Beautiful Me,* Gregory Maqoma comes downstage left, where each of three microphones on stands represents (we eventually learn) a different contemporary choreographer Maqoma worked with to create this piece: Vincent Mantsoe, Akram Khan, and Faustin Linyekula. All three are credited in the program as "artistic contributors" and have provided portions of the choreography. The first one Maqoma addresses is Linyekula: "Hi Faustin. We had many conversations about space and I know that space is important to you. I think I should first tell you where I am." At this point, Maqoma moves center stage, the lights come up, and he directly addresses the audience by saying the name of the venue and city where he is performing. His conversation with Faustin continues away from the microphone: he is speaking to us, the audience, as though we were Faustin.

This "dialogue" (which is actually a monologue) becomes embodied through dance performed center stage. The image of a compass is projected on the floor. To the accompaniment of live musicians who repeatedly sound four descending notes, Maqoma systematically positions himself at different points on the compass. He speaks the names of leaders at different periods of history in both his country and Linyekula's. He kneels, slices the air with his arm, and points his hand along a particular line as though aiming a weapon or conducting a land survey. Through repeated moves across the compass, landing each time low and crouched in readiness along a particular axis, he conveys with his words how lands have changed hands and names over the course of a century: "Joseph Marie René Rutten, the governor-general of the Belgian Congo, 1923–1927." "Thabo Mbeki, president of the Republic of South Africa, 1999." "Daniel F. Malan, prime minister of South Africa, 1948–1954 . . ." Punctuating the interludes between the invocations of the named leaders, Maqoma spins abruptly and expansively across the center of the compass and improvises turns, swirls, gestures, and

Fig. 17. Gregory Maqoma in *Beautiful Me,* 2007. (Photo by John Hogg.)

fleet footwork before he crouches to invoke another name: "Mobutu Sese Seko, president of Zaire, 1930–1997." "Johannes Paulus Kruger, president of the Transvaal, 1883–1948." "Jan Christiaan Smuts, prime minister of South Africa 1919–1924, 1939–1948." "Pieter Willem Botha, prime minister of South Africa, 1978–1984, state president of South Africa 1984–1989." "Joseph Kabila, president of Democratic Republic of Congo . . ." Maqoma then resumes his more casual conversation with Faustin (i.e., us, the audience): "We talked about . . . that if we change, get rid of these names. How do we know who we are? How do we know where we come from? How do we confront ourselves, each other?"

Suddenly Maqoma shifts tempo again. Bounding in the air repeatedly, slicing the air with each alternating arm stretched long, he shouts: "I am Faustin Linyekula Ngoy, I come from the Democratic Republic of Congo, the former Zaire, the former Free State of the Congo, the former Léopoldville, former private property of Leopold the 2nd, King of Belgium. Yes!" Is he Gregory or Faustin? We no longer know who this "me" is.

Beautiful Me is an excavation of self and past with many strata. This is a self who stands on layered soil. "My name is Gregory Vuyani Maqoma, an African dancer, I have plenty of exotic stories to sell. Which one would you like to hear tonight? Which one?" We are uncertain who the "I" is anymore: Is it Gregory or Faustin? We are not sure we know how to speak of the past, what to call a place, a country, or a person when names and natures shift so often. Which one? Which one? "I am an African dancer, I sell exotic stories to survive," Maqoma tells us, bluntly naming the terms of our encounter. His words echo previous utterances by Faustin Linyekula in works such as *Le Cargo* (2011) and *Festival of Lies* (2005), during which he asks the audience repeatedly "which one?" when he attempts to lead them in singing the national anthem of his country. There have been many previous anthems in Linyekula's homeland. Which one will be sung tonight?

As Gregory Maqoma dances a conversation in *Beautiful Me*, his interlocutors are geographically and chronologically wide ranging. Some are among the living, and others are among the dead; some are worldwide luminaries, and some are intimate relations. These interlocutors include Nobel laureate playwright Wole Soyinka from Nigeria, whose voice is heard via a recording of a speech he gave at the Africa Remix exhibition at the Centre Pompidou in Paris in June 2005; Michael Jackson of Los Angeles (now an ancestor); Linyekula from the DRC; and London-based British-Bengali choreographer Akram Khan. *Beautiful Me* engages Khan as a Kathak-trained dancer whose London company produces work rooted in Kathak and modern dance. The show also engages South African choreographer Vincent Mantsoe, whom Maqoma has known since childhood. Raised alongside Maqoma in Soweto, Mantsoe is a longtime childhood friend and dance colleague who, like Maqoma, came up through the ranks as a dancer in Sylvia Glasser's Moving into Dance Mophatong in Johannesburg.

At its core, *Beautiful Me* is an embodied dialogue between Gregory Maqoma and fellow choreographers Akram Khan, Vincent Mantsoe, and Faustin Linyekula.[81] Each is known for forging new choreographic aesthetics that derive from specific dance lineages in the Global South, but at the same time, they position their work in a global present that has radically heterogeneous influences and routes of circulation. Each presents work that intentionally reckons with the afterlives of colonial injustice. Each creates dances that audiences and critics have difficulty putting in any particular box. Johannesburg reviewer Moira de Swardt said, "I don't think it matters which other choreographers Maqoma chose for his collaboration."[82] But I disagree. The specificity does matter. It's the whole point.

What all three choreographers share is a history of colonialism in their home countries and an indeterminacy about the genres of their artistic work. No one is quite sure what to call the forms, genres, and styles they are creating. Linyekula is ambivalent about which terminology to use to describe his work. Khan, a British-Bangladeshi choreographer, is known for forging a new form of interculturalism, one that far suprasses the facile label "contemporary kathak" that has sometimes been applied to his work. Rather than fusion, he embraces confusion. Mantsoe has forged a unique aesthetic that is sometimes described as an Afrofusion that focuses on "freeing the spirit of our ancestors" and assimilates and incorporates a range of disparate movement vocabularies.[83] Notably, Sylvia Glasser trained Maqoma and his peers in her syncretic technique of Afrofusion, which was influenced by her longtime interest in African rhythms, rituals, and dance forms and informed by her training as an anthropologist. This syncretic technique included her approach to cultural appropriation, which she believed could be done with appreciation and respect.[84]

Yet using the word *fusion* to describe contemporary dance in South Africa has been controversial. As Lliane Loots explains, "Doing classical ballet to the sound of the African drum, while giving us all a warm feeling of wished for 'simunye' [we are one], does not (and did not) address the very real political and cultural questions" of the postapartheid era, such as the unequal distribution of resources, access to performance and rehearsal space, and access to training.[85] Fusion has also been used to describe Akram Khan's dances. He is forging a distinctive style that brings together Kathak's subtle interplay between stillness and speed, technical virtuosity, use of the floor as a percussive instrument, and narrative expressiveness, with contemporary modern dance techniques and styles from Europe and America. Often labeled as an innovator of contemporary Kathak, Khan rejects this label and that of fusion: he finds both to be too formulaic, too predetermined to express the deeper work of synthesis, exploration, discovery, and improvisation that he considers to be central to his process and aesthetic.[86] Khan has chosen instead to call what he does "confusion," a neologism not unlike Maqoma's self-description of his style as a "cultural cocktail."[87] There is a fluidity to both terms that isn't captured by other terms like interculturalism or the interweaving of performance cultures. Yet neither term seems fully adequate to the task of describing the complex and historically fraught nature of what these artists are forging through their artistic work, especially as they wrestle with the afterlives of injustice.

In addition to these three choreographers, the conversation that constitutes *Beautiful Me* includes the show's director, Gerard Bester (the same Gerard Bester who played the comic, anxious master of ceremonies in Robyn Orlin's *Daddy, I've seen this piece six times before and I still don't know why they're hurting each other*); the costumer, Sun Goddess, who has clad Maqoma in a distinctive priest-like robe of black and deep red; and the musicians, an exceptional ensemble who provide "astounding collaborative input" during the live show, in reviewer Rita Felciano's words.[88] Poorvi Bhana (sitar), Bongani Kunene (cello), Isaac Moleleka (violin), and Mandienkosi Nhlapo (percussion) are assembled upstage right, directly opposite the three microphones downstage left, the symbolic channels through which Maqoma speaks to his choreographic cocreators. The musicians propel Maqoma throughout the piece, extending and punctuating his actions sonically, reacting to his pops and shimmies and glides, and driving him into new actions, new modalities, new moods. The arrangement of musicians upstage right and microphones downstage left creates a strong diagonal axis that cuts directly through the space and Maqoma's movements center stage. In very specific moments, Maqoma comes directly downstage, right up to the fourth wall that separates the audience from the performers. While the conceit in much concert dance is that the performers don't "see" the audience, at deliberate moments in this work Maqoma highlights or breaks and then reestablishes that frame. Sometimes he just calls attention to it. Early in the work (at the end of a section that I think of as the "prelude" before direct conversations with absent co-choreographers begin), he comes up to the edge of the stage and blows. He blows and blows, looking almost like a fish that is attempting to break free from an aquarium. Spectators sitting in the front row (as I was when he performed at the Yerba Buena Center in San Francisco) can actually feel his breath and the moisture from his plosive soundings. "Knock, knock. I am here. I don't see you, but I am coming," this moment seems to suggest.

The "me" of *Beautiful Me* is not a self in isolation: the stage is crowded with others, both seen and unseen, the musicians upstage and other people whom Maqoma invokes. And we, the audience, form still more others who are part of Maqoma's "me." In a section labeled in the program as "Conversation with the Audience and Superpowers," Maqoma has a sequence of imaginary encounters with world leaders. He imagines being in front of the queen. "What would I say? What is it like? What is it like to be a real queen?" He imagines what he would do in front of Jacob Zuma, who was then president of the Republic of South Africa. Zuma gained notoriety for singing "Umshini Wam" (My Machine Gun) in 2005 when he was still deputy president.[89] Maqoma mimics how Zuma sang this song at a political rally, leaping from side to side, pulling his arms up close, bent at the elbows. Maqoma sings it as a sotto voce melody, as if it were a secret or a threat—"umshini wam, umshini wam"—slightly higher in tone each time he jumps to the other side. This moment is a layered allusion to a well-known liberation song, to Zuma's controversial rendition, and to invocations of this song during Zuma's trial for rape, a courtroom encounter Elizabeth Gunner has so provocatively analyzed.[90] Maqoma then alludes to the specious claims Zuma made at that trial about showers being an effective way to prevent HIV infection. Maqoma asks: "How many times do you take a shower in a day?" Then, imagining himself to be in front of George Bush, Maqoma asks: "Why don't you pull the trigger yourself?" Then he imagines he is in front of the pope. "What would I say?" The next imaginary interlocutor is more personal: "In front of my father?" What would Maqoma say? "I don't play football," he says, alluding to an ongoing source of tension and controversy between a father who had normative expectations of his son and a son who gradually discovered that he was a queer dancer.

These moments are fragments of monologues, really, as Maqoma gets no response from history. He also speaks to us, the audience, as though we, too, could be part of this conversation. He turns to us and asks: "If I was in front of you, what would I say?" The tension builds as he faces us, seeming to await our response. Like the world leaders he has been invoking until now, we don't respond. After an awkward pause, he breaks the tension with humor: "I forgot the lines!" he says, and he skips off to the side with a sly, playful sway of his hips.

Another important interlocutor is Nobel laureate Wole Soyinka. We hear Soyinka speaking about an "irrecoverable . . . aspect that emerges when there is a physical or mental break with the past."[91] A recording of him reading the paragraph I quoted in this chapter's introduction focuses on the question of colonial rupture, how a culture can navigate in the wake of an invading and colonizing force, especially one that has denigrated Indigenous languages and forms, saying they are not valid. This instruction demands a period of experimentation, when artists, writers, and leaders are all casting about for ways to reconceptualize creativity. An acceptance that the colonial is purely a rupture forms its own delusion, for the process is far more messy than that. Some artists respond by trying to salvage and reconstruct the precolonial past, the "anterior forms." But that is a futile endeavor, because all cultures evolve and change. The invading force and culture is now part of the current circumstance. As Soyinka advises, "I'm afraid it's a problem that has to be approached from many forms. I will never suggest one approach is superior to the other. I will like to judge what results from the approach as being valid, maybe, for that particular artist, or for that particular time."[92] In an early version of *Beautiful Me*, Maqoma walks to these words, his pacing shaped by Soyinka's vocal cadence. Maqoma even begins mouthing Soyinka's words, lip-syncing as Soyinka defines and addresses the "problem" of cultural ruptures in places that have been colonized, the impossible situation of trying to navigate a way out or a way forward through layers of the past: acknowledging and respecting the precolonial without romanticizing it or insisting that it serve the needs of the present when it may not; recognizing the traumas of the colonial without becoming entrapped by them; and then breaking into something else, something beyond the abyss and the rupture. What might the "totally new" matrices of creativity be? And how does an artist discover them? In the most recent iteration of *Beautiful Me*, a revival that Maqoma mounted at the 2019 Holland Festival in Amsterdam, this staging was revised. A sharp, focused overhead light in the shape of a severe rectangle was cast directly downward on the stage. In this narrow corridor of light, Maqoma's hands flowed and turned, perpetually moving with such velocity that they became a kind of flesh-toned liquid levitating before our eyes. It was an arresting apparition, a kinetic vortex that was at once thoroughly human and otherworldly.

This recording from Soyinka cuts to the core of what both Linyekula and Maqoma are tackling in their creative work. Both are interrogating inherited forms—the circle and the proscenium, *ndombolo* and *isicathamiya,* a form practiced by migrant black laborers in South Africa that has particularly influenced Maqoma. Both artists approach the afterlives of injustice as embedded in inherited artistic forms, from whatever era, and both are forging new aesthetics that bridge past, present, and future by experimenting with a great variety of forms of movement, style, and staging. As Soyinka suggests, we must judge the results in a focused way, considering fully what is valid for each particular artist and each particular time. In that vein, let us focus on the time and place out of which Maqoma arises.

Gregory Maqoma was born in Soweto, a former township outside Johannesburg, in 1973, three years before the momentous 1976 Soweto student uprising that changed the course of the antiapartheid struggle and of Maqoma's life. For many in his generation, access to education was disrupted, blocked, or permanently suspended due in part to an awakening activism among a younger generation. These activists rejected the Bantu education system of the apartheid era and the government's ever-escalating methods of repression that included states of emergency and curfews, as well as perpetual assaults on the townships that suspended all semblance of normal life. Despite the historical tumult of the 1970s and 1980s, such as school closures after the uprising, Maqoma's parents retained upwardly mobile aspirations for their son: they wanted him to become a doctor. His father worked with computers, and his mother was a cashier and then the brand manager for a chain store.[93] His father pressured Maqoma to excel at soccer (or football, as it's called in South Africa), an expectation that he was unable to fulfill, despite his love of and gift for movement.

But none of the pressures Maqoma experienced as a child from his parents or his peers affected him as deeply as did two transformative encounters with movement. Both occasions awakened in Maqoma an awareness of all that a body could do. The first of these came while he was visiting the residents of the Dube Hostel in Orlando East, a dwelling for migrant male workers located next to Maqoma's home. Soweto hostels were spare, densely populated accommodations that often lacked any provisions for privacy, heat, or hot water. Segregated by language and ethnicity, residents came from the rural areas and often remained isolated from the urban populations that surrounded the hostels. "Hostel dwellers were never properly integrated into township life," notes Dennis Creighton. "Many of these hostels still remain in appalling condition even today."[94] And yet for Maqoma, visiting with the migrant workers during their leisure hours was not about witnessing their isolation or the toll of poverty on their lives. Instead, what he saw was a dance studio:

> At the time I thought a hostel was a special place that bred special dancers—clearly oblivious of the hostel dwellers' impoverished conditions. I was fascinated by what the hostel dwellers could do with their bodies, unaware that their dance routines were a coping mechanism. Occasionally I would join them during these dance sessions. I had this innocent, natural connection to dance and those hostel dwellers were my first and biggest inspiration.[95]

In time, Maqoma came to realize that for these men, dancing was not just about the joy of movement. Dance for these migrants was an embodied practice of psychic survival predicated on the capacity of dance to forge connections between the self and the other, between locations far and near, between times present and past, and even between the living and the dead.

In a TED Talk, Maqoma tells a story about his childhood visits to the hostels. He performs this story as a duet with dancer and singer Xolisile Bongwana, who accompanies Maqoma's tale with deep-throated, dual-tone singing that evokes traditional song, precise gestures, and dance moves. Maqoma recalls:

> Every time I would watch men who were coming from different parts of Southern Africa living in the hostels, they would be competing amongst themselves with very organized traditional Xhosa and Zulu and Basotho dances. These men will be dancing about the place they come from, connecting their stories of displacement to the story of the place they were in. I was amazed by the intricate nature of their choreographies, sweat dripping down their muscled bodies, a harsh descent of a leg drumming the floor. The euphoria of movement engulfed my mind. And I realized later on that their movement was not just the movement of euphoria. But it holds true to the place they come from. It's the story of men and women leaving their households coming to big cities like Johannesburg seeking opportunities. It is the story of men digging deep down in the belly of the earth searching for a shiny metal stone that they may never own. It is a story of men who are using their dance as a form of connecting—connecting to themselves, connecting to the lives they are living—in these atrocities in the places that didn't give them the decency of life. I believe very strongly that this connection, my exposure to the traditional forms, helped me to have some compassion toward the other, toward their tradition, toward their culture, toward their aesthetic, toward their form.[96]

In witnessing and participating in performances among migrant laborers in the Dube Hostel, Maqoma came to understand that dance was fundamentally about connection to others, especially in an apartheid world that otherwise atomized and isolated black individuals. In such a situation, dance was a survival strategy in the face of dehumanizing conditions. Group dance forms practiced by the migrant workers, such as *ngoma* and *isicathamiya,* were a way for the body to serve as a sovereign nation even when it was located in and circumscribed by an authoritarian, racist state.[97]

The second transformative experience, which Maqoma has narrated often—in print, in lectures, in interviews, and in his performance *Beautiful Me*—is seeing Michael Jackson dance on television. Television came late to South Africa, and images of Michael Jackson's videos did not began appearing in the townships until the 1980s. Maqoma recalls,

> I grew up as a child, I think when I was nine or ten years old, I think the one person that really influenced me was Michael Jackson. Because at that time we had a lot of chaos in our township, for the first time I was seeing someone who was black on our television screen who was portrayed in a positive manner. And that became a very immediate connection. When I saw *Thriller*, I said I want to take dance to create the same kind of emotion that I felt.[98]

When Jackson's mercurial steps, side glides, pelvic thrusts, crotch grabs, and levitating moon walks were broadcast on South African television in the 1980s, the young Maqoma witnessed for the first time a positive image of black identity in popular culture. While by this time in Jackson's career many in the United States had come to question Jackson's racial identity given the whitening of his skin and the anglicization of his facial features, in Maqoma's eyes, Jackson was decidedly black, and Maqoma was immensely proud of this racial identity.[99] Immediately, Jackson's videos infected Maqoma with a desire to dance. And so he did. He danced with his friend Vincent Mantsoe. "Their feet started moving during the early 1980s to the beats of pop icon Michael Jackson," the *South African* reports. "The pair were so inspired that they started a five-man group called the Joy Dancers sporting tinted hair, faded denims and torn t-shirts."[100]

These two exposures to dance forms—South African group dance forms that we might think of as "traditional" and the popular African American dance moves Michael Jackson performed—synthesized in Maqoma's mind into a distinctive conglomeration. He combined these influences into what became his signature choreographic style. As Maqoma says of these two encounters: "That was when I actually created a dance aesthetic by fusing traditional and contemporary styles."[101] Critic Hayley Kodesh describes Maqoma's movement vocabulary as one that captures "a tension of opposites: fluidity and truncation, holding and releasing, depth and lightness, momentum and control."[102] One sees in his works a liquid explosion quickly retracted and contained, a pop to the side suddenly pulled inward and held, a bottled energy quivering and threatening to explode, a mercurial, undulating movement also capable of astonishing and sudden stillness. These aspects of his choreographic vocabulary can also be used to describe both the dances of Michael Jackson and *isicathamiya*, as the latter form is defined by performing on tiptoe, "walking like a cat" while punctuating this restrained movement with determined and fast high kicks.

Critic Alan Urlich describes Maqoma's dance vocabulary in *Beautiful Me* in this way: "He begins the evening in a pool of light, isolating his arms, which in one moment seem to embrace the universe and in the next wrap the performer in their tentacles and in the next slice through the air with startling vehemence. Once you have seen Maqoma navigate the forum space, his torso twisting, his feet stamping out an obsessive rhythm, he is not easy to forget."[103] Adrienne Edwards has described Maqoma's performance in the subsequent *Exit/Exist* (2013, a piece about his name and his namesake, his ancestor Chief Maqoma, who played a major role in the Xhosa wars of the nineteenth century) in a similarly mercurial vein: "Maqoma takes the stage in a gold suit, his back to the audience, lithely flowing through his supple solo with dynamic rhythms stamped out from the soles of his feet. His wrists and fingers ephemerally caress the air as the core of his being undulates, tilts and flexes."[104] One can readily see the affinity with the defining features of Jackson's movement vocabulary, as *New York Times* dance critic Anna Kisselgoff described it in 1988:

> Notice how many times Mr. Jackson takes your breath away with his rapid-fire flat-footed turns, his staccato gestures, his burst of movement from any part of the body and you will see that the steps and sequences are often repeated. But their rhythms and phrasing are changed along with the studded jackets; the words shower the same dances with a torrent of varying emotion while laser beams light up the imagined sky.[105]

The affinity Maqoma recognized between Jackson and traditional South African dance forms was not an epiphany that was uniquely his. Michael Jackson's dandy figure in "Smooth Criminal" gained immediate traction with South African *isicathamiya* performers. In particular, Ladysmith Black Mambazo (of Paul Simon's *Graceland* album fame) actually performed two songs in Jackson's signature 1988 film *Moonwalker* (they can be seen in the "Smooth Criminal" and "The Moon Is Walking" sections at the end).[106] Preeminent scholar of *isicathamiya* Viet Erlmann provides a detailed analysis of how that dance's walking steps (*istep*) and shoe tapping (*isicathulo*) are superimposed and intercut with Jackson's running, airplane moves, and whirling.[107] Erlmann sees the partiality of diasporic forms coming together in this video as key to the "transcendent power" of black interrogations of modernity.[108] While Maqoma does not articulate his aesthetic amalgamation as an interrogation of modernity, mass culture, or capitalism, there is something in the alchemy of his mash-up of Jackson's slides and the high kicks of rural South African dance forms that resonates deeply with Erlmann's analysis. This aesthetic conversation transcends tired boundaries, typical expectations, and formulaic theories about cultural encounters.

In Maqoma's *Beautiful Me*, his conversation with Vincent Mantsoe is about the latter's sustained engagement with ritual and the ancestors. Yet at the same time, the majority of the Mantsoe section in *Beautiful Me* is actually about Michael Jackson. The spoken text that Maqoma delivers downstage at the "Vincent" microphone is about childhood memories as Maqoma and Mantsoe discovered dance by emulating and imitating Michael Jackson. The speaker of the following text is unclear: is this speaker Mantsoe talking to Maqoma or Maqoma talking to Mantsoe?

> If you see him or he gets to see you in America or Europe—I mean Michael, "Jacko"—tell him we could only afford one pair of white gloves, we would have loved to have the ones that sparkle in the lights, so we had to share. Tell him we would flip a coin to see who gets to wear the right hand, tell him you always got the right hand and I had to improvise with the left. Tell him how we used to cut our pants into three quarters to show off our white socks. Tell him how we got into trouble because we stonewashed all of our jeans in Jik. Tell him how we used to practice in your mum's backyard in Diepkloof, Soweto, to enter those competitions at that one club in downtown Johannesburg, Club Image. Tell him how we used to entertain friends at parties and weddings. You can also tell him how we used to fight over his steps.[109]

Maqoma moves center stage, and soon we see dance allusions to several memorable Michael Jackson phrases: the moonwalk, the left-to-right elbows-bent monster moves from "Thriller," the slide glide of "Smooth Criminal." But this sequence is not mere imitation; Maqoma is mediator of Jackson's spirit. And suddenly we see all of his movement vocabulary and syntax in *Beautiful Me* in a whole new light. Like Jackson, Maqoma has his own distinctive ways of taking our breath away with rapid-fire flat-footed turns, staccato gestures, and bursts of movement from any part of the body.

Maqoma has often narrated these defining encounters he had as a young boy. While both elements—Michael Jackson and *isicathamiya*—are embedded in work throughout his oeuvre, the two forms came together overtly in a piece he recently created for William Kentridge's venue, the Centre for the Less Good Idea. Maqoma's piece *Requiem Request*, which premiered in Johannesburg in March 2017, was a study for a larger work he was creating called *Cion* (2017), an adaptation of a novel by Zakes Mda about a professional mourner.[110] *Requiem Request* was created for an ensemble of *isicathamiya* singers called Phuphuma Love Minus, and two dancers, Thulani Chauke and Xolisile Bongwana. The choir begins in a balcony above the audience, beating out a rhythm on a cement railing. While the tempo is distinctive, one might not immediately recognize that it is the insistent rhythm of Ravel's *Boléro*. TA-DUM ta-ta-ta, ta-ta-ta TA-DUM ta-ta-ta, ta-ta-ta. *Isicathamiya* choirs usually perform in a straight line, a convention that dates back to the nineteenth century; this South African form has roots in touring English blackface minstrelsy. *Isicathamiya* performers usually wear two white gloves, and they usually dress in suits and ties. But in *Requiem Request* the performers, who eventually descend the stairs and enter the stage area, are shirtless, and they have only one glove—a checkered glove on their right hands. I see this attire as a nod to Michael Jackson. Before the choir enters, we see onstage a mummy-like figure encased in tape. Gradually the singers descend from the balcony, and as they come into view, they circle the raised platform on which the mummy stands. The rhythm seems to be calling the encased figure, enticing him to move and break free. The chorus moves around him, forming an intimate healing circle, a definite break from the standard line and flat proscenium staging that is typical of *isicathamiya*. As with Linyekula's work, we see a tension here between the circle, which is inward focused on a circumscribed community, and the proscenium, which is presentational to an audience that is separate from the performers. Gradually another dancer joins the encased figure as he is breaking free. This second figure, Xolisile Bongwana, who performed with Maqoma in his TED Talk, climbs on top of the mummy figure, wraps himself around him, moves between his legs, and catapults over his shoulder as the wrapped man is breaking free from the constraints.

Does the tape symbolize paralysis from grief? Fear? Loss? Bongwana expresses an incredible range of vocalizations as he moves: wails, screams, long sustained cries that build from near silence to full-out shouts, all to the accompaniment of the *isicathamiya* choir's insistent clapping of the *Boléro* rhythm. Like Linyekula's *more more more . . . future, Requiem Request* deliberately upends expectations—of a proscenium in *isicathamiya* performances, of suits and ties, of a line dance of high kicks and hand waving, here replaced with an act of communal mourning. And all the while, Michael Jackson is somehow there in those single gloves, signifying something other than the pairs of white minstrel gloves that have for so many decades defined the *isicathamiya* form. We can see in this more recent work of Maqoma's a sustained exploration of these two defining encounters with dance in his childhood: with the Dube Hostel performances by migrant men in Orlando West and with the broadcast of the King of Pop on South African television. Is the result of Maqoma's synthesis something we should call fusion, contemporary African dance, a cultural cocktail, a new interculturalism, or a form of confusion? None of these terms seem adequate to the task of analyzing what Maqoma is doing here. But it seems to me that *Requiem Request* and *Beautiful Me* achieve what Soyinka foretold: a "new matrix of conceptualization of creativity, of education, and consequently of reproducing your own existence." This creativity hinges on slowing down and opening up the contradictory impulses embedded within the form of *isicathamiya*. Nhlanhla Mahlangu, musical director for *Requiem Request* and for the subsequent *Cion*, says: "I am interested in the irony of *isicathamiya*, the music that was born as a colonial response yet later became our heritage, the music that was born out of 'trying not to be heard' and its dance born out of 'trying not be seen.'"[111] *Isicathamiya* was created by combining Zulu traditional dance forms and their loud foot stomping with European and American minstrel forms that came to South Africa in the nineteenth century. In the mines, migrants needed to dance softly, on tiptoe, to not make noise with their feet. Hence the contraditions that Mahlangu identifies about being seen or heard.

I have spoken only briefly of the third co-choreographer of *Beautiful Me*, Akram Khan. What I can say of the Khan portion of the piece is that Maqoma adopts and makes his own myriad elements that are central to Khan's practice and to the tradition of Kathak: the interplay of speed and stillness, the use of the floor as percussive instrument, mathematically elaborate footwork that is a masterful expression of devoted training, mercurial arm movements anchored to a pelvis that rarely moves. And like Kathak, *Beautiful Me* is a solo with a narrative to tell.[112] This section of *Beautiful Me* offered some of the most complex and transcendent choreography, as one reviewer noted:

> It's in the Kathak section that Maqoma was at his most spectacularly expressive, topping his heel and flat-footed beats with butterfly Flamenco wrists, scooping and slicing arms that disappeared in a blur of motion like accelerating propellers. More than once his body simply became another musical instrument. At one point the vibration of his footwork created a bass rumble beneath soaring string melodies. You watched the energy soar in his torso, and the ground started to respond. The way he traveled downstage in a narrow beam of light only to intersperse the close to the body movements with simple strides and running patterns spoke of freedom and discipline all combined in one human being.[113]

But more than the emulation of Khan's movement and translation of it into Maqoma's personalized idiom, what this section realized so exquisitely through movement was a core principle of Khan's choreography: that in dance one "approaches othering as a self-reflexive exercise in an attempt to 'locate and identify the innumerable others' in one's own self," as Khan scholar Royona Mitra has observed.[114]

While many selves are encapsulated and expressed in *Beautiful Me*, including the three choreographic contributors Linyekula, Mantsoe, and Khan, the work is framed by Maqoma's own body in silence and his spoken and danced conversation with his father. *Beautiful Me* begins in the dark. A violin plays a repeated sequence of four plaintive notes. Then silence. The lights come up gradually to reveal a man, Gregory Vuyani Maqoma—the choreographer, the "me" of the dance's title—in an isolated pool of light, upstage and remote. The overhead illumination creates a tightly circumscribed and confining square on the floor rather than a diffuse and generous round pool of light. Within this focused confinement, Maqoma's arms lift to his side, poised like those of a conductor about to begin a symphony.

His arms undulate and flutter—hands, wrists, elbows, fingers, forearms moving with liquid grace, as though his ligaments and tissues have no underlying structure of bones. Quick shudders of movement are punctuated by pauses. Gradually these shudders crescendo with his arms upward in a posture of surrender. All movement stops. Arms straight and rigid above his head, palms out. Maqoma's pose evokes the "hands up, don't shoot" gesture from the #BlackLivesMatter movement. However, *Beautiful*

Me premiered in 2007, seven years before Michael Brown, an unarmed African American man, was shot dead by police in Ferguson, Missouri, sparking protest and outrage across the United States, long before the "hands up, don't shoot" gesture assumed its viral symbolism. But 2014 was hardly the first time a black man was frozen with his hands up. Maqoma's allusion might well be to the humiliating group medical examinations and strip searches routinely forced on South African black laborers in the mines under apartheid, as photographers Peter Magubane and *Drum Magazine*'s Bob Gosani powerfully documented.[115] As Sikhumbuzo Mngadi says, "There is a particular photograph that comes to mind when the issue of black masculinity in South Africa is raised. It is the 1968 picture by Peter Magubane depicting more than a dozen black men, lined up and naked in what appears to be a dimly lit shower room."[116] The photo's representation of black men with arms in the air in a pose of surrender has become iconic. These disciplines of black male identity in apartheid South Africa are part of the somatic archive that fuels Gregory Maqoma's unique movement vocabulary.

At the start of *Beautiful Me*, Maqoma speaks in isiXhosa, addressing "Baba," his father. He comes toward us, the audience, speaking lines that are translated only in the printed program: "Baba, I am a peacock, I am a peacock, I have beautiful feathers, red, black, white. I will like to get closer to you. I dream of flying."[117] He moves downstage to an illuminated area that is larger than the first area but is still a box. This tightly defined space (a room? a dormitory? a cell?) contains and delimits the dancer's sphere of action.[118] He is alone, elegantly clad in a black-and-red smock. His movements are gestural and graceful, impulsive and fluid. Discrete body parts appear in isolation, moving fleetingly. A wrist flips, and an arm cuts over, quickly, before another flash of movement in which we see an evolving conversation among the body's appendages. But before I grasp the body's sentence, the conversation has moved on. I can't follow it all.

A left wrist twitches and flows, a right elbow juts out, and then suddenly Maqoma's throat seems to be in conversation with this left knee. Momentum builds, a gathering foment, as his feet begin an animated dialogue with the floor. The rhythm steadily rises, and I stop thinking about language. The robed man before me is a monk, or a *sangoma*, and I am part of a ritual.

The dancer's moves are purposeful, abrupt and forceful, then alternately playful and sensually flowing. It's a Morse code of body parts communicating to someone I sense is far away but is also viscerally present and listening very, very intently, just as I am. The rhythms accelerate as musicians begin to play drums, strings, shakers. I think about the *ngoni,* the one-stringed guitar that griots in Mali use to tell ancient stories. The dancer accelerates. He seems to run in place. He seems to fly, yet he doesn't move from one place.

And as I listen and watch, I am aware that I am sitting next to others. We are spectators gathered in darkness, just as Maqoma was in darkness at the start of this show. We too are gradually emerging in the light, gaining definition, especially as we react to Maqoma, sometimes audibly as we sigh or sharply draw in our breath, other times physically as we shift our weight in a chair or lean forward. I am so close (or I imagine I am) that I can feel Maqoma's heat and moisture and the percussive gusts of air radiating out from him. He shifts to making plosive exhalations through his lips, like a shaman spraying water in the surrounding atmosphere.

We are getting to know each other. Do I know this movement? Have I seen this action before? Is this the movement of an animal, perhaps some slow-motion close-up of a migrating bird in flight that I saw once on the National Geographic Channel? Is this that traffic cop in a busy Accra intersection perched on a small cube, directing with a flash of his white-gloved hands a chaotic surging throng of traffic: go left! go right! stop! come forward! Do I know this language? The dancer begins to vocalize. What are these percussive sounds, these plosives without vowels? I am certain that I will understand. I am certain that I did once understand. I think this is a moth that accidentally flew into my window and now, as he tries to escape, frantically and persistently beats against the glass.

The dancer's movements are aquiline, birdlike. But for some reason I also think about a farmer sowing seeds in soil. I think about a woman cooking over an open hearth, her hands expertly flipping onions, stirring the boiling *banku*. Accomplished actions of grace, these express a confident, easy mastery of movements that may once have been difficult but now have become art. Elegantly beautiful, this "me."

Body parts, appendages, and limbs in conversation with one another suggest the multiplicity of "me." As one reviewer wrote of Maqoma, "His body is strung together in such a manner that he can compartmentalize it at will, as when only his torso is in play, or he reaches around in a double jointed manner and slaps his behind in a sassy spank."[119] Hands, neck, cheek, shoulder, now all work in collaboration, a many-part conversation that in totality forms a unitary self. So too do other people form the "me" that is at the center of Maqoma's autobiographical work.

Beautiful Me captures an interconnectedness, the way a "me" is the sum of one's many body parts and at the same time the sum of all the relationships we have had and our relationship with fraught histories. This work is a dialogic choreography that he literally constitutes alongside and with other choreographers in disparate geographic locations—Soweto/Republic of South Africa (Mantsoe/Maqoma), Kisangani/DRC (Linyekula), London/Bangladesh (Khan)—but all sharing an ongoing legacy of the afterlives of injustice. What does one do with these inherited names that carry so much baggage? What does one do with the insults and injuries of the present, the failures of past and contemporary leaders, the legacy of invading forces and the ruptures they have created? What does an artist do with inherited movement vocabularies, syntax, and style? How do the forms of the past—which often come with baggage, distortions, and fabrications—enter the present?

Maqoma's father, who died in 2008, just after *Beautiful Me* opened, is one of the most important interlocutors of all. He is the person first addressed at the opening, and he also frames the end of the show, as Maqoma reflects on the challenges of the first name his father gave him: "Gregory." We know that Maqoma's father wanted his son to "catch the ball, not dance with it."[120] We know his father made him wash all of his teammates' socks when they lost the match due to Gregory's "error" in the game.[121] In the last monologue of *Beautiful Me,* Maqoma tells how his father made Gregory write the letter *r* one hundred times so that he would be better able to wrap his mouth around and enunciate its difficult sound, a sound so central to the name he'd been given. Maqoma recalls: "When I was young, I think I was nine or ten years old, my father used to make me write the letter *r* a hundred times, and I will have to call it out back to him a hundred times. Rrrrrrrrrrrrrrr."[122] As I thought about his struggle with the letter *r,* the word Gregory seemed to suddenly have more than two *r*'s. "Greg-or-ry?" It seemed to have three. I was struck by the challenge Gregory's parents had given him: to wrap his tongue around this difficult sound multiple times just to enunciate his own first name. As with the name Faustin Linyekula, the name Gregory Vuyani Maqoma carries archival remains that are part of the afterlives of injustice. As Maqoma has said in an interview,

> I also bear the weight of my own name, Gregory, a Christian name very attached to colonialism, because according to the apartheid laws one had to carry a Christian name to be recognized as a person and a citizen. The traditional name of the house, Vuyani, was not recognized! I am identified as Gregory Maqoma and that's why I wanted my company to have my other name [Vuyani]. And at the

> same time I have to carry that name, Gregory, who is rich in historical connotations and defines my relationship with my father.[123]

Gregory's struggle to say his own first name is echoed in the way audiences outside South Africa struggle to pronounce his last name, Maqoma. (To pronounce the *q* in this Xhosa name, you must click your tongue on the roof of your mouth while also making the sound "o.") "Ma-[click]o-ma." The final segment of the show features a delightful call-and-response between Maqoma and the musicians, all rhythmically clicking the popping *q* sound of isiXhosa. *Beautiful Me* has traveled to many geographic locations. In some places, audiences struggle to say the *r*'s in Gregory's first name, while in other places, audiences struggle to twist their tongues into an unfamiliar palatal click as they try to make the popping *q* of isiXhosa. What does it mean when international audiences for this piece cannot properly pronounce the name of its lead artist? The encounter, if done with respect, demands a change of tongue, a commitment to wrapping one's mouth around utterances that are unfamiliar, to practicing what is unfamiliar, what may not come naturally but can be learned. What does it mean to not be able to pronounce one's own first name? In the case of Maqoma, this question is much harder answer. It is thoroughly embedded in the histories of his own parents and their navigation of South Africa's many colonial ruptures, their aspiration for their son to take an anglicized name that required him to annunciate sounds not common in either isiXhosa, his father's language, or Sesotho, his mother's first language.

Gregory Maqoma ends *Beautiful Me* with the startling admission: "I could never pronounce my own name: Gregory."

CONCLUSION

In identifying the cultural challenges faced by a world that is after the formal end of colonization but in which the afterlives of injustice remain very much alive, Wole Soyinka has said, "I'm afraid it's a problem that has to be approached from many forms."[124] In the performance works of Faustin Linyekula and Gregory Maqoma, we see each using a great range of approaches, and it might be tempting to talk about their work as "intercultural" or transnational performance artists or to think of them as among those who "interweave" influences or work in "hybrid" ways. Linyekula's performances derive from multiple sources: precolonial Congolese dances, popular contemporary social forms such as *ndombolo*, American contact improvisation, and other influences that range from the American Judson Dance Theater to German expressionism. Maqoma likewise draws on artists from many nations—Khan (UK/Bangladesh), Linyekula (DRC), Mantsoe (South Africa), Michael Jackson (United States), Soyinka (Nigeria)—and on "traditional" South African and South Asian forms such as *isicathamiya* and Kathak, each of which require years of immersive training. All the choreographers Maqoma engages in *Beautiful Me* are forging new performance aesthetics that draw on historical legacies of colonialism and a rich inheritance of movement vocabularies from past and present.[125] These vocabularies include contemporary Euro-American modern dance forms, transnational popular styles from around the globe (Michael Jackson is a pivotal inspiration for Maqoma, Linyekula, and Khan),[126] and locally sourced dances with deeper historical roots we might call "traditional" if the word weren't so problematic.

There is a breathtaking virtuosity in the ability of both Linyekula and Maqoma to have such authoritative command across so many forms. Yet I think so many of our current theoretical terms for talking about such permeable artistic endeavors across national boundaries and forms are too stiff and formulaic to capture the dynamic, hand-hewn, idiosyncratic, intellectually ambitious, physically protean, and politically charged nature of the new aesthetics these artists are forging in the crucible of the present, in the sovereign nation of their own bodies as they inhabit spaces very much permeated by the afterlives of injustice.

What do we call the dance styles contemporary choreographers from Africa like Gregory Maqoma and Faustin Linyekula are forging? By what name will their dances be known? Does the label "contemporary African dance" adequately represent this work? And why label this work at all? The reality is that the demand for names, for genres and categories, is almost as incessant as the projections of Africa, whether those of anomie or romantic exoticization. Linyekula is adamant that he is not an African dancer. He says: "When you take those two words together, for most people, the stress is more on the word 'African' than on the word 'dancer,' because of stereotypes and all that. The day that both words will be put on the same level, maybe then I can talk of myself as an African dancer."[127] Many other performing artists from Africa who tour internationally echo Linyekula's refusal.[128] The problem against which they are all fighting is the overdetermined nature of that label "Africa"; it comes with too much negative baggage. But not naming something doesn't solve the problem. Audiences will fill this ellipsis with expectations and assumptions, just as

Vienna audiences did when they first saw Linyekula and Maqoma perform at the Wiener Tanzwochen Festival in 2000.

Maqoma and Linyekula explore not just how certain subjects adopt names but how names are imposed by others and what that imposition means. Their work theorizes the naming of specific subjects—themselves—rather than a hypothetical, decontextualized subject. As Linyekula says, "My dance will be an attempt to remember my name."[129] His dances are future oriented ("will be") and provisional ("an attempt"). He has likewise said, "My dance *is* nothing more than an attempt to remember my name"—a change of tense from future to present, qualified by the modesty implied in "nothing more."[130] His dances are an occasion for both him and his audiences to ask this question: If names have the power to enact subjects as either agents or objects of oppression, how does one cross over from object to agent? To put this question differently, if the afterlives of injustice in places like South Africa and the DRC live on today embedded in names and in particular traditions of theatrical staging, how might artists and audiences name, construct, and stage things differently?

Both Maqoma and Linyekula create performances that are not reconciliations with the past: they are fierce and imaginative reckonings. Approaching names and frames as though on an archeological dig, Maqoma and Linyekula unearth long-buried forces and forms, asking what we *do* with these names and forms in the here and now. The past, as Soyinka underscores, is not dead yet. It lives on: through names, through staging conventions, through dance and movement, through various hangovers of those ruptures and abysses caused by invading forces, and through attempts to reconstruct a precolonial past in its anterior form. Instead of seeing any of these inheritances or approaches as necessarily good or bad, Maqoma and Linyekula ask how these inheritances might be deployed and redeployed in the here and now, perhaps for very different goals and agendas. How might one stage these names differently in order to grapple with the historical rupture of invading forces and the denigration of what came before and attempts to reappraise and rehabilitate that past? What might be the surprising possibilities when dance forms serve like force fields, a kind of "gravity assist" to do political work that was previously unimagined, for instance when a supposedly apolitical social dance form like *ndombolo* possesses someone's hips not to distract or deny or escape the difficulties of the present but rather to face the now with open eyes? If *ndombolo* can be deployed on Linyekula's stage "not to sustain dreams as thin as the cheap paper handkerchiefs sold in the streets of Kinshasa, but on the contrary to speak of the difficulties, dead ends, mistakes and the poor legacy of our fathers,"[131] then what other dance forms could be conjured and deployed in the present for both unexpected and urgently needed ends?

What is at stake performatively and politically in the process of naming something? I contend that both Maqoma and Linyekula are actually theorizing in and from the Global South through their performances, addressing this question with a great deal of ingenuity. My chapter has been an attempt to render these theories more visible and widely available. Through dances and embodied expressions, Maqoma and Linyekula interrogate names and frames as choreographers and as theorists in order to transform objects of oppression into subjects with agency. A foundation for their theory is an assertion of will, and this will is manifest in refusals: refusal to name or categorize the genre of their work, refusal to entertain, refusal to play soccer or perform conventional masculinity, refusal to follow a father's example, refusal to present a linear narrative, refusal to meet audience expectations, refusal to enact the circle, refusal to accept the unbreachable separation of audience and performer. What else is there to do but refuse? In exercising their will to refuse, Maqoma and Linyekula carve out a space for careful selection, respectful inquiry, and discovery of a new ordinary that asserts a future. If the afterlives of injustice in places like South Africa and the DRC live on embedded in names, and in conventions of staging, these artists are at the forefront of naming, constructing, and staging things differently. And yet, what they are doing may defiantly elude any attempt to name it.

Epilogue: Taking Them Back Home

In 2018, a monumental new opera, *The Head & the Load*, premiered at the Tate Modern in its expansive Turbine Gallery.[1] Created by white South African artist William Kentridge in collaboration with composers Philip Miller and Thuthuka Sibisi, choreographer Gregory Maqoma, and a veritable army of visual designers, musicians, vocalists, dancers, and actors, *The Head & the Load* commemorates the largely undocumented, unacknowledged, and unknown tale of the millions of Africans who gave their service and often their lives in World War I. When the war started in 1914, over 90 percent of Africa was ruled by Europe. So when Europe went to war, so did Africa. Many Africans served as porters—carriers of equipment, provisions, and armaments, their most grueling work performed when trains, trucks, boats, roads, and beasts of burden petered out, failed, or died. The show's master of ceremonies, Mncedisi Shabangu, enumerates the formulas that determined carrier allocations: "For every soldier, three carriers. For every officer, nine carriers. For every machine gun, twelve carriers. For every cannon, three hundred carriers." Among the millions of Africans who served, thousands died—of injury, accident, suicide, hunger, disease (typhus, blackwater fever, exhaustion, sleeping sickness, dysentery, "unknown"), or of even being mauled by lions. "For every man who dies from bullets, thirty-one die from disease," Shabangu tells us.[2]

The deeds and deaths of Africans who served Europe in World War I left very little imprint in the historical record. Sol T. Plaatje's recollections of the war from his legendary 1916 book *Native Life in South Africa, before and since the European War and the Boer Rebellion* are revealing. A quote from this book is read aloud during *The Head & the Load*: "Lest their actions merit recognition, their deeds must not be recorded." Plaatje's original quote is slightly different: "Nor must they carry arms, lest their behavior should merit recognition; their heroic deeds and acts of valour must, on account of their colour, not be recorded," a less efficient statement but one that brings into sharper focus the racialized nature of European fears: black Africans should never receive approbation.[3] Europeans feared giving Africans guns not because the firearms might be turned on their colonial masters but because the actions of Africans might prove meritorious.

The Head & the Load is an ambitious work that spans all of Africa and Europe, exposing with a broad historical sweep the systemic racism of European colonization. To date, the mostly black-cast performance has been presented to predominately white audiences in the Global North. Unlike Brett Bailey's *Exhibit B*, this production has so far not aroused controversy. Why is that?

Let us consider intent and method. *The Head & the Load* is a story of history's omissions and erasures and our consequent collective amnesia. Kentridge says his motivation in making *The Head & the Load* was twofold: to illuminate "what we've chosen not to remember" and, more personally, to express "frustration at my own ignorance."[4] Kentridge's aesthetic method is to tell an epic story through fragment and collage, staging disconnected scenes of mutual incomprehension during a war that was notable for its consistent breakdowns of communication—specifically Europe's inability to hear what Africa was saying. Kentridge turns to Dada, a high modernist movement that arose from World War I, an expression of how the war had stripped words of meaning, how the world had become unintelligible to itself.

Kentridge describes *The Head & the Load*, a tale designed with neither heroes nor clearly delineated characters, as "a historical drawing in performance."[5] This massive assemblage of music, vocalists, dancers, projections, costumes, set pieces, and random sounds stages a dark, absurdist cabaret enacted on an exceptionally wide stage that is the equivalent of half the length of a football field—so wide, in fact, that it is impossible for one person to visually take in all that transpires on stage. In New York city, the performance was held at the cavernous Park Avenue Armory; in London, at the Tate Modern Turbine Hall. The show's visual surfeit is matched by sonic excess. Through a collage-like soundscape, one hears Dadaist deconstructions—manifestos, phrases from a handbook for military drills, Setswana proverbs, sound poetry from Kurt Schwitters's *Ursonate* (1922–32), and quotations from Frantz Fanon and Aimé Césaire, as well as a babel of languages: English, French, Italian, German, Shangaan, Shona, Zulu, Pedi, Xhosa, Wolof, Madinga, and Swahili. The musical score is likewise an eclectic mash-up of traditional African melodies juxtaposed with a Viennese waltz, or a stuttered version of "God Save the Queen." The score also alludes to European composers from the World War I era such as Maurice Ravel, Erik Satie, Paul Hindemith, and Arnold Schoenberg.

One of the few approximations to a protagonist in *The Head & the Load*

Fig. 18. *From left:* Xolani Dlamini, Gregory Maqoma, and Thulani Chauke in *The Head & the Load* by William Kentridge, 2018. (Photo by Stella Olivier.)

is a role played by choreographer and dancer Gregory Maqoma. He appears several times throughout the show in threadbare coat, shorts, and battered boots—sometimes alone, sometimes flanked by one, two, or three other men (figure 18). Maqoma plays an anonymous archetype, a lean, hungry, haunted, anxious, tenacious, exhausted solider, one who perseveres despite all. At various moments in the opera, he twitches reflexively in response to unseen forces that jab and jolt him as war breaks out. Later on, he slaps and swats at harassing mosquitos and tsetse flies, the insects that carried malaria and other diseases that killed both man and beast during the war. He marches with his fellow soldiers, at first in studied rehearsal, as a neophyte, and later in a defiant stomping sequence that violently shakes both stage floor and the powerful projectors placed downstage, producing heart-stopping percussion that reverberates throughout the Armory's Drill Hall like firearms exploding. Maqoma orchestrates his compatriots in their march, blowing signals and directions through his whistle. Throughout the performance, Maqoma marches, marches, and marches—jogging and shuffling at a tenacious trot, sometimes fading to the side, nearly fainting with fatigue, or thrown to the ground by an explosion, but always climbing back up, marching on, an icon of fortitude and endurance.

In a moving sequence, Maqoma crosses the entire width of the stage—all sixty yards of it—dragging, assisting, propping up, and carrying his fellow performer Thulani Chauke, who struggles with exhaustion to stay on his feet. As one reviewer described, Maqoma "attempts to prop him up and slap him awake, knowing that if he falls, he will most likely be abandoned—a loose screw in a giant, unstoppable machine."[6] We see their slow procession, a stunning mixture of abrupt slaps and tender ministrations of care, these two men on a Sisyphean march to nowhere, their journey accompanied by singing and an exquisite, delicate kora solo played by Guinean musician N'Faly Kouyaté. The music invites us to reflect on the porters' devotion to each other during this epic journey, however pointless their journey might be.[7]

I wondered about Gregory Maqoma's motivation for being in this show. How does he understand its impact and its relation to his other performance works? In an interview, he told me that he sees *The Head & the Load* as completely aligned with his own creations such as *Exit/Exist* about the Xhosa chief Maqoma, his ancestor, who resisted British forces and was exiled to Robben Island; and *Cion*, an adaptation of a Zakes Mda novel about a South African professional mourner who traces the route of the American Underground Railway that slaves used to escape to the North. Like these works, *The Head & the Load* is a diasporic summoning of the afterlives of injustice, an embodied engagement with the past, and a very personal commemoration. It is an incantation that is danced, sung, shouted, declaimed, spoken, whistled, and thumped. It is a calling forth of the restless spirits of those who died without a name and without a grave.

"They are not men because they have no name. They are not soldiers because they have no number. You don't call them: you count them," says a narrator in *The Head & the Load*. Europeans did not acknowledge Africans who served and died in World War I by names or even by their numbers. That is why *The Head & the Load* concludes with a recitation of names. Delivered as both an elegy and a ritual, the names have been salvaged from historical records despite all odds. They testify that Africans who served in World War I came from all over the continent: South Africa, the Congo, Angola, Mali, Mozambique, Senegal . . .

The list of the dead:

Geelbooi Dinokee
Salif Beye
Momar Diagne from Dakar
William Ditshepo

Saucepan Moake
Ousmane Diagne
Omar Diahatti
Momar Diop from Kabrousse
Whisky Mahlaba
Papa Mar Diop from St Louis
Samba Gueye from Pout
Ibrahim who committed suicide . . .[8]

Given the centrality of names to the theorizations and performance works by Gregory Maqoma and Faustin Linyekula, I asked Maqoma whether he sees this calling of names in *The Head & the Load* as being part of the same conversation:

> Yes. I think the most powerful thing about this piece is to somehow record what was never recorded. Because their deeds were never recorded. Names were important because they give you an identity. And their identity was lost because they were never recognized as people.[9]

What does it mean to him to hear these names read aloud at the end of *The Head & the Load*? Is this moment about correcting history? Setting the record straight? Awakening awareness about racism? For Maqoma, his motivation is rather more spiritual:

> It feels as a ritual. I mean when you send somebody into . . . to join your ancestors, you need to call them by their name. Because then, when you are talking to ancestors, they need to recognize and open a path for that person to come and join. And it's the same thing I had to do when I created *Exit/Exist*. I was taken by the elders to the grave of Chief Maqoma to open up a path, and they had to call me by name, generation from generation. So there is a sense of lineage that is recognized. "Okay, so he comes from this line of people."[10]

The power of performance is realized through living, breathing human beings in the company of other living human beings, together performing a ritual whose purpose, ultimately, is to bring the unsettled back home. The recitation of names in *The Head & the Load* is an act that performatively confers honor and dignity. "Every night it feels like you are paying homage," Maqoma says. "When these names are being called, it's about bringing them home because most of them were never returned. So it's about taking them back home, returning them to their home, and giving them a little bit of dignity."[11] For Maqoma, the real work of *The Head & the Load* will not be realized until the performance comes to Africa. Currently there are discussions about possibly touring *The Head & the Load* in Nigeria, Ghana, and South Africa. Maqoma has lobbied William Kentridge for this tour, saying: "William, you need to find a way, because for me, the real honor for those soldiers will be to really perform this work at home because then we will have gone a full circle, to really return them back, to bring their spirits back home."[12] A performance in Johannesburg was scheduled for May 2020 as this book went to press. It had to be cancelled when the calamity of the coronavirus swept over and paralyzed the whole world.

I began *Performance and the Afterlives of Injustice* with an image of me swimming in a pool, at first quite innocently and, in time, with growing awareness of the afterlives of injustice lying below me, those unsettled Native American human remains stored in boxes under that pool. These hidden but nevertheless present remains testified to a long-denied history of California genocide and the epistemological obsessions of my own university, which saw humans as objects, as the basis of scientific investigation, but chose not to see our state's history of genocide as something to be actively remembered and taught. How could it be that at the world's most preeminent public university so few people on campus knew what resided under Phoebe Hearst's pool?

One may come to consciousness slowly, seeing a little at a time. As we swim above the afterlives of injustice, how might we intervene? What can a mere performance do, especially in the absence of the necessary actions of acknowledgment, apology, and redress? *Performance and the Afterlives of Injustice* illuminates how African performance artists are intervening in the face of such histories, how they are staging embodied performances that navigate caustic waters with care and precision and with clear-eyed awareness of the corrosive and toxic forces the afterlives of injustice can unleash. Not all attempts to intervene are successful. Some misfire, some fail, some boomerang back and strike the artist over the head. But still the work compels and goes on. These histories are bigger than we are.

The artists I have featured imagine otherwise possibilities while performing in ways that instantiate redress. They counter interpellations of apartheid's annihilation of black selves by staging willfulness as a conversion, the point when a potential becomes a threat.[13] Just as the Space Theatre invented in the 1970s a new grammar for South African theater to perform at the edge of the law under apartheid, contemporary movement and body-based performing artists are reinventing forms and genres, this time in the wake of apartheid. Sometimes they expose visions of the real hiding in plain sight, perhaps on a Johannesburg street corner, or they toy with our investment in the outcome of violence by refusing to end a performance until we walk away, as Sello Pesa has modeled. Others reveal the failure of political transition not just as an idea but as a lived, embodied experience in which a single person has agency to overturn a dysfunctional, precarious rainbow bench. What comes next may be, as Mamela Nyamza has shown, a rediscovery of the ordinary right between one's legs, as one woman takes possession of sexuality that has long been repressed and forbidden. White characters in these works sometimes upstage actors of color, talk too much, self-aggrandize, and mansplain, as Toni Morkel's character does in Robyn Orlin's *Daddy, I've seen this piece six times before and I still don't know why they're hurting each other* and John Cartwright's character does in Jay Pather's *Body of Evidence*. But both of these performances expose the presumptions of whiteness while working to decenter its corrosive and colonizing reach. The dance between the dances, as Jay Pather has shown us, has no set score.

Africa's inheritances from Europe are not all toxic—some, such as the proscenium stage, may turn out to be liberating shelters in a place of ruin, as Linyekula found. Likewise, art can repurpose frivolous escapes such as extravagant nightlife cultures that spring up in the midst of poverty to serve more revolutionary ends. Faustin Linyekula asks of the Congo's infectious *ndombolo* music: "Why not use the fantastic energy of guitars and voices, not to sustain dreams as thin as the cheap paper handkerchiefs sold in the streets of Kinshasa, but on the contrary to speak of the difficulties, dead ends, mistakes and the poor legacy of our fathers?"[14] Sometimes the way forward can be found in something so simple, so personal, so profound as a name, one's own name: excavating it, saying it, calling it out. Using names not only to articulate the self, but also to summon others who are not yet at rest, we can call forth, as Gregory Maqoma has, the "beautiful me"—or the many "mes"—among us.

Performance and the Afterlives of Injustice reveals contemporary South African artists' simultaneous invocations and refusals of coherence through their performances, which seems to me to be the point. In the face of South African anomie and the present distended state of an arrested decolonial project, the whole does *not* cohere. The story does *not* add up. The promises of a liberated, nonracial postapartheid order have *not* yet been fulfilled. Unresolved histories insert themselves in our times, yet their excess often surpasses both our comprehension and our ability to do something productive in the face of them, at least in a linear fashion. In such circumstances, the visions of artists featured here reveal what otherwise evades perception. As their art disorders the toxic real, they wedge open spaces where necessary new fictions can take root, gestate, and become sentient, living, breathing realities in the now. They invite us to sit with the ruins, the pieces of the past they have salvaged, to dwell in a state of confusion. Through these works we are invited to enter performed dreamscapes for the sleep-deprived, to unbecome ourselves, stop in our tracks, interrupt our habits, and sit with what is uncomfortable without trying to solve or resolve it. As they imagine new forms, these artists are helping audiences see the contemporary moment as it is, and to conjure, anticipate, and dream a world that is otherwise.

Acknowledgments

This book exists only because of the ingenuity and genre-busting creativity of the artists who made the works I have featured. Their artistic insights and fierce integrity in grappling with such difficult topics have given audiences so much to think about, and clearly have given me much to think about. I am inspired by how they dwell in the palimpsest that constitutes the contradictions of the present, resisting impulses to simply move on from colonialism, apartheid, and a host of related traumas visited on the African continent. I am inspired by their insistent and persistent expectations that things *should be otherwise* than what they are or have been.

South Africa is a long way away from Seattle and Berkeley, the places I lived while writing this book. Research trips to South Africa, New York, Los Angeles, and various European cities were essential, and these were made possible by generous funding and support. I was privileged to receive from the University of California, Berkeley, the Humanities Research Fellowship as well as Academic Senate research funds. The University of Washington, my more recent academic home, provided both research funds and leave time so I could assume a three-month fellowship at the Interweaving Performance Cultures Center at the Freie Universität in Berlin. That residency was utterly transformative for this project, giving me the space, time, and intellectual community needed to turn various strands of thought into a coherent book concept. I was privileged to receive a National Humanities Center Fellowship, and while circumstances did not allow me to take up residency at the center, I am grateful for the selection committee's vote of confidence. Books get written because people believe in the project; authors are uplifted by the belief that others convey through such tangible expressions of support.

Dance and theater are highly ephemeral forms, and therefore archives play an especially critical role for research scholars in these fields. I am grateful to the Lilly Library at Indiana University and the National English Literary Museum in Grahamstown, South Africa, for giving me access to their holdings on Athol Fugard. The Ar(t)chive at the Wits School of Arts in

Johannesburg, and especially Adrienne Sichel and Jessica Denyschen, was absolutely pivotal in providing access to key video recordings. I could not have written this book without this support. I also am appreciative of video resources I was able to consult at the Media Library for Dance and Theater at Mime Centrum in Berlin and at the New York Public Library for the Performing Arts. Kellen Hoxworth and Kimberly Richards served as brilliant research assistants, and I am grateful for their dedication, thoroughness, and collegiality.

During the course of writing this book, I benefited from opportunities to present the work to colleagues at the American Society for Theatre Research, African Theatre Association, and Dance Studies Association, as well as seminars and lectures at the University of Western Cape, Northwestern University, Amherst College, University of Marburg, Freie Universität, Brown University, Dartmouth College, Simon Fraser University, and Royal Holloway University of London. At the University of California, Berkeley, where I used to work, ideas for this book gestated in many forums: the Arts Research Center, TDPS Conflux gatherings, and the Department of African American Studies Colloquium series, as well as in my many undergraduate classes and graduate seminars. But perhaps the most generative experience of all was a 2011 invitation from Victoria Marks at UCLA's Department of World Arts and Cultures when she asked me to be an interlocutor for artist Gregory Maqoma's trip to campus to perform his *Beautiful Me*. This event was my very first major invitation to speak about dance, and to be honest, I was baffled and terrified. As a theater scholar, I watched the performance video of *Beautiful Me* over and over again, wracking my brain about what I was going to *say* about a performance that had so few *words*. Theater scholars are habituated to scripts! That UCLA speaking invitation was a breakthrough moment for this book. It forced me to discover a new writing voice, to find words to express how bodies move, and this discovery has been liberating, revelatory, and empowering.

Many colleagues have read and responded to chapters and sections of this book. This book became better due their feedback, questions, and suggestions, as well as occasionally letters of recommendation for fellowships. I am especially indebted to Kemi Adeyemi, Awol Allo, Anurima Banerjee, Gerard Bester, Rustom Bharucha, Catherine Burns, Brandi Wilkins Catanese, Joshua Chambers-Letson, Maryanne Constable, Lawrence Douglass, Laura Edmonson, Susan Foster, Nadine George Graves, Mark Griffith, Gillian Hart, Kellen Hoxworth, Yvette Hutchinson, Jasmine Johnson, Victoria Kahn, Suk-Young Kim, Megan Lewis, Mary Luckhurst, Susan Manning,

Victoria Marks, Jens Mierheinrich, Philip Miller, Emilie Morin, Mamela Nyamza, Tejumola Olaniyan, Jay Pather, Beth Piatote, Alan Read, Janelle Reinelt, Kimberly Richards, Sandra Richards, Joseph Roach, Mary (Polly) Nooter Roberts, Analola Santana, Austin Sarat, Adrienne Sichel, Helene Silverberg, Adam Sitze, April Sizemore-Barber, Elizabeth Son, Amara Tabor-Smith, Jane Taylor, Lynn Thomas, Martha Merrill Umphrey, Tria Blu Wakpa, William Worthen, Hannah Wiley, Patricia Ybarra, and Mlondolozi Zondi, as well as the anonymous readers solicited by the University of Michigan Press. All remaining shortcomings are entirely my own.

Hospitality of South African friends has meant a great deal to me. I especially want to acknowledge Catherine Burns and Keith Breckenridge for letting me stay with them, making me part of a long lineage of international researchers who have broken bread at their table. Had it not been for their galvanizing conversations during our shared time as graduate students at Northwestern University in the early 1990s, I doubt I would have found my way to South Africa as a researcher. I have also enjoyed many convivial meals in the homes of Malcolm Purkey, Liz Gunner, Isabel Hofmeyer, Janice Honeyman, and Liza Key.

Editor Kate Babbitt worked with me in the final stage of manuscript preparation. With precision and insight, she helped me not only to see the forest from the trees, but also to discern each branch, leaf, and speck of pollen while never losing sight of the expansive vistas this book attempts to cover. LeAnn Fields, sponsoring editor at the University of Michigan Press, has believed in this book from the beginning. To her and her fine staff who have shepherded the manuscript into becoming a bound book, I extend my profound thanks. Thanks also to Frederick L. Brown who created the index.

An earlier version of chapter 1 was printed in *Law and Performance*, edited by Austin Sarat, Lawrence Douglas, and Martha Merrill Umphrey (copyright © 2018 by the University of Massachusetts Press). Portions of chapter 4 on Gregory Maqoma's *Beautiful Me* were published in *African Arts* in Winter 2011. The text that appears as prologue here is a completely revised version of my essay "Representing Genocide at Home: Ishi, Again," published in *Theatre and Human Rights after 1945: Things Unspeakable*, edited by Mary Luckhurst and Emilie Moran, 128–50 (London: Bloomsbury Methuen Drama, 2015). My coverage of Sello Pesa's *Bag Beatings* and Robyn Orlin's *and so you see . . . our honourable blue sky and ever enduring sun . . . can only be consumed slice by slice . . . ,* starring Albert Silindokuhle Ibokwe Khoza, first appeared as part of a review of the 2018 Johannesburg Dance Umbrella that I published in *Theatre Journal* 70, no. 4, in 2018.

My family, Kwame Braun and Aaron Braun Cole, have endured my absences from home during long research trips as well as my preoccupations in my messy office during most days when I was home. Sometimes they have accompanied me on research trips, which made the lonely process of working on a book so much more fun. Daily, they ground me, anchoring everything in the rhythms of our shared domesticity. I could not have written this book without their support, company, and welcome distractions.

Notes

PROLOGUE

1. This prologue is written in honor of Beth Piatote's play *Antíkoni,* which premiered with readings at the Phoebe A. Hearst Museum of Anthropology on the campus of the University of California, Berkeley, on November 6–7, 2018. A longer version of this essay was published as "Representing Genocide at Home," with a focus on an entirely different play by a different author but on the same theme of the afterlives of unrepatriated ancestral remains held at the University of California, Berkeley. Like a stone repeatedly washing up on shore, this story returns, each time transformed yet each time somehow also tenaciously the same.

2. Butler, *Precarious Life,* 19–49.

3. Morrison, *The Source of Self-Regard,* 133.

4. Ellison, *The Invisible Man,* 6.

5. Brechin, "The Way We (Almost) Were"; Architectural Conservation, Inc., PGA Design, Michael Corbett, Architectural Historian, and SMWM, San Francisco, *The University of California, Berkeley, Hearst Memorial Gymnasium: Historic Structure Report,* September 2005, https://realestate.berkeley.edu/sites/default/files/hsr_hearst_gymnasium_sept2005.pdf

6. Steven Finacom, "Phoebe Hearst Remembered as Premier UC Benefactor," *Berkeley Daily Planet,* April 21, 2011, http://www.berkeleydailyplanet.com/issue/2011-04-20/article/37716?headline=Phoebe-Hearst-Remembered-As-Premier-UC-Benefactor

7. A version of this text was read in the Phoebe A. Hearst Museum of Anthropology on November 8, 2018, as part of a panel presentation.

8. Alvarez, *Native America and the Question of Genocide,* 113.

9. Tony Platt, "UC and Native Americans: Unsettled Remains," *Los Angeles Times,* June 18, 2013, http://articles.latimes.com/2013/jun/18/opinion/la-oe-platt-native-american-indian-remains-20130618; see also Platt, *Grave Matters.*

10. Qtd. in Platt, *Grave Matters,* 171.

11. The story of Ishi's "discovery" in Oroville and exploitation by settlers is deeply tied to the history of the University of California, Berkeley. For a comprehensive summary of key sources on Ishi, see James Clifford, "Ishi's Story," in Clifford, *Returns*, 91–191.

12. Rassool, "Restoring the Skeletons of Empire."

13. "Governor Newsom Issues Apology to Native Americans for State's Historical Wrongdoings, Establishes Truth and Healing Council," press release, Office of Governor Newsom, June 18, 2019, https://www.gov.ca.gov/2019/06/18/governor-newsom-issues-apology-to-native-americans-for-states-historical-wrongdoings-establishes-truth-and-healing-council/

14. Qtd. in Perry, "When the World Was New," 278.

15. Richard C. Paddock, "Native Americans Say Berkeley Is No Place for Their Ancestors," *Los Angeles Times*, January 13, 2008, http://articles.latimes.com/2008/jan/13/local/me-bones13

16. Qtd. in Paddock.

17. "As I listen, things once obscure began falling into place. Odd things, unexpected things. Such as the poster that reminded me of the tenacity which a nation's moral evasions can take on given the trappings of racial stereotypes, and the ease with which its deepest experience of tragedy could be converted into blackface farce." Ellison, *Invisible Man*, xvi.

18. Piatote, *Antíkoni*.

19. Coincidentally, also in November 2018, the time of the Camp Fire, Boalt Hall was finally divested of its colonial name and given a new one. See Karen Sloan, "UC Berkeley Law to Ditch Boalt Moniker over Namesake's Racist Legacy," *Law.com*, November 13, 2018, https://www.law.com/therecorder/2018/11/13/berkeley-law-to-ditch-boalt-name/

20. Jack Nicas, Thomas Fuller, and Tim Arango, "Forced Out by Deadly Fires, Then Trapped in Traffic," *New York Times*, November 11, 2018, https://www.nytimes.com/2018/11/11/us/california-fire-paradise.html

21. Qtd. in Alene Tchekmedyian, Maria L. La Ganga, and Rubin Vives, "Could the Northern California Fire Really Have Killed 1,000 People? The Staggering Number of Missing Haunts Paradise," *Los Angeles Times*, November 19, 2018, https://www.latimes.com/local/lanow/la-me-missing-paradise-fire-california-20181119-story.html

22. On deep-settler colonies, see Steyn, *Whiteness Just Isn't What It Used to Be*, xxiv.

23. Frederickson, *White Supremacy*, xi–xii.

24. "Governor Newsom Issues Apology."

INTRODUCTION

1. Achille Mbembe, "Achille Mbembe on the State of South African Political Life," *Africa Is a Country*, September 19, 2015, https://africasacountry.com/2015/09/achille-mbembe-on-the-state-of-south-african-politics/

2. See Marcus, "The Violent Fight for Higher Education"; and Rosa Lyster, "The Student Protests Roiling South Africa," *New York Times*, October 21, 2016.

3. Sipho Hlongwane, "News Analysis: We Are Dangling on the Edge of a Failed State," *Mail & Guardian*, October 17, 2016, https://mg.co.za/article/2016-10-17-00-news-analysis-we-are-dangling-on-the-edge-of-a-failed-state/; see also Sean Jacobs, "Postapartheid South Africa's Negative Moment," *Africa Is a Country*, May 18, 2016, https://africasacountry.com/2016/05/postapartheid-south-africas-negative-moment/

4. Jason Musyoka, "Why Post Apartheid Order Is Only Starting Two Decades On," *Mail & Guardian*, October 3, 2016, https://mg.co.za/article/2016-10-03-00-why-post-apartheid-order-is-only-starting-two-decades-on/

5. Van Bever Donker et al., *The Remains of the Social.*

6. Van Bever Donker et al., 7.

7. Sharpe, *In the Wake*, 18.

8. Sharpe, 18.

9. Morrison, *The Source of Self-Regard*, 133.

10. Steingo, *Kwaito's Promise*, 95. See also Achille Mbembe: "The racial state in South Africa combined two technologies of power. In relation to blacks, both techniques of power and profit were, ever since the founding of Johannesburg, centered on the body: the individual body of the migrant worker and the racial body of the populace. These bodies were serialized and subjected to various forms of spatial distribution and apparatuses of capture." Mbembe, "Aesthetics of Superfluity," 52.

11. Foster, *Choreographing Empathy*, 13.

12. Weheliye, *Habeas Viscus*, 11.

13. Weheliye, 12.

14. Crawley, *Blackpentacostal Breath*, 24. I am grateful to Jasmine Johnson for drawing my attention to Crawley's work.

15. Crawley, "Otherwise, Ferguson."

16. This is also true of much black performance in the United States as analyzed by DeFrantz and Gonzalez, *Black Performance Theory*, 9.

17. Qtd. in Bongeka Masango and Georgina Selander, "Born Rebels in Avignon," *Libération: Le Blog de Officiel du Safari Culturel*, July 16, 2013, http://blog-partenaire-safariculturel.blogs.liberation.fr/2013/07/16/born-rebels-in-avignon/

18. Hartman, *Lose Your Mother*, 6.

19. Hartman, 6.

20. Meister's capitalization is deliberate, signifying the "transformation of Auschwitz-based reasoning into a new discourse of global power that claims to supersede the cruelties perpetrated by both revolutionaries and counterrevolutionaries during the previous two centuries." See Meister, *After Evil*, 3.

21. Meister, viii.

22. Wenzel, *Bulletproof*, 14.

23. On the *ngoma* form, see Meintjes, *Dust of the Zulu*. On Bharatanatyam and Indian dance in South Africa, see Radhakrishnan, "Dancing the Rainbow Nation as It Bleeds."

24. Sichel, *Body Politics*, 22.

25. See Friedman, *Post-Apartheid Dance*; Sichel, *Body Politics*; and Katrak, *Jay Pather*.

26. Pather and Boule, *Acts of Transgression*.

27. Gurney, *The Art of Public Space*.

28. Kruger, *The Drama of South Africa*, 183–206; Krueger, *Experiments in Freedom*.

29. Lewis, *Performing Whitely in the Postcolony*.

30. Two other recent volumes document contemporary South African artists across media—from photography and cartoons to theater, gay archives, and artistic work by urban geographers: Anders and Krouse, *Positions*; and Heidenreich-Seleme and O'Toole, *Über(w)Unden*. Both books represent valuable journalistic overviews, but they do not provide sustained scholarly analysis.

31. Middeke, Schnierer, and Homann, *The Methuen Drama Guide to Contemporary South African Theatre*.

32. Friedman, *Post-Apartheid Dance*; and Samuel, *Proceedings of Confluences 8*. See also *Critical Arts* 20, no. 2 (2006), which was a special issue dedicated to dance that published some of the proceedings from the 2004 JOMBA! Contemporary Dance Conference, entitled "African Contemporary Dance? Questioning Issues of a Performance Aesthetic for a Developing and Independent Continent."

33. Loots, "Post-Colonial Visitations," 93–94.

34. See Werry, "Oceanic Imagination"; Bharucha, "Hauntings of the Intercultural"; and Farfan and Knowles, "Editorial Comment."

35. Pather, "Democratic, Intercultural Choreography," 132.

36. Qtd. in Murnik, "Jay Pather," 115.

37. Roach, "Kinesis: The New Mimesis," 2.

38. See Fuchs, *Playing the Market*; and Orkin, *At the Junction*.

39. Pather, pers. comm., February 11, 2019.

40. Sichel, "Dance Is Where Theatre Was."

41. Cima, "Postconflict Nostalgia." In a similar vein, James Davies complained that "every *award-winning* theatre piece I saw at the Grahamstown Festival in July 2011 only massaged the old-hat identity politics. History was a big theme ('race histories')—a wreck of stereotypes: black actors masked as white, whites impersonating black, English as Xhosa, Zulus as English, performing and reperforming shopworn tribalisms over and over *ad infinitum* amen. It was only that these happy essentialisms were now repackaged for liberal Festival consumption, circling in a pattern designed to keep an apparently consoling status quo airborne for as long as humanly possible." See Davies, "The Fifth Congress of the South African Society for Research in Music," 192.

42. Sichel, "Grappling with South African Physical Theatre," 42. On Magnet Theatre, see Lewis and Krueger, *Magnet Theatre*.

43. Adrienne Sichel sees many of these artists as doing "conceptual" dance. See Sichel, "Grappling with South African Physical Theatre," 48–49.

44. Samuel, "Black Bodies Matter," 116.

45. See Desai, "An Exploratory Critique of the Notion of Social Cohesion"; Molefe, "Review of 'A Report on Ubuntu'"; Matolina and Kwindingwi, "The End of Ubuntu"; Watkins, "Simunye, We Are Not One"; Roome, "Transformation and Reconciliation"; and Hlongwane, "Simunye (We Are One!)."

46. "We are all one" is an English translation of "simunye," which was widely popularized as a slogan of national unity. See Hlongwane, "Simunye (We Are One!)."

47. Friedman, *Post-Apartheid Dance*, 10.

48. Qtd. in Masango and Selander, "Born Rebels in Avignon."

49. Hlongwane, "Simunye (We Are One!)," 3.

50. Krueger, *Experiments in Freedom*, xiii.

51. Krueger, 230.

52. Krueger, 230.

53. Krueger, 198.

54. Steyn, *Whiteness Just Isn't What It Used to Be*.

55. Racial blindness may sometimes masquerade as good manners, as Brandi Wilkins Catanese has persuasively argued in her book *The Problem of the Color[Blind]*, yet it may also masquerade as a principled ideological disavowal. Catanese identifies "the problem of the colorblind" in America as follows: "In this schema, race is the unruly chin hair on the face of an otherwise unblemished America: only bad manners would compel anyone to bring it up, and the

politest among us will instead do others the favor of not mentioning a thing that can only cause embarrassment, discomfort, or shame." Catanese, *The Problem of the Color[Blind]*, 5.

56. Krueger, *Experiments in Freedom*, xv. Mbembe, "Achille Mbembe on the State of South African Political Life."

57. Barry Bearak, "South Africa's Poor Renew a Tradition of Protest," *New York Times*, September 6, 2009, https://www.nytimes.com/2009/09/07/world/africa/07protests.html; Hazel Friedman, "Orlin against the World," *Mail & Guardian*, September 22, 1995, https://mg.co.za/article/1995-09-22-orlin-against-the-world

58. Christine Hauser, "'Fees Must Fall': Anatomy of the Student Protests in South Africa," *New York Times*, September 22, 2016, https://www.nytimes.com/2016/09/23/world/africa/fees-must-fall-anatomy-of-the-student-protests-in-south-africa.html; Norimitsu Onishi, "Students in South Africa Protest Slow Pace of Change," *New York Times*, September 8, 2015, https://www.nytimes.com/2015/09/09/world/africa/student-protests-in-south-africa-highlight-dissatisfaction-with-pace-of-change.html; Onishi, "South African Students Clash with Police in Cape Town over Tuition," *New York Times*, October 21, 2015, https://www.nytimes.com/2015/10/22/world/africa/south-africa-university-students.html

59. Adam Withnall, "Library Torched in 'Nazi-Style' Book Burning," *Independent*, September 7, 2016, https://www.independent.co.uk/news/world/africa/ukzn-south-africa-university-protests-nazi-style-library-book-burning-rape-brutality-a7230296.html

60. For perspectives on performances deemed by some to be failures and misfires, see Cima, "Postconflict Nostalgia"; and John Matshikiza, "Drama in the Streets," *Mail & Guardian*, March 14, 2007, https://mg.co.za/article/2007-03-14-drama-in-the-streets

61. Niren Tolsi, "Nice Work, Shame about the Lack of Insight and Risk," *Mail & Guardian*, July 8, 2011, https://mg.co.za/article/2011-07-08-nice-work-shame-about-the-lack-of-insight-and-risk. On the aesthetics of the previous struggle era, see Ndebele, *Rediscovery of the Ordinary*.

62. Krueger, *Experiments in Freedom*, 116.

63. Nduka Mntambo, "How 'Marikana: The Musical' Has Contributed to Cultural Amnesia," *Conversation*, August 17, 2017, http://theconversation.com/how-marikana-the-musical-has-contributed-to-cultural-amnesia-82651

64. Lewis, "Power Plays in the Cradle of Humankind."

65. Ellison, *The Invisible Man*, 6.

66. Achille Mbembe, "The Spear That Divided the Nation," *Cape Times*, June 5, 2012.

67. African National Congress, "Memorandum to the Goodman Gallery and Brett Murray," press release, May 30, 2012, reproduced at *Polity*, https://www.polity.org.za/article/sa-anc-memorandum-to-the-goodman-gallery-30052012-2012-05-30. Quotes come from the joint settlement agreement and statement between President Zuma, the ANC, Brett Murray, and the Goodman Gallery. For additional analysis of this controversy, see Hart, "Exposing the Nation"; Hassim, "Violent Modernity"; Pauwels, "Post-Struggle Art"; and Stupart, "Old Wounds, Fresh Meat."

68. Hassim, "Violent Modernity," 168.

69. Georgina Gratrix, qtd. in Stupart, "Old Wounds, Fresh Meat," 103.

70. Comaroff and Comaroff, *Theory from the South*.

71. See, for instance, Boehmer, "Endings and New Beginnings"; Clingman, "Writing the Interregnum"; Barnard, "Rewriting the Nation"; Jamal, *Predicaments of Culture in South Africa*; and De Kock, *Losing the Plot*.

72. Sichel, "Gate-Crashing Prejudices and Perceptions."

73. Lawless, "Souvenir," 147.

74. Colleran, "Re-Situating Fugard," 43.

75. Sörgel, *Contemporary African Dance Theatre*.

76. Qtd. in Krueger, "Gazing at 'Exhibit A,'" 5.

77. Anker, *Fictions of Dignity*, 2.

78. Anker, 74.

79. Habib, *South Africa's Suspended Revolution*, 27. See also Bundy, *Short-Changed?*; and Marais, *South Africa Pushed to the Limit*.

80. Habib, *South Africa's Suspended Revolution*, 13.

81. Habib, 24.

82. Meister, *After Evil*, 10.

83. See Gramsci, *Prison Notebooks*, 32–33. See also Gordimer, "Living in the Interregnum."

84. On the notion of cure in disability studies, see Shakespeare, *Disability Rights and Wrongs Revisited*; Hamraie, "Historical Epistemology as Disability Studies Methodology"; and Garland-Thomson, "Integrating Disability, Transforming Feminist Theory."

85. De Kock, *Losing the Plot*, 11.

86. Dillon, *New World Drama*, 50.

87. Qtd. in Murnik, "Jay Pather," 113.

88. Pather, "Negotiating the Postcolonial Black Body," 139.

89. The idea of interweaving, which is motivated by a "beyond postcolonialism" sentiment and attempts to recuperate and resuscitate interculturalism within performance theory, has many similarities with the "letting go" framing in South Africa. See Fischer-Lichte, Jost, and Jain, *The Politics of Interweaving*

Performance Cultures. The notion of "beyond" seems as preposterous as "post" when the afterlives of apartheid's and colonialism's injustices continue to froth, seethe, agitate, and thrive today.

90. Nuttall, *Entanglement*, 1.

91. See Desai, "An Exploratory Critique of the Notion of Social Cohesion"; Molefe, "Review of 'A Report on Ubuntu'"; Matolina and Kwindingwi, "The End of Ubuntu"; Watkins, "Simunye, We Are Not One"; Roome, "Transformation and Reconciliation"; and Hlongwane, "Simunye (We Are One!)."

92. Friedman, "The Impact of the Tourist Gaze," 102.

93. Frederickson, *White Supremacy*, xi–xii.

94. DeFrantz and Gonzalez, *Black Performance Theory*.

95. Young, *Illegible Will*, 7.

96. DeFrantz and Gonzalez, *Black Performance Theory*.

97. Zondi, review of *Black Performance Theory*, 281.

98. Schneider, *Performing Remains*.

99. Schneider, 180.

100. Auslander, *Liveness*; Phelan, *Unmarked*; Taylor, *The Archive and the Repertoire*.

101. Snyder-Young, *Theatre of Good Intentions*; Dolan, *Utopia in Performance*; Thompson, *Humanitarian Performance*; Thompson, *Performance Affects*; Edmonson, *Performing Trauma in Central Africa*.

102. Carlson, *The Haunted Stage*; Schneider, *Performing Remains*; Roach, *Cities of the Dead*.

103. Cole, *Ghana's Concert Party Theatre*; Cole, *Performing South Africa's Truth Commission*.

104. Ndebele, *Rediscovery of the Ordinary*.

105. Bank, *Theatre Culture in America*, 2.

106. Sexton, "Afro-Pessimism: The Unclear Word."

CHAPTER 1

1. "Coloured" in apartheid South Africa meant "mixed race." I use South African spelling in this chapter to draw attention to this historically and culturally specific usage. Black Consciousness, a movement begun by activist Steve Biko, introduced the idea that "black" meant all people of color, including those categorized under apartheid as "coloured." It is for this reason that later in this chapter I at times refer to the character Errol as "black."

2. Achille Mbembe, "Rule of Property versus Rule of the Poor?," *Mail &*

Guardian, June 15, 2012, https://mg.co.za/article/2012-06-15-rule-of-property-versus-rule-of-the-poor

3. Althusser, "Ideology and Ideological State Apparatuses," 118.

4. Butler, *The Psychic Life of Power.*

5. Dolar, "Beyond Interpellation"; Butler, *The Psychic Life of Power,* especially chapter 4, "'Conscience Doth Make Subjects of Us All': Althusser's Subjection," 106–31.

6. Dolar, "Beyond Interpellation," 76.

7. Dolar, 87.

8. Butler, *The Psychic Life of Power,* 129.

9. Bunch, "The Unbecoming Subject of Sex," 50.

10. Bunch, 53.

11. Agamben, *Homo Sacer,* 6–7.

12. Weheliye, *Habeas Viscus,* 4.

13. Butler, *Precarious Life,* 68.

14. See Hartman, *Scenes of Subjection.* Hartman's research on nineteenth-century America reveals how operations of terror could be found in quotidian practices where terror could hardly be discerned—self-fashioning, dancing in the slave quarters, or the comic inversions and exaggerated body contortions of the minstrel stage.

15. Fugard, *Notebooks, 1960–1977,* 132–33.

16. Vandenbroucke, *Truths the Hand Can Touch,* 203.

17. Colleran, "Athol Fugard and the Problematics of the Liberal Critique," 390.

18. Fugard, Kani, and Ntshona, *Statements: Sizwe Bansi Is Dead, The Island, Statements after an Arrest under the Immorality Act.* This volume was originally published by Oxford University Press in 1974 and subsequently republished by Theatre Communications Group in 1986. All citations in this chapter refer to the latter republication. Note that the incorrect spelling of "Banzi" as "Bansi" appeared in both versions.

19. Wertheim, *The Dramatic Art of Athol Fugard,* 69.

20. For summary of titles from theatrical reviews of this play in South African press, see Read, *Athol Fugard: A Bibliography.* One review is Owen Williams, "Honesty, Integrity, but Dullness in Play," *Cape Times,* 29 March 1972, 17.

21. Fugard, *Notebooks, 1960–1977,* 196.

22. Fugard, *Statements after an Arrest,* 81.

23. Fugard mss., Box 1, Folder 28, Notebook 1971 to 1972/10, entry dated June 5, 1972, Papers of Athol Fugard, 1918–1997, Lilly Library, Indiana University, Bloomington, Indiana (hereafter "Fugard mss.").

24. Fugard mss., Box 1, Folder 28, Notebook 1971 to 1972/10, entry dated May 7, 1972.

25. See South African Parliament, "Act to Prohibit Illicit Carnal Intercourse between Europeans and Natives and Other Acts in Relation Thereto," March 26, 1927, https://en.wikisource.org/wiki/Immorality_Act,_1927

26. See South African Parliament, "Act to Amend the Immorality Act, 1927, So as to Prohibit Illicit Carnal Intercourse between Europeans and Non-Europeans, and to Provide for Matters Incidental Thereto," May 1, 1950, https://en.wikisource.org/wiki/Immorality_Amendment_Act,_1950

27. Colleran, "Re-Situating Fugard," 43.

28. Fugard mss., Box 1, Folder 30, Notebook 1972/11.

29. Fugard mss., Box 4, Folder 29, typescript of draft of *Statements after an Arrest* with holograph insertions and changes. Handwritten note appears after page 13.

30. Fugard, *Statements after an Arrest*, 80.

31. Wertheim, *The Dramatic Art of Athol Fugard*, 72.

32. Fugard, *Statements after an Arrest*, 81.

33. Orkin, *Drama and the South African State*, 110.

34. Davis, *Voices of Justice and Reason*, 150.

35. Brian Astbury, pers. comm., August 7, 2019.

36. Fugard, *Statements after an Arrest*, 82.

37. Fugard, 85.

38. Fugard, 93–94.

39. Fugard, 89–90.

40. Fugard, 91.

41. Fugard, 82.

42. Fugard, 84–85.

43. Fugard, 93.

44. Errol rejects Mladen Dolar's claim that love can be beyond interpellation, just as Judith Butler does. See Butler, *The Psychic Life of Power*, 127–31. See also Kahn, *Law and Love*.

45. Fugard, *Statements after an Arrest*, 96.

46. Fugard mss., Box 1, Folder 30, Notebook 1972/11.

47. Fugard mss., Box 1, Folder 28, Notebook 1971 to 1972/10, entry for August 8, 1972.

48. Fugard, *Statements after an Arrest*, 96.

49. Fugard, 96.

50. Fugard, 96.

51. Fugard, 98.

52. Fugard, 99.

53. Fugard, 101–2.

54. Fugard, 102.

55. Fugard, 103.

56. Fugard, 104.

57. Fugard, 101.

58. Fugard, 105.

59. Fugard, 105.

60. His journey would seem to contradict Dolar's hypothesis that perhaps the interior register of love is beyond interpellation. See Dolar, "Beyond Interpellation," 85.

61. Fugard, *Statements after an Arrest*, 106.

62. Fugard, 106.

63. Fugard, 107–8.

64. Fugard, 108.

65. Butler, *The Psychic Life of Power*, 130.

66. Dillon, *New World Drama*, 50.

67. States, *Great Reckonings in Little Rooms*, 20.

68. See Slaughter, *Human Rights, Inc.*; and Anker, *Fictions of Dignity*.

69. Davis, *Voices of Justice and Reason*, 145.

70. Qtd. in Fuchs, *Playing the Market*, 30.

71. Meierhenrich, *The Legacies of Law*, 112.

72. One can trace the play through its evolving form in the several versions of the play manuscript held in the Papers of Athol Fugard at the Lilly Library at Indiana University, Bloomington.

73. Orkin, *Drama and the South African State*, 165. This restriction is likely why one never sees the guards or prison wardens in one of the other key *Statement* plays, *The Island*, an adaptation of the Antigone story set in the notorious prison of Robben Island.

74. Fugard, *Notebooks, 1960–1977*, 196.

75. Fugard, 196.

76. Uys, *No Space on Long Street*.

77. Uys, 26.

78. Uys, 32.

79. Uys, 33.

80. Uys, 31. Note that Brian Astbury, founding producer of the Space Theatre, claims that Pieter-Dirk Uys's memory deceives him: while the theater was raided on several occasions, no raid happened during *The Glass Menagerie*. Brian Astbury, pers. comm., August 7, 2019.

81. Uys, *No Space on Long Street*, 32.

82. Uys, 29–30.

83. Fugard, *Statements after an Arrest*, 108.

84. Ahmed, *Willful Subjects*, 11.

85. Ahmed, 23.

CHAPTER 2

1. Mamdani, "Beyond Nuremberg."

2. Sitze, *The Impossible Machine*.

3. Saidiya V. Hartman coined the phrase "afterlives of slavery" in her book *Lose Your Mother*. Christina Sharpe subsequently amplified and expanded on the term in her book *In the Wake*. For insightful overviews on the state of contemporary South Africa, see Reddy, *South Africa, Settler Colonialism and the Failures of Liberal Democracy*; Hart, *Rethinking the South African Crisis*; and Pithouse, *Writing the Decline*.

4. Nixon, *Slow Violence and the Environmentalism of the Poor*.

5. Caelainn Barr, "Inequality Index: Where Are the World's Most Unequal Countries?" *Guardian*, April 26, 2017, https://www.theguardian.com/inequality/datablog/2017/apr/26/inequality-index-where-are-the-worlds-most-unequal-countries

6. Reddy, *South Africa, Settler Colonialism and the Failures of Liberal Democracy*.

7. Charlotte England, "South Africa's Murder Rate Climbs 4.9 Per Cent to 51 People Killed Every Day," *Independent*, September 3, 2016, https://www.independent.co.uk/news/world/africa/south-africa-murder-rate-51-killed-every-day-rise-49-per-cent-a7224176.html

8. Enwezor, "The Enigma of the Rainbow Nation."

9. Derek Yu, "The Lesser Known and Scarier Facts about Unemployment in South Africa," *Conversation*, September 3, 2017, https://theconversation.com/the-lesser-known-and-scarier-facts-about-unemployment-in-south-africa-83055

10. Greg Nicolson, "South Africa: Where 12 Million Live in Extreme Poverty," *Daily Maverick*, February 3, 2015, https://www.dailymaverick.co.za/article/2015-02-03-south-africa-where-12-million-live-in-extreme-poverty/

11. Pithouse, *Writing the Decline*, 71.

12. Bundy, *Short-Changed?*, 50.

13. Bundy, 140.

14. Bundy, 41.

15. Jamal, *Predicaments of Culture in South Africa*.

16. Habib, *South Africa's Suspended Revolution*.

17. Habib, 13.

18. Achille Mbembe, "Rule of Property versus Rule of the Poor?," *Mail & Guardian,* June 15, 2012, https://mg.co.za/article/2012-06-15-rule-of-property-versus-rule-of-the-poor

19. Sharpe, *In the Wake.*

20. Ndebele, *Rediscovery of the Ordinary,* 52–53 (italics in the original).

21. Sachs, "Preparing Ourselves for Freedom." See also Sachs and respondents, *Spring Is Rebellious.*

22. Pieterse, "Post-Apartheid Geographies in South Africa," 1.

23. See chapter 4 in Steingo, *Kwaito's Promise,* for a thoughtful reflection on the navigation of urban space in Soweto and the way the vestiges of apartheid still pattern movement and paths of travel today.

24. Kruger, "Black Atlantics, White Indians, and Jews," 113.

25. Frenkel and MacKenzie, "'Post-Transitional' South African Literature in English.

26. Frenkel and MacKenzie, "Conceptualizing 'Post-Transitional' South African Literature in English," 2.

27. Flockemann, "Little Perpetrators, Witness-Bearers and the Young and the Brave," 21.

28. Weheliye, *Habeas Viscus,* 12.

29. Anderson and Menon, *Violence Performed,* 4. Italics in the original.

30. On hieroglyphics of the flesh, see Spillers, *Black, White, and in Color.*

31. Weheliye, *Habeas Viscus.*

32. Caroline Smart, "Body of Evidence," *Artsmart: KZN Arts News,* October 17, 2009, http://news.artsmart.co.za/2009/10/body-of-evidence_17.html

33. Pather, "Laws of Recall," 337.

34. Fairbanks, "'I Have Sinned against the Lord.'"

35. Qtd. in Fairbanks.

36. Fairbanks.

37. South African gumboot dancing is associated with mine labor, as rubber boots were worn by workers underground, and the dancing form that evolved—of rhythmic slapping on boots and body parts—was also a way to communicate in the dark. Eventually mine owners exploited this dance form by having troupes perform for visitors. See Muller and Farigon, "Gumboots, Bhaca Migrants, and Fred Astaire."

38. Jay Pather, "Artist's Statement for *Body of Evidence,*" Grahamstown National Arts Festival, Official Program, 2009, 42.

39. Pather, 42.

40. Shakespeare, *Disability Rights and Wrongs Revisited,* 137.

41. Shakespeare, 145.

42. Garland-Thomson, "Integrating Disability, Transforming Feminist Theory," 264–65.

43. Sparks, *Beyond the Miracle*.

44. For additional scholarship on Mamela Nyamza, see Feltham, "Decolonising the Stage"; Johnstone, "Looking behind the Mirror"; and Mahali, "Rites of Passage."

45. Gottschild, *The Black Dancing Body*.

46. Claire Keeton, "Captivated by Mamela Nyamza," *Sunday Times* (Johannesburg), June 10, 2018, https://www.pressreader.com/south-africa/sunday-times/20180610/283124249588849

47. Mahali, "Rites of Passage," 1.

48. Mike Anderson, "Review: *Hatched* (Mamela Nyamza/Canstage)," *Mooney on Theatre*, April 15, 2015, https://www.mooneyontheatre.com/2015/04/15/hatched-mamela-nyamzacanstage/ (italics in the original).

49. Zaza Hlalethwa, "Nyamza's Hatchling Comes into His Own," *Mail & Guardian*, July 6, 2018, https://mg.co.za/article/2018-07-06-00-nyamzas-hatchling-comes-into-his-own

50. Ahmed, *Willful Subjects*, 23 (italics in the original).

51. Ballet's colonizing and white supremacist legacies have been a focus for many choreographers in South Africa, as Sichel illuminates in *Body Politics*.

52. Siya Ngcobo, "The Elitism of Ballet Tackled with Attitude," *Cue*, July 3, 2015, http://cue.ru.ac.za/the-elitism-of-ballet-tackled-with-attitude/

53. Steven Weisz, "Review of Mamela Nyamza's *The Meal*," *Dance Journal*, April 23, 2015, https://philadelphiadance.org/dancejournal/2015/04/23/review-of-mamela-nyamzas-the-meal/

54. Weisz.

55. *Mamela Nyamza: Choreographer, Dancer, and Performer—South Africa*, accessed September 9, 2018, http://mamelanyamza.com/

56. Annie Kelly, "Raped and Killed for Being a Lesbian: South Africa Ignores 'Corrective' Attacks," *Guardian*, March 12, 2009. https://www.theguardian.com/world/2009/mar/12/eudy-simelane-corrective-rape-south-africa

57. I saw this work on Friday, July 8, 2011, at the National Arts Festival.

58. Johan Myburg, "Intimate, Inward and African," *Cue*, July 15, 2011, reprinted at *AllAfrica*, http://allafrica.com/stories/201107151077.html/

59. Myburg.

60. Sachs, "Preparing Ourselves for Freedom."

61. For a fuller analysis of this performance, see Sizemore-Barber, *Prismatic Performances*.

62. Pithouse, *Writing the Decline*, 43–47, and 73.

63. "The crisis consists precisely in the fact that the old is dying and the new

cannot be born; in this interregnum, morbid phenomena of the most varied kin come to pass," said Gramsci, *Prison Notebooks*, 32–33.

64. Analysis in this text is based on a video of the opening of this show taped on February 24, 2017, and made available to me by the Ar(t)chive at the University of Witwatersrand (Wits University).

65. On vamping as a larger dynamic in black vernacular dance, see Jackson, "Improvisation in African-American Vernacular Dancing."

66. Adrienne Sichel, "Testifying for Humanity," *JOMBA! Contemporary Dance Experience*, August 22, 2017, https://medium.com/@JombaDance/testifying-for-humanity-876a8c177185

67. See I Am Woman Leap of Faith, season 2, episode 2, "Mamela Nyamza," directed by Miki Redelinghuys, April 13, 2013, YouTube video, 24:33, https://www.youtube.com/watch?v=SkeP3aCoEwE, especially starting at 12:00.

68. Sarah Roberson, "*De-Apart-Hate*: Intricate and Difficult," *Critter*, October 7, 2016, http://thecritter.co.za/?p=1712/

69. Robyn Sassen, "Chapter and Verse of Dogma and Sex, and a Little Something to Take Home with You," *My View by Robyn Sassen*, February 25, 2017, https://robynsassenmyview.com/2017/02/25/chapter-and-verse-of-dogma-and-sex-and-a-little-something-to-take-home-with-you/

70. Masego Panyane, "#NAF18's '*Phuma-Langa*' Mime Act Is a 'Silent Scream' with Subtle Nuances," *IOL*, July 4, 2018, https://www.iol.co.za/entertainment/whats-on/naf18s-phuma-langa-mime-act-is-a-silent-scream-with-subtle-nuances-15824758

71. Nicola van Straaten, "*De-Apart-Hate*: Mamela Nyamza," *People Are Dancing Here*, January 12, 2017, https://peoplearedancing.wordpress.com/2017/01/12/de-apart-hate-mamela-nyamza/

72. Achille Mbembe, "Achille Mbembe on the State of South African Political Life," *Africa Is a Country*, September 19, 2015, https://africasacountry.com/2015/09/achille-mbembe-on-the-state-of-south-african-politics/

73. Ahmed, *Willful Subjects*, 11.

74. See isiZulu and English translation of the lyrics of this song at "'As'phelelanga' by Vusi Nova and Jessica Mbangeni," *Musixmatch*, accessed August 22, 2019, https://www.musixmatch.com/lyrics/Vusi-Nova-feat-Jessica-Mbangeni/As-phelelanga/translation/english

75. Mpho Raborife, "ANC Conference Kicks Off with Battle of the Songs," *News 24*, June 30, 2017, https://www.news24.com/SouthAfrica/News/anc-conference-kicks-off-with-battle-of-the-songs-20170630

76. See "ANC Delegates Don't Sing from Same Songbook," *ENCA/DStv Channel 403*, July 1, 2017, https://www.enca.com/south-africa/anc-delegates-battle-in-song-ahead-of-policy-conference

77. Sassen, "Chapter and Verse of Dogma and Sex."

78. Mamela Nyamza, pers. comm., August 16, 2019.

79. Ngũgĩ wa Thiong'o, *Decolonising the Mind*; Ndlovu-Gatsheni, *Epistemic Freedom in Africa*.

80. "De-Apartheid," *Mamela Nyamza: Choreographer, Dancer, and Performer—South Africa*, accessed August 19, 2018, http://mamelanyamza.com/creations/de-apartheid.html. *Ubuntu* is an isiZulu word that is often translated as "I am because we are," and that indicates an essential dynamic of humaneness. The concept was central to South Africa's Truth and Reconciliation Commission.

81. Fugard, *Statements after an Arrest*, 106.

82. Young, *Illegible Will*.

83. Gurney, *The Art of Public Space*, 109.

84. I saw the Dance Umbrella performance at the Wits Downstairs Theatre on Thursday, March 15, 2018. A video of the 2017 version staged at the Centre for the Less Good Idea can be seen online, though it bears little resemblance to the Dance Umbrella version, for which there was no live music or projection prelude. Nor did the Dance Umbrella version transpire on a raised platform in a boxing ring, and perhaps because of the absence of the rope barrier, the audience was more directly implicated. There were moments of humor, yes, but the show was a more direct, aggressive, extreme and visceral experience and also just longer. The first iteration was 11 minutes, and later versions ran 75 minutes—a slow evisceration of the audience's confidence that they were separate from the spectacle or the action. For the 2017 version, see *Bag Beatings* [Full], *Centre for the Less Good Idea*, Vimeo video, 2017, 10:52, https://vimeo.com/211480785. South Africa's Dance Umbrella was founded in 1989 and the original sponsor was AA Life, followed by sponsorship from IGI Life (1989–93), and then First National Bank (1994–2010). After 2010 First National Bank (FNB) withdrew its sponsorship and naming rights. See Sichel, *Body Politics*, 154.

85. Mary Braid, "Truth at the End of the Rainbow," *Independent*, June 14, 1998, https://www.independent.co.uk/arts-entertainment/truth-at-the-end-of-the-rainbow-1164853.html

86. Jason Burke, "South Africa: Murders Surge by More than 7% in a Year," *Guardian*, September 11, 2018, https://www.theguardian.com/world/2018/sep/11/south-africa-murders-surge-by-more-than-7-percent-in-a-year

87. See chapters 1 ("The May 2008 Programs") and 9 ("Only Protected on Paper") in Pithouse, *Writing the Decline*, 7–15, and 43–47.

88. See Andersson, "Mpumelelo Paul Grootboom"; and Sobiso, "Paul Grootboom and the Quest to Reroute South African Theatre."

89. For an overview of Grootboom's oeuvre, see Andersson, "Mpumelelo Paul Grootboom."

90. Ndebele, *Rediscovery of the Ordinary*.

91. Robyn Sassen, "Welcome to the Scene of the Crime," *My View by Robyn Sassen*, March 16, 2018, https://robynsassenmyview.com/2018/03/16/welcome-to-the-scene-of-the-crime/

92. Boxing is also a motif in Pather's *Body of Evidence* (2008), and it was the subject of one of the most famous productions of early South African theater, the 1959 work *King Kong*, which featured the young Hugh Masekela and Miriam Makeba. This musical, modeled on *Porgy and Bess*, was about a legendary black South African boxer.

93. Kelly, "Raped and Killed for Being a Lesbian"; Reality Check team, "South Africa: How Common Are Xenophobic Attacks?," *BBC News*, April 7, 2019, https://www.bbc.com/news/world-africa-47800718

94. See Gurney, *The Art of Public Space*, 1–2; Siegenthaler, "Aesthetic Shifts in a Transforming City."

95. Siegenthaler, "Aesthetic Shifts in a Transforming City," 90.

96. Gurney, *The Art of Public Space*, 35.

97. I would be remiss if I did not acknowledge that I soon called my wait off and went back inside the theater to see if I could find a more reliable alternative. I was most grateful to receive the offer of a ride by none other than Dance Umbrella director Georgina Thomson.

98. A phrase derived from Mbembe, "Rule of Property versus Rule of the Poor?"

99. Morrison, *The Source of Self-Regard*, 133.

100. See Muñoz, *Disidentifications*, 21 (and this chapter's epigraph).

101. Schneider, *Performing Remains*, 1–26.

102. Bank, *Theatre Culture in America*, 2.

103. The phrase "vistas of capacity" comes from Ndebele, *Rediscovery of the Ordinary*, 52.

CHAPTER 3

1. Peter Crawley, "The Trials of Brett Bailey: 'I Was Seen as a Racist South African. That Typecast Me.'" *Irish Times*, July 11, 2015, https://www.irishtimes.com/culture/stage/the-trials-of-brett-bailey-i-was-seen-as-a-racist-south-african-that-typecast-me-1.2280455. See online petition written by Sara Meyers at Change.org, last updated September 24, 2014, https://www.change.org/p/withdraw-the-racist-exhibition-exhibition-b-the-human-zoo

2. See Bain, "Hypertheatrical Performance on the Post-Apartheid Stage," esp. 146 and 161n3.

3. Krouse, "A Staccato Movement of Expansive and Neurotic Individuals," 134.

4. Sichel, "When Jay Pather Shook Johannesburg in 2003."

5. Larlham, "Brett Bailey and Third World Bunfight," 13.

6. Achille Mbembe, "Decolonizing Knowledge and the Question of the Archive," unpublished essay, 2015, https://wiser.wits.ac.za/system/files/Achille%20Mbembe%20-%20Decolonizing%20Knowledge%20and%20the%20Question%20of%20the%20Archive.pdf

7. Krueger, "Celebrating the Spirt of Tragedy," 229.

8. Krouse, "A Staccato Movement of Expansive and Neurotic Individuals," 135.

9. Krouse, 137.

10. Roslyn Sulcas, "Pointed Choreography, Rooted in South Africa," *New York Times*, February 10, 2011, https://www.nytimes.com/2011/02/11/arts/dance/11orlin.html; Hazel Friedman, "Orlin against the World," *Mail & Guardian*, September 22, 1995, https://mg.co.za/article/1995-09-22-orlin-against-the-world

11. Judith Mackrell, "Out of the Darkness," *Guardian*, July 15, 2002, https://www.theguardian.com/stage/2002/jul/15/dance.artsfeatures

12. Rudakoff, "Why Did the Chicken Cross the Cultural Divide?" 81; Larlham, "Brett Bailey and Third World Bunfight," 9.

13. Cue Editor, "Welcome to the Circus," CueOnline, July 4, 2009. http://cue.ru.ac.za/2009/07/welcome-to-the-circus/

14. Rudakoff, "Why Did the Chicken Cross the Cultural Divide?"

15. The Siwela Sonke Dance Theatre started, in 1997, with an equal number of men and women. The five men were black, and the women consisted of one Indian, two Africans, and two white people. Both the black African women have remained all these years; the white woman and the two Indian women have left. As these three women were replaced over the years, white women seldom stayed. After a while, as the number of company members and funding dwindled, one of the remaining women, Neliswa Rushualang, took on a group of *pantsula* dancers. (*Pantsula* is a highly energetic street dance form.) Rushualang trained this all-Zulu male group as contemporary dancers. Jay Pather says, "This was a massive game changer for the company as the quality of her teaching kept these dancers as the core of the company and they went on to also create their own companies (Khanyiso Kunene and Sandile Mkhize), while the others remained under the direction of Neli Rushualang and Ntombi Gasa. There are now three men and four women, all black." Jay Pather, pers. comm., December 6, 2018.

16. Flockemann, "Spectacles of Excess."

17. See Larlham, "Brett Bailey and Third World Bunfight," 7.

18. See Lei, "Interruption, Intervention, Interculturalism."

19. Peter Machen, "'Body of Evidence': Jay Pather at the Playhouse," *Artthrob: Contemporary Art in South Africa*, October 2009, http://www.artthrob.co.za/Reviews/Review_of_Body_of_Evidence_by_Peter_Machen_at_The_Playhouse.aspx

20. Brenda Dixon Gottschild, "'My Africa Is Always in the Becoming': Outside the Box with Faustin Linyekula," 2007, https://brendadixongottschild.files.wordpress.com/2010/07/outside-the-box-with-faustin-linyekula.pdf

21. See Bharucha, *Theatre and the World*.

22. See Robyn Orlin, *Daddy, I've seen this piece six times before but I still don't know why they're hurting each other*, RobynOrlin.com, accessed November 3, 2018, http://www.robynorlin.com/productions/Daddy/prod_Daddy01.htm. My analysis of *Daddy* is based on a video at the Mime Centrum in Berlin of a performance at the Montpellier Danse Festival on January 1, 2000. See Robyn Orlin, *Daddy, I've seen this piece six times before but I still don't know why they're hurting each other*, video of dance performance, Montpellier Danse Festival, January 1, 2000, 25 minutes, http://archiv.mimecentrum.de/videos/MCB-DV-4404. I have also referenced a video that was shot at the Dance Factory in 1999, when the show first premiered. My sincere gratitude to Jessica Denyschen from the Ar(t)chive at the University of Witwatersrand in South Africa for giving me access to this historic video. *Daddy* is an improvisatory work that morphed and changed over time, so these two video records are not entirely consistent.

23. The cast list I provide here is from the Montpellier Danse Festival performance. Regretfully, I was not able to see a performance of this work live. In South Africa, beyond the 1999 premiere, *Daddy* was performed at the Market Theatre in 2002 and 2012. The work has been performed all over Europe—besides its performance at the Montpellier Danse Festival, for instance, it has been performed at the Théâtre de la Ville (Paris), the Lille Opera (Lille), the Centre National de Danse Contemporaine (Angers), and the Barbican Centre (London).

24. Orlin has said, "I hate talking about my work and having to explain it, so titles really function as programme notes for me. They also allow for a lot of free association on the part of the audience, and that makes for healthy viewing." See Donald Hutera, "Introducing Robyn Orlin, an Unorthodox Beauty," *LondonDance.com*, August 12, 2013, http://londondance.com/articles/features/an-unorthodox-beauty/

25. Krouse, "A Staccato Movement of Expansive and Neurotic Individuals," 131.

26. Nelisiwe Xaba is also known as Nelisiwe Xaba, a name she more commonly adopted later in her career.

27. These six performers made up the cast for the production that traveled internationally from 2000. There have been variations in the cast over the life of the production.

28. This reference in the 1999 performance anticipated an upcoming performance by the company at a festival in Madagascar. So instead of coming from there (like the ducks), the company was going to Madagascar.

29. *Daddy* went on to win third place at the Festival of African and Indian Ocean Choreography, held in Antananarivo, Madagascar, in 1999, a recognition that propelled the work to international visibility. That festival later became known as Choreographic Encounters of Africa and the Indian Ocean and is now entitled Danse l'Afrique danse.

30. Mackrell, "Out of the Darkness."

31. South Africa's relatively peaceful transition to democracy is often spoken of as a "miracle." See Sparks, *Beyond the Miracle*.

32. Steyn, *Whiteness Just Isn't What It Used to Be*, xxxi (italics added).

33. Fischer-Lichte, Jost, and Jain, *The Politics of Interweaving Performance Cultures*.

34. Bharucha, "Hauntings of the Intercultural."

35. Werry, "Oceanic Imagination," 97.

36. Catanese, *The Problem of the Color[Blind]*, 5.

37. Mbembe, "Decolonizing Knowledge and the Question of the Archive" (italics in the original).

38. John Hogg's photo of Neli's solo in *Daddy* took second place in 2000 in the World Press Photo competition. See "John Peter Hogg," *World Press Photo*, 2000, https://www.worldpressphoto.org/collection/photo/2000/32049/1/2000-John-Peter-Hogg-AE2

39. Katzke, "Probing the Politics of the Female Body," addendum A, extracts from an interview conducted with Robyn Orlin in 2012.

40. See *The History of Xibelani* (trailer), directed by Maya Wegerif (Sho Madjozi), March 6, 2018, YouTube video, 2:38, https://www.youtube.com/watch?v=zYRSQDgAfXI; Sichel, "Dance Is Where Theatre Was."

41. On the verticality of Western classical dance and its contrast with African movement, see John Perpener, "Jawole Willa Jo Zollar," *Jacob's Pillow Dance Interactive*, accessed December 22, 2018, https://danceinteractive.jacobspillow.org/themes-essays/african-diaspora/jawole-willa-jo-zollar/. See also chapter 4 ("Butt") in Gottschild, *The Black Dancing Body*, 144–87.

42. Gottschild, *The Black Dancing Body*, 18.

43. Mackrell, "Out of the Darkness."

44. Qtd. in Krouse, "A Staccato Movement of Expansive and Neurotic Individuals," 140.

45. Krouse, 141.

46. John Matshikiza, "The Politics of Performance," *Mail & Guardian*, May 7, 1999.

47. Hlongwane, "Simunye (We Are One!)," 3.

48. Stephanie Jason, "Nelisiwe Xaba Makes Her Moves on the Politics of Exoticism," *Mail & Guardian*, March 3, 2015, https://mg.co.za/article/2015-03-03-nelisiwe-xaba-makes-her-moves-on-the-politics-of-exoticism

49. Cole, "Johannesburg Dance Umbrella."

50. The 2016 Montpellier Danse Festival program lists the credits as "Proposition de Robyn Orlin avec Albert Ibokwe Khoza." The 2018 Johannesburg Dance Umbrella Festival program presented the credits as "a piece by Robyn Orlin with Albert Khoza and Léopard Frock." Frock was the costume designer.

51. Krouse, "A Staccato Movement of Expansive and Neurotic Individuals," 144.

52. On the frictions of coauthorship with *Sizwe Banzi Is Dead*, see Cima, "Resurrecting 'Sizwe Banzi Is Dead' (1972–2008)."

53. This and the two subsequent artist quotes from Yende and Moremi are from Marilyn Jenkins, "Going with Robyn Orlin," *Citizen*, September 13, 2000.

54. Interview with Robyn Orlin in the program for the Winter School's Festival 2000, author unknown, exact date unknown; produced in the addendum of Katzke, "Probing the Politics of the Female Body," v–vii (brackets in original).

55. Bain, "Hypertheatrical Performance on the Post-Apartheid Stage."

56. Lewis, *Performing Whitely in the Postcolony*, 13.

57. *Encyclopedia of South African Theatre and Performance*, s.v. "Siwela Sonke Dance Theatre," accessed August 21, 2017, http://esat.sun.ac.za/index.php?title=Siwela_Sonke_Dance_Theatre

58. On "dance between dances," see Pather, "Democratic, Intercultural Choreography," 131.

59. Linyekula and Patel, "My Dance Is Nothing More Than an Attempt to Remember My Name," *Pambazuka News: Voices for Freedom and Justice*, February 28, 2006, https://www.pambazuka.org/arts/%E2%80%98my-dance-nothing-more-attempt-remember-my-name%E2%80%99

60. Pather, "Shifting Spaces, Tilting Time," 441–42; see also Pather, "Laws of Recall," 327–31.

61. Pather, "Laws of Recall," 329.

62. Richard Pithouse, "Only Protected on Paper," The South African Civil Society Information Service, March 30, 2011. https://sacsis.org.za/s/story.php?s=534

63. Shembe is an African religion that combines Christianity with aspects of Bantu religion. The San are the oldest inhabitants of South Africa; San or Khoisan are non-Bantu Indigenous peoples of Southern Africa.

64. The misspelling of *beautiful* expressing a nascent command of written English in a country still largely without access to literacy.

65. See Katrak, "Jay Pather, South African Artist of Indian Ancestry," 153.

66. The majority of people of Indian descent in South Africa can trace their family lines back to indentured laborers brought to South Africa from India to work on sugarcane farms in the late nineteenth and early twentieth centuries. As Desai argues, "In proposing the identity of 'Black' to unite all whom apartheid oppressed [including Indians], the BCM [Black Consciousness Movement] activists tried to break out of apartheid identities and congeal this into a new identity," one that both disassembled and reassembled unity. See Desai, "Indian South Africans and the Black Consciousness Movement," 39.

67. Pather and Jazzart Dance Theatre, "Dance in Search of Commonality," 85.

68. Pather and Jazzart Dance Theatre, 85.

69. Pather, "Negotiating the Postcolonial Black Body."

70. Alexander, *The New Jim Crow*.

71. Pather, "Negotiating the Postcolonial Black Body," 139.

72. Pather, 139. For more on South African inequality, see Greg Nicolson, "South Africa: Where 12 Million Live in Extreme Poverty," *Daily Maverick*, February 3, 2015, https://www.dailymaverick.co.za/article/2015-02-03-south-africa-where-12-million-live-in-extreme-poverty/

73. Jay Pather, "Artist's Statement for *Body of Evidence*," Grahamstown National Arts Festival, Official Program, 2009, 42.

74. Pather, "Negotiating the Postcolonial Black Body," 148.

75. Pather, "A Response: African Contemporary Dance?," 10.

76. Garland-Thomson, "Integrating Disability, Transforming Feminist Theory," 264–65.

77. Michael Ignatieff, qtd. in Hayner, *Unspeakable Truths*, 21. See also Cole, *Performing South Africa's Truth Commission*.

78. Qtd. in Machen, "'Body of Evidence': Jay Pather at the Playhouse."

79. Jay Pather, "A Love Affair with Spaces," TEDxUCT, University of Cape Town, February 27, 2015, YouTube video, 14:21, https://www.youtube.com/watch?v=1kgNZ3G8lMY

80. This quality is part of the reason that I am taking the long view of Pather's work, thinking across the works for their composite aesthetics and styles.

81. Pather, "Shifting Spaces, Tilting Time," 439.

82. Qtd. in Machen, "'Body of Evidence': Jay Pather at the Playhouse."

83. Pather and Jazzart Dance Theatre, "Dance in Search of Commonality," 91.

84. Pather, "Democratic, Intercultural Choreography," 131.

85. See Katrak, "Jay Pather Reimagining Site-Specific Cartographies of Belonging."

86. Drewal, "Object and Intellect," 72.

87. Cue Editor, "Welcome to the Circus."

88. Pather, "Shifting Spaces, Tilting Time," 436.

89. For more on Pather's site-specific work, see Katrak, "Jay Pather Reimagining Site-Specific Cartographies of Belonging."

90. Pather, "Democratic, Intercultural Choreography," 131.

91. Kealinohomoku, "An Anthropologist Looks at Ballet as a Form of Ethnic Dance."

92. Qtd. in Van Wyk and Giesler, "Ballet Blanc to Ballet Black?," 333.

93. Erlmann, *Nightsong*.

94. Pather, "Laws of Recall," 340.

95. Akrofi, "Zulu Indigenous Beliefs," 1.

96. See Simonson, Leelai, and Ladysmith Black Mambazo, *On Tip Toe*.

97. Craighead, "Shifting Spaces in the 'New South Africa,'" 29.

98. Qtd. in Castelyn, "A Feminist Poststructuralist Examination," 106.

99. Pather, "Democratic, Intercultural Choreography," 132.

100. Qtd. in Valencia Govindasamy, "Artful Action: Private Bodies in Public Spaces," *IOL*, June 30, 2015, http://www.iol.co.za/entertainment/whats-on/durban/artful-action-private-bodies-in-public-spaces-1878402

101. Machen, "'Body of Evidence': Jay Pather at the Playhouse."

102. Miller, *Slow Motion*, 132.

103. Machen, "'Body of Evidence': Jay Pather at the Playhouse." *Sangomas* and *inyangas* are traditional healers, diviners, and herbalists.

104. Qtd. in Murnik, "Jay Pather," 115.

105. Qtd. in Miller, *Slow Motion*, 138.

106. Pather, "Shifting Spaces, Tilting Time," 440.

107. Qtd. in Miller, *Slow Motion*, 138.

108. Pather, "Shifting Spaces, Tilting Time," 440.

109. Craighead, "When the Rainbow Is Not Enough," 272–73.

110. See Farigon, "The Gumboot Dance"; and Muller and Farigon, "Gumboots, Bhaca Migrants, and Fred Astaire."

111. Osborne, "The Gumboot Dance," 53.

112. Osborne, 70–71.

113. See Farigon, "The Gumboot Dance"; and Muller and Farigon, "Gumboots, Bhaca Migrants, and Fred Astaire."

114. Pather, "A Response: African Contemporary Dance?," 14.

115. Castelyn, "A Feminist Poststructuralist Examination," 52.

116. Pather, "Democratic, Intercultural Choreography," 131.

117. Pather, 129.

118. Qtd. in Machen, "'Body of Evidence': Jay Pather at the Playhouse."

119. On the importance of respect in intercultural encounters, see Gray, "The Question of Cultural Appropriation."

120. Qtd. in Craighead, "Shifting Spaces in the 'New South Africa,'" 91.

121. Kundera, *The Book of Laughter and Forgetting*, 3.

122. See Atkin, "Looking at the Other/Seeing the Self"; Bain, "Hypertheatrical Performance on the Post-Apartheid Stage"; Bradford, "Review: 'The Plays of Miracle and Wonder'"; Ben Chikha and Arnaut, "Staging/Caging 'Otherness' in the Postcolony"; Flockemann, "Spectacles of Excess"; Hoxworth, "Tour(ist)ing Post-Apartheid South African Theatre"; Hutchinson, "Zones of Occult Instability"; Jamal, ". . . Nothing Is / But What Is Not"; Keevy, "Interracial Mumbo Jumbo"; Krueger, "On the Wild, Essential Energies of the Forest"; Krueger, "Celebrating the Spirt of Tragedy"; Krueger, chapter 21 ("The Dionysian Theatre of Brett Bailey") in *Experiments in Freedom*, 153–70; Larlham, "Brett Bailey and Third World Bunfight"; Rudakoff, "Why Did the Chicken Cross the Cultural Divide?"; Sieg, "Toward a Civic Contract of Performance"; Singleton, "Censorship and Sensitivities"; Wenzel, *Bulletproof*, 207–20; and Wetmore, "Brett Bailey." Bailey is also the only contemporary artist I cover in this book who has published an anthology of dramatic texts: Bailey, *The Plays of Miracle and Wonder*.

123. Bailey, *The Plays of Miracle and Wonder*, 10.

124. Bailey, 10.

125. For more on Artaud, see Bharucha, *Theatre and the World*, 14–15; Foley, "Trading Art(s)"; and Knowles, *Theatre & Interculturalism*, 16–21.

126. Krueger, "Celebrating the Spirt of Tragedy," 243.

127. "Review: House of the Holy Afro," *Sunday Times Live*, June 20, 2010, https://www.timeslive.co.za/tshisa-live/tshisa-live/2010-06-20-review-house-of-the-holy-afro/

128. Hoxworth, "Tour(ist)ing Post-Apartheid South African Theatre," 112. See also Roach, "World Bank Drama."

129. Brent Meersman, "Blazing New Directions in Drama," *Mail & Guardian*, September 7, 2012, https://mg.co.za/article/2012-09-07-00-blazing-new-directions-in-drama

130. Hoxworth, "Tour(ist)ing Post-Apartheid South African Theatre," 43.

131. I am indebted to Yvette Hutchinson for this careful parsing of the history of this performance. See Hutchinson, "Zones of Occult Instability."

132. Bailey, *The Plays of Miracle and Wonder*, 9.

133. Larlham, "Brett Bailey and Third World Bunfight," 9.

134. Wenzel, *Bulletproof*, 208.

135. Wenzel, 208.

136. On nostalgic revivals, see Cima, "Postconflict Nostalgia."

137. Matshikiza, "The Politics of Performance."

138. Matshikiza.

139. Pather, "Democratic, Intercultural Choreography," 133.

140. Jay Pather, pers. comm., February 11, 2019.

141. Pather, "Democratic, Intercultural Choreography," 133.

142. Gray, "The Question of Cultural Appropriation."

143. Gray.

144. Qtd. in Murnik, "Jay Pather," 115.

145. Soske and Walsh, "Thinking about Race and Friendship in South Africa," 18 (italics in the original).

146. Bailey, *The Plays of Miracle and Wonder*, 10.

147. Bradford, "Review: 'The Plays of Miracle and Wonder,'" 234.

148. Wenzel, *Bulletproof*, 208.

149. Wenzel, 214.

150. Wenzel, 234.

151. Even Anton Krueger sees that there is an inherent and irreconcilable contraction at the core of Bailey's work: "There seems to be a paradox here, in that Bailey appears to endorse both essentialism (in claiming African roots), while remaining irreverent about traditions. . . . Which is it then? Does Bailey appeal to whichever view is expedient for his purposes at any given time and place? And if so, would this be problematic?" Krueger, *Experiments in Freedom*, 164. Citing Nietzsche's endorsement of hypocrisy, Krueger concludes that it ultimately does not matter whether Bailey is simultaneously venerating and making fun of Xhosa traditions if his interest is both "authentic" and expedient. For further justification, he cites a cadre of white male theater gurus, including Peter Brook, Richard Schechner, and Jerzy Grotowski, without indicating any awareness of the legacy of cultural criticism attached to these paradigmatic white male figures.

152. I saw *Exhibit B* at the Galway International Arts Festival in Ireland in Galway's Black Box Theatre, July 15, 2015.

153. Ben Chikha and Arnaut, "Staging/Caging 'Otherness' in the Postcolony," 672.

154. Yvette Gresle, "Brett Bailey, the Barbarian and the Black Britons," *Africa Is a Country*, October 2, 2014, https://africasacountry.com/2014/10/brett-bailey-the-barbican-and-black-britons/

155. Brett Bailey, "Yes, *Exhibit B* Is Challenging—but I Never Sought to Alienate or Offend," *Guardian*, September 24, 2014, https://www.theguardian.com/commentisfree/2014/sep/24/exhibit-b-challenging-work-never-sought-alien ate-offend-brett-bailey

156. For a summary of references to these critiques, see Gresle, "Brett Bailey, the Barbarian and the Black Britons."

157. Qtd. in Crawley, "The Trials of Brett Bailey."

158. Bailey, "Yes, *Exhibit B* Is Challenging."

159. Bailey.

160. Brett Bailey, "EXHIBIT B: Here is a full report on events in St Denis thus far. It was to have been in today's South African Sunday Times, but wasn't," *Facebook*, November 30, 2014, https://www.facebook.com/brett.bailey.543/posts/10205249583468120:0, reprinted as Brett Baily, "Blood on the Tarmac: Brett Bailey Speaks," *Mail & Guardian*, December 2, 2014, https://mg.co.za/article/2014-12-02-blood-on-the-tarmac-brett-bailey-speaks

161. Ben Chikha and Arnaut, "Staging/Caging 'Otherness' in the Postcolony," 675.

162. Ellison, *The Invisible Man*, 6.

163. Crawley, "The Trials of Brett Bailey."

164. Soske and Walsh, "Thinking about Race and Friendship in South Africa."

165. Bailey, *The Plays of Miracle and Wonder*, 9.

166. Armah, *The Beautyful Ones Are Not Yet Born*, 10.

CHAPTER 4

1. Comaroff and Comaroff, *Theory from the South*, 1.

2. Qtd. in Maqoma, *Beautiful Me (Performance Video*, DVD, Pantin, France: La Centre National de la Danse, 2008. Copy in author's possession.

3. Many decades ago, Frantz Fanon theorized along similar lines, saying that mere reclamation of precolonial forms, traditions, and practices is not sufficient to enact decolonization. See Fanon, *The Wretched of the Earth*.

4. Linyekula, "An Artist/Activist Moving (across) Borders," 138.

5. See Banham, *A History of Theatre in Africa*.

6. Ngũgĩ wa Thiong'o, *Decolonising the Mind*.

7. Qtd. in Brenda Dixon Gottschild, "'My Africa Is Always in the Becoming': Outside the Box with Faustin Linyekula," 2007, https://brendadixongottschild.files.wordpress.com/2010/07/outside-the-box-with-faustin-linyekula.pdf

8. Qtd. in Gottschild.

9. Seibert, "Faustin Linyekula."

10. Linyekula's *more more more . . . future* also toured to the Yerba Buena Center for the Arts in San Francisco, which is where I saw it in October 2011.

11. I saw *Beautiful Me* first at the Yerba Buena Center for the Arts in San Francisco on November 6, 2009. Two years later, I participated in an artist's visit with Maqoma at the University of California, Los Angeles, on February 17, 2011, during which he presented an excerpted and condensed version of the piece. I once again had the privilege of seeing the work on June 11 and 12, 2019, at the Holland Festival in Amsterdam.

12. Wilderson, "Grammar & Ghosts," 122.

13. Wilderson, 122.

14. Qtd. in Smaranda Olcese-Trifan, "Interview with Gregory Maqoma" [in French], *Paris Art*, n.d., http://www.paris-art.com/gregory-maqoma/, translation by Jenner Mandel).

15. Maqoma, "A Response," 37.

16. Maqoma, 37.

17. Gregory Maqoma, pers. comm., December 14, 2018, New York City, Park Avenue Armory.

18. Maqoma, "Identity, Diversity, and Modernity in an Urban Cultural Cocktail," 71.

19. Maqoma, 66.

20. Maqoma, "A Response," 37.

21. My transcription from performance video, Maqoma, *Beautiful Me (Performance Video*, DVD, Pantin, France: La Centre National de la Danse, 2008. Copy in author's possession.

22. Qtd. in Dirks, "Editorial," 4.

23. Qtd. in Douglas et al., "Under Fire," 110.

24. Qtd. in Douglas et al., 110.

25. Linyekula, "An Artist/Activist Moving (across) Borders," 139.

26. Linyekula, 139.

27. My transcription from performance video.

28. Austin, *How to Do Things with Words*, 57.

29. Kodesh, "For Arts' Sake?," 35.

30. Gottschild, "My Africa Is Always in the Becoming."

31. Hardy, "Islands of Beauty," 64.

32. Hardy, 63.

33. Linyekula, qtd. in Kear, *Theatre and Event*, 188.

34. Scholarship on Linyekula's work is just now coming to the fore. Major works include Bradley, "Corporeal Resurfacings"; Frosch, "One Story, One Movement (R)Evolution"; Gottschild, "My Africa Is Always in the Becoming"; Haitzinger, "Afro-Futurism or Lament?"; Hardy, "Islands of Beauty"; Kear,

chapter 5 ("De-Creating the Step of the World") in *Theatre and Event*, 186–215; Köpping, "Performing 'Africa'"; Osterweis, "Geo-Choreography and Necropolitics"; Scott, "Performing Acupuncture on a Necropolitical Body"; Sörgel, "The Global Politics of Faustin Linyekula's Dance Theater"; and Sörgel, "Transnationalism and Contemporary African Dance." Laura Edmondson also has work in development on Linyekula. I am grateful to all these scholars, for I certainly stand on their shoulders.

35. Program notes, *more more more . . . future*, Faustin Linyekula and Studios Kabako, REDCAT, Los Angeles, October 5, 2011, in author's possession.

36. Qtd. in Hardy, "Islands of Beauty," 65.

37. Qtd. in Hardy, 60.

38. Faustin Linyekula, "Corks and Memories," unpublished essay written as part of a workshop at the Institute for Choreography and Dance in Cork, Ireland, 2005, http://www.kabako.org/txt-entretiens/Corks.html

39. Faustin Linyekula and Shailja Patel, "My Dance Is Nothing More Than an Attempt to Remember My Name," *Pambazuka News: Voices for Freedom and Justice*, February 28, 2006, https://www.pambazuka.org/arts/%E2%80%98my-dance-nothing-more-attempt-remember-my-name%E2%80%99

40. Linyekula, "An Artist/Activist Moving (across) Borders," 137.

41. "Artist Talk: Faustin Linyekula," Walker Art Center, Minneapolis, September 22, 2011, *YouTube* video, 1:00:53, https://www.youtube.com/watch?v=tIdABul4wpA

42. Linyekula, "An Artist/Activist Moving (across) Borders," 137–38.

43. Hardy, "Islands of Beauty," 68. Video clips of *more more more . . . future* are available online. See MCA Chicago, October 2011, *Vimeo* video, 1:34, https://vimeo.com/30384295; and also Hexagone SN de Meylan, June 15, 2011, *YouTube* video, 3:24, https://www.youtube.com/watch?v=2X5LithJxmQ

44. Qtd. in Hardy, "Islands of Beauty," 68.

45. Program notes, *more more more . . . future*, REDCAT, 3.

46. Program notes, 7.

47. Andy Horwitz, "Faustin Linyekula at the Kitchen—October 12," *Culturebot: Maximum Performance*, October 17, 2011, https://www.culturebot.org/2011/10/11477/faustin-linyekula-at-the-kitchen-october-12/

48. Hardy, "Islands of Beauty," 66.

49. Osterweis, "Geo-Choreography and Necropolitics," 273.

50. Program notes, *more more more . . . future*, REDCAT.

51. Program notes, *more more more . . . future*, Faustin Linyekula and Studios Kabako, Museum of Contemporary Art, Chicago, October 21, 2011, in author's possession, 5.

52. "Artist Talk: Faustin Linyekula."

53. Program notes, *more more more . . . future*, REDCAT, 3.

54. Antoine Vumilia Muhindo, *more more more . . . future* (poetry libretto).

55. Muhindo.

56. Muhindo, "That Does Not Encounter Me," in *more more more . . . future* (poetry libretto).

57. Muhindo, "The Dawn of the Idols," in *more more more . . . future* (poetry libretto).

58. Muhindo, "The Dawn of the Idols."

59. Muhindo, "Like the Prophets," in *more more more . . . future* (poetry libretto).

60. Muhindo, *more more more . . . future* (poetry libretto).

61. Worley, *No Future*.

62. Program notes, *more more more . . . future*, REDCAT, 3.

63. Gottschild, "My Africa Is Always in the Becoming."

64. Gottschild.

65. Claudia La Rocco, "Messages from Prison to an Irresistible Beat," *New York Times*, October 14, 2011, https://www.nytimes.com/2011/10/15/arts/dance/more-more-more-future-at-the-kitchen-review.html

66. Horwitz, "Faustin Linyekula at the Kitchen—October 12."

67. Linyekula, "An Artist/Activist Moving (across) Borders," 146.

68. Horwitz, "Faustin Linyekula at the Kitchen—October 12."

69. See "Artist Talk: Faustin Linyekula"; and Faustin Linyekula, "Knowing Dance More: Faustin Linyekula," lecture performance, Re-PLACE-ing Philadelphia Project, October 14, 2015, *Vimeo* video, 1:11:57, https://vimeo.com/143649336

70. Linyekula, "Knowing Dance More."

71. "Artist Talk: Faustin Linyekula."

72. Linyekula, "Knowing Dance More."

73. This movement phrase is also a recurring motif in Linyekula's piece *Festival of Lies*.

74. Muhindo, "Like the Prophets," in *more more more . . . future* (poetry libretto).

75. Program notes, *more more more . . . future*, Museum of Contemporary Art, 8.

76. Laura Bleiberg, "Dance Review: *more more more . . . future* Performed at REDCAT." *Los Angeles Times*, October 6, 2011, https://latimesblogs.latimes.com/culturemonster/2011/10/dance-review-more-more-more-future-performed-at-redcat-.html

77. Kear, *Theatre and Event*, 215. The internal quote is from Linyekula, a conversation with Michikazu Matsune, 2010.

78. Muhindo, "Nobody Knows!" in *more more more . . . future* (poetry libretto).

79. Program notes, *more more more . . . future*, REDCAT, 3.

80. A much earlier version of some of the following text was published as Cole, "Beautiful Me/We."

81. All three choreographers are listed as artistic contributors in the program notes for *Beautiful Me*, Gregory Maqoma and Vuyani Dance Theatre, REDCAT Theater, Roy and Edna Disney/CalArts Theater, Los Angeles, October 21–24, 2009, in author's possession.

82. Moira de Swardt, "Local Dancer and Choreographer Gregory Maqoma Gets a Standing Ovation in His Hometown," November 7, 2009, rev. qtd. in Görtz, "Linguistic Markers as Evidence for Cultural Awareness," 82–83.

83. See Mitra, *Akram Khan*; and Pickett, "Akram Khan." On Mantsoe, see Vedel, "World Dance. Trance Dance"; and Vedel. "Vincent Mantsoe."

84. I am grateful to Adrienne Sichel for the historical context for Glasser.

85. Loots, "Voicing the Unspoken," 52.

86. Mitra, *Akram Khan*, 9–10.

87. Maqoma, "A Response."

88. Rita Felciano, "Roaming to Find Your Voice," *danceviewtimes*, November 8, 2009, http://www.danceviewtimes.com/2009/11/roaming-to-find-your-voice.html

89. See "Jacob Zuma Sings Umshini Wam," uploaded August 4, 2008, *YouTube* video, 2:40, https://www.youtube.com/watch?v=lof6XJ8b1SU

90. Gunner, "Jacob Zuma, the Social Body and the Unruly Power of Song."

91. Qtd. in program notes for *Beautiful Me*.

92. Qtd. in Maqoma, *Beautiful Me (Performance Video)*.

93. Sam Mathe, "Saluting an Exceptional Career in Dance," *African Independent*, January 5, 2016, https://www.africanindy.com/culture/saluting-an-exceptional-career-in-dance-1427730

94. Dennis Creighton, "Housing in Soweto," *Soweto.co.za*, accessed April 4, 2018, http://www.soweto.co.za/html/i_research_doc1.htm

95. Qtd. in Mathe, "Saluting an Exceptional Career in Dance."

96. Gregory Maqoma, "Beyond the Euphoria of Movement," TEDxJohannsburgSalon, October 18, 2016, *YouTube* video, 16:20, https://www.youtube.com/watch?v=XubYaoshp6s

97. See Erlmann, *Nightsong*; and Meintjes, *Dust of the Zulu*.

98. Qtd. in "STGtv: Journey with Gregory Maqoma," Seattle Theatre Group, February 14, 2014, *YouTube* video, 7:59, https://www.youtube.com/watch?v=XStE1xrZ2x8

99. As Veit Erlmann says, "Of all the superlatives that are routinely attached

to Michael Jackson's name, none appears to surpass those connected with his alleged racial features, with the complete whiteness of his skin and utter thinness of his lips, or the profound blackness of his music. . . . No other performer divided public opinion more sharply over question of racial identity than Jackson." Erlmann, *Music, Modernity, and the Global Imagination*, 268.

100. "Beautiful Dance," *South African* (blog), June 12, 2007, https://www.thesouthafrican.com/beautiful-dance/

101. Qtd. in Mathe, "Saluting an Exceptional Career in Dance."

102. Kodesh, "Cultural Cocktails," 46.

103. Alan Ulrich, "Maqoma's Sinewy Search for Kinetic Identity," *San Francisco Chronicle*, November 7, 2009, https://www.sfgate.com/entertainment/article/Maqoma-s-sinewy-search-for-kinetic-identity-3211359.php

104. Adrienne Edwards, "Kinetic Maxim: The Experimental Movements of Gregory Maqoma," 2013, unpublished essay, https://www.ontheboards.org/sites/default/files/GregoryMaqoma_Essay_KineticMaxim_AdrienneEdwards.pdf

105. Anna Kisselgoff, "The Dancing Feet of Michael Jackson," *New York Times*, March 6, 1988, https://www.nytimes.com/1988/03/06/arts/stage-the-dancing-feet-of-michael-jackson.html

106. Ladysmith Black Mambazo, "The Moon Is Walking" (music video), uploaded February 1, 2011, *YouTube* video, 3:47, https://www.youtube.com/watch?v=AqU5oEz_xAs

107. Erlmann, *Music, Modernity, and the Global Imagination*.

108. Erlmann, 280.

109. My transcription from performance video, Maqoma, *Beautiful Me*.

110. Gregory Maqoma, *Requiem Request*, Centre for the Less Good Idea, Johannesburg, 2017, *Vimeo* video, 20:34, https://vimeo.com/211473195

111. Qtd. in Kwanele Sobiso, "A Requiem for the World's Dead," *Mail & Guardian*, September 5, 2019, https://mg.co.za/article/2019-09-05-a-requiem-for-the-worlds-dead

112. Mitra, *Akram Khan*.

113. Felciano, "Roaming to Find Your Voice."

114. Mitra, *Akram Khan*, 25.

115. See Mngadi, "Rereading and Resistance."

116. Mngadi, "Rereading and Resistance," 7. See Magubane's image of mine workers at "Post-Apartheid Africa Kills Its Miners," *Shahidul News*, accessed August 12, 2019, http://www.shahidulnews.com/post-apartheid-south-africa-kills-its-miners, article originally published in *New Age*, September 10, 2012.

117. Transcription and translation available in Melissa Berry, "'Beautiful Me':

Gregory Maqoma/Vuyani Dance Theatre at REDCAT," *Examiner.com*, November 11, 2009, http://www.examiner.com/cultural-events-in-national/beautiful-me-gregory-maqoma-vuyani-dance-theatre-at-redcat.

118. I attended a live performance of *Beautiful Me* at San Francisco's Yerba Buena Center for the Arts on November 6, 2009, and viewed a DVD of a performance taped at Centre National de la Danse (National Center of Dance) in Paris. I also participated in an artist's residency with Maqoma on February 17, 2011, in the Department of World Arts and Cultures, University of California, Los Angeles. The piece was first performed in 2007, at Johannesburg's FNB Dance Umbrella Festival, which commissioned the work.

119. Berry, "Beautiful Me."

120. Maqoma, "Beyond the Euphoria of Movement."

121. Maqoma.

122. Maqoma.

123. Qtd. in Smaranda, "Interview with Gregory Maqoma."

124. Qtd. in Maqoma, *Beautiful Me (Performance Video)*.

125. In terms of the post-1949 modern dance trajectory in South Africa, the Laban method came first (at the University of Natal's Speech and Drama Department, Durban), according to Adrienne Sichel (pers. comm., November 20, 2018). According to Sichel, Laban remains one of the cornerstones of South Africa's contemporary dance development, and the country notably had both European and American imported forms as well as the Alexander Technique (adopted first at Jazzart Dance Theatre from 1976).

126. Akram Khan's mother, Anwara Khan, recalls her son learning Bangladeshi folk dance at age three, at the same time that he became fascinated by Michael Jackson. Khan himself has recalled, "If Michael Jackson hadn't been there, I don't know if I would have been a dancer. He was the first person I connected with. I remember when I saw *Thriller*, I was terrified. I'd never seen anything so frightening in my life, but [it] was also incredibly exciting. It had everything—music, storytelling, dance." Qtd. in Mitra, *Akram Khan*, 34. Khan also speaks about how emulating Jackson on the dance floor helped him avoid being a target of bullying for effeminacy. Jackson, for him, removed the stigma of the male dancing body.

127. Qtd. in Gottschild, "My Africa Is Always in the Becoming."

128. See for instance the many choreographers interviewed in Joan Frosch and Alla Kovgan's 2009 documentary film *Movement (R)Evolution Africa*.

129. Linyekula, "Corks and Memories."

130. Linyekula and Patel, "My Dance Is Nothing More Than an Attempt to Remember My Name" (italics added).

131. Program notes, *more more more . . . future*, REDCAT, 3.

EPILOGUE: TAKING THEM BACK HOME

1. Subsequent performances took place in 2018 at the Ruhrtriennale in Germany and the Armory in New York City, and in 2019 at the Holland Festival. More performances are planned for the future.

2. My transcription from production video. This video was for a brief time streamed on the Tate Modern website.

3. Plaatje, *Native Life in South Africa*, 266–67.

4. Qtd. in Maya Jaggi, "Decolonizing Commemoration: New War Art," *New York Review of Books*, November 14, 2018, https://www.nybooks.com/daily/2018/11/14/decolonizing-commemoration-new-war-art/

5. Park Avenue Armory, "*The Head & the Load* by William Kentridge with Music Created and Conceived by Philip Miller, Makes North American Debut at Park Avenue Armory This December," press release, October 2, 2018, http://armoryonpark.org/downloads/press/William_Kentridge_Release_10.2.pdf

6. Stewart Zachary, "*The Head & the Load* Tells the Hidden History of World War I in Africa" *Theatre Mania*, December 5, 2018, https://www.theatermania.com/off-broadway/reviews/review-head-and-the-load-park-avenue-armory_87226.html

7. The kora, an instrument from Mali and West Africa, often serves as accompaniment in the telling of epic tales, such as the *Sundiata Epic* from the thirteenth century.

8. William Kentridge, *The Head & the Load*, libretto, 48, in my possession.

9. Gregory Maqoma, pers. comm., December 14, 2018, New York.

10. Maqoma.

11. Maqoma.

12. Maqoma.

13. See Ahmed, *Willful Subjects*, 11.

14. Program notes, *more more more . . . future*, Faustin Linyekula and Studios Kabako, REDCAT, Los Angeles, October 5, 2011, 3, in author's possession.

Bibliography

Agamben, Giorgio. *Homo Sacer: Sovereign Power and Bare Life*. Translated by Daniel Heller-Roazen. Stanford, CA: Stanford University Press, 1995.

Ahmed, Sara. *Willful Subjects*. Durham, NC: Duke University Press, 2014.

Akrofi, Eric. "Zulu Indigenous Beliefs: To What Extent Do They Influence the Performance Practices of 'Isicathamiya' Musicians?" Paper presented at the African Arts Education Conference, South Africa, 2001.

Alexander, Michelle. *The New Jim Crow: Mass Incarceration in the Age of Colorblindness*. Rev. ed. New York: New Press, 2012.

Althusser, Louis. "Ideology and Ideological State Apparatuses (Notes towards an Investigation)." In *Lenin and Philosophy, and Other Essays*, 85–126. Translated by Ben Brewster. New York: Monthly Review Press, 1971.

Alvarez, Alex. *Native America and the Question of Genocide*. Lanham, MD: Rowman and Littlefield, 2014.

Anders, Peter, and Matthew Krouse, eds. *Positions: Contemporary Artists in South Africa*. Auckland Park, South Africa: Jacana Media, 2010.

Anderson, Patrick, and Jisha Menon. *Violence Performed: Local Roots and Global Routes of Conflict*. New York: Palgrave Macmillan, 2009.

Andersson, Muff. "Mpumelelo Paul Grootboom." In Middeke, Schnierer, and Homann, *The Methuen Drama Guide to Contemporary South African Theatre*, 241–57.

Anker, Elizabeth S. *Fictions of Dignity: Embodying Human Rights in World Literature*. Ithaca, NY: Cornell University Press, 2012.

Armah, Ayi Kwei. *The Beautyful Ones Are Not Yet Born*. Oxford: Heinemann, 1988.

Atkin, Lara. "Looking at the Other/Seeing the Self: Embodied Performance and Encounter in Brett Bailey's Exhibit B and Nineteenth-Century Ethnographic Displays." *Safundi: The Journal of South African and American Studies* 16, no. 2 (2015): 136–55.

Attwell, David, and Derek Attridge, eds. *The Cambridge History of South African Literature*. Cambridge: Cambridge University Press, 2012.

Auslander, Philip. *Liveness: Performance in a Mediatized Culture*. 2nd ed. New York: Routledge, 2008.

Austin, J. L. *How to Do Things with Words*. 2nd ed. Cambridge, MA: Harvard University Press, 1975.

Bailey, Brett. *The Plays of Miracle and Wonder: Bewitching Visions and Primal High-Jinx from the South African Stage*. Cape Town: Double Storey Books, 2005.

Bain, Keith. "Hypertheatrical Performance on the Post-Apartheid Stage." In *Shifting Selves: Post-Apartheid Essays on Mass Media, Culture and Identity*, edited by Herman Wasserman and Sean Jacobs, 145–65. Cape Town: Kwela Books, 2003.

Banham, Martin. *A History of Theatre in Africa*. Cambridge: Cambridge University Press, 2004.

Bank, Rosemarie K. *Theatre Culture in America, 1825–1860*. New York: Cambridge University Press, 1997.

Barnard, Rita. "Rewriting the Nation." In Attwell and Attridge, *The Cambridge History of South African Literature*, 652–75.

Ben Chikha, Chokri, and Karel Arnaut. "Staging/Caging 'Otherness' in the Postcolony: Spectres of the Human Zoo." *Critical Arts: South-North Cultural and Media Studies* 27, no. 6 (2013): 661–83.

Bharucha, Rustom. "Hauntings of the Intercultural: Enigmas and Lessons on the Borders of Failure." In Fischer-Lichte, Jost, and Jain, *The Politics of Interweaving Performance Cultures*, 179–200.

Bharucha, Rustom. *Theatre and the World: Performance and the Politics of Culture*. London: Routledge, 1993.

Boehmer, Elleke. "Endings and New Beginnings: South African Fiction in Transition." In *Writing South Africa: Literature, Apartheid, and Democracy 1970–1995*, edited by Derek Attridge and Rosemary Jolly, 43–56. Cambridge: Cambridge University Press, 1998.

Bradford, Helen. "Review: 'The Plays of Miracle and Wonder': Bewitching Vision and Primal High-Jinx from South the South African Stage." *Kronos* 30 (2004): 230–34.

Bradley, Rizvana. "Corporeal Resurfacings: Faustin Linyekula, Nick Cave and Thornton Dial." PhD diss., Duke University, 2013.

Brandstetter, Gabriele, and Holger Hartung, eds. *Moving (across) Borders: Performing Translation, Intervention, Participation*. Bielefeld, Germany: Transcript Verlag, 2017.

Brechin, Gray. "The Way We (Almost) Were: The Rise and Fall of the Hearst Memorial." *California Monthly*, November 1993, 12–15.

Bremser, Martha, and Lorna Sanders, eds. *Fifty Contemporary Choreographers*. 2nd ed. New York: Routledge, 2011.

Bunch, Mary. "The Unbecoming Subject of Sex: Performativity, Interpellation, and the Politics of Queer Theory." *Feminist Theory* 14, no. 1 (2013): 39–55.

Bundy, Colin. *Short-Changed? South Africa since Apartheid*. Athens: Ohio University Press, 2014.

Butler, Judith. *Precarious Life: The Powers of Mourning and Violence*. London: Verso, 2004.

Butler, Judith. *The Psychic Life of Power: Theories in Subjection*. Stanford, CA: Stanford University Press, 1997.

Carlson, Marvin. *The Haunted Stage: The Theatre as Memory Machine*. Ann Arbor: University of Michigan Press, 2001.

Castelyn, Sarahleigh. "A Feminist Poststructuralist Examination around the Utilisation of the Body as a Contested Site of Struggle for Meaning in Contemporary Theatre Dance in South Africa." MA thesis, University of Natal, 2000.

Catanese, Brandi Wilkins. *The Problem of the Color[Blind]: Racial Transgression and the Politics of Black Performance*. Ann Arbor: University of Michigan Press, 2011.

Cima, Gibson. "Postconflict Nostalgia: Postapartheid South African Theatre, 1990–2010." PhD diss., University of Washington, 2012.

Cima, Gibson. "Resurrecting 'Sizwe Banzi Is Dead' (1972–2008): John Kani, Winston Ntshona, Athol Fugard, and Postapartheid South Africa." *Theatre Survey* 50, no. 1 (2009): 91–118.

Clifford, James. *Returns: Becoming Indigenous in the Twenty-First Century*. Cambridge, MA: Harvard University Press, 2013.

Clingman, Stephen. "Writing the Interregnum: Literature and the Demise of Apartheid." In Attwell and Attridge, *The Cambridge History of South African Literature*, 633–51.

Cole, Catherine M. "Beautiful Me/We: Gregory Maqoma and Ubuntu." *African Arts* 44, no. 4 (2011): 22–25.

Cole, Catherine M. *Ghana's Concert Party Theatre*. Bloomington: Indiana University Press, 2001.

Cole, Catherine M. "Johannesburg Dance Umbrella: Thirty Years On." *Theatre Journal* 70, no. 4 (2018): 539–42.

Cole, Catherine M. *Performing South Africa's Truth Commission: Stages of Transition*. Bloomington: Indiana University Press, 2010.

Cole, Catherine M. "Representing Genocide at Home: Ishi, Again." In *Theatre and Human Rights after 1945: Things Unspeakable*, edited by Mary Luckhurst and Emilie Moran, 128–50. London: Bloomsbury Methuen Drama, 2015.

Colleran, Jeanne. "Athol Fugard and the Problematics of the Liberal Critique." *Modern Drama* 38, no. 3 (1995): 389–407.

Colleran, Jeanne. "Re-Situating Fugard: Re-Thinking Revolutionary Theatre." *South African Theatre Journal* 9, no. 2 (1995): 39–49.

Comaroff, Jean, and John L. Comaroff. *Theory from the South, or How Euro-America Is Evolving toward Africa*. Boulder, CO: Paradigm, 2012.

Craighead, Clare. "Shifting Spaces in the 'New South Africa': Site-Specific Performances as an Intercultural Exploration of Sites, Using as Examples Jay Pather's *Cityscapes*, Durban (2002) and *Home*, Durban (2003)." MA thesis, University of KwaZulu-Natal, Durban, 2006.

Craighead, Clare. "When the Rainbow Is Not Enough: Site-Specificity, the Body as a Site, Multiculturalism and Intercultural Practice in Jay Pather's *CityScapes* (Durban 2002)." *South African Theatre Journal* 24, no. 1 (2010): 259–78.

Crawley, Ashon. *Blackpentacostal Breath: The Aesthetics of Possibility*. New York: Fordham University Press, 2016.

Crawley, Ashon. "Otherwise, Ferguson." *InterFictions Online* 7 (October 2016). Accessed August 19, 2019. http://interfictions.com/otherwise-fergu sonashon-crawley/

Davies, James. "The Fifth Congress of the South African Society for Research in Music (Report)." *SAMUS: South African Music Studies* 30/31 (2011): 191–94.

Davis, Geoffrey V. *Voices of Justice and Reason: Apartheid and Beyond in South African Literature*. New York: Rodopi, 2003.

DeFrantz, Thomas F., and Anita Gonzalez, eds. *Black Performance Theory*. Durham, NC: Duke University Press, 2014.

De Kock, Leon. *Losing the Plot: Crime, Reality and Fiction in Postapartheid Writing*. Johannesburg: Wits University Press, 2016.

Desai, Ashwin. "An Exploratory Critique of the Notion of Social Cohesion in Contemporary South Africa." *PINS: Psychology in Society* 49 (2015): 99–113.

Desai, Ashwin. "Indian South Africans and the Black Consciousness Movement under Apartheid." *Diaspora Studies* 8, no. 1 (2015): 37–50.

Dillon, Elizabeth Maddock. *New World Drama: The Performative Commons in the Atlantic World, 1649–1849*. Durham, NC: Duke University Press, 2014.

Dirks, Anja. "Editorial." In *Presence of the Colonial Past / Afrika Auf Europas Bühnen: A Reader on the Focus of the Theaterformen Festival Braunschweig 2010*, edited by Anja Dirks, Caroline Farke, Sylvia Franzmann, Silke Kaufmann, Felicitas Kotzias, and Kathrin Veser, 4. Hanover, Germany: Theaterformen Festival Braunschweig, 2010. https://issuu.com/festivaltheaterformen/docs/pcp-onlinepub-deutsch/

Dolan, Jill. *Utopia in Performance: Finding Hope at the Theater*. Ann Arbor: University of Michigan Press, 2005.

Dolar, Mladen. "Beyond Interpellation." *Qui Parle* 6, no. 2 (1993): 75–96.

Douglas, Gilbert, Adrienne Sichel, Adedayo M. Liadi, Kettly Noël, Reggie Danster, Augusto Cuvilas, and Faustin Linyekula. "Under Fire: Defining a Contemporary African Dance Aesthetic—Can It Be Done?" *Critical Arts: South-North Cultural and Media Studies* 20, no. 2 (2006): 102–15.

Drewal, Henry John. "Object and Intellect: Interpretations of Meaning in African Art." *Art Journal* 47, no. 2 (1998): 70–72.

Edmonson, Laura. *Performing Trauma in Central Africa: Shadows of Empire*. Bloomington: Indiana University Press, 2018.

Ellison, Ralph. *Invisible Man*. New York: Vintage International, 1995.

Enwezor, Okwui. "The Enigma of the Rainbow Nation: Contemporary South African Art at the Crossroads of History." In Perryer, *Personal Affects*, 23–43.

Erlmann, Veit. *Music, Modernity, and the Global Imagination: South Africa and the West*. Oxford: Oxford University Press, 1999.

Erlmann, Veit. *Nightsong: Power, Performance, and Practice in South Africa*. Chicago: University of Chicago Press, 1995.

Fairbanks, Eve. "'I Have Sinned against the Lord and against You! Will You Forgive Me?'" *New Republic*, June 18, 2014. https://newrepublic.com/article/118135/adriaan-vlok-ex-apartheid-leader-washes-feet-and-seeks-redemption

Fanon, Frantz. *The Wretched of the Earth*. New York: Grove Press, 1963.

Farfan, Penny, and Ric Knowles. "Editorial Comment: Special Issue on Rethinking Intercultural Performance." *Theatre Journal* 63, no. 4 (2011): i–iii.

Farigon, Janet Topp. "The Gumboot Dance: Sell-Out or Symbol?" *Música Oral Del Sur: Revista Internacional* 3 (1998): 107–11.

Feltham, Kymberley. "Decolonising the Stage: Reflecting on Mamela Nyamza in a Canadian-Hosted South African Performance Festival." In Hutchinson and Okoye, *African Theatre*, 45–66.

Fischer-Lichte, Erika, Torsten Jost, and Saskya Iris Jain, eds. *The Politics of Interweaving Performance Cultures: Beyond Postcolonialism*. New York: Routledge, 2014.

Flockemann, Miki. "Little Perpetrators, Witness-Bearers and the Young and the Brave: Towards a Post-Transitional Aesthetics." *English Studies in Africa* 53, no. 1 (2010): 21–34.

Flockemann, Miki. "Spectacles of Excess or Threshold of 'Newness'? Brett Bailey and the Third World Bunfight Performers." *Kunapipi* 24, no. 1–2 (2002): 272–90.

Foley, Kathy. "Trading Art(s): Artaud, Spies, and Current Indonesian/American Artistic Exchange and Collaboration." *Modern Drama* 35, no. 1 (1992): 10–19.

Foster, Susan Leigh. *Choreographing Empathy: Kinesthesia in Performance*. New York: Routledge, 2011.

Frederickson, George M. *White Supremacy: A Comparative Study in American and South African History*. New York: Oxford University Press, 1981.

Frenkel, Ronit, and Craig MacKenzie. "Conceptualizing 'Post-Transitional' South African Literature in English." *English Studies in Africa* 53, no. 1 (2010): 1–10.

Frenkel, Ronit, and Craig MacKenzie. eds. "'Post-Transitional' South African Literature in English." Special issue, *English Studies in Africa* 53, no. 1 (2010).

Friedman, Sharon. "The Impact of the Tourist Gaze on the Voice of South African Contemporary Dance." In Friedman, *Post-Apartheid Dance*, 87–105.

Friedman, Sharon, ed. *Post-Apartheid Dance: Many Bodies Many Voices Many Stories*. Newcastle upon Tyne, UK: Cambridge Scholars, 2012.

Frosch, Joan D. "One Story, One Movement (R)Evolution: An Archival Study of Faustin Linyekula." PhD diss., Texas Woman's University, 2011.

Frosch, Joan, and Alla Kovgan, dir. *Movement (R)Evolution Africa: A Story of an Art Form in Four Acts* (film). Watertown, MA: Documentary Educational Resources, 2009.

Fuchs, Anne. *Playing the Market: The Market Theatre, Johannesburg, 1976–1986*. Amsterdam: Rodopi, 1990.

Fugard, Athol. *Notebooks, 1960–1977*. New York: Theatre Communications Group, 1984.

Fugard, Athol. "Sizwe Banzi Is Dead (Memoir)." In *A Night at the Theatre*, edited by Ronald Harwood, 26–32. London: Methuen, 1986.

Fugard, Athol. *Statements after an Arrest under the Immorality Act*. In Fugard, Kani, and Ntshona, *Statements*, 76–106.

Fugard, Athol, John Kani, and Winston Ntshona. *Sizwe Bansi Is Dead*. In Fugard, Kani, and Ntshona, *Statements*, 1–44.

Fugard, Athol, John Kani, and Winston Ntshona. *Statements: Sizwe Bansi Is Dead, The Island, Statements after an Arrest under the Immorality Act*. New York: Theatre Communications Group, 1986.

Garland-Thomson, Rosemarie. "Integrating Disability, Transforming Feminist Theory." In *The Disability Studies Reader*, edited by Lennard J. Davis, 257–73. 2nd ed. New York: Routledge, 2005.

Gordimer, Nadine. "Living in the Interregnum." *New York Review of Books*, January 20, 1983. http://www.nybooks.com/articles/1983/01/20/living-in-the-interregnum

Görtz, Ann-Christin. "Linguistic Markers as Evidence for Cultural Awareness: A Critical Examination of International Critiques of a South African Dance Company." MA thesis, University of Stellenbosch, 2011.

Gottschild, Brenda Dixon. *The Black Dancing Body: A Geography from Coon to Cool*. New York: Palgrave Macmillan, 2003.

Gramsci, Antonio. *Prison Notebooks*. Vol. 2. Edited by Joseph A. Buttigieg. Translated by Antonio Callari. New York: Columbia University Press, 2011.

Gray, Briahna Joy. "The Question of Cultural Appropriation." *Current Affairs*, September 6, 2017. https://www.currentaffairs.org/2017/09/the-question-of-cultural-appropriation

Gunner, Liz. "Jacob Zuma, the Social Body and the Unruly Power of Song." *African Affairs* 108, no. 430 (2008): 27–48.

Gurney, Kim. *The Art of Public Space: Curating and Re-Imagining the Ephemeral City*. New York: Palgrave Macmillan, 2015.

Habib, Adam. *South Africa's Suspended Revolution*. Athens: Ohio University Press, 2013.

Haitzinger, Nicole. "Afro-Futurism or Lament? Staging Africa(s) in Dance Today and in the 1920s." *Dance Research Journal* 49, no. 1 (2017): 24–36.

Hamraie, Aimi. "Historical Epistemology as Disability Studies Methodology: From the Models Framework to Foucault's Archeology of Cure." *Foucault Studies* 19 (June 2015): 108–34.

Hardy, Susan. "Islands of Beauty." In Heidenreich-Seleme and O'Toole, *Über(w)Unden*, 56–69.

Hart, Gillian. "Exposing the Nation: Entanglements of Race, Sexuality, and Gender in Post-Apartheid Nationalisms." In *Spaces of Danger: Culture and Power in the Everyday*, edited by Heather Merrill and Lisa M. Hoffman, 53–76. Athens: University of Georgia Press, 2015.

Hart, Gillian. *Rethinking the South African Crisis: Nationalism, Populism, Hegemony*. Scottsville, South Africa: University of KwaZulu-Natal Press, 2013.

Hartman, Saidiya V. *Lose Your Mother: A Journey along the Atlantic Slave Route*. New York: Farrar, Straus and Giroux, 2007.

Hartman, Saidiya V. *Scenes of Subjection: Terror, Slavery, and Self-Making in Nineteenth-Century America*. New York: Oxford University Press, 1997.

Hassim, Shireen. "Violent Modernity: Gender, Race and Bodies in Contemporary South African Politics." *Politikon* 41, no. 2 (2014): 167–82.

Hayner, Precilla. *Unspeakable Truths: Transitional Justice and the Challenge of Truth Commissions*. 2nd ed. New York: Routledge, 2011.

Heidenreich-Seleme, Lien, and Sean O'Toole, eds. *Über(w)Unden: Art in Troubled Times*. Auckland Park, South Africa: Jacana Media, 2012.

Hlongwane, Gugu. "Simunye (We Are One!): Discourses of Nation-Building in South African Texts." PhD diss., York University, 2002.

Hoxworth, Kellen. "Tour(ist)ing Post-Apartheid South African Theatre: The Works of Brett Bailey, Yael Farber, and Mpumelelo Paul Grootboom in (Inter)National Production." MA thesis, University of Pittsburgh, 2012.

Hutchinson, Yvette. "'Zones of Occult Instability': A South African Perspective on Negotiating Colonial Afterlives through Intercultural Performance." In McIvor and King, *Interculturalism and Performance Now*, 153–79.

Hutchinson, Yvette, and Chukwuma Okoye, eds. *African Theatre: Contemporary Dance*. Woodbridge, Suffolk: James Currey, 2018.

Jackson, Jonathan David. "Improvisation in African-American Vernacular Dancing." *Dance Research Journal* 33, no. 2 (2001): 40–53.

Jaggi, Maya. "Decolonizing Commemoration: New War Art." *New York Review of Books*, November 14, 2018. https://www.nybooks.com/daily/2018/11/14/decolonizing-commemoration-new-war-art/

Jamal, Ashraf. ". . . Nothing Is / But What It Is Not: Macbeth in Africa." *South African Theatre Journal* 18 (2004): 31–38.

Jamal, Ashraf. *Predicaments of Culture in South Africa*. Pretoria: University of Pretoria Press, 2005.

Johnstone, Kristina. "Looking behind the Mirror: Challenging Representation in Contemporary Dance in Postcolonial African Contexts." In Hutchinson and Okoye, *African Theatre*, 23–44.

Jones, Amelia. "Naming the Power of the Name: Janez Janša Performs the Political in/for the Art World." In *NAME Readymade*, 31–50. Ljubljana: Modern Galerija and Aksioma Press, 2008.

Kahn, Paul W. *Law and Love: The Trials of "King Lear."* New Haven, CT: Yale University Press, 2000.

Katrak, Ketu H. *Jay Pather, Performance and Spatial Politics in South Africa*. Bloomington: Indiana University Press, 2021.

Katrak, Ketu H. "Jay Pather Reimagining Site-Specific Cartographies of Belonging." *Dance Research Journal* 50, no. 2 (2018): 31–44.

Katrak, Ketu H. "Jay Pather, South African Artist of Indian Ancestry: Transforming Society in Post-Apartheid South Africa through His Theatre-Dance Works." In *African Theatre 15: China, India and the Eastern World*, edited by James Gibbs and Femi Osofisa, 153–69. Woodbridge, Suffolk: James Currey, 2016.

Katzke, Cecilia Johanna. "Probing the Politics of the Female Body: Robyn Orlin's Deconstruction of the Classical Ballet Canon." MA thesis, University of Cape Town, 2014.

Kealinohomoku, Joann. "An Anthropologist Looks at Ballet as a Form of Ethnic Dance." In *Moving History / Dancing Cultures: A Dance History Reader*, edited by Ann Dils and Ann Cooper Albright, 33–43. Middletown, CT: Wesleyan University Press, 2001.

Kear, Adrian. *Theatre and Event: Staging the European Century*. New York: Palgrave Macmillan, 2013.

Keevy, Jacqueline. "Interracial Mumbo Jumbo: Mpumelelo Paul Grootboom and Brett Bailey's Theatre." PhD diss., University of KwaZulu-Natal, 2008. http://researchspace.ukzn.ac.za/bitstream/handle/10413/1012/Keevy_J_2008.pdf

Knowles, Ric. *Theatre & Interculturalism*. New York: Palgrave Macmillan, 2010.

Kodesh, Hayley. "Cultural Cocktails: The Choreography of Gregory Maqoma." *Critical Arts: South-North Cultural and Media Studies* 20, no. 2 (2006): 39–60.

Kodesh, Hayley. "For Arts' Sake? Contemporary Dance in South Africa." PhD diss., University of Witwatersrand, 2006.

Köpping, Klaus-Peter. "Performing 'Africa': Linyekula's Re-Vision of 'La Création du Monde.'" In Brandstetter and Hartung, *Moving (across) Borders*, 55–78.

Krouse, Matthew. "A Staccato Movement of Expansive and Neurotic Individuals: Robyn Orlin's Search for the Expression of Contemporary Dance." In Anders and Krouse, *Positions*, 131–45.

Krueger, Anton. "Celebrating the Spirit of Tragedy: The Theatre of Brett Bailey." In Anders and Krouse, *Positions*, 226–48.

Krueger, Anton. *Experiments in Freedom: Explorations of Identity in New South African Drama*. Newcastle upon Tyne, UK: Cambridge Scholars, 2010.

Krueger, Anton. "Gazing at 'Exhibit A': Interview with Brett Bailey." *Liminalities* 9 (February 2013): 1–13.

Krueger, Anton. "On the Wild, Essential Energies of the Forest: An Interview with Brett Bailey." *South African Theatre Journal* 20 (2006): 323–32.

Kruger, Loren. "Black Atlantics, White Indians, and Jews: Locations, Locutions, and Syncretic Identities in the Fiction of Achmat Dangor and Others." *South Atlantic Quarterly* 100, no. 1 (2001): 111–43.

Kruger, Loren. *A Century of South African Theatre*. New York: Methuen, 2020.

Kruger, Loren. *The Drama of South Africa: Plays, Pageants and Publics since 1910*. London: Routledge, 1999.

Kundera, Milan. *The Book of Laughter and Forgetting*. New York: A. A. Knopf, 1980.

Larlham, Daniel. "Brett Bailey and Third World Bunfight: Journey into the South African Psyche." *Theater* 39, no. 1 (2009): 7–27.

Lawless, Annemarie. "Souvenir." In van Bever Donker, Truscott, Minkley, and Lalu, *Remains of the Social*, 146–71.

Law-Viljoen, Bronwyn, ed. *Light on a Hill: Building the Constitutional Court of South Africa*. Johannesburg: David Krut, 2006.

Lei, Daphne. "Interruption, Intervention, Interculturalism: Robert Wilson's HIT Production in Taiwan." *Theatre Journal* 63, no. 2 (2011): 571–83.

Lewis, Megan. *Performing Whitely in the Postcolony: Afrikaners in South African Theatrical and Public Life*. Iowa City: University of Iowa Press, 2016.

Lewis, Megan. "Power Plays in the Cradle of Humankind." *PAJ: A Journal of Performance and Art* 35, no. 3 (2013): 55–60.

Lewis, Megan, and Anton Krueger, eds. *Magnet Theatre: Three Decades of Making Space*. Bristol, UK: Intellect, 2016.

Linyekula, Faustin. "An Artist/Activist Moving (across) Borders." In Brandstetter and Hartung, *Moving (across) Borders*, 135–49.

Loots, Lliane. "Post-Colonial Visitations: A South African's Dance and Choreographic Journey that Faces Up to the Spectres of 'Development' and Globalization." *Critical Arts: South-North Cultural and Media Studies* 20, no. 2 (2006): 89–101.

Loots, Lliane. "Voicing the Unspoken: Culturally Connecting Race, Gender and Nation in Women's Choreographic and Dance Practices in Post-Apartheid South Africa." In Friedman, *Post-Apartheid Dance*, 51–71.

Mahali, Alude. "Rites of Passage: Separation, Liminality and an Initiation into Being in Mamela Nyamza's *Hatched*." *South African Theatre Journal* 29, no. 1–3 (2016): 1–14.

Mamdani, Mahmood. "Beyond Nuremberg: The Historical Significance of the Post-Apartheid Transition in South Africa." *Politics & Society* 43, no. 1 (2015): 61–88.

Maqoma, Gregory. "Identity, Diversity, and Modernity in an Urban Cultural Cocktail." *African Arts* 44, no. 4 (2011): 66–71.

Maqoma, Gregory. "A Response: Beyond Ethnicity." *Critical Arts: South-North Cultural and Media Studies* 20, no. 2 (2006): 34–38.

Marais, Hein. *South Africa Pushed to the Limit: The Political Economy of Change*. London: Zed Books, 2011.

Marcus, Jon. "The Violent Fight for Higher Education." *Atlantic*, March 8, 2017.

Matolina, Bernard, and Wenceslaus Kwindingwi. "The End of Ubuntu." *South African Journal of Philosophy* 32, no. 2 (2013): 197–205.

Mbembe, Achille. "Aesthetics of Superfluity." In *Johannesburg: The Elusive Metropolis*, edited by Sarah Nuttall and Achille Mbembe, 37–67. Durham, NC: Duke University Press, 2008.

Mbembe, Achille. "The Spear That Divided the Nation." *Cape Times*, June 5, 2012.

McIvor, Charlotte, and Jason King, eds. *Interculturalism and Performance Now: New Directions?* Cham, Switzerland: Palgrave Macmillan, 2019.

Mda, Zakes. *Nothing But the Truth*. Johannesburg: Wits University Press, 2002.

Meierhenrich, Jens. *The Legacies of Law: Long-Run Consequences of Legal Development in South Africa, 1652–2000*. Cambridge: Cambridge University Press, 2008.

Meintjes, Louise. *Dust of the Zulu: Ngoma Aesthetics after Apartheid*. Durham, NC: Duke University Press, 2017.

Meister, Robert. *After Evil: A Politics of Human Rights*. New York: Columbia University Press, 2011.

Middeke, Martin, Peter Paul Schnierer, and Greg Homann, eds. *The Methuen Drama Guide to Contemporary South African Theatre*. London: Bloomsbury, 2015.

Miller, Andie. *Slow Motion: Stories about Walking*. Aukland Park, South Africa: Jacana Media, 2010.

Mitra, Royona. *Akram Khan: Dancing New Interculturalism*. New York: Palgrave Macmillan, 2015.

Mngadi, Sikhumbuzo. "Rereading and Resistance." *Afterimage* 26, no. 3 (1998): 7–8.

Molefe, Motsamai. "Review of 'A Report on Ubuntu' by Leonhard Praeg." *Acta Acadademica: Critical Views on Society, Culture and Politics* 46, no. 2 (2014): 157–64.

Morrison, Toni. *The Source of Self-Regard: Selected Essays, Speeches, and Meditations*. New York: Alfred A. Knopf, 2019.

Muhindo, Antoine Vumilia. *more more more . . . future* (poetry libretto). *Heinrich Böll Stiftung*. May 7, 2014. http://heimatkunde.boell.de/2014/05/07/more-more-more-future

Muller, Carol, and Janet Topp Farigon. "Gumboots, Bhaca Migrants, and Fred Astaire: South African Worker Dance and Musical Style." *African Music* 7 (1999): 88–109.

Muñoz, José Esteban. *Disidentifications: Queers of Color and the Performance of Politics*. Minneapolis: University of Minnesota Press, 1999.

Murnik, Tracy. "Jay Pather." In Perryer, *Personal Affects*, 108–15.

Ndebele, Njabulo S. *Rediscovery of the Ordinary: Essays on South African Literature and Culture*. Scottsville, South Africa: University of KwaZulu-Natal Press, 1991.

Ndlovu-Gatsheni, Sabelo. *Epistemic Freedom in Africa: Deprovincialization and Decolonization*. New York: Routledge, 2018.

Ngũgĩ wa Thiong'o. *Decolonising the Mind: The Politics of Language in African Literature*. London: James Currey, 1986.

Nixon, Rob. *Slow Violence and the Environmentalism of the Poor*. Cambridge, MA: Harvard University Press, 2011.

Nuttall, Sarah. *Entanglement: Literary and Cultural Reflections on Post-Apartheid*. Johannesburg: Wits University Press, 2009.

Orkin, Martin, ed. *At the Junction: Four Plays by the Junction Avenue Theatre Company*. Johannesburg: Wits University Press, 2001.

Orkin, Martin. *Drama and the South African State*. Manchester: Manchester University Press, 1991.

Osborne, Jane. "The Gumboot Dance: An Historical, Socio-Economic and Cultural Perspective." *South African Theatre Journal* 4, no. 2 (1990): 50–79.

Osterweis, Ariel. "Geo-Choreography and Necropolitics." In *Choreographies of 21st Century Wars*, edited by Gay Morris and Jens Richard Giersdorf, 269–86. New York: Oxford University Press, 2016.

Pather, Jay. "Democratic, Intercultural Choreography: Searching for the Dance between Dances." In *Proceedings of the Second South African Dance Conference, Confluences 3: "Articulating the Unspoken,"* edited by Elizabeth Triegaardt, Sharon Friedman, and Aileen Berry, 129–33. Cape Town: University of Cape Town School of Dance, 1999.

Pather, Jay. "Laws of Recall: Body, Memory and Site-Specific Performance in Contemporary South Africa." In *New Territories: Theatre, Drama, and Performance in Post-Apartheid South Africa,* edited by Greg Homann, 317–44. Brussels: Peter Lang AG, 2015.

Pather, Jay. "Negotiating the Postcolonial Black Body as a Site of Paradox." *Theater* 47, no. 1 (2017): 139–61.

Pather, Jay. "A Response: African Contemporary Dance? Questioning Issues of a Performance Aesthetic for a Developing Continent." *Critical Arts: South-North Cultural and Media Studies* 20, no. 2 (2006): 9–15.

Pather, Jay. "Shifting Spaces, Tilting Time." In *Rogue Urbanism: Emergent African Cities,* edited by Edgar Pieterse and AbdouMaliq Simone, 433–43. Aukland Park, South Africa: Jacana Media, 2013.

Pather, Jay, and Catherine Boule, eds. *Acts of Transgression: Contemporary Live Art in South Africa.* Johannesburg: Wits University Press, 2018.

Pather, Jay, and Jazzart Dance Theatre. "Dance in Search of Commonality." *Staffrider* 9, no. 4 (1991): 85–92.

Pauwels, Matthias. "Post-Struggle Art: Its Vicissitudes and Atavisms, Reconsidering the Political Value of Brett Murray's Hail to the Thief Works." *South African Journal of Philosophy* 35, no. 2 (2016): 171–83.

Perry, Jean. "When the World Was New: Ishi's Stories." In *Ishi in Three Centuries,* edited by Karl Kroeber and Clifton Kroeber, 275–92. Lincoln: University of Nebraska Press, 2003.

Perryer, Sophie, ed. *Personal Affects: Power and Poetics in Contemporary South African Art.* New York: Museum of African Art, Spier, 2004.

Phelan, Peggy. *Unmarked: The Politics of Performance.* New York: Routledge, 1993.

Piatote, Beth. *Antíkoni.* Unpublished play in author's possession, 2018.

Pickett, Stacey. "Akram Khan." In Bremser and Sanders, *Fifty Contemporary Choreographers,* 194–201.

Pieterse, Edgar. "Post-Apartheid Geographies in South Africa: Why Are Urban Divides So Persistent?" Paper presented at Interdisciplinary Debates on Development and Cultures: Cities in Development—Spaces, Conflicts and Agency, Leuven University, Leuven, Belgium, December 15, 2009.

Pithouse, Richard. *Writing the Decline: On the Struggle for South Africa's Democracy.* Auckland Park, South Africa: Jacana Media, 2016.

Plaatje, Sol. T. *Native Life in South Africa, before and since the European War and the Boer Rebellion*. New York: Negro Universities Press, 1969.

Platt, Tony. *Grave Matters: Excavating California's Buried Past*. Berkeley: Heyday, 2011.

Radhakrishnan, Smitha. "Dancing the Rainbow Nation as It Bleeds: The Surialanga Dance Company in Post-Apartheid South Africa." *South Asian Diaspora* 11, no. 2. Published ahead of print, January 19, 2019. https://doi.org/10.1080/19438192.2019.1568457

Rassool, Ciraj. "Restoring the Skeletons of Empire: Return, Reburial and Rehumanisation in Southern Africa." *Journal of Southern African Studies* 41, no. 3 (2015): 653–70.

Read, John, ed. *Athol Fugard: A Bibliography*. Grahamston, South Africa: National English Literary Museum, 1991.

Reddy, Thiven. *South Africa, Settler Colonialism and the Failures of Liberal Democracy*. London: Zed Books, 2015.

Roach, Joseph R. *Cities of the Dead: Circum-Atlantic Performances*. New York: Columbia University Press, 1996.

Roach, Joseph R. "Kinesis: The New Mimesis." *Theater* 40, no. 1 (2010): 1–3.

Roach, Joseph R. "World Bank Drama." In *Shades of the Planet: American Literature as World Literature*, edited by Chee Dimock and Lawrence Buell, 171–83. Princeton, NJ: Princeton University Press, 2007.

Roome, Dorothy. "Transformation and Reconciliation: 'Simunye,' a Flexible Model." *Critical Arts: South-North Cultural and Media Studies* 11, no. 1/2 (1997): 66–94.

Rudakoff, Judith. "Why Did the Chicken Cross the Cultural Divide? Brett Bailey and Third World Bunfight's 'iMumbo Jumbo.'" *TDR: The Drama Review* 48, no. 2 (2004): 80–90.

Sachs, Albie. "Preparing Ourselves for Freedom: Culture and the ANC Constitutional Guidelines." *TDR: The Drama Review* 35, no. 1 (1991): 187–93.

Sachs, Albie, and respondents. *Spring Is Rebellious: Arguments about Cultural Freedom*. Edited by Ingrid de Kock and Karen Press. Cape Town: Buchu Books, 1990.

Samuel, Gerard M. "Black Bodies Matter: With Apologies to Beyoncé." In Samuel, *Proceedings of Confluences 8*, 109–99.

Samuel, Gerard M., ed. *Proceedings of Confluences 8: Negotiating Contemporary Dance in Africa*. Cape Town: University of Cape Town, 2015.

Schechner, Richard. *Between Theater and Anthropology*. Philadelphia: University of Pennsylvania Press, 1985.

Schneider, Rebecca. *Performing Remains: Art and War in Times of Theatrical Enactment*. London: Routledge, 2011.

Scott, Ariel Osterweis. "Performing Acupuncture on a Necropolitical Body:

Choreographer Faustin Linyekula's Studios Kabako in Kisangani, Democratic Republic of Congo." *Dance Research Journal* 42, no. 2 (2010): 11–27.

Seibert, Brian. "Faustin Linyekula: Remember His Name (and Country and Past)." *New York Times*, September 5, 2017.

Sexton, Jared. "Afro-Pessimism: The Unclear Word." *Issue* 29 (2016). https://doi.org/10.20415/rhiz/029.e02

Shakespeare, Tom. *Disability Rights and Wrongs Revisited*. New York: Routledge, 2014.

Sharpe, Christina. *In the Wake: On Blackness and Being*. Durham, NC: Duke University Press, 2016.

Sichel, Adrienne. *Body Politics: Fingerprinting South African Contemporary Dance*. Johannesburg: Porcupine Press, 2018.

Sichel, Adrienne. "Dance Is Where Theatre Was." *The Start Tonight*. September 11, 2000.

Sichel, Adrienne. "Gate-Crashing Prejudices and Perceptions: The Enduring Legacy of Arts and Dance Festivals in Post-Apartheid South Africa." In Friedman, *Post-Apartheid Dance*, 107–25.

Sichel, Adrienne. "Grappling with South African Physical Theatre." *South African Theatre Journal* 24, no. 1 (2010): 41–50.

Sichel, Adrienne. "When Jay Pather Shook Johannesburg in 2003." *Dance Umbrella Gazette*, no. 1 (2015): 2.

Sieg, Katrin. "Toward a Civic Contract of Performance: Pitfalls of Decolonizing the Exhibitionary Complex at Brett Bailey's 'Exhibit B.'" *Theatre Survey* 40, no. 3 (2015): 250–71.

Siegenthaler, Fiona. "Aesthetic Shifts in a Transforming City: Performative Acts and Gestures in the Urban Space of Johannesburg." In *Cities in Flux: Metropolitan Spaces in South African Literary and Visual Texts*, edited by Olivier Moreillon, Alan Muller, and Lindy Stiebel, 73–99. Zürich: Lit Verlag, 2017.

Simonson, Eric, Demoz Leelai, and Ladysmith Black Mambazo. *On Tip Toe: The Music of Ladysmith Black Mambazo*. Video. San Francisco, CA: California Newsreel, 2000.

Singleton, Brian. "Censorship and Sensitivities: Performing Tolerance in Post-secular Britain." In McIvor and King, *Interculturalism and Performance Now*, 213–33.

Sitze, Adam. *The Impossible Machine: A Genealogy of South Africa's Truth and Reconciliation Commission*. Ann Arbor: University of Michigan Press, 2013.

Sizemore-Barber, April. "Prismatic Performances: Queer South African Identity and the Deconstruction of the Rainbow Nation." PhD diss., University of California, Berkeley, 2013.

Sizemore-Barber, April. *Prismatic Performances: Queer South Africa and the Fragmentation of the Rainbow Nation*. Ann Arbor: University of Michigan Press, 2020.

Slaughter, Joseph. *Human Rights, Inc.: The World Novel, Narrative Form, and International Law*. New York: Fordham University Press, 2007.

Snyder-Young, Dani. *Theatre of Good Intentions: Challenges and Hopes for Theatre and Social Change*. New York: Palgrave Macmillan, 2013.

Sobiso, Kwanele. "Paul Grootboom and the Quest to Reroute South African Theatre." In Anders and Krouse, *Positions*, 61–74.

Sörgel, Sabine. *Contemporary African Dance Theatre: Phenomenology, Whiteness, and the Gaze*. London: Palgrave MacMillan, 2020.

Sörgel, Sabine. "The Global Politics of Faustin Linyekula's Dance Theater." In Brandstetter and Hartung, *Moving (across) Borders*, 79–92.

Sörgel, Sabine. "Transnationalism and Contemporary African Dance: Faustin Linyekula." In *Emerging Bodies: The Performance of Worldmaking in Dance and Choreography*, edited by Gabriele Klein and Sandra Noeth, 83–92. New Brunswick, NJ: Transcript Verlag, 2011.

Soske, Jon, and Shannon Walsh. "Thinking about Race and Friendship in South Africa." In Walsh and Soske, *Ties That Bind*, 3–30.

Sparks, Allister. *Beyond the Miracle: Inside the New South Africa*. Chicago: University of Chicago Press, 2003.

Spillers, Hortense. *Black, White, and in Color: Essays on American Literature and Culture*. Chicago: University of Chicago Press, 2003.

States, Bert O. *Great Reckonings in Little Rooms: On the Phenomenology of Theater*. Berkeley: University of California Press, 1985.

Steingo, Gavin. *Kwaito's Promise: Music and the Aesthetics of Freedom in South Africa*. Chicago: University of Chicago Press, 2016.

Steyn, Melissa. *"Whiteness Just Isn't What It Used to Be": White Identity in a Changing South Africa*. Albany: State University of New York Press, 2001.

Stupart, Linda. "Old Wounds, Fresh Meat." *Art Review*, no. 61 (2012): 96–103.

Taylor, Diana. *The Archive and the Repertoire: Performing Cultural Memory in the Americas*. Durham, NC: Duke University Press, 2003.

Thompson, James. *Humanitarian Performance: From Disaster Tragedies to Spectacles of War*. London: Seagull Books, 2014.

Thompson, James. *Performance Affects: Applied Theatre and the End of Effect*. Basingstoke: Palgrave Macmillan, 2009.

Uys, Pieter-Dirk. *No Space on Long Street*. Unpublished playscript, 2000. *Pieter-Dirk Uys* (website). http://pdu.co.za/no%20space.html

van Bever Donker, Maurits, Ross Truscott, Gary Minkley, and Premesh Lalu, eds. *Remains of the Social: Desiring the Postapartheid*. Johannesburg: Wits University Press, 2017.

van Bever Donker, Maurits, Ross Truscott, Gary Minkley, and Premesh Lalu, eds. "Traversing the Social." In van Bever Donker, Truscott, Minkley, and Lalu, *Remains of the Social*, 1–39.

Vandenbroucke, Russell. *Truths the Hand Can Touch: The Theatre of Athol Fugard*. New York: Theatre Communications Group, 1986.

Van Wyk, Steven, and Christy Giesler. "Ballet Blanc to Ballet Black? Unpacking Whiteness in South African Ballet." In *Confluences 6: Physicality and Performance*, edited by Beth Dutton and Lauren McGeorge, 328–39. Cape Town: University of Cape Town School of Dance, 2011.

Vedel, Karen. "Vincent Mantsoe." In Bremser and Sanders, *Fifty Contemporary Choreographers*, 233–40.

Vedel, Karen. "World Dance. Trance Dance: A Contextualized Look at Vincent Mantsoe's Solo in 'Men-Jaro.'" *Nordic Theatre Studies* 19 (2007): 90–99.

Walsh, Shannon, and Jon Soske, eds. *Ties That Bind: Race and the Politics of Friendship in South Africa*. Johannesburg: Wits University Press, 2016.

Watkins, Lee. "'Simunye, We Are Not One': Ethnicity, Difference and the Hip-Hoppers of Cape Town." *Race & Class* 43, no. 1 (2001): 29–44.

Weheliye, Alexander G. *Habeas Viscus: Racializing Assemblages, Biopolitics, and Black Feminist Theories of the Human*. Durham, NC: Duke University Press, 2014.

Wenzel, Jennifer. *Bulletproof: Afterlives of Anticolonial Prophecy in South Africa and Beyond*. Chicago: University of Chicago Press, 2010.

Werry, Margaret. "Oceanic Imagination, Intercultural Performance, Pacific Historiography." In Fischer-Lichte, Jost, and Jain, *The Politics of Interweaving Performance Cultures*, 97–118.

Wertheim, Albert. *The Dramatic Art of Athol Fugard: From South Africa to the World*. Bloomington: Indiana University Press, 2000.

Wetmore, Kevin, Jr. "Brett Bailey." In Middeke, Schnierer, and Homann, *The Methuen Guide to Contemporary South African Theatre*, 259–76.

Wilderson, Frank B., III. "Grammar & Ghosts: The Performative Limits of African Freedom." *Theatre Survey* 50, no. 1 (2009): 119–25.

Worley, Matthew. *No Future: Punk, Politics and British Youth Culture, 1976–1984*. Cambridge: Cambridge University Press, 2017.

Young, Hershini Bhana. *Illegible Will: Coercive Spectacles of Labor in South Africa and the Diaspora*. Durham, NC: Duke University Press, 2017.

Zondi, Mlondolozi B. Review of *Black Performance Theory*, edited by Thomas F. DeFrantz and Anita Gonzalez. *Text and Performance Quarterly* 37, no. 3–4 (2017): 278–81.

Index

Page numbers in *italics* refer to illustrations.